SEEKER

TOR TEEN BOOKS BY VERONICA ROSSI

Riders

Seeker

SEEKER

VERONICA ROSSI

A TOM DOHERTY ASSOCIATES BOOK
NEW YORK

This is a work of fiction. All of the characters, organizations, and
events portrayed in this novel are either products of the
author's imagination or are used fictitiously.

SEEKER

Copyright © 2017 by Veronica Rossi

A Tor Teen Book
Published by Tom Doherty Associates
175 Fifth Avenue
New York, NY 10010

www.tor-forge.com

Tor® is a registered trademark of Macmillan Publishing Group, LLC.

The Library of Congress Cataloging-in-Publication Data
is available upon request.

ISBN 978-0-7653-8256-6 (hardcover)
ISBN 978-1-4668-8780-0 (e-book)

Our books may be purchased in bulk for promotional,
educational, or business use. Please contact your local bookseller
or the Macmillan Corporate and Premium Sales Department
at 1-800-221-7945, extension 5442, or by e-mail at
MacmillanSpecialMarkets@macmillan.com.

First Edition: May 2017

Printed in the United States of America

0 9 8 7 6 5 4 3 2 1

SEEKER

CHAPTER 1

⟶ DARYN ⟵

You don't know what anger is until you've spent time with a mare in a truly foul mood.

Shadow is *livid*.

I've been back for two days now but she's still mad at me—and determined to let me know it. Usually I can sense what she's feeling by intuition. No need for that right now, with the tantrum she's throwing. Twelve hundred pounds of black mare ripping the earth open with her hooves isn't exactly tough to read.

As Jode would say if he were here, Shadow's off her trolley.

She rounds the far side of the enclosure and loops back, breaking into another charge and coming right at me. In the stormy afternoon light she almost looks like a normal horse. If you didn't know her, you might look past the unusual blackness of her coat and the smoky wisps that trail behind her lean body. You might not even notice that she's too fast, and just a little too elegant. But the prolonged eye contact she makes with me and the intelligence in her eyes? Total giveaway.

As she closes in, she lowers her head and shows no sign of slowing down. I brace my feet and prepare to jump back behind the fence. Shadow would never hurt me intentionally, but then I never meant to hurt Gideon and Sebastian.

Sometimes you hurt people even when it's the last thing you want to do.

With only a few feet left between us, she stops suddenly, her hooves gouging the mud, kicking up a wave of wet spatter that flies right at me.

"Wow." I wipe my face, spitting out bits of mud. "Thanks, girl!"

Her level stare makes it clear she's in no mood to joke around.

Do you see? Do you see how scared I was when you left me? Do you see how you upset me?

"I know, Shadow. You're furious and you have every right to be. Tell me all about it. I'm listening."

I hope she senses how sorry I am. I hated leaving her for a week, knowing how much she's suffered after we lost Sebastian. She went from being totally confident and calm to sensitive about almost everything. Other people can set her off. So can airplanes and cars. Fortunately there's almost none of that out here in Wyoming.

I'm the only one she trusts—and I left her. But my road trip to Georgia gave me the answer I needed. After so many months of indecision, I know what I need to do. When you're putting your life in danger, it's only right to be positive about it.

I'm positive.

Shadow snorts. I expect her to kick into another rampage but she looks past me just as I hear the screen door bang closed behind me. Turning, I see Isabel. My friend, roommate, mentor, and fellow Seeker steps off the porch of the cabin we've been renting.

Home, Daryn.

I've been here eight months. You'd think I could call it that by now.

Isabel lifts the edges of her wool poncho to keep them from dragging in the mud as she walks over. She takes her time, choosing her steps around the puddles with care. Iz never rushes through anything. Behind her the line of smoke struggling up from the chimney is erased by a storm gust, only to struggle up again. We'll get either snow or freezing rain tonight. Again. As far as I can tell, spring in Wyoming is a misnomer.

"This looks promising," Isabel says. "Have you two made up?" She props her arms on the fence beside me and smiles, her broad cheeks like rising mountains. She has a face for looking into sunsets and windstorms and futures—which she does as a Seeker. Which I used to do too, until everything changed after my epic fail last fall.

"I think we're getting there." Shadow has backed up and turned toward the river, striking a pose like we'll be sketching her, rant concluded for now. I stuff my cold hands into my pockets and make myself ask the question I've been holding all day. "What about you? Have you forgiven me?"

I left Isabel for a week, too. She's not my mother. I didn't need to ask her permission. But I could've run it by her.

"I was never angry with you, Daryn." Isabel brushes a lock of her hair behind her ear, most of it having already escaped from the bun she swept back before her morning shift at Franklin Ranch, where we both work. She regards me with bright eyes, goldish green at the edges and warm brown at the very center. "I was worried. There's a big difference. And the note you left helped."

I wonder how much good it really did. I didn't tell her where I was going or how long I'd be gone—only that I needed to figure something out. I still haven't told her anything, but I should. After all she's done for me, I owe her some answers. As long as they don't give away too much.

"So . . ." Where to begin? How far back does my regret extend?

Isabel's eyebrows lift. "So . . . ?"

"I was on the computer at the ranch about two weeks ago doing some research."

"Research?"

"On the friends I used to have until I disappointed them horribly? Gideon, Jode, and Marcus? I wanted to see how they're doing. Whether they're okay." *And hopefully not as miserable as I am,* I add silently. "I came across an announcement. An event where I knew they'd all be, and I couldn't resist. I had to go see them in, um . . ." *On three, Daryn. One, two,* three. "In Georgia."

Saying it out loud makes it sound even more extreme and I almost wince, but Isabel doesn't react.

"Why Georgia?" she asks, like she's not at all surprised that I drove four thousand miles in nine days.

"Marcus enlisted. It was a graduation celebration for him from the Ranger program—the one Gideon was in, too. I knew Gideon and Jode would be there for it. They'd never miss something that important."

I couldn't miss it, either. For several reasons.

"And how was it? Did you get a chance to talk through everything? Were they angry with you?"

She knows this is my greatest fear. That Gideon, Marcus, and Jode will blame me for what happened to Sebastian. I mean, *I* blame me. Why shouldn't they? It's a fear that's kept me immobilized here for more than half a year. That, and no longer having visions to tell me where I'm needed.

Right after the battle against the Kindred, aka my epic fail, they completely stopped. I've been totally cut off from the future. Without visions, I've felt incomplete. I've felt this constant quiet dread, like I've forgotten something important. Except it's not that I can't *remember* what I should know. It's that I can't *foresee* it.

"No, they weren't angry with me."

"That's good," Iz says, brightly.

"Not really. It's not anything." Isabel's smile fades. I can't look at her anymore, so I look at Shadow. With the daylight fading and the darkness reaching for her, anxiety curls low in my stomach. Her coat is so black, so deeply black, I've always had an irrational terror of losing her at night. "I didn't talk to them."

My words sound confessional and they hang in the stormy silence. A cold breeze sweeps across our property, stirring the trees at the edges of the field and lifting a lone hawk into the unsettled sky.

"Daryn . . . You went all that way and you didn't speak to them?"

"I chickened out, Isabel! I couldn't figure out what to say! 'Sorry'? What good would that do? I'm the one with the Sight. *Was* the one. I knew we'd have that showdown with the Kindred. I should've had a better plan. I should've anticipated every outcome. But I didn't and Gideon lost his hand because of me and Sebastian's hurt or possibly dead but definitely trapped in a realm with a demon. A realm *I* opened. How do you apologize for that? For making a mistake that big? What could I have said to make any kind of difference?"

Isabel carries a meditative quiet about her. I love it. I used to try to emulate it. She taught me that the quieter you are, the more you hear and see and understand and even feel. Quiet lets you fill yourself up. There's wisdom to be found in listening, in silence. But since my screwup, I'm not always quiet. I have a new volume, a yelling volume. It comes out of nowhere too, like those air horns people bring to sporting events. Just hit the right nerve and WAAHHHH!

It's awful. Isabel doesn't deserve it. Neither does Shadow. She takes a few steps toward me before she realizes I'm fine. Mostly fine.

My throat feels raw and I'm biting down so hard I may crack my own teeth. Isabel reaches over and squeezes my wrist with her strong potter's hand. I watch the hawk riding the storm winds as I wait for the tears that have welled up to be reabsorbed into my eyes. To the west the clouds have broken and are spilling themselves open. Unlike me.

"This is as close as I got." I slip my phone out of my pocket and pull up the only photo I took during my week away. I've looked at it five hundred times and every time it hits me with a different feeling. This time it triggers an aching, wishing feeling, like I want to be that hawk up there, gliding through a storm like fear is just a myth.

Isabel takes the phone. "Is this Gideon?" She must see the answer on my face, because she turns back to the phone and studies the photo. I wonder if she's looking for his prosthetic hand. You can't see it in the photo. I could barely see it in real life. "He's handsome."

"It's a picture of his back." He was turned away and standing in a crowd about forty feet away from where I lurked like a stalker. Which I technically was.

"Yes, but I can tell."

A smile rises inside me. This should be good. "How can you tell, Iz?" I waggle my eyebrows. "Does he have a handsome back? Do you think his *butt* is handsome?"

She rolls her eyes. "If you must know, he has a handsome *bearing*. He holds himself like he's comfortable with the moment. I extrapolated from that." She hands the phone back. "And I'm right, aren't I?"

"Kind of. 'Hot' fits him better than 'handsome' does, but . . . whatever." Appreciating Gideon's handsomeness is like standing in front of a bakery window full of the most delicious things I've ever seen—then trying the door and realizing it's locked. *And* realizing I'm the one who locked it.

"I know this has been hard for you, Daryn."

"I only wish I hadn't sucked you down with me." I've wondered if I'm her current mission as a Seeker. Maybe her Sight told her how much I'd need her?

"You haven't."

"Well, regardless, thanks. For everything. For being marooned here with me." I scan the vastness that's all around me. So beautiful and isolating.

"You don't have to thank me, you know that," she says easily, but there's a rare intensity in her gaze. She pats my arm, glancing toward the cabin. "It's getting dark and I've got soup on the stove. Come inside? We'll talk some more over dinner."

"I'll be right in." I listen to her trudge away, the bang of the screen door telling me she's inside.

Shadow moves closer, bobbing her head, her eyes never leaving me. Somehow I can feel that she knows more, senses more, than even Isabel.

What aren't you saying? What are you planning?

I climb off the fence and sweep my hand down her strong neck. The curls of her darkness wrap around my fingers, following my movement. She feels like sun-warmed silk. Like steadiness.

"We're going after Sebastian tonight, girl," I tell her. "It's time to make things right."

CHAPTER 2

"Hate to say it, Cordero," I say, dropping into the chair in front of her desk. "But I'm a little disappointed."

Natalie Cordero, PhD in criminal forensic psychology, my ex-interrogator and current boss, looks up from her laptop, peering over the frame of her glasses. "Morning, Gideon. I don't remember asking you to come in here."

"That's okay, I'll be quick." I rest my prosthetic hand on the arm of the chair, in plain view. I'm not above using it as propaganda if it helps get Sebastian back. If there's a better reminder of what the Kindred did to him, I don't know what it is. The Kindred got me, too. Just not as badly. "We need more resources. More drones. More geniuses. More of everything, and we need it quickly." After eight months, we finally have a shot at getting Sebastian back, but it hinges on finding Daryn. She's our way into the realm where Bas is trapped. Daryn not only *has* the key; she's also the only one who can use it. But none of that matters if we don't find her. "We're at four days," I continue. "And you know what they say about cold trails."

"What?"

"They say—" I rub my jaw, buying a second. She's the criminologist. I thought she was going to fill in the answer for me. "They say that cold trails suck."

"Elegantly put, but the trail isn't cold yet. We're getting close. Some of the top analysts in the world are on this. We're gaining ground."

Her eyes move past me, into the warehouse space where

the team is huddled around desks, laptops, easels. We took over this place—an abandoned food-distribution hub—as our command center right after Daryn's appearance at Fort Benning a few days ago. Since Cordero's in charge she's set up in here, the old manager's office, which somehow smells more like frozen meat than the rest of the warehouse. The rest of us are working in an office supply flotilla in the middle of forty thousand square feet of open space.

It's kind of unbelievable. Three PhDs from MIT out there, but where do they set up our desks? Right at the center, so we can trip all over extension cords and have the worst possible lighting and ventilation.

"I understand you're motivated, Gideon, but adding people isn't necessary," Cordero says. "Or even realistic. The security clearance alone would take months. Even if I could expedite it, bringing new people up to speed would only slow us down. We don't need anyone else. We're making progress. We'll find her."

She pauses, probably expecting me to keep pressing, but the truth is I'm actually not sure more resources *would* help. No one does the disappearing act like Daryn.

I stand. "All right. Good talk."

"Gideon, hold on a second. Now that you're here, there's something I want to discuss with you."

I ease back into the chair, but now I'm on my guard. "What's up?"

Cordero closes her laptop and sits back, giving me her full attention. It's only now that I notice my right hand is in a fist. Cordero notices this as well. "Want to close the door?" she asks.

"Do *you* want me to close the door?"

"If it'll make you more comfortable."

"Are you going to psychoanalyze me?"

"Not intentionally."

"Then open's fine."

"Open it is."

My knees are almost pressed against her desk, so I push the chair back and try to relax. Jode's laugh carries from the warehouse behind me, rising above the patter of tapping keyboards and humming generators. He has a high chuckle that reminds me of a little kid's laugh—a psychotic little kid's laugh.

Our team's technically nonmilitary. Totally off the grid and comprised of three out of four horsemen—me, Marcus, and Jode—plus Cordero; her assistant, Ben, who's one of three MIT prodigies; Sophia and Soraya, the other two; and eight special-ops soldiers who were with us in the final showdown against the Kindred—the rebel group of demons we shut down in the fall.

Almost shut down. Samrael's still out there. Still *in* there, to be precise. In the realm he managed to open by coercing Daryn. And by cutting off my left hand. Which he's going to regret the hell out of next time I see him.

Not a day's gone by that I haven't thought about Bastian and how to get him back. I think Cordero's motivations for going after him are professional. She never met Bas, but she's been studying occult and paranormal phenomena her entire career. This whole task force was created for that specific purpose. I couldn't care less what her motivation is, though, as long as she helps us. For Marcus, Jode, and me, this is personal. Bastian's one of us.

Cordero removes her glasses and sets them down on her desk. "How are you doing today, Gideon?"

"Great. You?"

"Good."

She nods, so I nod.

Actually I've struggled to keep my frustration under control today. I have a feeling that's what this little chat is about.

Everyone feels it when I get riled up. A fun part of being an incarnation of War is that my anger's literally contagious, so. I'm kind of a liability. Fortunately over the past six months, Cordero has developed a solid toolbox for disarming the Gideon rage bomb. "How about we run through what we know again?" she suggests.

Ah. Redirection. Refocus my attention toward something productive. This is awesome when it works. "Sure."

"You saw your sister standing alone at Marcus's graduation. Tell me again what made you go to her?"

"Twintuition."

Cordero's smile is faint, almost exclusively in her eyes. A couple of months ago, she told me all about the research paper she did as an undergraduate at Yale about telepathic connections between twins. Anything that defies explanation, Cordero loves.

I actually do feel super connected with Anna sometimes, so it's weird that she doesn't know about any of this stuff. My sister has no clue that I'm War. Or that her boyfriend's Conquest.

Jode, man. Talk about the worst guy for your sister to be with. It's not right.

The best the guys and I can tell, we're incarnations of the horsemen not because we're bringing about the end times, or Judgment Day. We are what we are as a kind of lesson. Me, for example. It'd be fair to say I have anger issues. It would also be fair to say I've had my share of internal unrest. As War, I've had to learn to deal with it. *Really* learn. Same goes for Jode, aka Conquest, who's got his superiority issues to deal with, and Marcus, who, as Death, has had to fight harder than anyone I know personally for a good life. We're walking metaphors, you could say. Human works in progress—but we are progressing. Every one of us has grown in character and in faith because we wear our weaknesses so openly.

"Give me more," Cordero prompts. "You saw Anna and noticed something unusual. What was it?"

"Hey, Cordero. Doesn't this remind you of the time you were questioning me but you actually secretly wanted to take my head off?" This entire moment, me sitting here and answering her questions, brings back bad memories of when one of the Kindred, a shape-shifter, impersonated her and interrogated me.

"That wasn't me, so of course I don't remember it." Her eyes narrow just slightly. "Do you want to talk about it?"

"No, thanks. I'm good." It's not that I don't trust Cordero. It's just that it's hard to *forget.* "You were asking about Anna. Why I went over to her." I lift my shoulders. "I just knew. She had this look on her face like something was going on. She told me a girl had come up to her and that she'd looked nervous. She introduced herself as a friend of mine and asked Anna to give me the key."

My attention is pulled to that very key, which sits between Cordero's computer and her glasses. It's heavier than an ordinary key, like something ancient. Daryn wore it around her neck for weeks. The guys and I had thought it was so important. A sacred key, to open heavenly gates. But we'd been wearing the real key all along without realizing it—divided and disguised as wrist cuffs. Four cuffs that were misused. That opened a splinter realm, under Daryn's control, when she was coerced by one of the Kindred. "I instantly recognized the key as the decoy when Anna gave it to me and—"

"I think I've got something!" Ben, one of the MI Trio, barrels into the office with a sheet of paper crammed in his hand. He drops it on the desk. For a second we all look at it, this paper-spider; then Ben dives back in. "Shoot, sorry," he says, palming it flat. "That's from a gas station sixty-five miles north of here. Oh, hey, Gideon," he says, finally noticing me.

Cordero picks up the rumpled page to get a better look.

I've stopped breathing mid-exhale. Totally stopped. I also seem to have spontaneously developed X-ray vision, because through the fibers of the paper I can make out the faded image of the girl.

The disappointment is gutting.

I let out my breath. "That's not her."

Cordero frowns and flips the paper around. "You're sure?"

"Yes." The girl in the photo has long blond hair and she's about the right age, seventeenish. Other than that, she looks nothing like Daryn.

"It's a grainy image," Ben says. "I can sharpen it up."

"Then it'll be a sharper picture of not her."

Cordero cuts a look my way. I know she wants me to be more encouraging. Everyone's working nonstop. We have cots set up outside and most of us sleep here rather than trek back to the motel. "Keep working, Ben," she says, handing the paper back to him.

"You're doing great, man," I add, to be more encouraging. "But try to do better. Faster, too."

"Definitely. You got it," Ben says, super earnestly. Then he jogs back to his desk. Literally jogs.

I can't keep the smile off my face. "See that? That's an A-plus effort, Cordero. Everyone should work that hard."

She shakes her head. "You take such advantage."

I laugh. "What'd I do?"

"Never mind. It's my fault. I should never have allowed them to see you as War."

"Nah. They loved it." Aside from Daryn, who's not here, and some extremely high-up government people, the people in this warehouse are the only ones who know what we are. Who we are? Whatever.

Until last night, though, the techs only knew in theory, so we did the full kit reveal for them here in the warehouse, calling up weapons, armor, and horses. It was Cordero's idea. She thought it would motivate the team, and did it ever. We made an impression, Marcus especially. When you get a look at Death, you feel something. I only wish we'd recorded their reactions.

Cordero and I pick up where we left off. This must be the tenth time I've answered these questions, but we're working on my frustration and it's also her investigative process. I know she thinks she'll stumble on a clue.

Marcus and Jode stroll in as we're going through it. Jode takes the chair next to mine, his watch flashing as he drops his hand on the arm. As Conquest, he's an incarnation of the white rider. Even in street clothes the hints are there if you know what you're looking for. Under the fluorescent lights, Jode's blond hair has just a little too much shine. Same with his watch, his fingernails. He's got some flash. Jode—James Oliver Drummond Ellis by birth—is English, smart as a well-bred and highly educated Englishman, and one hundred percent lethal. None of us would be here if not for ole Drummy. The world might not even be the same. When we fought the Kindred, Jode fired an endless supply of arrows from the back of his white stallion, keeping us from getting overrun by demons. There were a lot of heroes that day but Jode was center podium.

Marcus leans against the wall behind Cordero, gravitating to the back as usual. He trains his glass-colored eyes on me. Quiet, steady eyes. Death stare. Before I got to know him I saw that look as completely hostile. Total turnaround now. Marcus and I are connected like Anna and me—like words aren't necessary. He had it rough growing up in foster homes around Chicago. He doesn't say much about it, but it was hard-core survival. Every day. I lost Dad last year, and nothing will ever replace him, but I got Marcus right around the same time. A brother. It was meant to happen, I think. Mom and Anna needed him, too.

Marcus crosses his arms and listens, his gaze moving from me to Cordero. Jode's attention's more like a satellite: unfocused and landing nowhere specific but taking in everything. I wrap things up, describing how I'd sprinted after Daryn—the direction Anna indicated—getting the attention of the military police on base, but coming up with nothing. Daryn had disappeared again. Even now I feel the echo of that moment. Brutal.

"Okay," Cordero says. "What do we know for sure?" She steeples her fingers and taps them together as she thinks. I used to be able to do that. "We know she didn't come solely to give you the key. It has no real value and she could've found a much easier way to deliver it if that was all she wanted to do. She came for another reason. What was it, and what caused her to veer from her plan?"

"How do you know she veered from her plan?"

"I'm making an assumption based on the distress your sister picked up on."

"You think she saw a threat of some kind and changed her mind?"

"Or had a change of heart."

Cordero and Jode exchange a look. Marcus drops his head and stares at his feet.

I don't like this. "Spill, Ellis. Marcus . . . ? Someone, talk."

Jode looks at Cordero. I think I see a slight nod of approval from her. "What if she didn't come because of Sebastian?" he asks.

"Daryn might have come for strictly personal reasons," Cordero adds.

"Ah. Got it. You think I'm the personal reason. Solid the-. ory, but you're wrong. Daryn would never show up for that reason. She's dedicated. All Seeker business all the time." Why are they saying this—to test me? Or do they really think it's a possibility? "Anyway, this part of the discussion isn't up for discussion."

"Maybe it should be," Cordero offers. "Maybe you should consider that she might've shown up to see you and left because she wasn't ready."

Marcus crosses his arms. "She could've seen your prosthetic."

"You mean this?" I raise my robohand. It's capable of fifty distinct gestures, but the bird's one of my top-used ones.

Marcus is already smiling. He knew it was coming.

"It might have taken even less," Jode adds. "One look at you could've sent her running."

An image flashes through my mind. Daryn seeing me, then doing an about-face and hauling ass like she's in a B horror film.

I have to laugh. It's just so sad. "How is this relevant to anything?" I'm sweating and I can't sit any longer. I stand and brace my hands on the back of the chair. "Hey, Ben," I call into the warehouse. "How's your personal life? You got any rejections you want to dissect with our psychologist-boss?"

Ben jumps up and rounds his desk. "Definitely. I'm the king of rejection."

"Dude, then I'm your co-monarch."

"Blake," Cordero warns.

"We'll talk later, Ben. Keep after it. You're doing great."

Ben spins and goes back to his desk.

Cordero sighs. "This is a relevant line of inquiry, Gideon, because her appearance the other day could be a false lead. She doesn't seem to want to be found. We have to consider that she might want no involvement in the search for Sebastian. And since she controls the key . . ."

I shake my head. "I'm not on board with this line of thinking. If Daryn isn't willing to go after Bastian, we're nowhere. And I'm not throwing in the towel before we even find her. We assume she showed up because she wants to go after Sebastian, or what's the point?"

"All I'm trying to understand is why she'd leave without approaching you if she wanted your help."

"Because that's what Daryn does."

At this, Cordero's antennae go up. It's subtle, a quick blink, like she's afraid she might miss something. "Explain what you mean by that."

"She's not the most open book out there."

"Can you elaborate for me?"

"If she were a book, you'd only be able to read a few pages."

"Elaborate better."

I pull in a deep breath, then let it out. How can I say this without throwing Daryn under the bus? "She's not one to ask for help when she needs it. She's . . . I don't know. She's skittish."

"So she might, for example, attempt to approach you for help, then get cold feet and back away?"

Marcus and Jode both look at me. We all know where this is going.

"She might do that."

"And then?" Cordero asks.

"She'd go after it on her own."

The silence that falls over us feels like it reaches out to the warehouse. Like the team out there has felt a shift, too.

"Do you believe it's possible she might go after Sebastian alone?"

It's exactly what Daryn would do. Exactly.

Before I can reply, Ben jogs into the room carrying his laptop this time. He sets it down on Cordero's desk. Instantly, I know this isn't a false alarm. My heartbeat starts pounding in my ears as we crowd around it.

The screen is divided into four squares. My eyes pull to the top right quadrant first. It's a photo.

Of Daryn.

A close-up shot of her in an old Ford pickup. She's leaning slightly out of the driver's window as she hands money to a tollbooth operator. Her hair is up in a ponytail and she's wearing sunglasses with lenses in the shape of hearts, which seems weird and unlike her but then again, I haven't seen her in six months, aside from seeing her in my head all the damn time, so maybe she's changed. Maybe I never knew the real Daryn. Maybe everything that happened between us was fake.

Whatever. Doesn't matter.

Good. So that quadrant's out of the way.

The one below it has a shot of license plates with the registration information. It's registered to Isabel Banks of Moose, Wyoming. Which takes me to the left two quadrants. Both are maps. One is the projected route Daryn drove, or is still driving, from Georgia to Wyoming. The other is a map with Isabel Banks's last known address.

125 Smith Ranch Road, Moose, Wyoming

Daryn is in Wyoming.

Has she been there this entire time? Just miles from where I last saw her?

The name Isabel Banks sounds familiar. Daryn told me once that Seekers have a tight network. They help each other with connections, travel, boarding, money. That's how we think she got into Fort Benning.

I remember. Isabel was the Seeker that mentored Daryn when she first started having visions. *She's like an aunt to me,* Daryn told me.

"I got it right," Ben says. "That's her, isn't it?"

I can't answer him. My jaw feels welded shut and I'm back on quadrant one, a hundred thoughts racing through my head, not a single one sticking.

Cordero looks up, waiting for confirmation.

"That's her," Marcus says.

"That's Daryn," adds Jode.

"Ben, get us a flight to Wyoming." Cordero grabs her laptop and stands. "Let's go track her down."

I'm already out the door.

CHAPTER 3

⊸ DARYN ⊸

Daryn? Are you all right?"

"Yes, I'm fine," I reply automatically. I pop a piece of cornbread into my mouth, buying a second to figure out what I just missed. Isabel was telling me about something at the ranch. "No kidding, a black wolf?" I say, catching up.

It's raining outside. Actually, it's *pouring*. A quiet roar fills the cabin like the hushed sound of my noise-canceling headphones times a million. I missed when that started, too.

Isabel takes a sip of her tortilla soup and nods. "Yes, right behind the ranch. Caitlin and Samantha were clearing trails for summer and almost ran right into him. They said he was ten feet away and so enormous they thought he was a black bear at first." She smiles. "He gave those girls the scare of their lives."

This bit of news is actually noteworthy. There are tons of wolves in Wyoming but you never see them. They're too good at keeping their distance, which I admire. But a black wolf is *especially* rare. Ordinarily this would hold my interest but as Iz fills in the details, I feel myself slipping into my own thoughts again. Because what's more rare than a rare black wolf sighting?

Going to rescue a friend who's stuck inside a realm with a demon.

As soon as Isabel leaves, I'm doing it.

Fifteen minutes from now, I'm finally going to right some major wrongs.

As we finish our soup, I do my best to nod and reply at the correct moments but my thoughts keep straying to the things I'll need to bring with me tonight. What does one wear into an alternate dimension? Warm clothes, phone, rope, knife— wait, *knife*?

Yes. Knife. The goal is to come out of this alive, and with Sebastian.

"You sure you don't want to come tonight?" Isabel asks as we start on the dishes. She washes a glass, her movements flowing into one another—scrub, rinse, drain—like they're words in the same sentence. I've always loved the way she moves, so gracefully, still bearing the mark of her younger years as a dancer. Even her features are graceful, a mix of Japanese and Spanish traits that make her look like a living watercolor. I'm practically an ogre next to her. Tall. Muscular. Cloddish, with my Norse roots and crazy blond hair that's not straight but not curly, either. Little Vikings, Dad used to call Josie and me.

"Things are picking up," Iz continues. "We're fully booked this week. And you know the teen boys won't dance unless you're there."

"Hah. Even when I'm there, I wouldn't call what they do 'dancing.'" Franklin Ranch is a high-end resort for city slickers who want to ride horses and fly-fish in the summer and ski in the winter. Isabel waits tables there and I work in the children's program, which means walking little kids around the indoor arena on ponies, teaching them to rope calves, aka stuffed teddy bears, and doing crafts with them. It's not my life's passion but it gets me out of the cabin and I needed something after earning my GED in December. Being a shut-in who does nothing but read and watch the snow level rise sounded great at one point but I only ended up marinating in regret all day. Working with little kids and horses keeps you "in the moment," as Iz likes to say. It's helped.

It's Tuesday night, though. Square-dancing night. The staff is encouraged to come to the ranch and pair up with guests, since they don't know the steps. Isabel and I usually dress up in Old West clothes and lend a hand for a few hours—and earn a little extra cash. The season's just started but I've already allemanded and do-si-doed with way too many thirteen-year-old boys. It's agony. They smell like hormones, sweaty gym clothes, and Axe products. And they don't know where to look. That was one thing about Gideon. He always looked right at me with those soulful blue eyes, like he had a secret he couldn't wait to tell me. Like he couldn't wait to hear mine.

That look terrified me. But I also loved it.

"So? Will you come?"

"To square dancing?" *Come on, Daryn. Focus. Just a few more minutes.* "I'm going to pass. Still kind of tired from driving so much. I'll come next week when I'm back full-time."

"Okay. I'll let them know." Isabel dries her hands with a towel and passes it to me, then watches me as I dry mine. Rain hammers at the window, warping our reflections in the glass. "I'm worried about you."

"I know. But don't be. I'm fine." I need her to believe me. *Then stop wringing the dish towel, Daryn.* "Really, I'm fine. Seeing the guys stirred up some of the old stuff, that's all."

"I can imagine you miss them even more now."

"Yeah." Everything is sharper since I saw them, not just the "missing." The longing and the guilt have ratcheted up. And the emptiness in me, the part of me that used to be fulfilled by the Sight.

"Keep being patient. You'll know when it's time to move forward."

"Right." I hope that sounds less glib to her than it does to me. I've waited for a vision to show me the way forward for almost eight months. Patience has gotten me nowhere. The time to move forward is now—even if I don't have the assurance of knowing what's coming.

"Okay." Isabel nods, like it's settled. She takes her heavy coat off the hook by the front door and pulls it on, then tucks her purse under her arm and pulls the door open. Rain blows in, pushing back her hair and her coat like she's at the helm of a ship. She looks at me just before she steps outside, and I see it. The sadness that's probably on my face, too. This is the first time we're lying to each other. We're both holding something back.

In my room, I open the trunk at the foot of my bed and push aside my old running shoes and the dozens of letters I've written to Mom, Dad, and Josie and never mailed, unearthing my backpack from the bottom.

This battered leather bag traveled the world with me as I drifted from place to place guiding the lost. Protecting the small. Connecting those who needed help with those who could offer it. I loved what I was until the Kindred came along. I'd always done good with my Sight up until that point.

Unzipping the main compartment, I remove the blue oxford I permanently borrowed from Jode in Norway and unwrap the orb from the soft material, my heart squeezing tight as the memories threaten to flood back.

This sphere is small, only about the size of an apple, but infinitely layered with colors and depths, with skies and suns and seas swirling and dancing within it.

Beautiful.

Immeasurably so.

And incredibly powerful.

This orb is the key that opened the realm and started everything.

After Bas disappeared and Gideon was hurt, I spent weeks

curled up on my bed staring at it, reliving those awful moments in painful detail. I kept seeing Gideon's face when Bastian was stung by the demon Ronwae. Seeing Bastian's face as he sacrificed himself to take down Samrael, sending them both to a place that I can only imagine. Seeing Jode and Marcus looking like they'd lost part of themselves. But lately when I look at this orb I don't feel remorse. I feel outright panic.

I brush the glassy surface, running my thumb across the crack that appeared two weeks ago.

I'm not sure what this is—this fault line or tear—but little by little it's been growing deeper and longer. That can only mean one thing: Time is running out.

This is why I drove to Georgia.

Look at this, I wanted to tell the guys. *Our window to go after Bas is closing.*

But then how would I explain the eight months it took me to go for *them*?

The Sight. I was waiting for the Sight.

I've been lost without it, and I didn't want to risk any of you getting hurt again.

I just didn't trust myself.

In my head, they sound like weak excuses. In my heart, they've felt real and justified. But after days of thinking on the drive to Georgia and back, I realized I don't need anyone's help to go after Sebastian—or even want it.

I can do this alone. It's dangerous, but what part of this hasn't been? And if something goes wrong this time, I'll be the only one who will pay the price.

I slide the orb into the outer pocket and move around my room, gathering my rain parka, phone, notebook. When Bastian and Samrael went through the portal last fall, I saw impressions of a frozen landscape, ice and snow and jagged mountains like the Tetons, so I pack gloves, my wool beanie, and a scarf.

In the kitchen, I grab a bottle of water and a couple of granola bars, then hesitate over the knife drawer, open it, close it, open it, grab a three-inch paring knife.

If you run into trouble, are you going to peel your attacker?

For that matter, why bring the notebook? Do I really think there will be breaks to sit down and write?

The journal stays because it's my security blanket, but I switch the paring knife for a longer cutting knife, which I have even less confidence in. I'm strong and fast, but I'm not exactly Katniss. I have no experience of any kind in fighting, but it's no time for hesitation. I zip up my pack and I'm out the door, rain slapping at my shoulders as I jog to the barn.

Shadow watches me with alert eyes as I tack her up. Like all the guys with their mounts, Bas could get Shadow to call up her otherworldly tack. He could also get her to shift into threads of darkness, taking him with her. *Folding,* they called it. But without Bas, Shadow hasn't done any of that. She's been stuck in her horse state, so I have to use a regular harness, bit, and saddle. My hands start shaking as I fasten a lariat to her saddle, the reality of what I'm doing sinking in, but I get it done and bring her out into the rain. Then I mount up and we're off.

Shadow settles into a confident trot, navigating the mud puddles, rocks, and fallen branches without a stumble, despite the storm and the darkness.

She's much more confident than I am. I have to keep reminding myself to loosen my grip on the reins and stay gentle with her mouth.

As I ride toward the Snake River, the headlights from the main road are the first to disappear, then the porch light of the Smith Cabin.

Home, Daryn.

Will you ever call it home?

By the time I find the trail that follows the river, there's no sign of mankind and I'm soaked in spite of my raincoat. All I hear is water—rushing, dripping, and flowing. My backpack thumps against my lower back, heavy with the weight of the orb, and the grass blurs beneath me.

I'm so caught up in being alternately amazed at my bravery and furious at my recklessness that the ride passes quickly and I reach the stand of long pines sooner than I expect. The trail is overgrown and harder to see at night, but I find it and take Shadow up the hill, stopping at the top—a perfect secluded spot with no houses or roads around for miles.

Dismounting, I scan the night to make sure I'm alone. Then I say a quick prayer for Isabel, Bas, and for Shadow and me, before I reach inside my backpack for the orb.

It feels unnaturally heavy in my left hand. I take Shadow's reins firmly in my right.

When I opened the realm before, I knew I could do it. Knew in my soul how to do something I'd never done. I remember that moment—Samrael blackmailing me. Bas's life at stake. As I opened the portal, I felt Samrael poisoning the beautiful energy that had run through me. I felt him tainting the portal with his evil just before Bas sacrificed himself, launching into Samrael, sending them both hurtling into the realm.

That was how last time went. This time I'm on my own.

"Okay. Here we go." My pulse thundering, I draw a final fortifying breath and ask the orb to open, a request that whispers through my soul.

The orb's energy stirs and I feel it. Buzzing warmth that seeps into my hand and then hums down to my elbows, spreading through my chest and down my legs until it's a continuous wave, rolling through me.

In my palm, the orb is a small maelstrom of everything. Twisting fire and flowing water. Cold black granite and pillowy clouds. Earth, sky, stars. Laughter and tears. All churning with a speed I shouldn't be able to track, but easily do.

The orb lifts off my hand, light as a bubble floating into the air. It hovers over my palms and unravels like a ball of yarn, threads of fire swirling with green grass, twisting with streams of white feathers and veins of blood. It floats away from me, unraveling and growing in size, doubling and tripling until I no longer feel the rain, my drenched clothes or freezing hands, or even my fear.

I feel only love and connection—a connection that's immense and infinite. So like how I felt when I had the Sight, connected to the necessity of everything. Even *me*. In some remote part of my mind it registers how long it's been since I've felt this way. Necessary.

The orb unravels to twice my height and the swirling pattern solidifies into a tunnel like it did all those months ago. A portal with no end, no visible other side, but with walls that are stars and sun-seared deserts and the faces of every person in every time that ever was.

It moves toward me, or I move toward it, and one thread grows wider, liquid and glimmering like a sunstruck stream. Beside me, Shadow fades between her physical and ethereal form, smoky one moment and solid the next. I can't see beyond the thread, but Shadow pulls on the lead and I sense in my gut that it's the way to Bas.

I step forward.

It's instant agony—a cleaving inside me. Mind shredding away from body, heart pulling away from soul. Relentless pain, like a rift tearing through every part of me, and I know this is the poison that shouldn't be here, the poison Samrael brought to something that should be pure. I'm just beginning to wonder if it'll ever end when, with no warning, I lurch forward and go somersaulting over and over, no idea which way is up or down, no concept of where my body ends, until I finally stop.

Shaken, I climb unsteadily to my feet.

Dizziness hits me and almost sends me back down. A salty

taste slides over my tongue and I feel a deep throbbing ache begin at the base of my skull, like my heart has relocated there. I take a few deep breaths, waiting for it to go away, but it only lessens. Knowing I'll have to experience that again to leave here, dread starts to creep in. I can't focus on that now, though.

Shadow stands a short distance away. She's trembling and wide-eyed but looks unharmed.

The orb hovers a few feet away from me, spinning slowly and bright as a star. I pluck it out of the air and it immediately begins to dim in my hand. My breath catches as I notice that the crack on its surface looks longer, angrier.

Did I damage it by coming here? Have I broken it?

Panic bolts through me, but it's another thing I can't dwell on.

"It's okay, Shadow. We're okay." I run my hand over her neck, trying to give her reassurance I need myself.

I've arrived in a forest—not the arctic landscape I'd expected—and I've left the rain behind. The trees that surround me are ancient and gnarled, as much snaking roots as arching branches. I turn in a circle, still wobbling on my feet. I don't recognize what species of tree. Nothing I've ever seen before. They're everywhere—all I see.

That's when I notice the stillness.

Every single branch is motionless.

Even every *leaf*.

There's no wind here, no breeze, and it's dead silent. Soft moonlight filters down through the treetops like powdered chalk, and a subtle earthy smell surrounds me.

Shadow lets out a whinny and I jump, startled.

"What is it, girl?" Her ears flip forward and back. "Okay, Shadow. Easy. We're just going to see what happens for a minute."

It scares me that she's nervous. What's she sensing that I'm not?

I listen for what feels like an eternity. All I hear is Shadow's breathing and my own. Disappointment settles in, but what did I think would happen? That Bas would be right here, waiting for me to show up? Maybe this isn't even the right place.

Shadow nudges me in the back.

"Good idea." I remove my heavy coat and tie it to the saddle. Then I mount up and put her into a walk, alert to any sign of Bastian. Extra alert to signs of Samrael. He came through the portal too; I can't lose sight of that.

Under the canopy, the thud of Shadow's hooves on the loamy forest floor sounds close, like it's right beside my ears. The throbbing at the base of my skull has evened out to a noticeable but painless weight, like a hand resting on the back of my head.

Which isn't creepy, Daryn. Just a concussion, probably.

I pass tree after tree, and nothing changes. It's almost as though I'm on a treadmill. Moving with no visible progress. After a while—how long?—I stop Shadow and dismount. Time feels strange. When I check my phone to see how long I've been here, I discover that it's dead.

Of course. Of course it is.

I slide it back into my pocket and resist reaching for the knife stashed in my backpack.

It's too quiet here, too creepy, but I can't leave without Bas. Just the thought tightens my lungs. It makes my breath shallow and irregular, like a gear that won't catch.

This is how I felt as a girl when Mom was sick and I couldn't do anything to help her. The feeling is fuller here somehow. It's 3D despair. Despair that floats around me.

"Where is he, Shadow? Can you smell him?" All I want is

a clue that he's alive. "Sebastian! Bas, where are you? Please be here."

Something pale catches my eye at the base of a tree in the distance. I drop Shadow's reins and sprint over.

Growing under one of the sprawling trees, between two roots that look like outspread arms, is a patch of white flowers. The petals are mutedly bright in the darkness, like teeth are at night.

I kneel in the soft dirt and touch the furry leaves.

White begonias.

Mom's favorite flowers. She had them planted all over our yard in Connecticut.

At home.

Home.

The pressure at the base of my skull pulses harder, matching the drumming of my heart.

It's been eighteen months since I left home. When depression had her, *really* had her, it was like a dimmer switch had been turned down inside her. I couldn't reach her. Neither could Dad or Josie. Sometimes we couldn't do anything at all for her but watch her suffer. After my visions started, there was no point in staying. My problems would only have detracted from the care she needed. But I never meant to be away so long.

How has it been a year and a half?

I spot more clusters of begonias up ahead. They weave a path, making a trail that's almost bioluminescent in the dimness. I don't even think twice. I follow it, conscious of Shadow walking close behind me.

Soon I come to a break in the woods where a field of begonias glows under direct moonlight. A figure sits at the very center, surrounded by the white blooms. I can't see well in the low light but the figure looks small. Not lanky like Bas.

It's not him.

Then . . . who is it?

As my eyes begin to adjust, I see that it's a woman with honey-colored hair that rests on straight shoulders. Her long white dress pours over her legs and feet, and blends with the flowers that surround her. She's wearing a gold necklace with two charms that rest close to her heart. Though I'm too far to see the letters engraved in them, I know they're "D" and "J."

And as I near, she smiles like she's been expecting me.

My blood freezes. I stop.

It's not possible.

"Mom?"

"Daryn, my sweet daughter," she says. "I knew you'd come home."

CHAPTER 4

– GIDEON –

Twenty minutes out. Probably less," Travis Low says as he peels out of the tiny airport that serves Jackson Hole. The SUV fishtails on the soaked road but Low regains control and pushes past eighty miles an hour in a matter of seconds.

I look through my window. Rain clouds hide the tops of the mountains in the distance. The Grand Tetons. I flew over them in the fall. On the back of a demon that had taken the form of a dragon. I also lost Bas here and got my left hand cut off.

Lots of fun memories in Wyoming.

It's hard to believe that roughly three hours ago we were still in Georgia. Moving a team this fast takes money but if there's a limit to the unit's budget, I haven't seen it yet.

In the passenger seat, Jared Suarez checks his GPS. "Thirty minutes is probably closer. Traffic a mile up."

Between swipes of the windshield wipers, a string of red brake lights appears up ahead. "Drive around it, Low," I say, thumping the back of his seat for emphasis.

Suarez shoots me a dark look. "This is the United States, Low. Don't drive around it."

"Drive around it, Low," I repeat. "That's an order."

He laughs. "Blake's full of it today, ain't he?" he says to Suarez, loading his Texas drawl with all the sarcasm it'll hold, which is plenty. He meets my eyes in the rearview mirror, chewing his gum in slow motion. "Yes sir, Blake sir."

We're all on equal footing under Cordero so I shouldn't be

giving orders to anyone, least of all a commando thirteen years older than me. Travis Low has a hell of a lot more relevant experience than I do. Life experience, in general. Fortunately, Low and I go way back. Jared Suarez, too.

Last fall they were "Texas" and "Beretta" to me, respectively. The guys who stood guard while I was interrogated by a demon disguised as Cordero. They saved my life from that demon.

Low's a six-foot-five, two-hundred-fifty-pound lethal giant. Like Bas, he's always looking for his next laugh. Low doesn't take anything seriously except missions and his three-year-old son back in Texas. The guy drops everything when his kid calls and gets this heartbroken, happy look on his face. I've wondered if my dad felt that kind of pain when he talked to Anna and me back home while he was deployed.

Jared Suarez is ninja-quiet and calculating. He was a blue-chip high school baseball recruit—a catcher like I was. In a way, it's still Suarez's vibe. When Cordero's not calling the shots, Suarez steps in with the strategy and manages things. With the exception of Jode, who needs to question air before he breathes it, the rest of us pretty much follow Suarez's lead.

After fighting the Kindred with them and spending the past months in Cordero's unit, I have solid history with these guys. Marcus and Jode do, too. The respect and smack talk flow in equal measure in all directions.

As we approach the stalled traffic, Low doesn't slow down. He pulls onto the gravel shoulder and bears down on the gas, sending a hail of rocks and rain into the windshield. Low passes car after car with an expression on his face like he's supremely bored as Marcus and I bounce around like popcorn in the backseat.

When we're past the stalled car that caused the slowdown, I turn around. The other Suburbans with Jode, Cordero, Ben, and the rest of the team are obeying the law and have fallen behind.

"Jode," Marcus says, a smile tugging at his mouth. He won't like being left with the slowpokes.

"That's what he gets for sucking up," I say. But Jode doesn't really suck up. He just happens to be Cordero's favorite because they're extremely compatible. I mean, I'm Cordero's real favorite for sentimental reasons, but Jode's her favorite intellectually. They nerd out regularly by discussing the latest studies in science, technology, medicine. Et cetera. It all sounds the same to me. Like Wikipedia talking to itself.

The phone in Suarez's hand rings. He answers on speaker. "Suarez."

"Hold at a staging location off property," Cordero says. "Ben's sending you the address now. We'll regroup before we approach."

"Yes, ma'am. We were going to wait."

I don't want to wait. I've been waiting months for this already.

"Is that so?" Cordero says. "Then why roar past that traffic like your brakes don't work?"

Suarez looks at Low, who does a bad job of laughing silently. "We wanted to wait at the property."

"Tell Low we're discussing his driving later," Cordero says.

"Yes, ma'am." Suarez hangs up. "Morons," he says, addressing all of us. Then he checks the GPS again, inputting the address Ben sent. "Fifteen minutes out."

I settle back in my seat, trying to relax.

I've thought about Daryn a lot these past months. Pretty constantly. But I didn't focus on how to handle seeing her again. I spent my mental energy imagining that things were good between us instead.

I approached it like a math calculation.

Take away all the times she told you she just wants to be friends because she's afraid she might like you *too much*. I mean, *what*? How is that a reason? But it doesn't matter when you're imagining. Minus one confusing excuse—check.

Take away the memory of the look on her face when she saw you with one less hand. Maimed. Incomplete. Don't need that either, so. Get rid of it, too.

Take away the fact that she left one of your best friends to die in a realm *with your nemesis*. Tougher to delete. More brainpower required but I could get there. I could imagine it never happened.

Take all that out of the equation and what was left was good.

Without it, Daryn and I are incredible in my imagination. Tons of chemistry of all kinds. Physical. Mental. Emotional. Physical. Straight-up chemistry lab. Highly combustible.

I thought it would get old to picture us that way. Didn't happen. Wasn't able to get into hanging out with other girls, either. Anna brought her friends over. Marcus made an effort not to monopolize female attention. But being around other girls felt like killing time before the real deal. Before this.

"G?" Marcus says.

"Yeah, I'm cool," I say automatically. I look at my hands. They're in fists. Flesh and bone on the right, and magnesium alloy on the left. I open them. "Suarez, how close?"

"Five minutes."

Shit. I need a plan.

CHAPTER 5

⟶ DARYN ⟵

I have to be imagining this—it's the only explanation.

How else could it be possible?

But she looks so real.

So happy and *real*.

"Daryn, honey. It's me."

"It can't be. You can't be in here."

"I am, Daryn." She rises to her feet and spreads her hands. Like she's waiting for me to come to her, to hug her. Like she has nothing to hide. "It's me."

"It is?" My throat's squeezed up so tight, I can barely get the words out. And I still can't move. After eighteen months, only two dozen steps stand between us—but I can't even take one.

Burbling into my thoughts are memories of Malaphar, the demon that could take the form of others. Who fooled Gideon and the rest of us in the fall. But Malaphar was slain then, and demons can't see into my mind as a Seeker. How would they know about my mom?

I can't see how this could be a trick, so . . . maybe it's really her? But if it's really her, then how? Did *Samrael* bring her here?

"Yes, Daryn, it's me. I'm right here," she says, her smile going wider. "You've gotten so beautiful. I can't believe how grown you are."

Reflexively I look down, like I'll be able to see myself through her eyes.

Have I changed? I've never thought about it. I've only

thought about the things that were changing at home. The things *I've* missed.

"I've . . . I've seen a lot since I left." I only recognize the double meaning in my words after I've said them.

I *have* seen a lot in the past year. A lot of the world. Of people. Of suffering and pain—and of love, and grace, and good, too. And, as a Seeker, I've *seen*.

Mom's smile wobbles and her eyes well with tears. "I'm sure you have. You've been gone for such a long time."

"I know, Mom." When did I accept that this is *her*?

"I've missed you so much, sweetie."

"Me too." I'm about to step toward her, about to explain, to apologize, to hug her and start to bridge all the days and months we were apart, when her expression hardens.

"How could you do that to me, Daryn?"

The question steals the breath from my lungs.

"Where have you been?" she continues. "What could have been more important than me? More important than your sister and your father? How could you have left us? Didn't you think we'd worry? Where did you *go*?"

"Mom, I—" In my worst nightmares, these are the things she says to me.

"You thought I'd be better off without you."

"Yes."

"You were wrong. I needed you. I needed you, and you weren't there."

My heart shatters into pieces.

I want to run to her. I want to feel her hold me, and I want her to forgive me, and I want her to be okay, and me to be okay, but I can't move, can't take a step toward her because do I even deserve a chance? Do I even deserve her forgiveness?

"Daryn, you have to go. Right now."

"What? Mom, *no*! I'm not leaving you again." I don't understand her abrupt tone until I notice that the branches around me are shaking. Finally, there's a breeze here—no, stronger. Leaves rustle as wind sweeps past, and the begonias' white petals shudder.

"Listen to me. You need to leave."

"No," I insist, noticing that Shadow is braced, standing at high alert. "I'm not going without you—" When I look back at her, the white flowers at her feet are fluttering like butterflies. They're *moving*. Not just from the wind.

They rise up off the ground and settle over her white dress. Covering it. Blending in. White dissolving into white. Quickly reaching her waist and then moving higher. I don't understand what's happening, or why she's just standing there.

I drop my backpack and run.

Faster than I ever did when I ran track. Faster than I did when I was running for my own life in the fall.

I'm too late.

The flowers cover her. They wash her away like a wave. By the time I reach the spot where she was, they're receding. Returning to the patches along the forest floor.

I look down at the crushed petals under my boots.

They're all that's left.

I drop to my knees and rip, tugging them out of the dirt like I can bring her back, my vision blurring with tears. I want to let myself cry, but I'm afraid I won't stop.

And the wind is still rising, turning into powerful gusts. They shear through the branches and carry an acrid, wet smell that coats my throat like sludge.

Fear slices through me, bringing me to my feet.

All around me branches groan and toss, shedding their leaves. The gusts seem to come from every direction.

I sprint back to Shadow, snagging my backpack by one strap and grabbing the horn of the saddle to swing myself up.

Shadow squeals and jolts forward.

My shoulder yanks, nearly tears out of its socket. I miss the saddle, dragging beside Shadow before my grip gives and I hit the dirt.

Turning, I see the horror that scared her.

From the branches above where I'd just stood, a dark figure drops to the ground.

It lands on all fours. Soundlessly, like a spider. Then it straightens slightly onto its hind legs.

It's a haunting thing, cloaked and hooded, with a drawn face that's darkly wrinkled, a slack mouth full of razor teeth, and no eyes that I can see—just sockets that are fathomless pits. Its black cloak is ragged and swirls around it weightlessly, fluidly, like it's underwater. Its bony hands are tipped with long curved nails that are more like talons. They're the moldering yellow color of death.

Maybe it was human once. Not anymore.

It takes one step, and then another, hunkered as it comes, like it's preparing to spring at me. A low, purring sound gutters from its mouth.

"Stop! Don't move!"

It keeps coming, step after step.

Knife. I have a knife in my backpack.

The backpack I dropped. The backpack that's closer to the nightmare than it is to me.

Shit!

Beside me Shadow grunts to get my attention.

Get on my back. Get on, get on, let's go!

In a fraction of a second, I judge how close she is, how fast I am, how high I can jump—and then I leap.

My legs used to have the speed and strength to run hurdles.

They don't fail me. I grasp the horn and pull up, landing squarely in the saddle.

Shadow's turning before I jam my feet in the stirrups, accelerating in three powerful strides.

When I look behind me, the nightmare is bounding after us, cloak flapping, bony limbs churning.

It's fast—so fast it catches up, and launches into the air with that spidery weightlessness—the pounce of a predator bringing down prey.

Shadow sees.

She jumps to the side as I duck, wrapping my arms around her neck.

Something hooks into my lower back and drags across. Heat slashes over my skin, but I stay in the saddle as the thing flies past me.

Shadow keeps going but the creature doesn't pursue.

Why did it stop? Where is it going?

Dread hits me in the gut when I realize it's going after *my backpack*.

The orb's in there. I'll never get out of here without it.

I turn Shadow and grab the lariat tied to the saddle, the hemp smooth with use from lassoing teddy bears.

Dear God, really? *This* is what I'm doing?

As I get the rope circling over my head, Shadow rides true and smooth, like we've done this a thousand times before.

The nightmare sees us coming and sinks down in self-defense, but my throw is good—perfect.

The lariat slips right over the creature's head and falls past its shoulders. I yank hard, both of my palms burning as I draw it tight. Then I pitch the slack over a thick branch, catch it, and wrap the end around the horn a few times. Shadow does the rest, using her immense power to pull until the thing is hanging from the air, arms pinned to its sides, wicked feline hisses spraying from its mouth.

When I jump to the ground, my legs are shaking so badly that I almost collapse. I run to my backpack, pull out the knife, and throw the pack on. Pain flares in my lower back and blood runs a warm trail down my spine.

Holding the knife in front of me, I step closer. The creature stops struggling and swings gently, its black cloak oblivious to gravity, drifting on invisible tides.

This close I still don't see an end to those hollow eyes. It's like looking into two wells, so deep the bottom is unseeable. In appearance, the thing isn't a skeleton and it's not human—it's somewhere in between. But its movements are too eerily twitchy and sharp.

"What are you? Why did you attack me?" I ask the questions without expecting a response. The sounds the creature has made are too animal; there's no way it can speak. But speak it does.

"You won't find him," it says in a rasping voice.

Before I can think, I press the knife right beneath its jaw. "Sebastian? What do you know about him? Where is he?"

A wicked grin spreads over its face. The stench emanating from its mouth is like breathing grave. "You won't succeed until you fail. You won't win until you lose."

"What does that mean? What are you saying?"

"Your only hope is surrender." Another gust stirs past, shaking a million leaves. "Have more rope for my friends?" asks the creature, its attention moving past me. "Shame, shame. I fear you don't."

The smell carrying on the wind hits me again—that stale burnt stench. It's too dark to see beyond twenty feet in any direction, but I sense movement all around me. Sense it drawing in.

"Where is he?" I back away from it. "Is Sebastian alive? Is he all right?"

"Alive? Yes, more than me. All right? Perhaps, more than me."

Reaching Shadow's side, I mount up. Then I lay the edge of the knife on the rope. I have to cut it loose if I'm going to get out of here. But cutting the rope feels like it's also cutting hope.

The rustling of the trees is still growing louder and I hear coarse hissing sounds rising in the air. There must be dozens of them.

I can't face that many. I barely survived one.

I dig the blade into the hemp and cut the rope.

The creature drops, landing on its feet. It looks at me almost expectantly, showing no sign of wanting to attack again. But then it doesn't have to.

In moments, I'll be surrounded.

"Look, Seeker," it says, empty eyes panning the woods. "More than me."

There's only one option that doesn't get me killed.

I trade the knife for the orb. Then, faster this time, I coax the orb to unravel, praying it's not too damaged to still work.

It's not.

The spinning tunnel of limitlessness forms before me—a passage out of here that swirls with threads of all that's possible.

As I hurriedly lead Shadow inside, I brace myself for the tumbling, tearing feeling that will assault me. When it does, I tell myself over and over that it will end, that I can survive this.

I find the place where I came from—the thread linking to rain and melting spring snow. To Isabel, and the high peaks of the Tetons, and the little Smith Cabin with the noisy screen door, and even that black wolf out there somewhere.

Though I know it'll break my heart, I reach for it, doing the only thing I'd sworn not to do.

I leave without Sebastian.

CHAPTER 6

⊸ GIDEON ⊸

Because of the confidential nature of things, Cordero has Suarez direct the team in setting up a security perimeter when we reach the cabin.

The property is substantial, so this takes fifty minutes. I hate every one of those minutes, but at least they give me a chance to solidify a plan.

This mission is one hundred percent about getting Sebastian back, so. Working with Daryn is exactly that—work.

No more and no less.

Simple enough. Clear enough.

With the perimeter set, Cordero finally gives me the green light to approach. Marcus and Jode come to the door with me but they let me do the honors.

We set off a motion-sensor light as we step up to the porch.

With most of the team watching, I feel like I'm on a stage.

As I reach up to knock, I hesitate and go through a lightning-quick debate—prosthetic or right hand? Which makes no sense because I'm way past this. I stick with robohand, knocking a little harder than necessary.

Seconds pass.

I look at my boots, noticing the worn doormat.

There's a bear image on it, beneath which it says, *Please pause to wipe your paws.*

It's something Bas would love, this doormat. Guy never met a pun or a play on words he didn't appreciate.

"Gideon," Jode says.

"Right. I'm going."

Cordero has pulled the requisite clearance for us to enter, so I check the doorknob. It's unlocked, which is good and it sucks. *Safety, Daryn? Give it a try.*

Turning it, I step inside.

"Daryn? Isabel?" No answer again. I flip the lights. As Jode and Marcus slide past me to check the rest of the house, I take in the small living room. The faded furniture and stuffed bookshelves. The hunting trophies on the walls—elk, bison, buck, and so on. Lots of formerly living things in here.

Marcus and Jode return, confirming the house is empty. Relaying that to the rest of the team with radios.

I'm still stuck in the same gear—checking out this living room like I'm an anthropologist trying to figure out what kind of human lived here.

Except I know.

Daryn grew up with money. She never said so outright, but it was easy to pick up. Connecticut. Chief surgeon for a father. Mother who spends her time fund-raising for others instead of earning a living to care for her own kids, like my mom.

What did she think of these tired carpets and wood-paneled walls? All these hunting trophies staring down at her with shiny dead eyes?

The rest of the team starts to arrive. Cordero. Two of the MI Trio—Sophia and Soraya. We fan out, looking around in silence. Checking the notes on the fridge, the stack of bills on the coffee table. Searching for clues as to Daryn's where-abouts.

The roof is thin enough that I hear the rain drumming. The wood floors squeak as the team sweeps the cabin, but it's otherwise quiet. Until Ben storms through the front door.

"I found Isabel Banks!" We don't react quickly enough for him. "Daryn's mentor? Isabel? I know where she is right now." He pulls off his glasses and dries the lenses with a corner of his shirt as he talks. "She works at a nearby ranch as a waitress. A city-slicker-type place. Kind of fancy? I couldn't track her down there at first. She's not supposed to have the night shift, but—"

"Good, Ben. Great work." Cordero looks at Jode, then Low. "Go with him."

They leave with him to get her.

As I move through the kitchen, I see an open pack of Twizzlers on the counter. Daryn's sweet tooth obviously hasn't changed.

I head into the first bedroom. It's small. A twin bed and a dresser made of thick cabin pine. A nightstand and trunk—also pine.

Daryn's room. It smells like her. A mixture of fabric softener, flowers, and that smell of fall nights when the weather's just starting to cool—the smell of good things coming.

An ache moves down my throat, like the scents I'm breathing and can't get enough of are poisonous.

Shit, this is intense.

The mirror over the dresser has papers taped and tacked around the edges of the frame. Some are paintings made on colored paper, clearly done by little kids. Mostly versions of the same thing. Kids holding Daryn's hand as they ride horses. Unicorns riding through fluffy clouds. Pretty cute, actually. One in particular. Stealing goes against my moral code, but I'm tempted to swipe the one of Daryn riding a winged horse over a rainbow. Pure awesome.

There are also lined notebook pages covered in handwriting I recognize as Daryn's. I read the first one that catches my eye. The title at the top reads, "Blue."

mind and heart at war
for war
sky blue above me
inside me
my mind is mine
my wild heart is not
blue is what you are
darken
surround me

A shudder rolls through me. I step back, shaking out my shoulders. Step in and read it again.

This is about me, right? It's definitely about me.

But what does it *mean*?

"G, there's some—" Marcus freezes at the door when he sees me.

I back away from the dresser again, busted for I don't know what. Feeling a shitload of confusing feelings. "What's up?"

"Jode just called. He's on his way with Daryn's friend, Isabel. He said she thinks your hunch was right and Daryn went after Bas. One other thing. There's a stable out back. I went out there to check for Shadow but . . ."

"No Shadow."

Marcus shakes his head. "Daryn must've taken her. We found some tracks leading away from the stable heading east."

Bad news on top of bad news but my mind's only on what's next. "I'll take Riot and go follow them." I head for the door.

Marcus doesn't step aside. "You can't."

"There's no one around for miles."

He just looks at me, still not moving out of the way. I haven't ridden Riot outdoors since the fall. Cordero's too paranoid. A burning horse is hard to miss. Especially at night. "Cordero's sending a drone up to take a look. Nothing for you to do." His eyes narrow. "Take a walk or something, man."

He's right—I need to chill—but I don't love being called out on it. "You know what, Marcus? I think I'll take a walk."

He finally clears the doorway. "Do that."

I head outside, passing Ben, Soraya, and Sophia, well entrenched behind half a dozen laptops at the tiny kitchen table, through the living room where Cordero, Low, and Suarez are staring at a screen that shows the drone's feed. As I stride past them, I'm conscious of the moment of silence I generate in my wake.

In the short time I've been inside, Cordero's had the team set up floodlights around the cabin. They illuminate a hundred yards of slanting rain and muddy fields but come nowhere close to reaching the edges of the property.

I hop down the porch and walk toward the river, my mind jumping from one thought to the next. From confusing poems to frustrating actions.

Knowing that Daryn went after Bas alone is maddening. If she gets hurt or somehow fails it wouldn't just be Sebastian we'd lose. It would be her. It would be any chance of ever finding either of them. Worst possible outcome.

I'm almost at the stable when movement to my right makes me jump a foot in the air. Luckily, I stop myself short of summoning my sword and swinging.

Maia, our sniper, is lying on bales of hay covered by a plastic tarp.

"Hey, Blake! Sorry, didn't mean to scare ya." She lifts the tarp so I can see her. "Chill-out walk?"

"I've been told I need it."

Maia tilts her head like she's listening for something. She has a half-eaten granola bar in one hand, the other curled around an M24. Maia in a nutshell, right there. "Yeah," she says, "you do."

I shrug. "Yep." I'm not apologizing every time I get worked up. It would never end. Not that it happens all that much anymore. I've been pretty chill for a long time. Until very, very recently. After Marcus's graduation from Ranger School about a week ago, I couldn't shake off how close Daryn had been and how I didn't see her. I guess I got angry. I guess it affected Maia. She ended up breaking up with her girlfriend in a superheated phone call, which we all heard. In the food warehouse, everyone could hear everything. Maia told me she'd had it coming but I know it was partly my fault.

"It's amazing out here, isn't it?" she says. "I love this state."

"Yeah. Amazing." My answer doesn't sound sarcastic, surprisingly.

"Bleh." She frowns at her hand. "I took one of your granola bars by accident. These taste like birdshit, Blake. How do you eat these?"

"Quickly." One of the benefits of being under Cordero's wing is that she's hyperinvolved on almost every level. When she learned about my digestive issues, she had it checked out. Turns out I have celiac disease, which is about as sexy as it sounds. Eating is less physically painful now, which is good. But the trade-off is the grief I get for it. I can turn into fire. I have a burning horse and sword. Given the context, I can see the humor in War having a sensitive tummy. "See ya, Maia."

I've only taken five steps when her radio crackles. She answers and I hear Low's drawl. "You with Blake?"

"He's right in front of me." Maia hands me the radio.

"Blake, over."

"The drone just found her. Looks like she's headin' back here."

"Is Bas with her?"

"No, it's just her. No one else."

Chapter 7

— DARYN —

For the longest time, I lie in a wet puddle. Curled up like it's my bed. Like I'm not freezing or aching, or so disappointed I want to step outside of myself. Leave all that's me behind.

My lower back stings as rainwater meets the gashes the creature gave me. And my palms are rope-burned. Neither compare to the throbbing at the base of my skull.

The pressure is receding in pulses. It is like a heartbeat of pain, lessening by the second.

Shadow ambles over and snuffles my ear, telling me it's time to move.

I force myself to sit up and wince as dizziness hits me.

When the world stops spinning, I climb to my feet and see the orb. Once again I pluck the glowing little ball from the air. As it dims in my aching palms, the crack that runs through it splinters and shudders, and a piece of the orb breaks off.

No.

No, no, no.

A small shard, curved and rose petal shaped, has chipped off the main orb.

I brush rain off the surface. There are more fractures now, too. Cracks all over it, like it's sunbaked earth.

There's no question about it anymore. With every use, it's becoming more fragile and compromised. I wonder if it'll eventually be damaged beyond use and won't open the portal at all. I have to assume so.

Panic flutters in my chest.

I'm not holding an hourglass in my hands, but it feels the same.

Carefully, I slip both pieces of the orb into my backpack. Then I hoist myself into the saddle and head for the Smith Cabin.

Home.

Shadow's stride is sluggish and defeated. She's as down-trodden as I am.

The storm is passing. The rain is lessening.

It feels like a betrayal.

My storm isn't passing. I haven't moved forward. I don't know which way I've moved. My mind feels too foggy and slow to process what I just went through.

What was that horrible creature that attacked me?

Why was *Mom* in there? Was it even *her*?

I'm so consumed by trying to make sense of things that I'm not prepared when Shadow rears up. I fly back, pitching off the saddle, and land on my side on wet grass.

Only then do I see it.

Something silver just whizzed past us.

Shadow casts one look at me like she's trying to shake it off, but the whizzing sound returns. I've never seen a drone—not in person—but I know that's what the tiny remote-controlled-looking plane is.

I know it's going to terrify my horse, too.

As the drone circles back, Shadow shoots off as fast as a bolt of lightning. In just a few of her long strides, I've lost sight of her. She's disappeared into the darkness.

I jump up. "Shadow!" I chase after her, but she's gone.

Vanished.

My girl. My connection to Bas and the guys. My connection to my *sanity*.

I keep running, sprinting home, the backpack slapping at the cuts on my back, tears lodged in my throat, but hoping,

hoping, hoping. Maybe she went to the Smith Cabin? Maybe she'll be there? *Please be there.*

But as I'm coming up on the property, everything looks wrong.

There are spotlights everywhere.

Cars everywhere.

People everywhere.

I know what this is. I know who's here.

My boots suck to the mud as my legs grow heavy. I push on. Forward. No matter how hard this will be.

As I walk up I feel exposed by the lights. Everything I want to hide, visible.

I don't have Sebastian ambling beside me with his long strides.

I don't even have Shadow.

I have nothing.

I have failure.

Failure is something I have to spare at this very moment.

I'm covered in mud and bleeding and could there possibly be a *worse* time for this?

Isabel stands on the porch. She's the only one I want to see. Around her are strangers strapped with weapons and wearing serious, unfriendly expressions.

Then I see Jode standing at the base of the porch steps. And Marcus right beside him. And if I let myself keep panning over it would be Gideon standing there with them.

As I reach them, stopping in front of Jode, I know what I don't want to say more than what I *do* want to say. "Shadow bolted. She threw me about a mile west of here. All these lights and people, and the drone—they scared her."

The line between Jode's eyebrows deepens. I know he's processing much more information than what I've just told him. He looks slightly older and more rugged, like some of the crisp blue-blood edges have worn away. All the memories of him from our time on trains and in fjords flutter right beneath my eyelids. Jode riding Lucent. Jode with his nose buried in a book. Jode with a wry smirk on his face.

"We'll have the lights shut off," he says, like this is natural conversation following the eight months we've spent apart. "And we didn't know the drone would scare her." Then he opens his arms. Jode, who's the least affectionate. The least likely to do exactly what he's doing.

I step in.

Our hug is firm, quick, and horribly unsatisfying.

When I step away I want to crawl under the slats of the porch but Marcus is right there, waiting.

The sight of him is almost enough to break my control. I don't know how to pretend around Marcus—we've never been anything but straight with each other—and if he asks me if I'm okay . . .

"We missed you, D." He wraps me into his arms.

"Me too," I croak into his shoulder.

Then I turn to Gideon and freeze. For a lifetime.

He's right in front of me but I can't seem to absorb seeing him. He's like the sun—only visible indirectly. Somehow we move toward each other.

His arms fold around me. I'm shaking, but I can't stop it. This feels so forced, so false. When he squeezes, he unknowingly presses right on the cuts on my lower back.

Reflexively, my lungs pull in and my back goes straight.

I feel him freeze, tensing, but I dart back and immediately shut it down.

The pain. The disappointment. The fear.

I did all I could. Now it's time to move on.

"We should go inside," I say to anyone who cares. "I have a lot to tell you."

CHAPTER 8

⤙ GIDEON ⤚

After months of not knowing, the time for answers has finally arrived.

Maybe.

This *is* Daryn.

With her, information is never a sure thing.

I lean against the living room wall between Maia and Suarez and listen to her describe the crumbling orb, the pain of going through the portal, and then arriving at the woods she discovered on the other side.

She speaks slowly, her eyes on the mug of tea in her hands that's no longer steaming. Occasionally she pauses for long stretches to either think or collect herself. I think I used to be able to tell.

"The pain subsided once you were through?" Cordero asks, posing one of few questions so far. She's kept her interruptions to a minimum, letting Daryn set the pace.

"Yes. It was tearing pain at first. It felt like . . ." Daryn shakes her head. "Like a rift. A break inside me. Once that passed, though, I still felt pressure in the back of my head. Not a headache exactly, just . . . pressure."

I glance at the owl clock on the wall in the kitchen. One thirty in the morning, but no one looks tired.

Ben and Soraya run voice and video recorders on the coffee table in front of Daryn. Cordero sits directly opposite her in a straight-backed chair. Isabel is next to Daryn on the couch. Jode, Marcus, Low, and a couple of the techs are scattered around the room. We've been doing this for over an hour but it feels like five minutes. I've never seen a dozen people keep still for this long.

I'm the only one who's not locked into every word. My mind keeps taking detours, trying to reconcile the Daryn I remember with the Daryn in front of me. It's like getting the same picture but with a better exposure.

And I also keep thinking about what she's hiding.

I know she's bleeding beneath the blanket pulled over her shoulders. After I hugged her, there was blood on my prosthetic.

Who hurt her? Samrael? Why hasn't she said anything about it?

When she describes the white flowers that she followed, her voice becomes quieter and more measured, and I'm in. She has my full attention.

"I followed them," she says. "It almost felt like . . . like they were creating a path for me through the woods. Then . . . then I saw her. My mother."

For a second, no one breathes. Then Isabel asks the question on all our minds.

"Daryn, your *mother*? She was there?"

"Yes." Daryn looks up from her tea. "She was there. I don't know if she was real or if I imagined her." She frowns, her eyes going distant. "She seemed real. I mean . . . it was exactly her. Her voice. Her expressions. She told me she knew I'd come for her. She said all these things . . . I was talking to her. But then the creature came and she disappeared."

"Creature?" Cordero says.

Daryn looks at her. "The one that attacked me."

There's a stir of surprise around the living room but I've been waiting for this. Still, my pulse starts to race as Daryn describes it.

"It was horrible. Worse than horrible. Harrowing," she concludes.

"Any idea what it wanted?" Cordero asks.

Daryn shakes her head. "I thought it wanted to kill me. It definitely tried at first. But then it went back for my backpack. That's where the orb was—inside."

"Did the creature get to it?"

"No. I lassoed it and strung it up in one of the trees."

Pause.

Pause, pause, pause.

Jode turns his ear. "Say again?"

"I lassoed it with a lariat I had tied to Shadow's saddle and hung it from a tree."

Marcus smiles. Low and Suarez look at each other, eyebrows rising.

Then, for the first time since we came inside the cabin, Daryn looks at me.

None of my planning works. I have no idea what to say.

What she did was completely badass and dangerous and I know she's hurt and probably almost died. But none of that comes out of my mouth. Nothing does. I just cross my arms, hiding my prosthetic like a coward.

Why do I keep doing this? I'm not embarrassed about robohand. Never have been before.

Cordero keeps us on track. "You restrained it with a rope. Then what happened?"

"It told me that I'd never get Sebastian. And it told me not to even try, that there were more of them, those harrowing things. Dozens or . . . or maybe more."

I push off the wall, anger bolting through me. "It told you that?" No one's stopping me from getting Bastian back.

"Not in those exact words."

"What exactly did it say? Did it say he's alive?" My voice comes out harder than I intend, and all eyes are on me.

I look at Suarez. A vein stands out on his neck. I look at Maia. She's about to bite through her lower lip.

The signs are there. Time for me to become absent again.
I pull open the door and step outside.

Fifteen minutes later, Marcus joins me on the porch. "Cordero's calling it. We'll pick up in the morning. Probably a good idea for people to take a break."

"Okay. Actually, no. Not okay. Bas is in there with those things, Shadow's missing, and we're taking a break to get some sleep?"

"We're looking for Shadow. And Daryn's fried, man. You saw her."

"It took her *eight months* to do something, Marcus. Sebastian's been in there this whole time. Wounded. On his own. What do you think's happening to him? You think he's *taking a break* to get some rest? Sorry, but I'm having a hard time feeling bad that Daryn's a little *tired* when Sebastian could be getting tortured or worse."

I don't know why I say it. It helps no one. I'm not even sure I mean it.

"I'm not the one who's calling this off tonight," Daryn says, right behind me. She overheard it all. "Cordero wants to stop."

I straighten off the porch rail and face her. "How does it feel to not be calling the shots for once?"

"What's that supposed to mean?"

I don't know what it means. I'm on autopilot. I catch Jode's eye over her shoulder. He shakes his head slightly, and I know I should walk away but I don't.

"You blame me for this." Daryn steps forward and stares right into my eyes. "Just say it, Gideon."

"I'm not doing this. I've got nothing to say to you."

"Yes, you do. You blame me for leaving Bas in there. Why can't you tell me the truth?"

Unbelievable. This, from the girl who hides everything and

disappears any chance she gets. "I don't give a shit about why you did what you did, Daryn. Only one thing matters and it's getting Sebastian back. That's the truth. There. Now you know."

It's three in the morning by the time we check into an inn in Jackson Hole. The team took the last available rooms. Marcus, Jode, and I will be crammed in a room with a queen and a rollaway cot. As we take the elevator up, Jode and Marcus argue about who's taking the floor.

I toss my duffel through the door. "I'll take it." I won't be getting much sleep anyway.

Jode looks at me like he's going to say something funny, but he doesn't. What's there to say?

Great to see you and Daryn back in form?

Nice to see some things never change?

Jode's phone rings. He slips it out of his pocket and smiles. "Anna," he says. He moves further into the room, his voice goofy and high like he's talking to a kitten instead of my sister.

This perfect capper on my day makes Marcus laugh.

I shake my head. "I hate you. I'm going to go destroy something."

"Emergency stairs at the end of the hall," he says, knowing what I really need. "There's roof access."

That's where I go.

I step onto a small patio with stacked plastic chairs and tables. Underneath the tables, a few grungy piles of snow have still held on. Empty kegs tied with bungee cords lean against the wall. This is probably a great place to hang in the summer.

The rain has stopped and the night has a chill. I move to the edge of the balcony. The small square at the heart of Jackson sits in mostly darkness two stories below. Only a few lights are still on.

Turning back to the patio, I feel the anticipation building. I'd get reamed if Cordero found out I summoned Riot here, in such an exposed location. If people found out about us, the horsemen, it'd be a nightmare. *Yes, we're Death, War, and Conquest, but our purpose is good! Promise!*

That's a losing PR battle, so. You could say keeping our identities confidential is a matter of global security. And you could say summoning a burning horse on the roof of an inn in Jackson Hole is asking for trouble. There are all kinds of things you could say, but no one's around and I need my horse or I'll lose my mind.

I reach for Riot.

I've summoned him hundreds of times before, maybe thousands. It's a process Cordero tried to understand for months. How the guys and I can make supernatural horses manifest. How we bring them forward—and our armor and weapons.

Scientifically, there's no explanation. We have this energy inside of us, this power that we can produce as easily as we can speak words or exhale our breaths. Our horses come from inside us, and retain part of us, but they are not actually *us*. It's something in the middle. And something that ultimately originates from a power that's much, much higher than any one of us. To my knowledge no one's managed to put hard science around faith or God. Cordero gave it her best shot. Then she just came around to accepting the unexplainable, like the rest of us.

Riot comes up in a quiet whirl of flames stirring on the concrete floor. They build into a small burning tornado that solidifies into thousands of pounds of smoldering horse.

Broad. Red. All raw power.

If he were a real horse, he'd be a medium draft horse, or a warmblood. Not a Budweiser Clydesdale, but you wouldn't see him winning the Kentucky Derby, either. The guys joke because he's the biggest of our mounts. A lightweight tank with an attitude. But he's the greatest companion. The best. I can't even picture what my life was like before he came along.

His amber eyes find me first, then look around, checking things out, eventually coming back to me.

I smile. It's not that I hear his thoughts. It's more that I *know* them.

Bad day, Gideon? That's too bad. But I'm here now so you'll be better. Hey, nice view.

"Come here, horse," I say, but I'm the one who goes to him. I call up my armor so I don't have to be careful about burning my clothes. Then I bury my hands deep into his mane, sending a shiver of embers into the night sky.

He makes a low deep sound, telling me he's listening. That I can tell him what I'd never say to anyone, not even Marcus.

"I screwed up, Riot. Didn't stick with the plan. Said some really stupid things. *Really* stupid."

Ohhh. That's not good, Gideon. But it happens. Especially with Daryn. Don't worry. Tomorrow you'll do your best and try to fix it. I like Wyoming.

I laugh. Then I let my face fall forward, and rest my forehead on his broad neck. Letting his fire spread over me, and through me, and around me.

Warm. True.

Like peace.

CHAPTER 9

~ DARYN ~

"Daryn?" Isabel raps softly on my bedroom door. "They're here."

"Okay. I'll be right out." I stand on my toes and twist, getting a glimpse of the gashes on my lower back in the mirror over my dresser. Blood is still welling from the three cuts the creature gave me, three nice parallel claw marks. At least it's not pouring freely like last night.

The worst part is that they drag right across the scars I already have from crawling under the fence when I broke out of the mental institution a year and a half ago. My lower back has become a tic-tac-toe board of scars from the worst days of my life. Perfect.

I thought about telling Isabel I was hurt last night after the house emptied but I couldn't do it. I just needed some time alone after everyone left. And what are cuts compared to seeing your mother swallowed up by flowers? Compared to Shadow still missing or what Bas must be going through?

I'm having a hard time feeling bad that Daryn's a little tired when Sebastian could be getting tortured or worse.

Ugh. That comment from Gideon keeps haunting me. I didn't want to stop working, either—it was Cordero's doing—but that moment keeps replaying in my mind. I see it with perfect clarity. The anger in his blue eyes. The scruff on his jaw and the glint of his prosthetic under the porch light.

I wanted to cry when he said that. And I wanted to headbutt him.

I shake my head at myself and pull on my gray shirt. Then I tie a flannel tight around my waist. I wince at the pain, but this is the best compression bandage I can create on my own.

My notebook is open on my bed with the list I started last night.

A list, not a journal entry or poem. But it was a night for firsts, apparently.

1. My faith in God
2. Seeing Mom again, no matter what she said to me
3. Finding Shadow and Sebastian
4. Isabel's warm hands and unconditional love
5. Marcus's smile, perfect
6. Jode's voice, the charm of it
7. ~~Gideon. How on earth I can manage to find him stunning even when he's being a total and complete~~ Photo I took of Gideon's back/bearing/butt

They're things that popped into my head, things that bolster me, that give me the courage to keep going after Bas.

I write *Reasons* across the top, since that encompasses pretty much everything, and stash my notebook in the trunk. Then I twist my wet hair into a knot and head for the living room, ready for battle.

M orning, Daryn," Natalie Cordero says.
I expected a dozen people packed into our cabin again but it's only her and Ben, the guy with the buzz cut and black glasses who looks like a young astronaut. Clean-cut and stupendously brilliant.

Cordero's not too far off. She's businesslike in her dark suit, but there's also a military assuredness to her actions. I get the feeling that when a situation takes a nosedive she knows where the emergency exits are and how to deploy the water slide.

The cabin still smells of the blueberry muffins Iz baked for me at five in the morning when we had some time alone. I'd tearfully apologized for entering the Rift without telling her, and she tearfully patted my hand and told me she forgave me.

Through the window I see a dozen people milling by the SUVs on the drive. Several of them are eating muffins off of napkins. I hope they appreciate how amazing those are. Like Isabel, blueberry muffins are among my favorite things in life.

"Shadow hasn't come back yet," I tell Cordero, skipping past the platitudes. "She won't come back with all these people around."

She nods. "I understand your concern. I took the security down to the safest possible level but I do need to have some people here. For your good and Isabel's, and for the safety of this mission." Her smile is placid. Appeasing. "I want to show you something this morning, so we'll be going for a ride. I've studied last night's transcript and made a list of questions. Ben and the rest of the team have supplemented with theirs. We'll go through them in the car in order to save time. Isabel, you're welcome to come, too. Shall we go?"

My face warms. I feel like I've been handled.

Outside, the crisp air hits me, and the weight of a dozen foreign stares. I was too shaken up to focus on "the team" last night but now I notice them all. To think that I brought these strangers in on my failures unsettles me.

As Isabel and I follow Cordero to a Suburban, I see Jode, Marcus, and Gideon talking by a car. Marcus looks over but Gideon doesn't. I feel like a pariah, like I've been voted out of the group.

Ben the baby astronaut opens the door for me and I climb inside, trying not to lean back on the seat because I can still feel my cuts bleeding. The huge guy with the rust-colored beard is in the driver's seat. I notice he's wearing an earpiece and humming a song to himself. "All My Exes Live in Texas,"

I think. The dark-haired girl in the passenger seat with a rifle resting across her lap isn't much older than me.

"I'm Maia," she says, turning. "This is Travis but we all call him Low."

He meets my eyes in the rearview mirror. "Pleasure."

"I'm Daryn."

"We know," Maia says. "We've heard a lot about you."

It could've been a rude comment but her smile is genuine and even a little teasing. She faces front again as soon as Cordero slides in beside me. Low starts the car, and the motorcade—that's the only real word for this—gets moving.

"Daryn, I checked and your mother is home in Connecticut," Cordero says, before we've even left the property. "I've confirmed that she was at home last night while you were in the realm."

"You *called* her?" A wave of heat rolls from my head to my fingertips.

"No, I apologize. I should've been clearer. Of course we didn't call her. We have other means of discovering what we need to know. We were simply trying to confirm whether you saw an illusion in the realm or a reality. I think we can safely say it was the former."

As she speaks, Isabel's hand slips into mine and squeezes.

It didn't feel like an illusion. It felt more real than this moment, having this woman knowing more about my family than I do. "Is . . . is my mother okay?"

"Yes. She's doing well at the moment. Your father and sister are, too."

Cordero says this with a trace of warmth but it smacks of professional training.

"What does that mean, they're 'well'?" I ask. Does she know about Mom's depression? Does this mean Mom isn't having an episode right now?

Natalie Cordero taps her manicured fingers on the leg of

her slacks as she gives me an assessing look. I know exactly what she's thinking.

Can she handle this?

"It means that, by my standards at least, they're all relatively content. Your sister is in her second year at Yale, but she goes home most weekends to see your parents. Your mother is training for a marathon and she's planted bulbs for the year. Twice, it seems. Your father is working long hours, which seems typical. Four weeks ago at a fund-raiser, he bid on a puppy and won. Apparently it likes to dig and is quite good at it. They're installing a dog run, well away from your mother's flower beds." Her eyes sharpen on me. "Perhaps I shouldn't have—"

"I wanted to know. I asked." I look out the window. *My God, I miss them.* I've missed so much. Josie is a sophomore. Mom is training for a marathon? She always hated running. She never understood how I loved it. And a dog? They never let Josie and me have one. Why now? Do they even want it? I try to picture muddy paw prints on our rugs and can't do it. "What did they name the puppy?"

"Chief. He's a rescue. The breed is unknown but the veterinarian believes he's a blue heeler–boxer mix."

"Helluva mix," Low mutters.

"Right?" says Maia.

I'm not sure what they mean but I don't ask. I feel turned inside out. Everything sacred and secret about me is viewable and open for discussion. And the things that I *should* know are all mysteries. Only Isabel understands. She clings to my hand, giving me roots, connecting me to something. I would float away without her.

Cordero steers the conversation away from my family, asking me to clarify some of the things I told her yesterday. I don't want to tell her any more than I already have. She's prying into every little part of my life. But I make myself do it.

In the sparkling blue-sky morning my answers sound unbelievable. "I felt this extreme emptiness looking into its eyes," I hear myself answer. "I don't know—it looked harrowing. That's why I called it that. And yes, the flowers rose like a wave over her and she disappeared." It sounds absurd and cringeworthy. I'm so self-conscious about it that I only notice where we've arrived as we're pulling up.

"Here?" I ask. "The site of the battle against the Kindred?"

"To start." Cordero shuts the yellow pad where she's been jotting notes on my replies and slips it into her bag. Up ahead, a tall cyclone gate on wheels is set into a grove of trees. A man in cargos and a black sweatshirt pulls it open and we drive through.

I've wondered about this place—twice daily, since I drive right by it going to and from work. The fence went up right after the battle and there's always someone in a car parked in the trees just inside, day and night. The rumor I heard was that there's a complicated lawsuit going on between the landowner and the US government, but I'm pretty sure they're one and the same. And that the "lawsuit" is really just a decoy.

Less than a quarter mile in, the trees thin and the landscape changes. The grass is withered and dry, and the trees look brittle, like the area has been affected by drought. Then it's like we've driven onto the surface of the moon. The closer we get to the place where I opened the portal, the more extreme the desolation.

Low drives right to the spot where I stood when Bastian was stung by Ronwae, the Kindred that could transform into heinous scorpion-like creatures. My heart begins to thump a quick beat in my chest.

We get out of the car without a word. The earth here is a husk. No trace of blade or bug. Even the dirt is ashen, leached of every nutrient. There were a series of cabins in a horseshoe arrangement around this field once—they're still here but they're mere piles of timbers. Shipwrecks.

"This is the epicenter," says Cordero. "The damage began here about twelve hours after the portal was opened. It spread for approximately two weeks and it's been slowly restoring since then. Believe it or not, what you see today is a vast improvement over a few months ago.

"I call this a signature—a unique mark left by the opening of the portal. I believe the energy from that realm bled through when it was open and left its mark here." She looks at me. "The same thing is happening at yesterday's location. I have the team working on containment there now."

"Is it harmful?" My voice sounds hoarse. I had no idea this would happen.

"The vegetation is a straight loss. Animals and humans tend to clear out—or else they suffer the effects of exposure."

"What effects?"

"Short-term, the effects are headaches, irritability, confusion, nausea. Similar to what you described feeling last night. Long-term, we're still analyzing the data."

"Were you here for that?" I ask Maia, who's standing a few feet away.

"Yeah. I felt awful for about a week. It sucked. We were all here. We all felt it."

I look around me, at Low and the half-dozen people here. Then wander off, feeling dazed. And *responsible*.

I opened the portal.

Marcus and Jode make their way over and join me.

"How you doing?" Marcus asks. He drops his arm across my shoulders and tucks me against his side, which makes my eyes blur.

"Apart from the fact that I unknowingly made this happen? I'm fantastic."

Jode stuffs his hands in his pockets and bunches his shoulders against the chill morning air. "Mad, isn't it?"

"Yes."

"None of us knew, Daryn."

"I know."

Gideon is with Low and Maia. As he gestures to the Tetons, sunlight flashes on his prosthetic hand. I ache to get a closer look at it. I ache to get a closer look at *him*. But I don't expect him to come over like Jode and Marcus, so I just say what I need to say.

"I lost the Sight right after this . . . after we were last here." I swallow the gritty emotion in my voice. "It just stopped and I didn't know if it would be wrong to go after Bas without it. And I didn't want to mess up. I didn't want either of you to get hurt, or Gideon, too. I mean more hurt, in his case. Even though I didn't know about his hand or about Bas in the fall. You know I'd *never*—I'd never have let that happen . . ."

I'm rambling. But Marcus saves me. "D, it's all right."

"You have to be so angry at me."

Jode rolls his eyes. "Would *we* ever hurt *you* on purpose?"

"Maybe *you're* not mad, but . . . Gideon."

They exchange a look. "Talk to him," Jode says.

"I don't see that happening." Regardless, something starts to patch together inside me. This is a good step with Jode and Marcus, at least. Suddenly I feel a rush of optimism. I want to catch up on the past eight months. "You looked handsome, Marcus."

He smiles. "Right now?"

"In your uniform at the ceremony in Georgia."

He laughs. "So not right now?"

"Yes, right now. But especially that day."

"Cease, Daryn, I beg you. Or we'll never hear the end of it." The smile fades from Jode's eyes as he looks past me. "Here come our marching orders."

Natalie Cordero walks across this devastation with a sure

stride and sensible heels. She's put on dark sunglasses and it unnerves me to not see her eyes. "It makes an impact, doesn't it?" she says. "I wanted to show you this so you'd have some sense of the effect of going into the Rift."

"The Rift?"

"Last night you used the word a few times when you described crossing over. My team liked it and we needed to call the realm something. They also adopted a variation of your description for the creature. They're calling it a Harrow."

Ugh. *Your* description. And *my* team. I hear what she's not saying, loud and clear.

Cordero removes her sunglasses and slips them into the pocket of her jacket. "Daryn, I know you want to go back for Sebastian. We all do. But as you can see, we can't do that here without causing serious damage to the surroundings, not to mention the danger it would mean if some of the Harrows were to escape. We need to move to a safer location where the signature won't be as evident and where I can stage a covert defense force.

"My analysts have recommended a site in the Nevada desert. It's desolate. The terrain won't show the signature, like here. And it's already government property, so it's secure. I have people setting it up. It'll be ready for us when we get there."

I try to wrap my head around what she just said. "You want to relocate everyone to Nevada?"

"I'm going to relocate everyone to Nevada. It's already happening." She checks her watch. "We fly out in two hours."

"Well, have a nice flight. I'm not going anywhere until I find Shadow."

"We found her. Rather, she came back to the ranch and we were able to bring her in. She was trailered to the airport ten minutes ago and loaded onto the plane."

"She's—*what*? What did you do?" I can't believe what I'm hearing. "You can't load her onto a plane! She's traumatized!"

Cordero's back straightens. "She resisted at first but she's on board, unharmed, and already en route."

"You sent her without me?"

I guess I'm yelling, because Isabel and Gideon rush over. The rest of Cordero's precious team has stopped what they're doing to listen.

"It's a short flight and you'll be right behind her," she replies. "As soon as we're all in Nevada, we can regroup."

I'm beyond anger. Beyond words. Shadow has become as close as my own soul. If there's one thing I've done right these past months, it's protect Sebastian's horse.

"What's going on?" Gideon asks as he walks up, his blue eyes sharp. For the first time, it feels like he sees me. Like we see each other.

"It's Shadow," Jode says, and starts to explain.

A sick, panicky feeling spreads over me. I interrupt him. "Where's the orb?" I know where it should be—where I stashed it last night, in my backpack in my trunk at the Smith Cabin. In two pieces. How could I leave it behind?

"It's secure," Cordero says. "Nothing will happen to it."

"You *took* it? You searched through my things?"

"I couldn't leave such a powerful and important object unprotected. It's safe. Much safer than where we found it."

"Who do you think you are?" I feel like I've just relinquished all my power. No—not relinquished. It's been *taken* from me. "You can't just show up and do anything you want!"

"I'm only trying to plan and execute our next rescue attempt as expeditiously as possible. A life is at stake, Daryn. Every second counts."

What can I say to that? I'm the girl who waited eight months to make a move.

"Then I guess we better get going." I walk away, thinking only of Shadow.

I have to get back to her side.

We make a quick stop at the cabin to pack.

I stuff clothes into my duffel and then shove my journal and my letters to my family in my backpack. I got so used to living on bare necessities while I was a Seeker that I don't own much, only things that have meaning.

The orb has meaning—and it should be right here.

A wave of anger at Cordero moves through me, but I zip up the pack and sling it over my shoulder, wincing as it bumps my lower back.

As I look around my tiny room, a feeling like pre-nostalgia moves through me.

I'll never come back here. I feel it somehow, this knowledge, and it makes me wistful. I've been incredibly sad within these walls, but they've protected me. This room has held my sadness. That's something.

There's a soft knock on my door, then Isabel steps in wearing a sad smile. For a few seconds we just stand there, saying nothing. Then she says, "I have to stay."

"Oh." The only reason she'd ever leave me is because the Sight has told her to. Because she's needed somewhere else. Not with me. But it doesn't change the way it makes me feel. Unmoored. Cut loose. Without her and without Shadow there's nothing for me to hold on to, and though I did that for a year, traveled the world alone, the idea of solitude now sends a swirl of anxiety through me.

"Are you sure it's a good idea to leave me unsupervised with Cordero?" My attempt at a joke falls flat. Isabel knows exactly how hard this is for me.

"Natalie is on your side, Daryn. Let her help you." She places her hands on my shoulders and squeezes. "And you have the guys—"

"I don't."

"Yes, you do. They're with you. But never forget that *you* know what you're doing."

"Do I? Do I know how to fight off dozens of freaky creatures with no eyes?"

"You don't have to fight. Fighting isn't the answer."

"You didn't see that thing. It was evil. You don't make friends with it."

"Friendship isn't what you need to offer. Daryn, evil is its own undoing."

"You mean they'll suddenly see the error of their ways? I don't think so."

Isabel sighs. Smiles. "Listen to your heart. Pray on it. You'll know what's right."

Jode calls from the family room, telling me they're ready to leave.

"Go," Isabel says. "And trust, even when it's difficult. *Especially* when it's difficult."

I hug her quickly. Then I grab my duffel and my backpack and hurry outside.

Trust? Trust *who*?

I should've asked.

CHAPTER 10

— GIDEON —

Our private charter is still ten minutes away when we get to the airport, so the team fans out around the small terminal to wait. We've spent the past few days hustling and we're all tired. No one passes up the chance to zone out or grab a few minutes of sleep.

I'm about to sit by Marcus and Jode when I see Daryn enter the women's room.

I should go talk to her. Clear the air. The sooner the better.

"The men's room is that way, G," Marcus says.

"But Daryn's not in the men's room," Jode adds.

Marcus's eyebrows climb. "Ohhh."

"Get your asses up and watch the door," I tell them. "And shut up? Like, preemptively shut up about anything you do or do not observe in the next ten minutes."

When I step inside, Daryn is splashing cold water on her face at the sink. She doesn't react at all when she sees me. Just grabs a paper towel and dries off.

"Um . . . are you lost?" she asks. Her eyes are red, and I can't tell if she's been crying or if she's just tired.

"No." I reach into my pockets and pull out the butterfly bandages and antiseptic I grabbed earlier from a medical kit. It was smart of her to wrap the flannel around her waist. You wouldn't be able to see the bloodstains on the plaid pattern unless you were looking. I was looking.

Daryn glances toward the door.

"No one'll come in."

Her shoulders relax. She unties her flannel slowly and sets it on the sink.

I stand behind her, putting the supplies on the counter.

The gray T-shirt she's wearing is sticking to the wound as she tries to lift it up. "Can you—?"

"Yeah, I got it." She props her arms on the sink and squeezes her eyes shut as I peel the fabric up.

I almost can't contain my reaction. Three gashes run sideways across her lower back where her spine curves. They're deep cuts. Angry.

Instantly, so am I. She dealt with this kind of danger. I wasn't there to help. None of us were. It's not right.

I draw a breath and concentrate on settling down. There's nothing I can do to change this right now except treat it. But when the times comes, whatever did this to her is going to suffer.

I notice there are also pale scars running perpendicular to the cuts, faint lines on her bronze skin. Daryn told me how she got them, escaping from the mental hospital where she ended up when she started having visions. She's been through a hell of a lot in the past couple of years. Most of it on her own.

"Is it bad?" she asks.

I clear my throat. "On a scale of one to ten this is probably a five."

"Will I live?"

I meet her eyes in the mirror. "Yeah. You'll live."

I clean her up with some wet paper towels, then use the gauze pads to stanch the bleeding. Since I'm standing right behind her she can't see robohand, but its whirring sound seems louder than normal, and bad. I use it as little as possible, ripping open the packaging for the butterfly bandages and gauze with my teeth.

As I treat the cuts, a whole other part of my mind is noticing unrelated things, like the white lace peeking above the waistline of her jeans. The goose bumps on her skin and all the ways her body curves. The clean, flowery smell of her hair makes my heart bang against my ribs.

I'll be revisiting these details at a later time, no doubt. And often.

When I apply the antiseptic, Daryn drops her head and laughs a shaky laugh. "Um, you said five? It hurts like a ten."

"Five was a preliminary number until I got a better look. This is a seven point five—that's an official diagnosis." In several spots the cuts graze muscle. I'd be howling if I were in her place. I'd be crawling up the walls and begging to be put out of my misery. "But the good news is you won't need stitches if you can keep these bandages on."

"I promise I won't rip them off." I know she's smiling but I keep my head down. Keep on task. "Can I ask you something? How do you work with Cordero? She's so pushy."

"She's not that bad. She can be bullheaded but her heart's in the right place. I know she screwed up with Shadow but I think she feels bad."

"How can you tell? Did she appoint someone on the team to feel feelings for her?"

"Nah. Some people just have a hard time saying they're sorry. They show it through their actions."

"They showpologize?"

"Exactly."

"I think I know someone like that."

"Oh, definitely. Marcus is the worst. He'll eat his shoes before he apologizes."

Daryn laughs. "Weird how I don't remember that about him at all." She twists her hair over her shoulder, doing this spiral thing I remember, and shifts her weight. "You and I have made some real memories in bathrooms."

I almost fumble the butterfly bandage in my hand.

She's bringing *this* up?

Last time we were in a bathroom together it was in Rome and we kissed. A lot. First and only time that happened. I have no idea why she's mentioning it and I don't want to know.

"That's right," I say, like I'd forgotten about it. "Okay. All done." I wad up the trash and toss it.

She turns to me and I shove my hand into my pocket. This hangup I have with her and my prosthetic is getting old. I'm not self-conscious about it. I wasn't, even when I first got it.

Daryn arches her back, testing out my patch job. "Thank you." Her shirt's still pulled up and my self-control doesn't kick in fast enough to stop me from sneaking a glance. Her stomach is bare and smooth. Amazing. Just . . . amazing. "It hurts more, which I think is a good sign?"

Sign. Hurts. Wound—her wound. "It'll feel better in a couple of hours. I'll check it later and change the dressing."

"That sounds good. Thanks."

"You're welcome." Did I just say "you're welcome" for something I haven't done yet? "You may want to change into a clean shirt."

Her mouth lifts on one side. "I'll do that after you leave."

Don't let me stop you. Go right ahead. "Okay."

I catch a glimpse of my reflection and want to bang my head against the mirror. I look insane. Partly like I want to jump her and partly like I'm watching the most incredible sunset I've ever seen. Time to get this under control. "Daryn, we need to be able to work together. For Bastian's sake. We have to be professional. Civil. Let bygones be bygones."

"Definitely." She nods. Frowns. "Professional and civil. Of course."

"Good." With that settled, I get myself out of there.

Apart from sounding like a moron a few times, I handled that much better than yesterday. Didn't yell or make stupid accusations. Did everything I planned to do, so. Successful mission.

Outside, Marcus runs a hand down his jaw. "Blake, man." He shakes his head.

"What?" I look from him to Jode. "*What?*"

Jode laughs his psycho-kid laugh, a short one like a hiccup. "You're a bloody idiot."

Because we have to go around some weather our flight lasts slightly longer than it should, an hour and twenty minutes. We land on an airstrip on a playa, a wide stretch of paper-flat desert framed by low mountains. As we taxi I can see our base—a series of trailers, semis, and vans. A modular building is going up at the center. A crew lifts huge light panels that flash in the sun, like ants carrying around leaves. Then I see the plane sitting on the opposite end of the runway.

Shadow is in there.

A few seats over, Daryn's watching it too, barely blinking.

The MI Trio are waiting for me as I deplane.

Soraya hands me a radio. "Just holler if you need anything."

"Thanks." I slide it into my pocket. A cool breeze blows past, carrying a slight scent of sulfur.

"Or push the button and tell us what you need," Ben says. "That thing's got a mile range. The whole point is you shouldn't have to holler!" He laughs way too much, his shoulders shaking like he's working a jackhammer.

"We're really tired," Sophia says.

Soraya nods. "Major sleep debt."

I thank them and jog to catch up to Marcus, Daryn, and Jode, who are already halfway to the other plane.

Daryn sees me coming and frowns. "Where's everyone else going?"

"Away," Jode says. "To make it easier for Shadow."

She squints up at Marcus. "You guys arranged this?"

"G did while you were gettin' packed."

"We all did." I tip my head at the guys. "They came with me to talk to Cordero."

Jode shrugs. "But it was your idea. Marcus and I simply stood there. You did all the talking."

"That's right. We just backed you up." Marcus nods a few times.

I telepathically inform them that I'll be kicking their asses as soon as the opportunity arises. "Shadow will have a stable by your RV," I tell Daryn. "It's being set up on the edge of camp opposite the generators, so hopefully it'll be quieter. It might not help much, but . . . maybe it'll help."

She doesn't say anything. I wonder if she's thinking, *Show-pology?*

I also wonder if it's working and if I'm hitting the bar we've set for professional, civil conduct.

As we near the ramp I remember Shadow and Bas on the plane we took to Rome last fall. Both of them tall and spindly. Bas wearing the goofy grin he always got around his mare, and saying, *You can lead a horse to Rome, Gideon. But you can't make it drink every day.* So random. I don't know why Bas made me laugh so much. He just surprised me all the time.

Bas and Shadow were the first to bond. He was always a few steps ahead of the rest of us without even trying. Things just come easily to Bas, like he's ad-libbing through life, no problem. That's how I know he's still alive. Bas is the least lethal one of us, but he's the real survivor.

I stop as soon as I hear loud, labored breathing coming from inside the plane. Shadow. It sounds like she's hyperventilating.

"Stay out here and keep the ramp clear," Daryn says. She

breaks into a sprint and plunges into the darkness of the cargo hold.

Seconds pass. A full minute.

Against the glare of the playa the hold is dark and I can't see anything.

"Should we go after her?" I ask Jode.

But then finally I hear Daryn's voice. "It's okay, girl. It's all right. It's just us. The guys are here to see you. Gideon and Marcus and Jode. They're right outside."

Shadow's long black legs emerge from the pitch dark. Shaking legs, moving one at a time. Then her powerful chest and long neck move into the sunlight.

I've missed her. But this isn't the horse I remember.

She looks broken. Eyes wild and unsettled. Ears laid back like she's ready to fight. Foam dripping from her mouth. Hardly any wisps of smoke curling off her legs.

She stops halfway down the ramp when she sees us and lets out a loud whinny.

Daryn is right beside her, human shoulder to horse shoulder.

"Is she looking for Bas?" I ask.

"No," she says. "She knows he's not here. I think she's looking for your horses."

I summon Riot without thinking. He torches up, rising from the ground ten feet in front of me, the only thing out here brighter than the desert. Until Jode calls Lucent. The white stallion manifests like a lightning bolt bursting up from the ground. Heavily built like Riot, but more flash and less trouble. Marcus calls his mare, Ruin, immediately after. She swirls up like gold dust and bronze ash, the most perfect of the four, built for speed and strength. Entirely beautiful.

For a long while we stand by our horses. Marcus's mare nickers softly. Lucent stamps twice. Riot looks at me like, *Just hold your horses. We got this.*

Then Shadow continues down the ramp, still terrified, one

shaky step at a time, Daryn right beside her, until they're standing with us.

"She was like this the first two months, after Bas," Daryn says, stroking Shadow's neck. "Worse, in the very beginning. But she got better over time. With me, anyway."

"Can you ride her?" Jode asks.

"Yes. But she can't fold. We both lost something that day. Besides Bas."

I know Daryn means her Sight. Jode told me earlier that she stopped having visions—that it's the reason she waited all this time to go after Bas. I can understand it now. All these months of waiting make sense.

Last year, when my dad died, I was seventeen. Already making my own plans, paving my own path. But when big decisions come up, I miss having him to talk to. Having that sounding board. Someone who I know would steer me right. Daryn didn't lose her father's voice—what she lost is divine, so it's different. Way different. On a whole other level. But it's a loss I can relate to.

My radio chirps. "Blake, what's with the horse show?" Suarez asks. "Cordero's blazing mad, man. She's starting to look like Riot. You weren't authorized to—"

I click the button. "Suarez . . . static . . . don't . . . over." I turn the volume all the way down and drop it back in my pocket. "What do you want to do, Daryn?"

"I think we can ride to the stable if we take a wide berth around camp."

"Okay. Let's horse up."

We mount up and leave the plane gaping behind us.

Shadow's skittish the entire way, tossing her head and shying like a racehorse approaching the starting gate. The other horses become anxious, too. Riot keeps wanting us to fold, to fly, and I have to keep shutting him down.

At the stable Daryn walks Shadow into the structure,

taking her time. I notice dozens of people watching from a distance.

When Shadow and Daryn are inside and finally out of sight, Riot lunges beneath me and takes off. I barely hold on, almost flipping over his back. Ruin and Lucent are on the same page; both horses tear after us across the playa, straight out into a whole lot of flat nothing.

Jode and Lucent fold first, becoming a blaze of light shooting across the blue sky. Then Marcus and Ruin blur into a stream of bronze ash. Riot and I are last. An eruption of flames sweeps me out of my physical body, to fire. Then we're shooting over white earth.

The desert and our base camp and the mountains grow smaller, farther away, as we eat up more of the sky. I catch Jode and Marcus and we accelerate to top speed, defying sound and gravity. Pushing beyond feeling.

Soaring.

When I'm with Riot this way I'm invincible, unstoppable. I know in my soul that God gave him to me—an ally, mentor, and friend. Riot is what I got for carrying the burden of being War. For having a red temper that I constantly have to manage. With Riot, I feel grace. I feel whole in a way that only Jode, Bas, and Marcus can ever really understand.

And maybe Daryn. I wonder if being a Seeker gave her this feeling of wholeness, which she'd have lost without the Sight. *Brutal.*

Bas, too. Without Shadow, he's gone without this for a long time.

Do you think Sebastian is like that, too? Wherever he is in the Rift, do you think he's as scared as Shadow was just now? As broken?

It's both my thought and Riot's. But I know we're *all* thinking it. Jode and Marcus, too. Lucent and Ruin. We're all feeling this worry, no way to fix it, no immediate way to get to some-one who needs us, so. We do this to make ourselves feel better.

We fly.

It almost works.

CHAPTER 11

— DARYN —

I find Maia waiting for me when I step out of the stable after getting Shadow settled.

"Is she okay?" she asks, adjusting the machine gun—rifle?—on her back as we walk. I never see her without it. I'm starting to think it's her equivalent to my notebook.

"She'll only be okay when we find Bas, but under the circumstances, yeah. She is."

"She's so pretty and badass. She's my favorite of the four horses. Don't tell Marcus."

"She's your favorite?" I smile. "Thanks. Mine, too. And I won't tell."

Maia escorts me to a meeting that's been called at the command center. Along the way she points out the sections of Corderoville—my term, not hers. There are the living quarters where the motor homes are lined up, and where Maia informs me we'll be sharing an RV. The supply zone, where semis loaded with provisions are parked and where the generators hum in the desert quiet. The real highlight, though, is the structure at the center where we end up—a kind of deluxe pop-up shelter.

It's the biggest thing out here, constructed of steel supports and pieces that look like heavy canvas, covered by a metal roof that shines as brightly as the sun. It looks modern and expensive, like something out of a futuristic film. It instantly annoys me.

I don't know why we need all of this. All we need are the

horses and the orb—which is in Cordero's possession. Which annoys me even more.

Giant Travis Low stands at the entrance with a wad of tobacco tucked into his lower lip. I don't realize I'm shaking my head in frustration until he pulls the door open for me and says, "Let 'em have it, whoever it is."

"Right?" Maia points a thumb at me. "We're friends *and* roommates so I'm safe."

"As long as you don't snore," I say.

Low likes this. He splits a grin and offers his knuckles. I knock mine into them, feeling like I've fist-bumped a cement block.

Inside, people are still plugging in extension cords and setting up laptops, printers, whatever. A power drill whines as it tightens screws. The people doing the work are single-minded, seeing nothing beyond what's in front of them.

A couple of tables have been pushed together at the center. Cordero is at the head, speaking in a slow, methodical voice to the entire team like she's delivering a presentation to the board of directors. She sees me as I take the empty seat between Marcus and Maia but she keeps talking, not missing a beat.

No, no, no. Don't wait for me to start, Cordero. I'm only the one who controls getting us into the Rift.

Carry on.

I listen for a little while. Her report covers this location. What can be expected from the weather—warm days, cold nights. Wind. Possible stray thunderstorms. Blah blah blah, we're not going on vacation, so why does this matter? She describes the security. There are teams at all of the main access points into the valley; drones will monitor everything else. We don't need to worry about planes, since this piece of land is an annex to an Air Force base a hundred miles south. Call me crazy, but I wasn't worried.

She's clearly proud of this place. Of having pulled this together. I struggle to care. I *should* care. But seeing as how this meeting started without me, and would have happened whether I was here or not, it's not easy.

My attention wanders to Isabel. Is she at the cabin? Waiting tables at the ranch? On her way to Peru on some other task as a Seeker?

Then it wanders to Gideon, who's sitting right across the table, tipping back in his chair.

I haven't had a chance to look at him, really do it, but now that we've reached a peace accord of sorts, I feel I can.

He's wearing a black baseball cap turned backward and I notice his honey-blond hair is long enough to peek beneath his ears and that his nose is pink with a light sunburn. He's gotten more muscular through the shoulders in the past few months. Broader. Not husky, but definitely stronger. That, and the newfound experience in his eyes, makes him look older.

I wonder if he runs or lifts weights, and if so, if it's tougher to do with his prosthetic or if it makes no difference.

I've always had this feeling around him like he's bigger than the space he occupies—that hasn't changed. Some people have presence like that. They're noticeable without trying to be. It's his innate confidence, I think. He looks like he never feels the need to be anyone other than himself. It's compelling. A spatially tangible confidence.

Gideon's eyelids have been growing heavier as I've been watching him. Desire kindles inside me and speeds up my pulse, just like when he treated my back. He's not *trying* to look sexy. But it's happening anyway. When he stifles a yawn, I find myself smiling.

Until his blue eyes slide over to me.

I look past him, like the power-drill action in the back is really interesting.

Civil and professional, Daryn. Civil and professional.

Cordero is still going on about "camp" like soon we'll be paddling in canoes and roasting s'mores. "No one goes anywhere after dark alone. Camp lights will run all night but this playa is one hundred and twenty square miles. Getting lost is still a real danger. Okay. Let's take a quick fifteen-minute break before we turn to the mission plan."

People start heading to the coffee station set up in the back.

"A break?" I say. "It's almost three. Shouldn't we get going?" Cordero looks up from her yellow pad. "Aren't we going back in tonight?"

"Hello, Daryn. We're going to make our foray into the Rift tomorrow morning."

"Why not this afternoon?"

"We're still getting set and we need to create a strategy. We're not going to charge in there without a plan."

The condescension in her voice is almost imperceptible. But it's enough to make the blood roar in my ears. "How long does it take to create a strategy?"

"Reasonably?" She smiles, but it doesn't reach her eyes. "Until tomorrow morning. There are a lot of variables to consider. Terrain assessment. Threat assessment. Search procedures. Contingencies. Communication between the two teams, and so on."

I'm so tired of hearing about teams I'm not part of. "What *teams*?"

"It's on the other side of your agenda," Ben offers.

I flip over the paper in front of me and see the breakdown. The three guys, which I had expected. But then I see Travis Low. Jared Suarez. Maia Goss. Natalie Cordero. Ben Halpern. "I don't understand. Are all these people going in, too? *Why?*"

"It's safer. We can get spread out and get more accomplished."

"It's not safer! We don't need them. They'll just end up getting hurt." I look at Marcus beside me. "It should just be us."

"But it won't be," Cordero says impatiently, like she's answering the questions of a simpleton. "You told me there are dozens of the Harrows. 'Maybe even more' were your exact words. Everyone on the list is highly trained and has experience in combat. And Ben and I will be gathering data that could prove indispensable."

"Okay, great. Sounds like it'll be a great party." I get up and toss the agenda on the table. "Enjoy your coffee and your fancy mobile center and your printed agenda. Let me know when you want to get Bastian. I'm ready."

I go right back to Shadow.

One of the military guys is posted at the portable stable. He wears reflective sunglasses and a deadly smile that reminds me of a crocodile. I have no idea who he is, but he lets me in without question, and says nothing when I bring her out ten minutes later, tacked up and ready to ride.

I mount up and take her straight out into the desert.

After a few minutes I feel her stride lengthening, her muscles loosening, and it feels good to be with her, only her, though I'm sure that up in the fading blue sky somewhere a drone is keeping tabs on me.

If I had the orb, I'd go back in there after Bas right now. Maybe I don't have what it takes to fight a bunch of terrifying Harrows, but I'd try. I've gone past the point of waiting. I've become allergic to wasting time. Finding Bas feels possible and urgent.

And I want to see my mother again. I need to tell her I didn't abandon her. That I didn't leave because I was trying to hurt her. I left because I love her. Because I couldn't stand to see her so sad and not know how to help.

Cordero said she was sure it wasn't Mom inside the Rift. But somehow it doesn't matter to me, I realize. She *felt* real. I just want to see her again. And right now, Mom inside the Rift is closer to me than Mom in Connecticut.

The sun is setting as I return to camp. I find the other horses in stalls by Shadow's. Riot, Ruin, and Lucent look ridiculous penned like normal horses, and I laugh as the steel walls of their enclosures begin to make sense to me, considering Riot. Someone must have thought it would help Shadow to be with them—and it's a great idea. I think it will help. And I think I know who the "someone" was.

I absorb the horses' presence for a moment. I haven't been alone with them since Norway. There's a hallowed feeling in the space around them. A sense of spaciousness and quiet, like standing in a cathedral.

All three of the horses watch as I brush Shadow and weave her silky mane into three thick braids. Lucent bobs his head like he wants to be next—such a fancy-pants, Jode's horse— but I'm starving, my body's tired from riding, and the cuts on my lower back are pulsing with pain. I'm pretty sure some of the bandages have opened. I hug Shadow's strong neck and leave them for the night. Food smells and the sound of conversation drift from the mess tent but I head for the RV Maia pointed out earlier as ours.

My duffel and my backpack are inside, on the full-size bed in the small room in the back. I grab them both and toss them on the twin bed set into an alcove in the narrow hallway, putting Maia's stuff in the bedroom. I don't need much space and I don't want to experience any form of luxury on Cordero's dime.

After a hot shower, I feel better but my back is bleeding again. Since my arms haven't gotten any longer, the best I can do is press tissues against it until my shoulder sockets ache. I throw on some sweats and find a bottle of water in the mini-fridge, taking it down in two tilts. Then I slide into the booth and send Isabel a text to let her know things are fine. I've just hit send when Maia climbs into the RV.

"Pizza," she says, raising the paper plate in her hand. "I figured you'd want to eat here. I hope Carnivore's Delight is okay. Not a lot of vegetarians around here."

"Yes, it's perfect. You're the best." I dig in immediately. "Did you bring anything sweet?"

"Only memories." She looks up, pretending to go starry-eyed. "Of this amazing scope I saw in Low's hunting catalogue at dinner."

"You're a unique person, Maia."

"Says the girl who opens realms. Oh, and I have this." She reaches into her back pocket and drops a rolled-up stack of papers on the table. "Minutes from the meeting. I had to bring them. It'd be great if you could read them at some point so I don't get fired. But do it later." She nods toward the door, which she left open to the night. "People are hanging out in one of the trailers. Why don't you come?" She gestures to my clothes. "You're all dressed up and everything."

I laugh. "Thanks, but I don't think so. I'm . . ." I don't have a great excuse. Or even a decent one. "I'm used to being anti-social. It's kind of my thing."

"Nice," Maia says. "You'd make a good sniper."

"I snipe with pen on paper."

"Badass, Martin. Okay. There's a radio on the counter if you need anything, and someone'll be patrolling outside twenty-four-seven. You good?"

"Yep. I'm good."

"I don't want to leave you but I'm the reigning blackjack champ and I need to defend my title."

"I totally understand. That's a big responsibility."

"Right? I knew you'd get it. Okay, Martin. I'm out. Party in solitude."

In less than five minutes I regret my decision and wish I'd

gone with her. *Seriously, Daryn. The social-recluse act is getting old.*

I pull out my notebook and try to add to "Reasons," but I'm too distracted and end up doodling around the margins. I try on Maia's sniper gloves, which she left on the kitchen table. The right index finger of one of them has been cut. Trigger finger, I realize. *Whoa.*

Then I rummage around the kitchen and find graham crackers, but I don't eat any. They're Josie's favorite and seeing them makes me miss my sister. It makes me picture her with her hair piled up, a pen clamped between her teeth as she pores over a textbook.

A knock on the RV door pulls me from my thoughts. I'm sure it's Maia coming to convince me to be social. I pull it open, already agreeing. "Okay, I'm in! You win!"

It's Gideon.

"Hey." His smile goes crooked with surprise and confusion. "What'd I win?"

"Oh, hey! Hi. I thought you were someone else."

"I knew it was too easy."

"Easy?"

"To win something for just showing up."

"Oh, right. Well . . ." I try to think of something to say that won't add to our communication meltdown. *You're a winner in my book. Winning isn't everything.*

He holds up a small black pouch, saving me from myself. "Dr. Gideon Blake, at your service. I'm here to literally watch your back."

"Great. Come in." I feel my face warm and I don't know why. We established a professional code of conduct. This is no big deal. I gesture to the kitchen. "Is here okay? The bathroom's tiny."

"Sure."

I turn and lift my baggy sweatshirt, wondering if he'll

comment. It's a San Francisco Giants sweatshirt. Not his, but exactly like the one he had that I borrowed a lot last fall. I had to get myself a replacement.

His fingers are warm as they trace the cuts. Every touch is like a tiny tremor that spreads through me. Small earthquakes of feeling. I'm instantly so nervous that words start building up in my throat, fueled by a need to create conversation and hopefully make wound care less sexy. "Does it look better?"

"Marginally."

"That sounds promising. Am I going to have to file a medical malpractice suit?"

"No way. I rocked this. Your dad couldn't have done a better job on these."

"You remember he's a surgeon."

"I have a good memory."

"For me or for everything?"

I hear him swallow. "Sometimes there's no difference, but . . . both."

All the words in my head disappear and my breathing goes shallow and quick. For a long time, all I feel is his touch on my back. It's the epicenter of all sensation.

"Forget I said that, Daryn."

"I'll never be able to."

"It doesn't change anything."

"Why not?"

"Things with Cordero seemed tense before. At the meeting."

"She's doing this all wrong, but don't change the subject."

"She's just thorough. You'll get used to her. You should read the minutes. They're epic."

"Please stop changing the subject."

"I'm all done here." He tugs my sweatshirt down. "The bandages should hold until morning. I'll leave this stuff with you. Maia can handle it next time."

I turn. He's already on his way out. "Gideon, wait. I really messed things up, didn't I?"

He stops at the steps that descend to the door. "No. We're on this. We're going to get him back tomorrow."

"I mean between us."

He freezes on the small landing at the bottom, hand on the door, his back to me like the photo I have of him at Marcus's graduation. His head falls to the side like he's relaxing, but I know he's not. "What are you doing, Daryn?"

I step down to him. He turns and his blue eyes find me. They're guarded, and suspicious.

I know exactly what I'm doing. I'm taking my foot off the brake. Just this once. Just to feel what I've imagined all these months. I lift onto my toes and bring my mouth to his.

I thought he'd hesitate or draw away, but he doesn't. He wraps his arms around me and we collide, connect, combine. His lips are surprisingly soft, his tongue softer, but the energy between us is hard, desperate. Every cell in my body charges with his strength, his energy, his clean alpine smell. His uneven breaths dance with mine, our hunger for each other raw and equal.

He pushes or I pull, and my back thumps into the wall.

"Your back."

"It's fine."

He bends to kiss me again and I steal glances, so I don't forget. I see slivers of sky through his long golden lashes. His wet lips, his eyebrows furrowed with intensity. It's all the friction and disharmony between us, reversed and multiplied and perfect.

"Daryn," he says hoarsely. "My hand."

"It's okay."

"But it's—"

"Fine, Gideon."

His hands slip under my sweatshirt and run up my sides, cool and hard on one side, warm and soft on the other. I want to tell him how he makes me feel but it seems impossible to describe. I pull his shirt up and he understands. Reaches over his back and it comes off and he stands, hair ruffled, eyes heavy. He moves toward me again, but I'm not done looking at him yet.

He's beautiful. It's possible that he was made for me. Strong and lean. Every line of him fascinating.

Tattoos. He has tattoos now. A cross on his right forearm. And script on the inside of his biceps, ornate and only three letters.

Bas

I look away before responsibility crashes back in. There's a black brace on his left arm. It wraps around his elbow and biceps, extending over his forearm and becoming the sculpted metal that's his prosthetic.

A sick feeling blooms in my stomach. Dread for all the things I'm trying to ignore. All the things we haven't said yet.

Gideon has gone stone still.

I look up.

The expression on his face is definitely, definitely not what I want to see.

His anger I can take. Not this.

"I was wondering how long it would take for you to regret this," he says. "Took a little longer than last time." He grabs his shirt off the step and leaps up to the hallway, disappearing into the bathroom. He leaves the door ajar and I hear the faucet run.

This regret, this mortification, whatever this is, makes my heart feel sick.

A knock sounds on the RV's door and I start in surprise.

"Don't answer it yet," Gideon says, shutting off the tap. "Give me a second."

Moments later, he appears at the top step, shirt on.

He looks hurt, and he should. We drew a line in the sand and I stomped all over it.

"Gideon, it's not that I don't want . . ." I don't know what to say. Apologizing feels wrong. Everything feels wrong.

"I know." He comes down and stops in front of me. This close, I feel his anger. It's a dull feeling, not sharp and pointed.

My ears burn and I notice a drop of water on his neck. Water is the essence of life. *He* is essential. He makes time stop, makes my mind rhapsodize.

I want us to disappear into each other like waves into sand.

"I've been trying to figure out what 'darken, surround me' means from your poem," he says. "The one called 'Blue.' Because I'd do it, Daryn. Whatever it is that means to you, I'd do it if I knew it was what you wanted. But you need to be sure first. Otherwise we'll just keep hurting each other." He pushes the door open, steps around Maia, and strides off into the night.

My list is what saves me. I add to "Reasons" until sleep slams the door on my mind.

8. Carnivore's Delight pizza, really good even cold

9. New friends, maybe? It's been so long

10. Butterfly bandages, gauze, antiseptic—sometimes healing is easy

11. White begonias

12. Puppies named Chief (what do you look like, little Chief?)

13. Shadow's bravery today

14. Kissing Gideon! Amazing. All-encompassing. Lips should not possess such limitless power. And the way he looked at me—ardently (!!!)

15. The Terrible End to #14—tragic, save for the discovery that a) he read my poem and remembered it, and b) he might actually understand me

16. Tomorrow, because we'll find Bas and this will all be over

CHAPTER 12

— GIDEON —

W hat's keeping them so long?" Jode tugs at his hair. "Have I gone completely gray yet? Do I look like Gandalf the Grey?"

Lucent shakes his massive white head, as impatient as his rider. He's ready to go, too.

"Yes," I say. "You're exactly like Gandalf, except a pop-star version. Lord of the Sing."

"This isn't good, man," Marcus says.

"Yeah, it was a reach." *Bas would have liked it, though.*

I reach down and check the saddlebag for Bas's weapon— the scales. Like Shadow, they didn't go through with him into the Rift. Cordero has kept them safe until now. Soon I'll be handing them back to him.

Marcus tips his chin, indicating the rest of the team. "How's this gonna work?"

We've been sitting in our saddles for an hour on the edge of camp under a bright morning sun, waiting for them. The problem is their horses.

Cordero, Ben, Maia, Low, and Suarez will be riding into the Rift on the five Arabians that were trailered here late last night. So far, integrating them with our horses isn't going well. Riot appears to be the main issue. The Arabians can't seem to make sense of a totally chilled-out, happily burning horse. We have ten people trying to figure out how to settle five horses, and everyone seems to have a different method.

Marcus's comment was only meant for us but Cordero hears it.

"Once we're inside we'll split up and give them some distance to your mounts," she says. "It'll work."

Seeing her in black tactical gear is kind of disorienting. Low, Suarez, and Maia pull it off, of course, but Ben and Cordero look like they're going trick-or-treating dressed up as ninjas. I remember what Daryn said yesterday—that Cordero's handling this the wrong way. But Cordero's smart and knows her stuff. She'll keep a solid chain of command. That's critical to the success of any mission. And whatever gets Bas back is what I want.

Cordero lifts her foot into the stirrup and swings up in a motion that's exaggerated. The mare dances beneath her, and Cordero does all the right things, turning the horse in a circle. Establishing who's boss. But I notice the mare's quivering muscles and wide eyes. Riot makes a low sound like he disapproves, and Marcus looks at me, sending the same message.

Ben's next, mounting up with Low holding his horse by the reins. Cordero insisted that everyone on the team take riding lessons when she first formed this team, so they're conversant in horsemanship. Conversant. Definitely not fluent.

Finally, with Young Gandalf about to lose his mind, everyone settles in enough for Daryn to bring Shadow out. Shadow's the last add by design, since she's already so jumpy.

Daryn rides up from the direction of the stable. I remind myself where my head needs to be. Not on what happened last night. I'm getting Sebastian back today. If I'm lucky, I'm getting some revenge, too.

Cordero gives the signal and the posse gets moving. I'm in front until Jode takes the lead. Conquest has to be first or he gets chippy.

After a little while I turn in the saddle, checking out the

group. Cordero was right. At the rear, the Arabians seem to be settling down.

In ten minutes base camp is a spot of brightness behind us, like a mirror in the sun. To the west, a small defensive military force has dug in. There's also a larger secondary line farther back, and air support if needed. This is a precaution Cordero arranged in case the Harrows come through during our crossing. The last thing we want is more demon trouble.

We reach our designated location for entering the realm—a spot that was marked with an orange flag by someone earlier today.

Suarez leaves his horse with Low and goes to Cordero. She removes a black box from her saddlebag, and keys in a code. Suarez brings the box to Daryn, who lifts the orb from inside. The process seems too formal or ceremonious. Especially compared to last fall, when it was just me, Daryn, and the guys, running from demons and camping out in the mountains of Norway.

"Where is it?" Daryn looks from the strongbox to Cordero.

Cordero says nothing for a long moment. "It's in your hand. You're holding it."

"The *other* piece. Where's the shard that broke off?"

"Ben?" Cordero asks.

He shakes his head. "First I'm hearing of it."

"You didn't think to tell us about a broken piece?" Cordero asks Daryn.

"I guess I forgot to submit it to your agenda, since no one told me when anything was happening."

Marcus looks at me. I know we're thinking the same thing. *Not good.*

"We'll look into it later," Cordero says. "Will the orb still work?"

"There's only one way to find that out."

"Then let's do it. We can't delay this operation, Daryn. We have to get into the realm now."

Daryn's eyes flash with anger as she nods. "I understand. All these people are here. We have a schedule to keep." She cues Shadow forward. Then something tumbles over the desert in front of her, and I realize it's the orb.

My first thought is that she dropped it, but then it rolls into the air. Rolls *up,* like gravity is nothing, until it's hovering at her eye level. Just spinning there, ten feet away.

Apparently it still works.

Someone behind me gasps as it begins to brighten and spin, unraveling. But most of us have seen this before. This is how we lost Bas—through this portal. It's where Samrael disappeared into, too.

On that thought, I call my sword. Samrael could be waiting on the other side with his bone blades and his mind tricks, ready to attack. Jode and Marcus must have the same idea. They summon bow and scythe.

A thundering crack shreds across the desert to a flash of blinding white. Then shadows slash across the brightness, streaks of darkness and color whirling around us. Spooling with images of every kind, every thing. Howling wolves and white-sand beaches. Pigeons scattering off rooftops, comets trailing across the sky.

Jode and Marcus are beside me, but I'm seeing them through a blizzard of flash and color. Ahead, Daryn stands before a thread flowing with images of trees. I recognize them from her description—gnarled and eerie.

There's a sudden jarring lurch and I'm moving at warp speed, sure I've left parts of me behind. My lungs and my thoughts. My eyes and my heart.

It's agonizing pain, splintering pain, and I understand why Daryn called it a rift. It goes on and on, and I'm reaching my breaking point when I come back with a jolt and rock forward.

My face smashes into Riot's neck. My teeth dig into the inside of my lip, unleashing a warm flood in my mouth.

Leaning down, I spit on the dirt by Riot's hoof, telling myself it's not a bad omen that I've bled here before I've even drawn a breath.

Straightening, I scan the woods.

Then I take a head count.

Everyone made it. And we're not in immediate danger, as far as I can tell.

I reach down and pat Riot, feeling the tension in him. He's disoriented and completely torched up, fire covering all of him and most of my legs. "It's all right, Riot. We're good. Except you split my lip."

He makes a low sound. *Maybe you should've moved out of the way. I don't like this place.*

"I hear you, Big Red."

The cut inside my mouth isn't half as bad as the ache that's melting out of my body. And I see that I'm not the only one having a hard time.

Low's cursing in English. Suarez's cursing in Spanish. Both Ben and Cordero look pained and it doesn't help that their horses stamp and struggle at their reins, wanting to bolt. Jode holds his bow at full draw. He looks ready to blow something up. Marcus has his scythe resting against one shoulder, waiting for the rest of us to pull it together.

Daryn has dismounted. The orb is in her hand, solid again. Still bright, but fading. "Everyone okay?" she asks.

"Not really," Maia says. She slides off her saddle, staggers a few feet, and vomits.

"Welcome to the Rift," Low mutters.

I pull in a deep breath. We've left behind the glare of the

desert for forest darkness. The air smells leafy, damp and cool. The long branches almost block out the sky—a purple sky, like fading dusk.

It's hard to believe I'm here. Where Bas has been for the better part of eight months.

"Gideon, I think you're bleeding," Ben says, grimacing like injuries don't compute in his mind.

"Just a cut." I wipe my mouth. "I'm fine."

Jode lowers his bow. Then he frowns at it. "Gideon, call away your sword."

I do it.

Try to.

"Gideon?" Cordero says.

"Nope." My connection is down. My sword is still right in my hand.

We all look at Marcus, but we know it'll be no different. He lifts the scythe off his shoulder and gives it a sweeping turn in the air—his favorite way of calling it forth and sending it back—but, like the bow and sword, the scythe goes nowhere. His mare, Ruin, starts to prance anxiously beneath him. "Nothing." Marcus sends me a pissed-off look. "We can't fold, either."

I reach for Riot anyway, asking him to go to fire. It's like we're in the dark, no way of finding each other. Riot bobs his head up and down, about as happy about this as I am.

This isn't good, Gideon. I can't protect you if we can't fold.

I rest my hand on his withers. "We're good, big guy. All good."

If our abilities as horsemen are gone, the only good news is we won't have to worry about my anger contagion in here. Marcus and Jode, too. Their effect on others would also be gone. Not that either of them struggle as much as I do. They're both way more adept at controlling fear and will than I am at controlling anger.

The only thing left to verify is whether we're still capable of rapid healing, but the cut inside my lip will answer that soon enough.

"GPS doesn't work," Low says. "Neither does my compass or my watch."

"Digital?" Cordero asks.

"Negative, it's windup. Both hands have stopped moving."

Everyone looks at me, and my gut sinks. I can't get my prosthetic to change gestures. It's stuck in a half-open position like a metal mannequin hand. But at least it came through with me. I'd worried it wouldn't. "Only one of my hands stopped moving," I say, to be hilarious.

"I told you about this," Daryn says to Cordero. "I told you my phone didn't work before."

"As we've verified." She looks at Suarez. "We'll have to adjust."

Lots of setbacks, but we do adjust. We're prepared.

Cordero takes the orb from Daryn to return it to the lockbox. "It's getting worse. The damage is more severe," she says, pausing to study it in her hand. There's a note of actual concern in her voice.

"Yes, it is. Take good care of it," Daryn says. "And don't lose any more pieces."

Marcus catches my eye and smiles.

We immediately break into two groups, as planned.

Cordero, Ben, Low, Suarez, and Maia will dig in here at our entry-point location. The rest of us will conduct the search. Jode will keep track of time using our riding pace. Marcus will mark the earth with his scythe, indicating our direction. All four of us will look for Bas.

"Let's bring him home," I say, and we ride.

CHAPTER 13

━ DARYN ━

We fall into a formation.

Jode in the lead, followed by Gideon, then me, and finally Marcus.

The plan is to search for forty minutes, then retrace back to the B Team, at which point we'll "assess," which I'm pretty sure means "Cordero decides what to do next."

We're looking for Sebastian but we know there are threats in the Rift, like the Harrows and probably Samrael, too. Which is why I didn't want all these people to be here, risking their lives, but that ship has sailed.

As we head away from the B Team, the trees close in, dampening sounds. Maia's voice vanishes quickly behind us.

I'm struck by an unsettling thought: We're no more than mice crawling under the folds of a cloak. Small and blind.

And scared.

It doesn't feel right leaving the others. And even my group feels wrong, like we're together but not *together*. It's no time for doubt, though.

"These trees," Gideon says, with the same awe I felt when I first saw them. The branches look like broken limbs, the knots like yawning faces.

"They look like they're going to come alive," Jode says.

The silence thickens even more. I feel it settling into my bones. The sound of the horses' hooves seems loud. So does my own breathing. And every shadow reminds me of the

Harrow, with its spidery speed and agility. Its depthless eyes and raspy voice, speaking in riddles.

You won't succeed until you fail. You won't win until you lose.

I don't know what it meant but I'm not losing. I'm not failing.

A dull ache has settled at the base of my skull, just like the last time I came here. It's more pressure than it is pain, but it's still distracting. I have to force myself to stay focused.

Cordero's briefing had a section on identifying signs of human presence. Any tracks, broken branches, or scratches in tree trunks are worthy of investigation—but as we ride I don't see anything.

Until the flowers.

As soon as I spot the sprinkling of begonias up ahead, I'm struck like a music cymbal. A tremor rolls through me. My hands start to shake and Shadow snorts, sensing my unease. The petals are brighter in the gloom than I remember, glowing from some internal source, like Lucent.

"You okay, D?" Marcus asks.

They've stopped with me—even Gideon, who's been avoiding me all day.

My cheeks start to burn under his gaze. Last fall I told him about my mother, and I know he's thinking about that conversation right now. As tense as things are between us after last night, I still feel connected to him. The bond between us may be damaged, but at this moment it feels indestructible. Crisis-proof. Or maybe crisis-bonded.

"I'm fine." I cue Shadow. "Let's keep going."

We ride on, and my heart riots inside my chest as I see that the flowers make several paths that curl through the trees in different directions. I want to break into pieces so I can follow them all.

Is my mom at the end of one of them? I need to see her

again. I need to apologize and tell her that I love her and I'm sorry I left her.

Beside me, I hear the hiss of Marcus dragging the blade of his scythe across the earth, leaving a groove to mark our direction. He settles the staff on his shoulder, the blade curving behind him like a steel wing.

"Daryn," he says.

"Yeah, what's up?"

Gideon and Jode have pulled slightly ahead.

Marcus runs his free hand over his close-shaved head. "The headache you said you got last time. I have it."

"You do? Have you had it since we got here?"

"No. Just started."

"*Ho—halt,*" Jode says in front of us.

Something is nestled in the white flowers in the distance, something glaringly different from the trees. I don't even think; I vault from the saddle and run. Gideon is beside me in seconds. He reaches over his shoulder to unsheathe his sword.

"What the hell?" I hear him say as we reach it.

The silver car is nestled in the tangle of roots between two close-set trees. It's an older-model Mustang, dented and scratched. With tinted windows and Chicago license plates. The driver's-side door is open. Inside, the darkness is deeper but I can see that it's empty.

Gideon slowly paces around it. "Why this?" he asks when he's circled back to me. His blue eyes are honed with intensity.

"I don't know. I have no idea." How do you explain a car here in the Rift? Parked like it's been here for ages? And it's not just any car. It's the one Marcus was driving when we found him in the Mojave Desert last fall. Marcus fled home in this car.

Gideon's gaze moves to Marcus and Jode, who are riding our way. "Shit."

Marcus dismounts. He stakes his scythe in the earth and strides up, his face emotionless. He reaches out slowly and rests his hand on the hood, like he needs to be sure it's real. I notice the shudder that rolls through his broad shoulders.

The Mustang looks as real as anything can ever be, solid and tangible. But it projects a presence too, like it's a living thing that's only dormant.

Marcus's expression darkens as he stands with his hand on the hood, and I can almost see the memories playing in his mind. This car is a reminder of one of the worst times in his life.

Last fall, Marcus told me he'd taken it from one of the five guys who had beat him to death—which had led to him coming back *as* Death. He had attacked the guys first. But he'd been retaliating on behalf of a friend who'd been assaulted by them—a girl. Brutalized by all five. *I* have nightmares about what he went through. I can't imagine how *he* feels. Not to mention his friend, the girl who suffered more than either of us. And who undoubtedly still suffers. Marcus had been driving for days when we found him. Out of money. Stranded in the desert. Terrified by what he'd become. Death.

I don't think anyone knows this except me—and Gideon, maybe. It's all Marcus has ever offered—not much. But I respect it. You don't always get the answers. The gaps don't always fill in. Sometimes you have to live with not knowing everything. I'm learning that.

Unquestionably, though, this car is a physical token of pain he carries inside him. Just like . . .

Mom.

The hair on my arms lifts and tears spring to my eyes.

"Shame to break up the fun," Jode says dryly, "but we're past time. We need to head back."

We stand a moment longer, the four of us, and I feel the focus shift away from the car to Sebastian.

We haven't seen a single sign of him.

The same feeling washes over me as when I came back to the cabin a few days ago—failure, starkly exposed. No shelter from it. No escape from the glare of disappointment.

The ride back is more infuriatingly monotonous trees. I don't expect anything else, not even after seeing the silver Mustang, so I'm not prepared when a structure comes into view through the scrim of branches and leaves.

A house?

No, a cabin.

The Smith Cabin.

My home in Moose, Wyoming, sits beneath the trees, the A-frame roof disappearing into the thick canopy.

It's exactly the same, with a porch and weathered green paint. Wooden shutters with the moose details carved at the center.

My fear cranks up to such a fever pitch that I go numb.

There's no question about whether we'll go to investigate. We quickly make a plan.

Jode will stay on watch, Marcus will look after the horses.

Gideon and I approach on foot once again. This time with caution.

I don't want to go anywhere near it. But what if Isabel is in there?

What if *Bas* is?

We step onto the porch and I lead, knowing which boards creak, which ones to avoid. When I see the doormat, it stops my heart. A black bear, with the words *Please pause to wipe your paws* beneath it—exactly like in Wyoming.

Gideon steps aside. "Door," he whispers.

He's holding the sword in his good hand, I realize. He needs me to open the door for him.

I reach for the handle and pull it open.

He rushes inside in brisk, practiced movements. I feel like I'm floating as I follow him. The curtains are drawn and it's almost pitch black and my heart can't possibly pound any harder than it is now.

We move through the kitchen and down the hall, plunging into darkness that's even more oppressive. In my room, I can't stand it anymore; I grab the curtains and yank them open. Gideon and I lock eyes for an instant. Then he slips out to continue searching the cabin.

I step to the mirror over my dresser. The pictures I taped around the frame are all here. My poems. Just how I left them.

I rush back into the living room, terror choking me.

Gideon's already there, sword sheathed at his back. "It's clear. We're good. We're the only ones here."

My eyes are starting to fill. I don't want to be this afraid inside these walls. I *live* here.

He takes a step toward me. "Daryn?"

"I don't know what this means. Why do these things keep appearing? How many will we see? Will it be something from your life next? From Jode's? And I don't know why we haven't seen Bas. I feel like I should know all of this. I feel like we're all here because of me and I should *know.*"

"Slow down a minute." His hand finds my elbow. "None of this is your fault and no one's expecting you to have all the answers. Let's just keep this simple. One thing at a time. We're here for Bas and we're going to find him. I'm not going to give up. Are you?"

"No. Never."

"Okay. You doing all right?"

For an instant I see him for what he is. An anchor. A marvel to me. "Yes."

He nods, relaxing his posture slightly. "Scary, isn't it? Seeing this stuff in these woods?"

"I hate it."

"Sums it up for me, too." His eyes dart to the door. "We should go. B Team will be waiting."

But neither one of us moves. I want to say something to make things better between us. To set the bone that's broken so we can start to heal, even though this is a terrible time to have that conversation. I have to do *something* though, so I reach for his hand. My fingers close around cool sculpted metal. "Thank you."

He frowns slightly. "No need, Martin. We look out for each other."

We share a beat of silence. Close and connected.

Not at all civil or professional.

Then chaos erupts outside.

Our horses squeal and Marcus shouts for us. Through the open door, I see the flash of Jode nocking an arrow and taking aim.

But it's the screams from the distance that chill me. I've never heard Ben or Cordero scream for their lives before, but I know it's them. And I know what's happening.

Harrows.

CHAPTER 14

⟨ GIDEON ⟩

It sounds like a massacre.

I push Riot to top speed, risking missing the directional marks Marcus left with his scythe. Riding slow isn't an option, though, or I'll be too late to save anyone.

The Arabians are screaming—horse sounds I've never heard before—and the Harrows are making a crazed pack-hunting noise—something between wolf and hyena howls.

Cordero and Ben were screaming, too. A little while ago.

Not anymore.

The pull I feel to fold with Riot is intense. And futile. We could reach them in seconds as fire, but we're stuck as horse and rider.

The woods have been dead still since the minute we came through, but now the wind is rising, shearing off leaves and making the branches bend and groan. A burnt wet smell like floods and fires stings my eyes and throat.

"It's them!" Daryn says, thundering beside me on Shadow. We weave through the trees, all four of us, our horses leaping over roots, smashing through smaller branches. "They've surrounded us."

Movement blurs past my peripheral vision—too heavy and fleet to be shadows.

Marcus, who's a few lengths ahead, looks back and catches my eye. "I'm going!"

"Yes, go!"

He sinks lower in the saddle and couches the scythe to his

side as Ruin accelerates and surges ahead, Daryn and Shadow following right behind him.

Jode, who's with me, our horses much slower, sends me a look. Splitting up is a mistake. But I need everyone to stay alive.

In moments I spot four Harrows closing in. Skeletons in hoods, ragged and bony. Loping on all fours with predatory speed.

"On my right!" Jode yells.

I look and see nothing, then realize he means "*Get on* my right" because, with my useless robohand, my left side is vulnerable.

Before I can make a move, something leaps directly in my path.

Riot twists to the side and collides shoulder-to-haunch with one of the Arabians. The horse caroms off Riot and hits the ground with the gritty sound of the air emptying from its lungs. It rolls over, legs thrashing in the air, and springs back up. Cordero's white horse freezes for a moment, looking at us, its saddle askew, blood staining its white neck; then it shoots off again in terror.

Looping the reins around my prosthetic, I push to catch up to Jode. The acrid stench is more powerful as we draw close, burning my throat. The reports of several handguns as well as Maia's rifle fill the air, and I hear Low shouting something over and over.

The fear in his voice shocks me.

When we fought the Kindred, Low kept his calm even when he was gravely wounded; I can't even think of what could scare him.

Then I see our group and I understand.

The B Team's on the opposite end of the clearing, where we came through, and is divided in two. Both groups are under siege by Harrows—an attack style that reminds me, suddenly, of crows diving on a bird's nest.

Suarez and Maia are with Cordero and Ben—the four of them huddled close. Suarez and Maia are firing at Harrows that bolt from all directions, charging to swipe at them with claws and snapping teeth. They're managing to hold off the bulk of the attack with a steady flow of rounds but I know our ammunition is limited.

Marcus is protecting them on one side with big swings of the scythe.

Forty yards away, Low is alone with the Arabians, making up the other part of the B Team. A force of one. He's trying to untether the horses, but it's chaos. The animals crash against each other and scream, tossing their heads, desperate to flee. As I watch, Daryn rides up and I see them shouting at each other.

Jode nocks an arrow and fires at a Harrow. It disintegrates along with the nearby trees to concussive cracks that fill the air and pop my ears. I haven't seen the full destructive power of his bow in months, but I haven't forgotten it. There's an instant of silence in the aftermath, like someone hit pause; then I hear the crackle of fire in the distance.

Jode looks at me, a quick frustrated expression crossing his face. His bow is too powerful for close-range combat, like taking out an ant with a bomb. He won't be able to do much without endangering the people we're trying to save.

We need to get out of here.

We need the orb.

I put my heels to Riot, going for Cordero. Then I sense the first Harrow coming at me from dead left, my weak side.

It has no eyes. I knew from Daryn's briefing, but seeing it is another thing, a chilling thing.

The Harrow leaps at me like it's weightless, on springs.

I wheel Riot as I swing my sword. It connects where the Harrow's neck and shoulder meet, the blade resisting more than I expect. The thing is all bone and sinew, like a body made of pure tendons, but it's mortal. It tumbles to the ground, writhes for a second, and stops moving.

Another comes from the left. Riot and I have done this before and we're good at it. I take the thing's head off and make my first offensive attack, picking off a Harrow that's working its way toward Marcus.

I'm still in my follow-through when Riot surges up. I know what he's doing—facing an attack from the front—but I'm twisted, shoulders turned like I'm loading up to swing a bat. I have no chance of staying on him. I fly back, lifting off the saddle.

The harness of my prosthetic yanks against my elbow, and for an instant I'm sure I'll lose my entire arm this time, but then the reins slide free. I somersault and land on the flats of my shoulder blades, sword thudding away as I tumble ass-over-head.

Finding my feet, I scramble for my weapon.

Riot is trampling the Harrow under his enormous hooves. As I run up, the thing's legs are mashed. I pin its neck with my prosthetic and stare into empty eyes.

"Where's Sebastian?" I growl, pressing the point of my sword into its armpit. "Where is he?" It breathes heavily through yellowed fangs. The brackish stench of its breath almost makes me gag. "Answer me! Where's Sebastian?"

It snaps at me, fangs scraping my metal hand.

I push myself up and Riot moves right in, finishing the job he began.

Then he looks at me, fire rolling up his broad chest. *Did he bite you?*

He didn't.

Get on.

No. We're two fighting if we stay separate, Riot. We can do more.

Riot's eyes flash as he stamps his hooves. I can tell he doesn't like this, but he lowers his head and tears after a Harrow.

The creature reverses so fast that it skids out and lands flat on its back, standing no chance.

Firming my grip on my sword, I think through my next steps as I sprint to Cordero's group. We need a secure position first. We'll be annihilated if we can't regroup somewhere.

"Suarez! Fall back!" My voice is drowned in the noise, but Suarez and Maia hear me. I point. "Cabin a hundred yards that way."

Maia is stemming the tide of howling oncoming Harrows with steady, deadly accuracy. Jode has concentrated his shots to one area. The woods there are glowing red and roaring.

"We're not mobile," Suarez says as I reach him. Cordero's hand is pressed to her neck, and blood flows through her fingers. She looks white as bone. Ben's shirt is covered in blood but I don't see a wound. "Someone needs to help Low. We need those horses."

"We need the orb," Cordero says. "None of it will help if we don't get the orb."

I don't want to believe what I just heard. "You don't *have* it? Where is it?"

"My horse's saddlebag. We heard trouble—we were trying to leave but the horse spooked."

I look at Suarez. He looks at me. There are no words for this shit sandwich.

"Gideon, I'll go!" I look up at Daryn, mounted on Shadow. "I'll get it!"

"Daryn, wait!" But Shadow lunges away in hungry strides.

This plan has serious flaws. Daryn has no weapon and we need her as much as the orb to get out of here. And I just need her alive, period.

I look for Riot but he's deep in the fight, biting and kicking anything that comes near. Too far for me to reach quickly. "Marcus!"

He looks at me, sees Daryn leaving, and then peels away from the clearing to follow her. As Ruin opens up her stride, a Harrow leaps into her path. She jumps and clears the Harrow easily. As she lands I see the flash of the scythe arcing, then the sickle hooking into the Harrow's back. Marcus drags it a few feet before he releases it.

Low thunders up on one of the Arabians. He jumps off and grabs the reins with one hand, waving at Cordero and Maia with the other. "Come on come on come on," he says. "Up up up."

I run over and hold the horse so he can boost Maia into the saddle. Cordero doesn't move.

"Cordero, let's go!" I yell.

She's swaying on her feet, and her eyes have gone distant. She'll bleed out if we can't get her help. "No," she says. "Send Ben. I'll go last."

Shit. This is no time to act noble.

But Low immediately adjusts. "Ben, get over here!"

Ben doesn't hesitate. He throws himself into the saddle and lands half on top of Maia, who scoots back.

"How far, Gideon? Which way?" he asks, taking the reins. "Is it close?"

"Easy, Ben. Head that way. Follow our tracks. You good?"

"I'm good," he says.

Maia loops an arm around his waist and pulls a 9mm from her leg holster with the other hand. She digs her heels into the Arabian's flanks, and the horse shoots away.

Low and I give each other cover as we sprint back to the three remaining Arabians. We need a horse for Cordero and Suarez.

"The red, Blake." He points to a chestnut mare that looks slightly less crazed than the other two. "Cut her loose."

The leads are braided together from the jostling the horses have done. There's no untangling them, so I wrap my left arm around the mare's head to hold her still and cut the leather. As soon as she's free, she springs away from me, but Low grabs her bridle.

"Whoa," he says. "Whoaaa. Settle down, little firecracker."

The mare's eyes go wide and she squeals in fear. A Harrow is barreling our way, teeth bared, claws tearing at the dirt. The horse wheels sideways and Low backpedals to get out of her way, but his feet catch and he goes down.

I lunge for the horse's mane, for anything to stop her from trampling Low. I swipe air twice before I remember my left hand is metal and useless.

Low rolls, somehow evading four churning hooves, and comes up unharmed. Already drawing his sidearm from his hip holster. "Go, Blake! Take her!"

Finally getting control of the mare, I swing up into the saddle. Being on a horse that isn't Riot feels like wearing someone else's clothes, but I get her settled and moving. In seconds, I'm back with Suarez, Jode, and Cordero.

In just the short time I've been with Low, Suarez has been viciously attacked. His thigh has been ripped open. Cordero is down on her knees, the wound at her neck flowing worse than before. All around, the Harrows continue with the incessant howling, slashing with claws that are curved and dripping deep red.

Suarez limps over.

"Can you get to the cabin?" I ask, jumping down.

"Yes." He hauls himself into the saddle to a fluid stream of Spanish curses.

I rush over to Cordero. "Okay, boss. Time to get outta

here." Her head lolls to the side as I lift her and carry her to Suarez. "You'll have to hold her," I tell him. Which means he won't be able to shoot.

"Jode, go with them," I yell. "They need cover."

Jode looks from Suarez to me. "So do you!"

"Get them back to the cabin, Jode! Do it!"

"Bloody hell!" he yells, but he lowers his bow and comes our way.

"Blake, you've got Low?" Suarez says as he negotiates his terrified horse and a limp Cordero. He looks across the clearing. *"Travis!"*

I've never heard Suarez yell, and it's so rare to hear Low's first name that it takes me an instant to process what's happening.

Low is in trouble.

He's on the ground, and a Harrow is dragging him into the woods.

The creature paces, like it's protecting a fresh kill. Low bucks and thrashes and digs his heels into the dirt, but the thing has claws hooked deep into his chest and enough strength to haul his huge body away with ease.

"Riot!" Across the clearing, my horse's bold amber eyes swing to find me. "Riot, to me!" He digs in, hauling over to me as I sprint to him. We barely slow as we reach each other. But by the time I'm in the saddle, I can't see Low anymore.

I bolt to where the Harrow was taking him. Riot senses the urgency, and each of his strides are like leaps.

It doesn't take long to find Low—I reach him almost right away.

But I'm not there quick enough.

I'm a lifetime too late.

CHAPTER 15

⤙ DARYN ⤚

Shadow and I retrace our path, searching the woods for the white Arabian that darted past us only minutes ago.

Cordero's horse.

The horse packing the saddlebag with the orb.

I scan left and right, the earth blurring beneath Shadow's hooves. The horse has to be here somewhere.

Behind me I hear the howls of the Harrows and the deep yell of either Low or Suarez. Every hair on my body lifts at the sounds—life and death, violence and fear—all present, adding up to a noise I know I'll hear in nightmares for the rest of my life, if there is a rest of my life.

I spot a Harrow huddled in the high branches of a tree up ahead. We're going too fast to divert our path.

I brace. Anticipate claws in my back again. A new set of hash marks.

I picture it. Every inch of my skin ripped open.

But as we pass beneath the Harrow it only smiles with its sharp rotten teeth.

"Like my friends?" it calls down, and I recognize it as the one from before. "More than me, don't you think?"

As I speed past it, I'm in instant crisis. That thing knew about Sebastian—*I should go back!* But if I don't find the white horse with the orb, everyone in the group could die.

I race on, something blackening and withering inside me as I return to searching for the white horse. In these dim woods she should be easy to spot. She should be as bright as the begonias.

"Daryn!"

Marcus shouts my name from somewhere behind me.

"Here! Marcus, I'm here!" I look for him through the blurring trees, but I don't see him.

I'm still turned when Shadow suddenly jerks to a halt.

I rock forward, almost catapulting out of the saddle. Then I see what stopped her.

The white Arabian stands just a few lengths away.

She's not alone.

A young man, dressed in dark clothing fitted to a long and lean build, stands beside the mare, holding her by the halter. His feet are planted in a stance that's slightly wide and his attention is fully on me, like he's been waiting.

Euphoria turns my heart into a rocket, shooting for the stars.

Sebastian.

His name almost leaps from my throat until I realize I have it wrong.

I *wanted* to see Bas. But it's not him.

It's Samrael.

Shadow begins to dance beneath me. *No, Daryn. Leave now. We need to leave now.*

I can't hold her still. I know she's scared for me, but I can't leave without the orb.

I'm vaguely aware of dismounting. Vaguely aware that all the moisture has left my mouth and that I've pressed my shaking hands flat against my legs.

My head feels like it's about five feet above my body. Like my consciousness is still mounted somewhere behind me, up on Shadow.

"I'm here to help," Samrael says in a resonant voice. A voice that's cool as a winter's breath.

"Do you think I'm stupid?"

"Quite the opposite."

I have no response to give him. If he's serious, it's a compliment I don't want from him. If it's flattery, I want it even less.

I notice that the white mare's saddle is unbuckled and almost sliding off her back, and that Samrael has tethered his own horse—a giant dapple-gray—farther back.

"Daryn . . ." He lets go of the mare and lifts his hands like he means no harm, but he's a demon. He *is* harm. "Hear me out."

It's been months since I've seen him. But unlike Gideon, Jode, and Marcus, who changed so much in that same stretch of time, Samrael hasn't changed at all.

He's still beautifully made, with wide-set green eyes and dark hair that bends like ocean waves. He has a lithe build, his athleticism like a panther's—speed and strength that are somehow evident even in his languid movements.

"You're in trouble," he continues. "I can help. I can take you to safety."

"Where's Sebastian?" My voice warbles over the words like rolling pebbles. "Do you know where he is?" That's all I want to know. That knowledge is the only thing he could ever give me that I'd want. "The Harrows said they have him."

"Harrows?" His eyes dart toward the direction of the struggle. "No, they don't. He's with me. He's safe. Sebastian is well."

"I don't believe you."

"It's the truth," Samrael repeats, his gaze steady as a frozen lake. "Bas is well."

A small gasp escapes me and my eyes blur. I think I believe him. I want so much to believe him. It's the way he said it. *Bas.* So familiar. Like he knows Sebastian.

"I'll take you to him," he says. "But we need to go now."

"Are you serious?" Samrael severed Gideon's hand. He had Sebastian poisoned. "You think I'll actually go with you?"

He says nothing. His eyes skim the woods again, warily.

The sounds of the Harrows could be growing louder; I can't tell. "We're running out of time."

"I'm not leaving without my friends!" I snap. Then I swallow the dryness in my throat. "I'm not leaving people behind."

"I understand."

"How could you possibly?"

Again, he says nothing for a long moment. "I would bring them as well if I thought they would come, but—" He smiles, a deadly smile, and shakes his head in frustration. "Do you think Gideon will ever follow me anywhere?"

"Never." Hearing his name jars me back to my goal. I need to get to Gideon, Jode, and Marcus. Cordero and the others. "I need that horse."

"Certainly," he says. He gives the mare a gentle prod and she darts over to Shadow, seeking safety in the familiar. But the saddlebag slides off her back and drops, landing almost at Samrael's feet.

My eyes fall to it inadvertently. Samrael notices.

He bends gracefully and lifts the bag off the ground, holding it up. "I suppose you need this as well," he says, more a statement than a question. Then he opens the leather buckle and removes the orb, and a bemused expression flashes across his features. "Quite a lot of trouble this thing has caused. And it looks worse for wear."

His eyes lift to me, but I've lost the power to speak.

I need that, I want to say. But of course he knows that.

Give it to me, I want to demand. But what good would that do?

Samrael slips the orb back into the saddlebag and buckles it. I see my chances of saving everyone, and of ever getting out of here alive, vanish. He'll take it. He knows that without it none of us will go anywhere.

I expect him to haul it over his shoulder. Instead he tosses it in my direction.

It lands with a soft thump a few feet in front of me.

"I would keep that on you at all times."

Is he being *wry*? I dart forward and grab it, greedy as a scavenger, and quickly remove the orb, stuffing it deep into my jacket pocket.

The howling voices are so close—definitely heading our way.

"Come with me, Daryn."

Something large flies past me, *whooshing* by my ear.

Marcus's scythe turns end over end as it sails through the air. Enormous. As if a helicopter has shed its propeller.

Samrael lunges aside and it misses him by inches, biting into the bark of a tree behind him with a crack.

Samrael dashes to his horse and mounts smoothly. "A message? For Sebastian?"

He's finally understood I'm not going with him.

"Tell him I won't give up. Tell him I won't stop until I bring him home."

"He already knows," Samrael says, turning his gray, "but I'll tell him."

I watch him ride away, wondering if I've made a terrible mistake.

Marcus rides up moments after. He sees Samrael's retreating form. Then his furious eyes find me. "You okay?"

I nod, but I honestly don't know. I'm shaking all over.

"The orb, D?"

"I have it."

He nods. "We got hit hard. We better get back." He retrieves the scythe. I loop my lariat around the white mare and we ride back toward the cabin.

My body never lets go of the fear. Every passing shadow makes me tense, anticipating the Harrows coming down on us. But the woods are eerily still. I don't see any Harrows anymore, yet I don't feel like they've left us, either.

Gideon is waiting in front of the cabin as we ride up. Jode stands to one side of the porch, Maia to the other. Gideon takes a long look at Marcus and walks up to me. There's blood on his cheek, four stripes like dragged fingers. And a fierce pain in his eyes that makes my stomach drop. "We need to go."

"What happened?" I ask.

Gideon grabs Shadow's reins to keep her steady and looks up at me, some emotion that I can't place burning in his eyes. Marcus has jumped off Ruin and disappeared into the cabin with Jode.

"Gideon, who's hurt? What happened?"

"We have to get home, Daryn." His voice is in shreds and his eyes begin to shine with tears. Marcus comes out of the cabin carrying someone over his shoulder. Then Jode does.

And I understand.

Not here. Not yet.

Home first.

With half of our team either slumped or strapped to saddles, I open the portal and bring us back through to Nevada, where blood is scarlet red under the bright desert sun.

CHAPTER 16

⊸ GIDEON ⊸

Jode takes a pull from the whiskey bottle and grimaces. *"Acid."* He presses the back of his hand to his mouth, wincing. "Or is this petrol?" He passes it to me. "I can't tell."

I reach across and take the bottle. Robohand's working again, now that we're back out. I'm not sure the rest of me is, though.

I don't feel right.

"If it gets the job done, does it matter?" I say, slurring all over the place. I don't drink. At all, really. I have a hard time with anger when I drink. Harder time. And it's murder on my stomach. But tonight there was no choice. Right now, life is pain—the kind you do anything to try to stop.

We're lined up on top of our trailer—the three of us—our legs hanging over the side. Below, the camp's spotlights illuminate about twenty feet of desert; then it's nothing but darkness and stars.

"Tell me how close you were to splitting Samrael open again," I say to Marcus.

Five minutes ago we were all staring at the ground and trying to figure out if we'd break anything if we fell. Marcus got dizzy, which is why he's lying back. Jode and I are still sitting. Even though I'm dizzy, too. Except the dizziness is somewhere inside me. My soul may have a concussion.

"I've told you three times already," he says.

"I'm trying to focus on happy things."

"Close. A couple inches."

"And you threw the scythe how far?"

"Don't know. Forty feet."

"That's really good, Marcus. But maybe get practiced up. So you don't miss if you get another chance."

"I'll do that."

He's joking. We're joking. You don't throw a scythe. But I bet he actually will practice. He wants to end Samrael. Almost as much as I do.

We've hit another conversational dead end, so I drink.

It's terrible. Like petrol.

Why am I doing this?

Oh, yeah. Because I don't want to think.

"Suarez is leaving in the morning," Jode says. "Soraya told me a little while ago. He's going to Texas to see Low's family."

I look at him. "You're just telling us this?"

"It didn't seem like a headline item."

That's true. The headline items of the day are hard to eclipse.

Things could've gone worse earlier. We *did* make it back out of the Rift. But we paid a steep price. We lost too much today.

Suarez had to have a blood transfusion and twenty-four stitches on his thigh. Maia had five on her forearm, seven on her shoulder. Ben's status is as yet unclear. He's had massive internal bleeding. Right now we're waiting. We just want good news. I was sure Cordero wouldn't make it. I thought she'd had her jugular or carotid nicked. But it was a wound in her scalp that caused all the bleeding. She got some staples, but she's fine. Physically she's going to be okay. But not Low.

Travis Low is dead.

Dead, but constantly appearing in my head. Joking around, and then yelling in fear. Unstoppable, and then in shreds.

I should know how fast it happens, after my dad. How

quickly you can lose someone. But I don't feel any more equipped to handle this.

"I don't want this. Here, take it." I hand the bottle to Marcus. My stomach's churning—it hasn't stopped churning since the second I caught up to Low and saw that I was too late.

"No," Marcus says.

"Yes. Take it."

"Don't want it."

"Why so difficult, Marc?"

"Who's Marc?"

"You are."

"Yeah? 'Sup, Gid?"

"If you're gonna shorten it, use Deon."

Marcus laughs. "Ohhh my God. You are messed up."

He's right. At this point Jack Daniel's has as much to say about what comes out of my mouth as I do. "Why aren't *you* messed up?"

He's quiet for a second. "Not a good idea."

I understand. On top of everything else, seeing the silver Mustang in the Rift got to him. Some things are better left in the past—and for him that's one of them.

What I *don't* understand is how it got in there. How did Daryn's Wyoming cabin or her mother, for that matter?

There's a whole part of this that we're not even tapping into yet.

I draw the cool night air into my lungs, filling them. All the stars in the universe are out tonight. Stars by the billion. It could've been a perfect night under different circumstances.

"Suarez is going to Texas, huh? It's the right thing," I say. He knew Travis for fifteen years. Better than anyone. They've been on the same track since boot camp. Low's ex-wife will be hurting. His kid, who's only three, will feel the loss for the rest of his life. Jared needs to be there for them. I didn't know Travis as well as Suarez but we went through plenty together these past months.

The stars start to blur and my throat goes raw.

Shit.

Jode sighs. He rubs a hand over his head. "What were we thinking, taking everyone in there?"

"Nuh-uh. I ain't lookin' back, Jode," Marcus says. "Why didn't we do this and why didn't we do that?" He shakes his head. "It happened. It's done."

I agree. But Jode just wants to understand. Processing information is how he copes. I've seen this before.

A phone buzzes. Jode pulls his mobile from his pocket, the screen illuminating the look of relief on his face. Jode's not close to his family. He has a pretty distant relationship with his parents and his sister. The only person who gets that reaction out of him is *my* sister.

"We're not supposed to take personal calls here," I say, like an asshole. I don't know why. Yes, I do. Maybe I want what they have.

"Cordero made an exception today."

"Makes sense. Enjoy talking to the person I share the most DNA with."

He smiles. "I will." He hops up and walks away. "Anna? Yes, I called. No, no, no, everything's fine. Only wanted to talk." He sells it pretty well until the very end. On the last comment, emotion makes his voice crack. "I do? No, it's nothing. Just a sore throat coming on. Tell me how you are."

His voice fades away as he climbs down the ladder and disappears into the RV. It's weird to hear him lie to my sister but it's part of the job. Part of what we promised we'd do. Still, I feel bad for him and I feel bad for Anna. My sister's too smart to be fooled. And today isn't a day for hiding things from the people you care about.

"You want to know something? This is the only time I've ever wanted them to actually be physically together. I mean in the same place. Not physical with each other."

Marcus smiles. "You want them to *get physical*, Blake?"

"This isn't the time, man. Really."

He laughs.

I grab the bottle from him and end up just staring at it, getting lost in a memory of the time Low toasted a piece of bread over Riot's mane. Big idiot.

"I'll see you, G." Marcus stands. "I'm gonna go see Daryn."

I launch to my feet. *"What?"*

"Were you goin'?" Marcus acts like he's surprised, but he's not. He's a terrible actor. "My bad. Didn't look like it."

"Dude, why? You could've just said, 'Go see her.'"

"Go see her."

"I'm going."

He steps aside. "Get it done, Deon."

I climb down and walk to Daryn's RV, not sure this is the right move, considering everything. But I want to see if she's okay. Except she won't be, because today no one's okay.

Why *am* I going to see her?

So she can act like she wants me, then change her mind and act like I'm the biggest mistake she's ever made?

Keep moving, Blake. Forward march.

I get lost for a while in the maze of RVs and trip on air a couple of times. Either the earth's having an earthquake or I'm having trouble walking. But I find Daryn's RV and knock.

Sophia answers the door. Her eyes are red from crying. Everyone's eyes are red. We're like a new subspecies of human.

"Hey," she says. Sad smile. She looks toward the kitchen, where Daryn's sitting at the table. "Call me if you need anything, okay?"

"Sure. Thanks," Daryn says.

Sophia leaves and I step inside.

Daryn is sitting at the booth, slumped forward, her chin resting on her arms. She's wearing an oversized sweatshirt and her hair's wet, like she just got out of the shower. The smell of her shampoo or lotion or something else amazing hits me as I sit in the bench across from her.

"How are you?" she says.

She has red eyes, too. Puffy red eyes. She still looks amazing. "Pretty shitty. You?"

"I cried for twenty minutes straight," she says. "I timed it by the microwave clock."

Why wasn't I here? Why didn't I come sooner? "I maxed out around five. But it was intense. I threw up."

"You did?"

I shrug. "It was more like heaving. I had nothing to give back, but you know my stomach. Any excuse to get attention."

"I know you cared about him."

"Do."

She nods. "Do." She brushes her hair behind her ear and reaches across the table, taking my hand. Her fingers are soft and cool. Much smaller than mine. Then her other hand comes to my prosthetic and she takes that, too.

It surprises me that I don't care. Right now my hand hang-up seems stupid, so. I just focus on how it looks. Her pretty hand holding my bionic hand.

It looks okay. Not as bad as I'd imagined. I adjust the gesture for a better position, but the whirring sound of its inner gears seems loud and makes me feel self-conscious. And stupid. I guess I do care.

Too late now. We're holding hands.

"What can I do to help?" Daryn asks.

Somewhere in camp a generator cranks on.

"This is good."

"Should we pray for Travis? For his family?"

This surprises me. "Sure."

We do that, silently but together. For Low. For his ex-wife and his son, who's got it much worse than me. I got eighteen years with my dad. Low's little kid—Austin, I remember—only got three.

Out of nowhere, I remember Suarez and Low a few days ago in the warehouse, talking over boxes of pizza.

Hey, Low. You missed it. Blake just made a joke.

He did? Man, that's inspiring. He's been trying for so long.

Low. There was no one else like him in the world.

Another one of the day's huge swells of emotion sweeps over me. I drop my head in my arms and count backward from a thousand.

Nine hundred and ninety-nine.

Nine hundred and ninety-eight.

Daryn slides into the bench next to me and lays her hand on my shoulder. The light pressure quickly becomes the only thing I feel. I want to face her, hold her, but that seems insane and like it could go bad, so I count.

She starts to run her hand up and down my back. It has a totally different effect than what I think she's going for so I just keep counting, feeling hot and jumbled up, all haywire and like I'm just an animal reacting to everything—life and death and lust.

I get to nine hundred and eighty before I feel confident enough to sit up.

I should leave, but I can't make myself. I want to stay, but my emotional brakes are burnt out. I look for distraction, something that doesn't mean anything. My eyes drop to the journal on the table. My name jumps out at me. It's in Daryn's handwriting.

"Wait, does that say—" I bring it closer and read it. Then I read it again. "How'd you get a picture of my *butt*? And when? And *why*?"

Daryn winces. "Give me that." She grabs for the notebook

but I hold on and we jostle for it. "Gideon, give it! It's embarrassing."

"'Reasons'?" I laugh, reading the title of the list. "What kind of reasons are these exactly?"

"I don't know *exactly*. They're just reasons. Reasons to be happy. Reasons to keep going. Reasons to live, laugh, love. To me, they're all kind of the same."

"Not to me. Are you *laughing* at my ass? Or *loving* it? Big difference."

"Do you really need to ask?"

I let go of the notebook and sit back. Instantly sober. No, better than sober. I'm bulletproof.

Daryn takes the notebook, but she doesn't close it. She slides it in front of us, smiling. "Great." She shakes her head. "I can't believe you saw this."

"It was open. I couldn't help it. But, like . . . it's *awesome*. I honestly didn't expect anything good to come of today."

She looks at me, her blue eyes going softer. "Glad I could help. Go ahead. You might as well read the rest."

I don't even hesitate. I dive right in.

The first few are great—they're exactly how I'd start my own Reasons list. Then I slow down. "Marcus's smile? It's that good?"

"Yes. He has a gorgeous smile. Stunning."

"Okay, easy. Take it easy." I keep reading. "Jode's weird Britishisms?"

"So good."

"I'm with you there." Her mother is on the list, of course. Her dad and her sister. Isabel. As I move down, it becomes apparent it's a mixture of people and keen observations. None of it surprises me much, which is cool. I know this girl. She tries to keep her distance, but I know her.

Then I get to another item with my name in it and my head explodes.

Is this for real? My lips have "limitless power"?

I've kissed her *twice*. Both times I was so shocked it was happening that I didn't even give my best effort. And *this* is my starting grade?

I can't even process. This tops everything. Out of everything I've ever accomplished, this is the best thing.

Daryn is giving me a level gaze, waiting for my reaction.

"This is a really good list, Martin. *Really* good. I especially like number fourteen."

"I was being hyperbolic. Exaggerating for literary effect."

"Just own it. No shame." She smacks my arm. I laugh. "I'm not kidding. Fourteen is the best item here by far. Except it also says that I look at you ardently, which isn't true. Whatever that even means."

"Yes, you do."

"No way." Do I? I remember my face in the airport bathroom mirror. "Nah."

"You're doing it right now. It's your eyes. They speak the truth."

"I'm just tired. It's been a bad day."

"Ardent."

I look back at the notebook before my eyes tell her she looks perfect right now, with her sleepy eyes and sexy smile. "There are sixteen items here. How many Reasons are there going to be?"

"I don't know. I hadn't thought about it. Maybe a hundred?"

"Nice. Can I add one?"

Her eyebrows rise. "Of course."

"You sure?"

"*Yes*. I want you to. Add as many as you want. It kind of feels like it's our list now."

"Well, I am all over it."

"Write, before I change my mind."

I take the pen she offers. Then I remember I've been left-handed my entire life until last year. "Daryn, my handwriting's not—"

"It'll be perfect. Go for it."

So I do.

17.   *Daryn's actual butt—not a photo of it, the real thing*

Daryn laughs. "Seriously?"

"Very seriously. Have you seen it?"

"My butt? Not really. It's kind of behind me."

"Well, it's a damn good Reason, and fair's fair." I move to the next line and write the entry I really wanted to add. It's shorter than the one I just wrote but it takes me longer because my eyes keep trying to wash out again. I get it done, though.

18.   *Low*

I sit back and take a tight breath and then another and another until I'm breathing normally again.

Daryn rests her head on my shoulder. We stay like this. Staring at Low's name.

The memories come. I keep thinking of all the things I'll miss about him.

I've done a lot of this.

I do this almost daily, with Dad.

Around the time he died, he was still laying into me regularly about leaving my dirty clothes on the floor of my bedroom. He wanted me to make my bed every day and screw the toothpaste cap back on and always stop to hug Mom or Anna anytime I walked through the door. Even if I just went out to pick up a pizza. It seemed insane to me, doing all that. Huge waste of time. I do it all now. He'll never see it, though.

That's the thing about death. You miss everything before

and everything after, too. You miss everything that should've been.

Daryn yawns and glances at the microwave clock. "It's almost three a.m. Are you going to try to sleep?"

"Probably." It'd be better than thinking depressing thoughts all night.

"Do you want to sleep here?"

Whoa.

"Yes."

She stands and I follow her, thinking we're going to the bedroom in the back, but she stops at the twin cubby into the hallway that's probably made for little kids or garden gnomes.

"The bedroom is Maia's. She's with Suarez right now, but she might come back tonight."

"This is great."

"I don't know." Daryn looks at me like she's measuring my height. "Are you sure you'll fit in here?"

"Yep. I'll just sleep in a cannonball position."

She laughs, hits the lights, and climbs in.

I knock my forehead as I climb in after her. *Easy, Blake. Settle down.*

Right away I realize the only way to accomplish this is as a team. "You should turn sideways. It'll give us more room."

"Like this?"

"Yes. How's your back? Can I put my arm around you?"

"Better—yes. Can I put my leg over yours?"

"Sure." *Pour yourself all over me. Really, I won't mind.* "And come closer. Bring it in, Martin. All the way in." We end up pressed together, me on my back, her resting her head on my shoulder. I can't straighten my legs so I hang my feet out into the hallway.

Since there are cabinets above and below us, the roof is really low. Wood paneling surrounds us on all sides, except along the hallway. I've never felt claustrophobic before but

I do right now. I'm incredibly uncomfortable—and incredibly turned on.

Her hair smells amazing. Her body feels amazing. I feel her heart beating fast, like mine, and I'm drowsy but awake. Wired. Wishing we weren't both fully dressed. And that this situation was more bedlike instead of like we've been thrown into solitary confinement together.

"Gideon . . ." Her voice is so close to my ear it almost makes me shiver. "Are you comfortable?"

"No. Are you?"

"No. Want to move?"

"No."

"Good. Me either." She shifts around against my chest, and any chance of me sleeping tonight vanishes. Game over. It's just not going to happen. "I keep thinking I should've stopped them from going into the Rift. I had a bad feeling about it from the start."

Maybe I will sleep tonight. "Yeah. I know you did. I should've listened to you." I peer down at her. "I should've trusted your judgment. You were right."

"I wish I wasn't." She blinks. "And I wish I weren't so wrong about other things." I wait for her to keep going. There's obviously more coming. "Gideon, what you said to me last night after we, um . . . in the RV?" She sighs, and then comes right out with it. "After I mauled you?"

"It was mutual mauling. Actually, I think I had the edge."

She smiles. "Debatable. Anyway—the things you said afterward. Do you remember?"

"Yes." I told her I wanted her. That, from my side of the equation at least, we're a go. "I was just trying to understand, Daryn. I just wanted to understand what's in our way. You don't have to tell me."

"I *want* to tell you. But not tonight. Some other time. Soon."

"Okay. To be continued."

"To be continued," she agrees. "We should probably get some sleep."

"Sure." But nothing changes. We lie there, our faces only a few inches apart. It's awesome. Just watching her blink. Feeling her breath. But after a little while my eyes won't stay open any longer. I let them close.

"Good night," she says.

"Night."

"I hope I dream about this . . . this exact moment."

Amazing thing to hear. Amazing. "I hope I dream about reason number fourteen. Pretty sure I will."

"Showing you that list was such a mistake."

"Martin, you have no idea."

CHAPTER 17

⟶ DARYN ⟵

The sound of Velcro unstrapping wakes me.

In the darkness, it takes a second for the disorientation to wear off. I'm on my bed in the RV. Creases of amber light frame the drawn shades in the kitchen area, warm with the desert's morning glow.

Gideon is up. Sitting over the side of the bed with his back to me. His shirt is off and he's pulling on the black harness of his prosthetic. He tucks it under his elbow, pinning it to his side as he tries to untangle the straps.

Maia's soft snoring filters through the cracked door of the bedroom.

I watch in silence as Gideon tries to work the strap free. His back is impressively cut. Sculpted with muscle. Tapering to a narrow waist. I could lie here and appreciate it for an hour if sadness didn't find me, bringing a dull ache to the back of my throat. He's struggling with the straps.

All the times I've seen him casually slip his prosthetic hand into his pocket, or cross his arms to hide it from me, pass before my eyes.

He thinks I don't notice. But I do.

Under some power that's beyond me, my hand moves to his forearm.

He freezes. Sharply, like I startled him. Then he turns slightly to me, sliding the harness from beneath his arm as he looks over his shoulder. He's hidden all evidence of this thing we haven't talked about.

"Did I wake you?" he asks, his voice pitched low.

"No."

"I know I did."

He's right. And this already isn't going well. What I want is more honesty between us, not less. "You did wake me. But I'm glad."

"Daryn, I'm going to go." He rises to his feet but I hold his arm. Stopping him. "Daryn . . ."

"Do you hate me because of it?" I whisper the question, though Maia's still snoring steadily in the bedroom. In the low light, all I see is the line of his jaw and sweep of his eyelashes.

"That's not even possible."

"Do you blame me, then?"

"I think I tried to in the beginning. For like a minute."

"I'd never have let it happen if I'd known. I'd have done anything to keep you safe."

"I know."

"Then why . . . ?"

"Why am I weird about it around you?" His head eases to the side and the muscles in his neck roll as he swallows. "Good question."

We fall into silence, tension making this tiny space feel even smaller. I know he's miserable. I can feel how much he wants to leave.

"Don't go, Gideon."

"I'm here."

"I want you more here." I pull him back by the arm. He resists at first, but then he relents and lies beside me on the mattress.

His prosthetic thumps to the floor.

He stares up at the low ceiling, his chest rising and falling, his stomach rising and falling. As out of breath as I am. "Are you trying to ruin me?"

"No." I don't know what the opposite of ruin is—the word

won't come to me—but that's what I want for him. The opposite of ruin. "Just let me."

"Let you what?" he asks.

But both he and I know the answer.

I run my hand down his right arm, over the tattoo of the cross. Then over Bas's name. Three letters but they're cursive, surprisingly fluid and beautiful.

Gideon balls his hand into a fist, the veins in his forearm standing out.

He shuts his eyes and I know I have his permission.

I look at his other arm. At how it ends at his wrist.

There's nothing odd about it. It's instantly normal—but normal how *he* is to me. Which isn't normal at all.

He's the furthest thing from that.

He's extraordinary. Strong. Beautiful.

"Are we done?"

"No."

His eyes part slightly and he looks at me through his lashes. "Does this—" He swallows. "Change anything? If you think it's gross—"

"It does, Gideon. It changes things."

His brow furrows, hurt digging in. But as I pull myself over him, planting my knees on either side of his hips, the hurt is replaced by surprise.

I tug my hair over one shoulder and tell my heart to stay put, to not break out of my chest quite yet. Then I bend and kiss him on the lips, once, softly.

As I draw away, the emotion in his blue eyes is the most vulnerable and human thing I've ever seen.

I keep moving, or I'll lose my nerve. I move down to his shoulder and kiss it, then his biceps, making a trail along warm skin and muscles that tense under my lips. All the way to the wrist that's resting on his stomach.

When I get there, I look up. He's holding his breath. His

eyes are closed again. It makes me want to cry to see how hard this is for him. How hard it's been.

I haven't gone through what he has, but I understand what it's like to miss part of yourself. I've struggled so much without the Sight. Without my family. I know what it's like to be without something you depended on, and even took for granted. Incomplete in some critical way.

"Gideon."

He shakes his head.

"Yes," I say. "Let me." I plant a long kiss on the strong bone of his wrist, feeling his breath stutter. I don't know if he can sense what I'm thinking, but I hope so. *You are perfect to me. Believe it.*

Then I retrace my path, kissing my way back up, stopping when I reach his mouth.

My plan is to spend some time here, but first things first. "I have a question."

"Ask." He looks at me intensely, ardently. "Anything."

"These." I tap my bottom lip. "In terms of power, how are they? Limitless?"

He yanks me against his chest, clamping his arms around me. "God, Daryn . . ." He kisses the top of my head. "*Yes.*"

When Maia starts to stir, Gideon leaves. If his goal was to make a secret exit, it doesn't work.

Soraya and Sophia show up as he's stepping out. I hear him talking to them outside.

"We don't know what to do," Soraya says.

"Or where to be," Sophia says.

"Yeah," he says. "I think there's going to be a lot of that today."

They talk for a little while, sharing medical updates on everyone. Then he leaves and they come inside, joining Maia and me.

We talk at the kitchen table. Then we sit and *don't* talk. We're all emotionally and physically wrecked. And aimless.

We move in a small pack the rest of the morning, pretending to eat breakfast. Wandering from the medical station to the RV and back as we wait for news of Ben, who was flown to a regional hospital.

I don't see Gideon again. He stays in his trailer with Jode and Marcus.

I wonder where things stand between us. We've had so many starts and stops—but he's right. That's on me. I've been the one slamming on the brakes. I've been so stupid. So determined to protect myself. Why have I been protecting myself *from him*?

Back at the RV, news arrives at eleven that Ben is stable. He lost a spleen, but spleens are optional. He's going to have a long road ahead, but the doctors think he'll make a full recovery.

Soraya and Sophia fly into a hug and dissolve into tears of relief.

Maia exhales a long breath through her teeth. "Okay. Good boy, Ben," she says, like he's right here. Then she looks at me. "I'm gonna go shoot. Wanna come?"

"Yes." I want to do anything that's *not* sitting around and worrying.

She commandeers a Jeep, and we spend an hour at the shooting range on the adjacent base. Maia gives me a lesson. Pointers on breathing, stance, technique. Much as I try, holding the weapon feels wrong, like I'm holding a chair instead of a rifle, whereas it looks like a natural extension of her body. Even with her leg stitched up beneath her cargos, she stands and shoots like a pro. It's impressive to watch her.

We head back when other people at the range start to notice how good she is.

"So, you and War?" she says, pulling the Jeep onto the

main road. "I saw that he spent the night. Plus all the eye hockey you two have been playing. Plus, we all knew something had gone on before."

"Yeah, we're . . ." I don't know what we are. I pass the water bottle we've been sharing back to her. "We're something."

Maia laughs. "Yep. That you are. Blake's a top-quality guy. Hot as Hades, too." I look at her. "Whoops. Is it okay I said that?"

"Of course. I'm just surprised that I feel good right now. I mean, I'm sad about what happened . . . but I'm also good." Part of it is Maia, I know. Being with her. Doing something random with her that I'd never otherwise do. Being out. Driving around. Sharing water. Just . . . accepting the missing pieces and *keeping going*.

"I hear you," she says. "Life's frickin' weird, ain't it?"

"So weird."

Back at camp, we're told to gather in the command center. Maia and I plop down next to each other. The seats around the table start to fill, but it's the absences I notice.

No Ben. No Suarez.

No Low.

Without them, it feels like we're half the number we were two days ago, even though that's not true.

Marcus walks in and looks at me. Jode follows behind him. Then Gideon, who I can't look at directly. Not even after I internally yell at myself for being a chicken. Not even when he sits right beside me and says, "Hey."

I mumble it back.

He must realize I've become mute, because he starts talking to Maia. "Heard you went shooting. How'd you do?"

Maia replies and then he replies and they talk like grown people, as I try to follow along while my brain feeds me an image of the way he looked smiling at me from the other side of the pillow.

"Daryn shot, too? How was it?" he asks, still carrying on like three of us are participating in this conversation.

Maia picks me up. She carries both of us, like she's my spokesperson. I sit like a lump of human, running my thumb over an imaginary scratch on the table. Because eye contact? Words? Not happening right now.

I feel too close to him. I've lost my protective shell, my ability to modulate, to hide or deflect or play it cool. I haven't felt this before. I'm afraid I won't properly shift gears back to civil and businesslike. I'm afraid I'll get up and crawl into his lap and look at him with hearts twirling around in my eyes instead of answering, *Yes, I shot a rifle for the first time and I didn't like it much*.

I'm rescued from my newfound awkwardness when Natalie Cordero enters. The quiet hum of conversation cuts off as she rounds the table and sits in her usual seat.

She's a mess. Her complexion's not far from the gray sweat suit she's wearing. Her head is bandaged and there are small cuts along her cheek.

Her eyes are sunken.

She looks like she's spent the entire night crying her eyes out, like the rest of us.

But Cordero has never been like the rest of us.

She folds her hands, and keeps her gaze on them as she speaks. "I'll get right to the point." Even her voice sounds broken. It's raw and almost inaudible. "I take full responsibility for what happened. Travis Low's death is on my conscience, so don't let it be on any of yours. The injuries to Jared, Ben, and Maia as well. It's all on my shoulders. That is likely no comfort to those of you who are suffering, but I apologize. Sincerely and deeply."

She sighs, letting that sink in.

Beside me Gideon sits forward, propping his elbows on the table.

"I've made a decision," she continues, "to discontinue this operation, effective immediately. Nothing more is required of you—" Her breath catches. "Consider yourselves relieved of your duties. Tomorrow, a crew will come to break down camp. Helos will be here in the morning to transport you. That said, if any of you wish to leave now, there are enough SUVs to accommodate everyone if you share rides, and the RVs are an option, too. Talk to Soraya to coordinate.

"As far as the future of this team goes, that decision remains to be made. Reports will need to be written and reviewed. An investigation will be conducted. Perhaps several. That will all take time. But I will notify you as soon as we have a directive." She pauses. "Does anyone have any questions?"

Jode speaks first. "You're dismantling everything? The search? What about Sebastian?"

It's the question on all of our minds.

Cordero turns a weary gaze on him. "The search is suspended until further notice."

"But there won't be further notice. Will there be?" Jode presses. "This isn't a suspension. It's a cancellation."

Cordero doesn't reply.

Anger rises inside me. Volcanic. Somehow I keep from exploding.

How can she abandon Sebastian?

"Cordero, you *saw* what was in there," Gideon says.

"Yes, Gideon. I *did*," Cordero returns. "That's precisely why this is over. The risks are too high."

"You're going to leave Bas?" he says. "You're going to leave him to those things?"

The expression on Cordero's face tells me what she won't say: She thinks Sebastian is dead.

"It's the only choice now. I won't expose any of you to that again. And I won't run the risk of those things crossing over to this side."

Gideon shoves his chair back and walks out. Marcus is a half step behind him, Jode right after. And suddenly I'm the only one still here.

Me. The one who never wanted any of this in the first place. Not the involvement of all these people, or this military-style circus in the middle of the desert.

The weight of a dozen stares presses on me. "You can't give up."

"Oh, I *can* give up," Cordero says. "If it means saving lives."

I shake my head. If there's one thing that can't happen, it's this. We can't leave Bas in the Rift. I desperately want and need to find my lost friend. I'll never be able to move on until I do.

"Are you going to tell me that I should've listened to you?" Cordero says. "Go ahead if it'll make you feel better."

It won't. Only one thing will.

I get up and leave.

I go right to the guys' RV, opening the door and letting myself in.

I find them standing in the kitchen, talking. All of them at once and in urgent tones. They strike me as imposing, the three of them. Like it's a child's table they're arguing around.

They fall silent when they see me.

"We were just discussing asking you about going into the Rift," Jode says. He glances at Gideon, whose full attention is on me. "You're aware of the danger."

"I am, and you don't have to ask me. I'm asking you."

"We're in, of course," Jode says immediately. "When?"

"Tonight," I say. "Just the four of us."

CHAPTER 18

─ GIDEON ─

We start planning to go back into the Rift right away.
With the security measures in place around camp,
we won't get away from here undetected without some help.

"Maia," Daryn suggests.

We all agree. Perfect.

Daryn grabs the radio on the kitchen counter and calls her.

Five minutes later, Maia steps into the RV and takes a slow
look around. Marcus is sprawled on the couch. The rest of us
are sitting at the kitchen table. Everyone is serious and quiet,
like we're processing Low's death, but she knows better. "What's
up, guys?"

"If we wanted to take the horses out tonight," Daryn says,
"would that be a problem?"

"Around what time?"

"Two?"

Maia bites her lower lip, her focus turning inward. "Let me
talk to Soraya and Sophia. I don't think it'll be an issue." She
stops at the door. "If any of you get hurt on this 'ride' of yours,
I'll kick your asses. So don't, okay?"

As soon as she leaves, we work on our strategy for inside
the Rift.

We can't identify what drew the Harrows to us, but we
agree that while we were traveling quietly, we went undetected. That's the course we'll keep: riding as a group, in silence, and maintaining a forward direction.

As far as finding Bas, we decide to let Daryn lead with

Shadow. Bas's horse is as sensitive to him as the rest of our horses are to each of us. Maybe he'll pick up Bas's scent and take us to him.

It's a thin plan. Definitely could be stronger. But it's something.

"What about the Mustang and the cabin?" Jode asks. "The white flowers?"

Daryn shakes her head. "I don't know. I've been thinking about them. It's like they're emotional triggers."

"To what end? Driving us out of the Rift?"

"I don't know." She looks at me. My emotions trigger. Lots of new developments to think about. Later, though. "I've been thinking about how Samrael could get into your minds," she continues. "And how, when he made me open the portal in the fall, I felt part of him seeping into it. It felt like he contaminated it."

Contaminated. Perfect word. That's exactly how I felt when he got in my head.

"You think that ability of his bled into the place?" I ask.

"It was just an idea," Daryn says. "But it doesn't explain the flowers or the cabin. He couldn't see into *my* head—just yours."

Silence falls over us. Jode scratches his chin. "If they're psychological attacks, we can't let them work."

"Agreed." It's a chorus. A pact. But I'm not sure how we'll keep it—the actual mechanics of how we won't "let them work."

Jode looks at me. "We haven't talked about Samrael yet, or what he said to Daryn."

"What is there to discuss, Jode?"

"He needs to die," Marcus says. "Done. What's next?"

"You don't believe what he told Daryn? That he knows where Sebastian is?"

Marcus shakes his head.

"Gideon?"

"As a rule, I don't believe anything a demon says."

"Daryn, you're the one he spoke to. What do you think?"

"I . . ." She sighs. "I'm getting tired of saying, 'I don't know.' Taking into consideration everything I know at this time, I'm undecided."

"Undecided. So you might believe him?" I shouldn't be this pissed about something that's not even *known* yet.

Color rises in her cheeks, but her eyes don't waver. "Yes, Gideon. That's what I said."

"All right, next question," Jode says quickly, moving us along. "Have we planned an exit strategy? How long do we think we'll stay inside?"

Daryn slides out of the booth and lifts her backpack off the floor. She removes the orb, holding it in her palms. "In the chaos of things, Cordero hasn't asked for it back yet. Not that I'd have given it to her even if she had."

We move in for a closer look.

"This might influence our decision," she says. "It's deteriorating so much. Every time I've gone through, it's gotten worse."

The orb looks like tectonic plates, its surface broken and cracking into pieces. It looks like it's about to fall apart. It actually *has* fallen apart. One of the plates is missing. There's an entire piece that's not there at all—the sliver that was misplaced somewhere in Wyoming.

"I'm not sure we'll be able to get in again after this," Daryn says. "Tonight might be our last chance."

"Will we able to get back out?" Jode asks.

"I hope so," Daryn says.

I look around me. We all hope so.

At two in the morning, we head for the stable. The moisture in the air is thick. Heavy clouds are rolling in like a dark wave, and thunder rumbles constantly.

By contrast, camp is quiet. No one's patrolling and the usual guard posts are vacant. As we approach the stable, I see a few people huddled beyond the glow of the floodlights.

I lift my hand, knowing it's Maia and whoever else she recruited to help us pull this off.

Inside, Daryn tacks up Shadow. The guys and I summon armor and tack. Then we ride into the desert under flashing thunderheads that are about to unleash a tidal wave of rain.

The storm breaks as we reach the spot where we entered last time. Under the strobing lightning, I see the dried blood, hoofmarks, and tire treads from yesterday. I'm glad that soon it'll all be washed away.

In spite of the weather, everything flows better this time. Daryn has the orb. The horses are calmer without the Arabians, especially Shadow. And so are we, even knowing the dangers inside. And knowing this might be our last shot at getting Bas.

Daryn was right. This is how it should've been all along.

I get that now. I feel it, and so does Riot.

This is much better, Gideon. Soon we'll be whole again. Together. I hate rain.

Daryn's faster with the orb. More confident. She flips it up like she's tossing a ball. It catches in the air, brightens and unspools, swallowing us up into a completely different kind of storm.

Going through is the same agony as before, ripping pain. Like being pulled apart. It's only slightly easier to bear, knowing there'll be an end. When it comes, I'm spit into the woods, barely staying in the saddle. Disoriented, nauseous, and with a pounding headache.

Like before, there's no geographical or weather correlation between where we were and where we are. We left the stormy desert behind us; now we're in quiet woods at night.

For a split second I don't see Daryn and my heart stops beating. Then the glint of her blond hair catches my eye.

Mounted on Shadow, and dressed in black, she practically disappears.

Jode pulls Lucent to my right, Marcus brings Ruin to my left.

Daryn cues Shadow forward and recovers the orb from where it's spinning in the air. "Let's go," she says quietly.

We go.

I'm not crazy about the darkness for a few reasons. We'll have a harder time spotting Bas or the Harrows. I ride a burning horse. Lucent glows like a paper lantern. And though Ruin isn't as bright, she still glints like copper. We're *extremely* conspicuous. The odds of achieving our goal are significantly hampered, but we don't have any alternative.

Barely five minutes in, we spot the white begonias.

Daryn keeps Shadow going, but Jode and Marcus exchange a look, and the weight of my sword becomes noticeable at my back.

Time drifts past. Slow time. Fast time. Measurable in breaths. In hoofbeats and trees. I don't hear the Harrows. I don't smell their burnt reek or hear the wind rising.

Just as the woods are becoming numbingly, painfully the same, I see something different up ahead.

A fallen tree, dried and leafless, resting on its side.

Marcus hops off Ruin and probes it with the scythe. It's strange. The bark is broken, and parts are shredded like corn silk. I don't see heartwood or sapwood—it's hollowed out. And the *inside* of the bark is blackened and burnt.

I have the discomfiting thought that it looks like a cocoon. Like something clawed its way out.

Marcus shakes his head. "Don't like it." He mounts back up.

We ride again.

My mind starts to want to wander. I catch myself and bring my focus back to Bas, to the Harrows, to listening and looking. But the sameness of the woods feels like staring at a blank wall, and doing that for hours is impossible.

Random stuff starts popping into my head, like the time Bas and I were having a discussion at the train station in Denmark over whether it was okay to order a Danish or not.

Gideon, it is rude. You'd never order an American, would you? Or an Australian?

If someone asked me for an American I'd say, "You got one right in front of you."

You're missing the point. They're asking because they're looking for food.

I'm pretty sure I taste amazing.

Okay. I dare you. Walk up to those girls over there and ask if they're hungry for an American.

I would've done it to make him laugh. But at that point I was already thinking about Daryn all the time. She was the only girl I would've allowed to cannibalize me.

I also find myself thinking about Airborne School. Remembering the double parachute malfunction that killed me, for a little while, after which I became War.

It would suck if I died for good here in the Rift.

Why? Why am I thinking about this?

I rub the back of my head. My headache hasn't faded; it's getting worse.

"G?" Marcus says.

I look at him. Then suddenly Riot jolts back—all the horses reel back as the ground starts to shake.

A loud noise like a boom of thunder comes from the thick woods up ahead. Trees shudder, and all I hear is the splinter and snap of branches.

We rush toward it. I have no idea what to expect.

Harrows? Samrael? Sebastian?

But the massive object that we approach is one I'd know anywhere. I recognize it instantly.

The C-130 is a workhorse of a military plane. Big and cumbersome. It's the plane I jumped out of about a year ago, and then fell to my death.

As we ride up, it's still rising out of the earth like a sprouting plant, the nose pressing through the treetops and disappearing beyond.

The shaking stops as suddenly as it started, and there it is. In front of us. All but the tail sticking out of the ground.

Silence rings in my ears. For a few seconds I have to just process.

Daryn told us about the flowers washing over her mom, but this is the first time I've seen something unbelievable with my own eyes.

"So." I lick my dry lips. "Wonder where that flew in from."

Marcus looks at me. Not laughing.

Everybody knows this is from my past. There's no point in even saying it.

I hop off Riot to check it out. Jode comes with me, nocking an arrow in his bow.

I touch the plane. The metal feels solid and real. Every detail is just as I remember it. All it's missing is people.

Jode finally lowers his bow and lets out a hissing breath. "Why?"

"Don't know. But I was thinking about it before."

"You were?"

"Yeah. It wasn't the only thing on my mind, though." I was thinking about Bas, too. About my mother and my sister. My dad.

"But it's the only thing that appeared."

"So far."

"Yes. So far." He shakes his head. "It's like we're meeting our own psyches."

As I catch Daryn's eye on my way back to Riot, it hits me how hard it must've been for her to see her mother here.

This stuff isn't real—not the plane or her mom—but it *feels* completely real.

If I came across my mom in the Rift, I'd lose it. But if my *dad* were here?

Just imagining it makes my stomach queasy.

"Good seeing ya, plane from my past," I say as I mount up.

Well done, Gideon. If you want to feel positive, be positive.

"Thanks, horse," I mutter, patting Riot.

Just as I'm shaking off the plane, we come across our next surprise; they're coming in quick succession now.

This time there's no shaking ground or snapping branches. Like Marcus's Mustang, we ride up and there it is.

Another car.

A Range Rover that's smashed into a tree. *Smashed* into it. Almost wrapped completely around the trunk.

"Mine," Jode says. "This belongs to me."

He jumps off Lucent and moves to investigate, peering into the mangled cabin. It's empty, but I'm sure he's imagining himself inside it, since I am.

I know this story. Jode died in this car. It's his version of the C-130.

I picture his last seconds before he crashed, died, and came back as Conquest. How much like *my* last seconds they must've been. Feeling all that regret over things you wanted to do and say and be, but never got around to. Nothing like those pre-death moments to give you perspective on life.

As Jode returns, his face is white but he tries a grin. "Quite a grand tour of our transportational tragedies."

"Not all of them. My mother was different," Daryn reminds us. "Her flowers, too. They're not all related to tragic accidents."

"Were you thinking about her beforehand?"

"I can't remember." Daryn frowns. "Were you thinking about this?"

"Yes. Gideon, too."

"I think I was too," Marcus adds. "I just remember a headache before the Mustang."

"I felt that as well before this," Jode says, tipping his chin at the Range Rover.

"Same for me before the plane."

"I've felt pressure the entire time I've been here," Daryn says.

Jode looks at each of us. "Well, let's be smart about this. We could be manifesting these anomalies through our thoughts. We can't dismiss the possibility. And the headaches could be giving us warning, so keep sharp, everyone."

"Yeah, but . . ." I shake my head. "Never mind."

"Say it, Gideon. We need everything right now. As much intelligence as we can use, let's use it."

"Daryn, you said earlier that you thought Samrael poisoned this place when you first opened the portal. He contaminated it. Those were your words."

"Yes," she says. "That was how it felt."

"Well, Samrael didn't just have the ability to *get into* my head to see what was there. He had a lot more guns than that. He could go hunting for my memories. And fears. He could put thoughts in my head, too. So if this place took some of him and has his ability, it's not just our thoughts that can manifest. We're wide open. It's open season on our worst fears."

No one says anything for a few seconds.

Then Jode shoves both hands into his hair. "Oh, *hell.* Bloody fabulous."

CHAPTER 19

‑ DARYN ‑

I don't know if what Jode and Gideon suggested is true.

Are these anomalies coming from our minds? Is the Rift peering into our heads and lobbing our fears at us?

It seems utterly unbelievable. Impossible.

But then again, we've seen the impossible too many times to doubt it can happen.

What I don't understand is *why*. What's the point of the Rift mind-torturing us? To get us to leave? That's not going to happen.

As we ride past a never-ending parade of woodsy sameness, I become semi-paranoid about my own thoughts, because now they may have physical power.

Random images shoot through my mind. They swoop in like sparrows. I can't stop them.

I see Shadow's inky black tail, swishing.

Isabel's warm hands wrapped around a teacup.

Josie's chocolate-chip cookies.

Dad, wiping his red face with a towel after his Tuesday-night tennis match.

Mom with her gardening gloves and sun hat, kneeling at her flower beds.

I keep scanning the woods, waiting for one of them to materialize. But hours pass until we see another—and it's nothing I've been thinking about.

It's a dog.

A tiny white dog, tied to the root of a tree with a thin purple leash. It has a snowy white coat and beady black eyes. A purple ribbon is tied around its neck.

I love dogs, and I've always wanted one. It's why I keep thinking about Chief—the puppy that would've been mine if only I were home in Connecticut.

In my entire life, I can't remember ever meeting a dog I haven't liked on sight. But this little ball of white fur starts to yap furiously and lunge at the leash as soon as we come near. Something about it instantly puts me off. A mean-spiritedness at odds with its adorable appearance.

Jode says, "Ah, lucky me. That's mine again. Well, he's my mum's. His name is Baudelaire. Bodie, for short."

"He seems . . . sweet," I say.

"Yes," Jode says. "Charming, as you can see."

By his strained expression, I can tell there's a story here. Maybe Baudelaire isn't part of a tragedy, like some of the other anomalies we've come across. But he's not part of many happy memories, either.

"Riot wants to eat Bodie," Gideon says. "Can I let him?"

Jode laughs humorlessly. "No."

"Then what's the plan? Are we taking him?"

Jode shakes his head. "We can't. He's too loud."

"Are we leaving him?"

"I can't. He's my mum's dog."

"Okay, so what are we doing?"

Jode looks from Bodie to Gideon. "This dog died five years ago."

"Oh."

Silence descends.

Baudelaire has stopped yapping. He pants as he looks at Jode, his tiny pink tongue lolling. Then he turns and runs right into the tree.

Into a hollow knot in the tree.

Into it.

Disappearing inside.

The leash snaps loose and trails after the little white dog like a kite streamer; then the knot closes, sealing shut. In seconds, an instant, there's no dog, no leash. No sound in the air.

Then Marcus says, "The tree just ate the dead dog."

"Yes," says Jode. "So it seems."

"Jode," I ask, "were you thinking about him? Before we found him?"

"He crossed my mind briefly. An hour ago, though. Not recently."

We look at each other, hoping theories will emerge. None do. All we have is questions, and we've already asked those.

The Rift, score a million.

Us, zero.

There's no further discussion necessary. What is there to say? We sit in our saddles and quietly try to file this away, accepting the anything-is-possible-ness of this place.

The hours string together, one after another. We don't see any planes or cars or dogs. We don't see my mother, only occasional patches of flowers winding through the trees.

Dawn breaks. The sun reaches its zenith. Dusk falls.

Nothing new has appeared, and neither has Bas. Tiredness seeps into my muscles, but my imagination shows no sign of slowing down. I imagine the trees growing eyes and mouths and taunting us with deep rumbling voices. I imagine them hiding small dogs inside them. I imagine *Sebastian* inside them. And Harrows. Harrows like rotten black maggots, packed and squirming inside.

I don't notice the chill in the air until Gideon speaks.

"It'll be dark soon. We need to lay camp," he says.

He looks unhappy with his own idea.

We've been riding for fifteen hours and haven't slept in twice as long. The horses don't tire, but we do. I'm sure I'm not alone in being exhausted.

As I dismount, my legs wobble and my stomach sinks with disappointment. We've accomplished nothing. And we're going to *sleep* here.

Necessary, sure. But somehow it seems foolish.

After weighing the pros and cons of making a fire to warm up, we decide to do it. We're already visually exposed, thanks to Riot and Lucent. A fire won't make that much difference. And we're not just trying to go undetected by the Harrows and Samrael. We want Bas to see us.

Jode and Marcus go in search of wood. Gideon takes a slow stroll around the clearing, like he might see something different from what we've seen all day.

I stay with Shadow, since the orb is in her pack and I'm not making that mistake again. I remove her tack and comb her mane out with my fingers, feeling her relax under my attention. "You'll tell us, won't you, girl? When Bas is close?"

She doesn't move. She doesn't twitch a muscle. But I know what she's thinking.

Of course. Of course I will.

"Hey," Gideon says.

I turn and he's there, tall and so different in armor from the Gideon who came to my RV last night in a long-sleeved T-shirt and jeans. As War, he's a little intimidating. He would be if I didn't know him.

"You doing okay?" His eyebrows are drawn. He looks serious, but his mouth is tugging up like he's thinking about smiling.

I feel it, too. Happiness. The flight of butterflies in my gut. The desire to laugh. Desire. So much of it. "I'm good, considering! My legs are still working." I sound a little too enthusiastic.

He looks at my legs. "Right. A lot of riding."

"It's *crazy*. How about you? Are your legs tired?" My gosh. *Calm down, Daryn.* What's wrong with me?

He eases his head to the side, smiling. "My legs are okay."

I nod. I don't look at his legs or comment on them. I just stare into his blue eyes and take a pass on talking, which seems like the smartest thing to do.

"All right over there?" Jode asks.

A moment ago, he and Marcus were stacking the wood for the fire. Now they're both watching us, big smiles on their faces.

"I didn't say anything to them about us, Daryn. They're just idiots." Gideon winces slightly with self-awareness. "I didn't mean that there's anything to say."

"Isn't there anything to say?"

Something settles in his eyes. A sincerity. A promise, like this moment is his and mine. Only ours. When he steps closer, my entire body buzzes to life. I feel actual voltage.

"I wasn't exactly sober last night," he says, pitching his voice low. "You may have noticed. But I wanted to say that I remember everything. And I meant everything."

"So did I."

He grins, and it's true and breathtaking. A smile I'll see again in daydreams and night dreams, I'm sure. "That's what I wanted to hear."

"Gideon, whenever you're ready to get your horse," says Jode. "We need a flame. This campfire won't start itself."

"Set us on fire, G." That's Marcus.

Then it's Jode again. "Yes, Gideon. You're so *hot*."

I laugh, but Gideon doesn't. "Be right there," he replies without looking away. He bends close to my ear. "This is going to be good, Daryn," he says. "I promise." Then he brushes a kiss against my cheek like it's the most natural thing in the world.

We claim spots around the fire and unpack blankets, fruit, crackers, cheese, and water, and then set to eating industriously.

There's no enjoyment. We need food, water, and sleep. We're just refueling before we can get back to searching. I'm hungry, but not hungry. Chewing is work.

The mood is subdued. My stolen moment with Gideon is like a brilliant canary in a cage. Nowhere to go. But still beautiful despite the grim context.

When we're finished we wrap ourselves in our blankets and stare into the fire with longing on our faces. For home. For Bas. For resolution.

The darkness presses into our golden circle and I keep imagining the Harrows out there beyond the light. Crouching on branches. Peering around the thick trunks. Watching us.

You won't succeed until you fail . . . Your only hope is surrender.

The words of the Harrow I slung to the tree circle in my mind like a riddle.

Then Samrael's. *He's with me. He's safe. Sebastian is well.* Was he telling the truth?

Finally, I hear the echo of Isabel's words from the last time I saw her. *Evil is its own undoing.*

They're pieces of a whole I can't quite fit together. A kaleidoscopic view of what's right in front of me.

Gideon shifts beside me, reclining on an elbow and crossing his legs at the ankles. His pose is unconsciously seductive. An athlete in repose. His face is painted in flickering amber and gold. Contrary to his serene posture, he's concentrating intensely. Somehow I know that whatever he's thinking, it's in the service of someone he cares about. All the intensity in him comes from love.

And from passion.

Heat builds on my cheeks at my own thoughts. It's so strange to feel this—whatever it is that's growing between us—in this place, at this time. How can something this good be happening in *here*?

Gideon becomes aware of my attention on him and his mouth lifts in a subtle, private smile. Caught, all I can do is smile back, my heart aching and stretching and expanding to make room to accommodate moments like this in my life.

Jode scratches the pale stubble on his jaw. He clears his throat, and I realize it's the first sound I've heard in a while, aside from the crackle of the fire.

"I'll keep first watch again," he offers. "I'm overtired. I haven't got much chance of sleeping anyhow."

No one argues. It wouldn't work anyway.

After a few minutes of willfully pressing my eyelids closed, I accept that sleep isn't in my near future either, and give up trying.

Sitting up, I pull my journal from my backpack. Marcus has disappeared into his blankets. Across the fire, Jode winks at me, then goes back to panning the woods. Gideon is asleep eighteen inches away from me. But who's counting?

I turn to a blank page and write Sebastian's name a few times in all its variations.

Sebastian. Bastian. Bas.

Seb, which he once told us was what his brothers in Nicaragua called him.

Then I write *Famine*. And then *hunger*, and I don't even look Gideon's way, but my heart starts racing anyway.

I page to "Reasons." It's become a habit to add to this list. Going to sleep without reflecting on the day's Reasons would feel incomplete. I reread the last few lines. I add to it.

19. *Humor, in the face of the frightening and bizarre*
20. *Conviction, in times when hope is scarce*
21. *"This is going to be good, Daryn. I promise."—I promise, too. I won't let fear stop me.*

I close my notebook and stash it in my backpack, double-checking to make sure the orb is safely tucked at the bottom. Then I twist my hair up, piling it on top of my head.

"For the record," Jode says from across the fire, "I think the recent developments I've observed are excellent."

I smile. "Thanks. I do, too. And who knows? Maybe he'll lighten up on the Anna thing now."

"One can hope," Jode says, in a wry voice, devoid of all hope.

In the interest of newly added entry number twenty-one, and of the bravery it'll require from me to keep my promise, I move to Gideon, lift the edge of his blanket, and burrow right against his back.

His armor isn't bulky—it's much tougher than leather, though just as thin and flexible—but it still makes him feel distant. I can't feel the life in him at all, but that's not the point.

The point is I'm here.

Gideon stirs, his body flexing with awareness. Cool metal slides over my hip, and he relaxes again.

For a while all I notice is his prosthetic on my hip. All I feel is surprise at how much I like it—this adopted part of him that makes him so unique. Then tiredness washes over me in waves. As I drift off, a blurry, brilliant happiness fills me.

He told me this would be good, and it will be. I won't run, like I usually do. Even if *he* hurts and I can't make it right, or even if *I* hurt and he can't make it right, I'll stay.

This will be good.

CHAPTER 20

— GIDEON —

Did I miss something? Did you ask them to leave?" Daryn asks, tipping her chin at Jode and Marcus.

"No. I didn't say anything." Instead of sitting with us by the fire this morning, they've wandered off about thirty yards to eat. I think they're giving Daryn and me some time alone before we get going again. There's no other logical explanation. "But, pretty cool of them, right? This is practically our first date."

She laughs. "It's certainly memorable."

"What do you want for breakfast?" I reach into one of our supply bags. "Trail mix, trail mix, or a granola bar—trail mix that's glued together? Keep in mind that we should probably get going in about five minutes."

"Hmm. Tough one." She squints at the sky in thought. "I'm going to have to go with my favorite. Trail mix."

"Good choice." As soon as I try to open the packet, I realize my mistake. The plastic is thin and slippery, but thick enough to be hard to tear. Level-ten challenge with only one working hand, and I'm not going to rip into it with my teeth.

I try to pin it with Robohand and tear with my right. I drop the packet a few times. Tug at air a few times.

Nothing's working and embarrassment's hitting hard. I feel the heat on my face and the rush of my heartbeat. I'm starting to sweat. And I'm hyperconscious of Daryn watching my hands, not saying anything.

Please don't say anything. Don't ask if I need help.

Just when I'm about to smash the entire thing, the plastic tears.

I hand her the open packet.

"Thank you." She leans over and kisses my cheek, then pours the contents out onto her palm.

Just accepting how things are.

How I am now. In here. In general.

It's the best thing. The best thing she could've done. A surge of gratitude and wonder sweeps over me. Too much to hold inside. I suddenly want to tackle her, kiss every bit of her, but she's hard at work picking out M&M's and sorting them by color. I can't make myself interrupt her.

"What's your order?"

She smiles. "Red first, of course. Then blue. Then usually yellow."

She goes through it all. The entire hierarchy of how she eats the trail mix. I start to zone out at cashews. She's just so pretty, all sleepy-eyed. And smart and cool. Generous and funny. A little weird. And *tough*. It just keeps hitting me how she's this incredible combination of all these different qualities.

Like trail mix.

I make myself laugh.

She laughs at me. "What?"

I'm about to tell her. I think I even open my mouth to tell her, when I realize my head's pounding. Headaches are our warning.

"Gideon, what is it?"

The flames in our campfire leap higher—suddenly, like someone threw gasoline on them.

Daryn and I lunge backward.

The logs shift. Instead of the ashes rising *up*, the logs sink *down*. The fire's burning a hole—*through the ground*.

The earth beneath our feet begins to rumble and break apart. Crumbling and giving out.

And we're going with it.

Daryn yanks my arm. "Gideon, go!"

We backpedal together, feet churning, but the dirt falls away. We have no chance of escaping this.

We're going into this sinkhole.

"Gideon! Daryn!"

Jode and Marcus stand above, looking down from the edge of a cliff that becomes steeper by the instant. Embers and ashes fly past, stinging the skin on my face and arms. Avalanches of roots and dirt scratch and fling themselves into my eyes and nose.

Marcus whips the scythe around and extends the base down to me, but I've got ahold of Daryn with my good hand. I'm not letting go of her.

Then it's too late. They're a hundred feet above. A thousand. Gone.

I can't see them anymore. Can't hear them yelling.

Darkness closes over us, but we keep falling. I wrap my arms around Daryn. Her body is rigid with fear. Seconds turn to minutes.

"When will it stop?" she yells, and starts coughing.

"I don't know."

I look down and there is no down. I don't see anything.

Falling is how my dad died. It's how I died, too.

A legitimate fear of mine. But now I know what's worse than falling to your death: falling indefinitely. Falling for the rest of your life.

Five minutes of this and I feel like I'm going insane. No power to move, to stop. Nothing but this gut-dropping descent. Then I see a shape shooting toward us from the darkness below.

As it speeds closer, I see that it's a sphere. Golden. Huge. We're going to smash into a planet. I see mountain ridges, then valleys. Then the ground speeding up.

"Hold on to me. Don't let go."

"I won't. I won't let go."

As we're about to hit, the same brutal thoughts shoot through my mind as last time, after my parachuting accident.

Wanting more of life. Wanting to do *better* at life.

I see grains of dirt, and then a jolt shoots through me.

Daryn and I rip apart, but there's no pain.

I'm blinded. I can't see anything. Can't *feel* anything. Then blurred images appear and begin to solidify around me.

Pressure builds across my chest, and I realize I'm sitting in a truck. Passenger seat. Seat belt on.

My dad's work truck.

Shit. Not this.

The air-conditioning in the truck is blasting, but I can still feel the outside heat of the summer day coming through the windows.

I'm wearing faded jeans and a sweaty T-shirt and in my hand is the cell phone I owned almost two years ago.

Daryn sits next to me in the driver's seat. The steering wheel in front of her is cracked and faded with use.

She looks lost. Confused.

There's no dirt on her, no ashes. No sign of the fall we just experienced on me, either. It's like it didn't happen.

We're parked in a residential neighborhood. The houses are small, tidy. Flower boxes under the windows. Newspapers on driveways. No people, though, like there were on that day. No birds or other cars, either.

I've seen this scene a hundred times. I've relived it each and every time. But not like this.

"Gideon," Daryn breathes, like someone will overhear us. "This is how your dad died."

"Yeah." We're parked in front of the yellow cottage where it happened. My eyes drift past the porch, past the two small bikes leaning against the wood rail, stopping at the spot on the brick walkway where Dad fell. He's not there.

I look up to the roof. Not there, either.

All I see is the warped shingle roof. Above it, clear blue sky.

"I saw this in a vision," Daryn says. "I saw this before I ever met you."

I always wondered if she had. As a Seeker, there were lots of things I thought she knew and kept to herself. But I don't know how to respond.

My body is still adjusting to not falling. I feel seasick—the falling equivalent. And I'm not sure if I'm dreaming or dead or if the Rift just upped its game significantly.

"We were here to bid on that roof," I hear myself say. "See the bend in the gutter above the window? He was standing right there when he had a stroke. I was in here texting my buddies when it happened."

"I know," she says.

"Right. You would know if you saw it." I'm struggling to draw air into my lungs. The street is wobbling up ahead. The lawns and trees, too. They undulate like they're behind heat waves in the desert. Checking the rearview mirror, I see that it's the same behind us. And above us. The shimmering is happening all across the sky.

"Any ideas on what's next?" I ask, though I'm not sure I want to know. We fell through the ground into one of my worst memories. What's next can't be good.

Daryn shakes her head absently, her attention elsewhere. She leans toward me, ducking to look at the roof of the yellow bungalow. "Gideon . . ."

I turn to see what she sees.

Someone *is* up on the roof, standing right at the edge where Dad stood that day.

It's a woman I've never seen before—but I know who she is.

Daryn's mother is in a white dress that blows in the breeze. Her shoulder-length hair is a lighter blond than Daryn's. Her complexion's lighter than Daryn's honey-colored tan, too. But she has Daryn's long legs and straight posture. And like Daryn, there's a quiet challenge in her eyes. Not hostile. Just daring you to put anything less than your best foot forward.

She steps to the very edge of the roof. She looks ready to jump.

"Mom?" Daryn says. *"Mom!"*

Fear crashes into me. Daryn yanks at the door handle. "It's locked! Gideon, it's locked!"

My side is locked, too. The lock is mechanical but it won't give. I slam my shoulder into the door. Daryn is screaming and hitting the driver's-side door, and there's no sound worse than the raw fear in her voice.

"Gideon, how do I get out? How do I stop her?"

I don't know. It kills me that I don't know. I keep throwing myself against my side, smashing my shoulder into it. It feels like it's made of concrete, and suddenly I know we're not meant to get out. Nothing we do will change what's going to happen.

Huge black clouds are tumbling across the sky. They come like waves, casting shadows across the street and the house, plunging us into instant twilight. Gusts roll past, lifting leaves and blowing them across the lawns.

In just seconds it's growing *dark*. The houses at the end of the street disappear. Then the ones closer to us.

"Don't do this, Mom," Daryn pleads. Her mom has inched closer to the edge of the roof. "I'll come home. I'll come home. I'm coming home, Mom."

I grab Daryn's hand. I've never felt more useless.

The last thing I see before darkness takes everything is the flash of her mother's hair as she steps off the edge—a gold flame that burns bright, then snuffs out.

In the silence of the truck, all I hear is Daryn's breathing and mine.

"Oh, God. What just happened?"

I can't answer that. I reach over and pull her onto my lap.

"Gideon, I don't understand. What happened? Did she jump? I didn't see. I didn't see her fall."

I bury my hand in her hair and bring her forehead to mine. I'm glad she can't see my face in the darkness. I went through this. I lived this. I *did* see my father fall. I don't want her to feel this. I don't want her to know this pain, too.

The truck begins to shake. We instinctively latch on to each other.

Here we go.

I hear the sound of metal bending and groaning.

Something rough and dry snakes over my wrists. Then my ankles. The smell of dirt invades my nostrils.

Roots. I'm being shackled by roots.

They twist around my legs and arms. Twist around Daryn, too. I feel us being plucked up. Lifted off the seats of the truck. I hold on to her and we keep rising, up, up, up. Like the hellacious fall, but in reverse.

Dirt falls over me. Into my eyes and my mouth.

Daryn coughs. I'm hacking too, trying to clear my throat, when we're thrust up violently.

We push through a wall I can't see—a wall that hits me everywhere. Then we break into air, cool air, daylight surrounding us. Trees all around.

Airborne for an instant.

A lifetime.

Then we come down hard. Daryn lands square on my chest; my back hits earth that's sealed shut behind me. Around us roots slither into the ground like retreating eels, disappearing.

Jode and Marcus run up, weapons drawn, cursing. Ready to do anything to help.

I'm still trying to make sure it's over. Whatever *it* is.

Daryn rolls away from me, still coughing. She brushes her hair out of her eyes and sits up, looking at me.

"It wasn't her," I tell her. "It wasn't real."

Empty words. They do nothing to ease the devastation on her face.

There's not a single thing in the world that actually seems worth saying.

I feel like I failed her. Like I should just walk away. At the same time, I feel like pulling her into my soul.

But neither can happen right now.

The trees are rustling with a breeze that smells like smoke. We know what that smell brings.

The last thing I want to see right now is the Harrows.

We mount up and ride.

My mood is off by a few thousand degrees, and Riot feels it.

He keeps us covered in flames, and won't pull back on them.

He burns so hot he leaves a trail of charred hoofprints, which is a problem. If the Harrows are out there trying to hunt us down, we don't need to become any easier to find.

I rest my hand on his withers, trying to convince him that I'm all right, but until I know Daryn's all right, I won't really be. It's a chain reaction.

An hour later, the burnt smell is gone. The wind has died down, and leaves hang still on the branches. Feeling relatively safe from the Harrows, we ride abreast so we can talk about what happened.

Marcus wants to know. Jode *really* wants to know. And they deserve to. They're at the mercy of this place, too.

I describe falling through the ground, then falling through darkness for ten minutes or maybe more, and finally ending up in Dad's truck with Daryn beside me.

"You saw your dad's death?" Marcus asks. He looks worried. He knows how that day still haunts me.

I shake my head. "He wasn't there. It was only the place. The house where it happened."

"You were in the truck. Then what?" Jode asks.

"It went dark. We were mauled by roots, and then we came back up." Something keeps me from telling them about Daryn's mom being the one on the roof of the yellow bungalow.

I glance at her and find her watching me, her eyes narrowed in anger. "You don't have to protect me, Gideon," she says. Then she gets Shadow moving and pulls ahead.

I want to go after her. But I need to figure out where I went wrong first.

Marcus looks at me. He cues Ruin, catching up to Daryn.

"Traitor," I mutter.

"Yes," Jode says in a deadpan. "He's ever so eager to betray you."

The day grows bright, even under the thick canopy.

Sunlight catches dust motes swirling in the air and peppers the forest floor with white spots, illuminating our tour through psychological land mines. Judging by what Daryn and I just experienced, the tour is now interactive.

We're ready for it. Every one of us feels a constant mild headache. It's so constant, we start to not notice it.

Game on, Rift. Bring it.

We come across a red canoe resting on the forest floor. It's made of real wood and looks authentic, handcrafted and old, like something passed down through generations.

I hear Daryn explain to Marcus that it's from her family cabin in Maine. "My sister and I spent a lot of summers in that canoe," she tells him. "My mom painted it."

She says nothing more, but I know she's thinking about what we went through this morning. I don't know how we rolled right into not talking about it. Ignoring it. Maybe it was me.

Did I make it this way?

We see my catcher's mitt in the dirt, just lying there. This thing that was a huge part of my life two years ago. Baseball was everything to me. I wanted to play in college. I was working my ass off trying to get scholarship looks, and things were heading in the right direction. Now I have no dad. I have one hand and a burning horse. A few hours ago, I thought I had a girlfriend—first one I've ever really wanted. Not sure about that anymore.

Marcus claims a thick flannel blanket draped over a branch, but he offers no story. Then we see a flute resting against the trunk of a tree. Jode lifts his land and says, "Mine. No further comments, please."

We start calling them relics, these physical objects. Relics from our pasts. But we don't fall through the ground or come face-to-face with death, so. That's a plus. This place is redefining my standards.

Hours pass. We've been so focused on staying alive and absorbed in the relics that finding Bas hasn't been our top priority—which is a major problem. And we're running out of food and water—also a major problem.

I'm starting to think we've lost another day when Daryn says, "Guys, look."

She points up ahead, where the woods thin.

Riding up, we find a field of fallen trees. Burnt trees like the one we saw yesterday. Broken open. Charred on the inside. Crumbling trunks and cracked bark lie scattered across the field like dead on a battlefield.

A burnt smell seeps into my nose. Of course, considering we're surrounded by fire damage. But my heart starts to thunder and I scan the edges of the field for any sign of rustling leaves or swaying branches.

"Guys, over here!" Daryn's halfway across the field already. She tucks in as Shadow breaks into a gallop.

Riot lifts off as soon as I cue him. We shoot after her, kicking up dead branches and vaulting over logs.

Daryn dismounts at the edge of the field. "Look." She strides up to a sheet of rough-edged paper nailed to one of the tree carcasses.

Tearing it free, she reads.

CHAPTER 21

⊸ DARYN ⊸

I read it twice.

As I'm finishing the second time, I can't stop myself from laughing, with this rising sun inside my heart.

"What is it?" Jode asks.

"It's . . . It's better if I just read it aloud." I lift the sheet and project my voice.

> *Jode, Gideon, Daryn, Marcus,*
>
> *I knew you'd come get me, but I still can't believe you're really here!*
>
> *It's too dangerous for me to tell you how to find me. Stay near the lake and I'll find you.*
>
> *Do you know where the lake is? I marked the way, just to play with safety.*
>
> *Thanks, you guys. I can't wait to see you and Shadow. I can't wait to go HOME!*
>
> *—Bas*

Gideon is the first to react. He jumps off Riot and reaches me in quick strides, peering at the paper. "It could be fake."

"It's not fake! It's from him."

He takes the paper and reads it. The grim expression on his face never changes.

He hands it to Jode, who reads it.

Jode hands it to Marcus, who reads it, too.

"Could be another relic," Jode says. "It could be just another false object."

"No! It's from *him*," I say. "That's from Sebastian. Look—he even wrote 'play with safety.' That's *him*. Only Bas would mangle that. He did it to prove to us it's him. I'm positive. This is how we find him. We go to this lake and we wait there. You guys . . . this is it."

Marcus and Gideon communicate in their silent language, but I know what they're worried about. I feel their skepticism. Jode's, too. They're on the verge of discussing ambushes and setups and a hundred other "what if" scenarios. But I'm not standing on the sidelines anymore. I'm not waiting for certainty to come through visions, or strategizing, or any other way. What kind of plan could ever feel solid here, in this utterly unreliable place?

Instinct. Faith. That's what I can count on. I don't know what will come of believing this letter. But I *do* know that I want to be the type of person who can believe in positive turns. Not everything has to be out to destroy us.

Like Isabel said, I'm trusting.

I take the paper from Marcus. "You guys don't have to go wait for him, but I am."

"Daryn, hold on."

"No, thanks." I keep walking. "I'm going. You can join me or not. Your choice."

As I walk to Shadow, I pray my momentum is enough to get them moving, to bring them with me.

It is.

Half an hour later, guided by the trail of broken branches Bas left to point the way, we find the lake.

We check the area, following the shoreline one way and then back the other, Jode never lowering his bow for more than seconds at a time. Apart from the begonias, which we're all becoming used to seeing, there's no sign of danger, or of Bas. We brush down the forest floor with branches to erase our tracks. Then we set up a campsite away from the banks.

By the time we finish it's growing dark, so Marcus and Jode gather wood to get a fire going. Gideon and I head to the lake for water.

We're quiet on the walk, but the silence isn't comfortable. We haven't really talked since we went through our ordeal— our joint nightmare. We should probably discuss it, but it's the last thing I want to do.

Gideon stakes his sword as we reach the gravelly shore. The lake is vast, the trees on the opposite shoreline miniature. The water shines dully under the starlight, like pewter, and whirls of fog curl across its surface. After so much time beneath the stifling green canopy, the view of the open water and of the stars blinking to life in the dusky sky fills my lungs with fresh hope.

"You think it's poisonous?" Gideon asks.

"The water? No. But just in case, you should probably drink it first."

Blue eyes slide over, and he smiles. "I wish you weren't kidding. Should we go together?"

"Sure."

We fill our canteens, count to three, and drink. It's delicious, cool water, and neither one of us dies.

"Well, that's a relief," he says.

"Yeah. But also oddly anticlimactic?"

"Right? Pretty small-time for this place. Wait . . . Oh no. Oh no." He drops to the gravel and bugs his eyes out, coughing and grabbing his throat comically. So I grab my stomach, and then do my poison death, shaking like a fish out of water.

We laugh for five minutes straight, unable to stop ourselves.

"Why was that so funny?" I ask.

"I don't know. 'Cause death's super possible here?" My legs ache as I stand to head back. "Daryn—wait. Stay a little longer?"

I sit back on the gravel shore. "Okay."

He regards me with a frank expression. Then he moves over and puts his arm around me. "Good?"

My body—pushed beyond exhaustion—melts against his chest. "Better than good. You make a great chair."

"I make a better bed. I'm serious," he says, when I start laughing. "My neighbor's cat sleeps on me all the time at home."

"You seem more the dog type."

"Well, I'm the horse type now. But I do love dogs. I'm going to get one soon. From an animal shelter or something. I've been thinking about it."

"That's awesome—you should. My parents just adopted a dog and they're definitely *not* dog people." He must hear the crack in my voice because his arms tighten around me. I close my eyes and feel his heartbeat drumming against my back. "Your heart's beating fast. Are you worried about it happening again?"

"Define 'it,' " he says.

"Falling through the ground. Going through another living nightmare."

"I don't want that to happen. But I'm not worried. There's nothing I can do to stop it. No point stressing." His lips press against the top of my head. "You really want to know what I'm worried about?"

"Yes."

"That I did something dumb earlier. Toward you."

"Which dumb thing are we talking about?"

"You've got a real wicked streak, Martin."

I laugh. "Sorry. What was it? Tell me."

"You think I censored what I was telling Jode and Marcus

to protect you. About what we saw . . . your mom. I *was* censoring, because it felt like your thing to share, not mine. I didn't mean disrespect. I just wanted to give you the choice."

Anxiety curls inside my chest. "I don't want to talk about this."

I start to stand, until he says, "I had a feeling you'd do this. It's like you're always ready to bolt."

I *am* always ready to bolt—I can't deny it. But now I can't leave or I'll only prove him right. I try to relax again. To find the comfort in his arms again. But now my heart is racing, too. "I probably deserve that reputation."

"Why do you do it?"

"Run?" Such a simple and yet terrifying question. "I don't know."

He doesn't say anything, but I feel his disappointment. *Tell him, Daryn.* I promised him I would. And as hard as it'll be to say, I want him to know. I clear my throat. "I told you about my mother, remember? When we were in Rome?"

"You told me she has depression."

"That's right. Sometimes, growing up—" He answered so readily and with such focus. Like he wants to ace the test on my background. It gets to me for a second, how much he cares. I have to start over. "Sometimes as I was growing up it got really bad. She'd be in her bedroom for weeks crying. It was really hard. *Really* hard. I hated seeing her that sad and I hated not being able to fix it. Sometimes there was no fixing it. It felt exactly like being in your truck, Gideon. Exactly.

"Time was the only thing that would get her through and give her back to us. Before we learned that, we tried everything. Dad took her to see every specialist in the country. Mom tried every kind of medication, every kind of therapy. Some things helped but like I said, there were times nothing worked.

"After a while, Dad just got worn down by it, I guess. Being so helpless. Seeing her in such bad shape. I don't think he could stand to be around her, so he started to spend more time at work. Days. Nights. Weekends. It got to be that we hardly saw him. With Mom sick, my sister Josie stepped in and ran the house. She made dinner, did the laundry, got straight As. Josie took care of us. Josie became my mom.

"I tried to stay out of the way. I thought that was the best thing I could do. I was around just enough so they wouldn't worry. I ran track and did well in school. But I was dying inside, watching my family fall apart.

"Then I started having visions. Once *that* happened, the focus switched to me. A daughter having paranoid delusions? That's intense. That'll steal the spotlight. I could see right away how much it scared my dad. Since he'd been through the psychiatric evaluations before with my mom, he knew all the best doctors, the best facilities. So you could say he fast-tracked me and sent me right to that institution I told you about— the one I broke out of.

"Except I knew all along that I wasn't schizophrenic. I was seeing the future. The visions were a blessing. But my parents were never going to believe me, considering our family history of mental illness. And by sticking around, I was only drawing from the resources that should've been going to my mom."

"So you ran."

"Yes. Awful, right? I bailed on them. I ran away and started traveling the world as a Seeker. I guess that's when the running started. I was on the move, physically and emotionally. Since then, it's been easy to walk away from stuff that feels too close. Safer.

"Gideon, I didn't get mad at you back there because you censored your story. I was mad because you hold this part of me now. This scary, secret knowledge that I've been terrified my entire life for my mom. Terrified. I'm just not used to . . . trusting people. Letting them in."

"I'd never abuse that knowledge, Daryn. You don't have to be afraid of trusting me. I'm not your parents."

"My parents? What are you saying?"

"They bailed on you, Daryn. You can see that, can't you?"

"My mom is sick, Gideon. Depression is an illness. *I* left *her*."

"Is hiding behind work an illness?"

"You mean my dad?"

He shrugs—a quick, frustrated gesture. "It's your family. I shouldn't say anything."

"Tell me. I want to know."

"What your dad did was wrong. You don't turn your back on your kids because you're in too much pain to deal. He was the adult in the situation and he abandoned you. Your mom did, too. Maybe she couldn't help it because she was sick, but they left you before you ever left them. It sucks that that happened to you. If you felt the way you did in my truck your entire childhood, scared like that—and your dad was nowhere to help? I want to punch something when I think about it. It may be your dad if I ever meet him."

Emotions rise up and clash inside me like cymbals. Anger, banging against a deep, deep desire to heal, to go home.

I look up at the stars, my eyes blurring.

"I knew I should've kept my mouth shut," he says.

"No. I wanted to hear what you think. And . . . you're right." All this time I've been thinking about how I let them down, but Dad let *me* down, too. He gave up on me. I don't know why I never realized it before. Why I felt like I should've been stronger. I was scared out of my mind. And I had no one. And yet, I miss him. How can I miss him *and* feel abandoned by him? "I think I need to go home."

"You'll do it. You'll go home and get it worked out."

He makes it sound so simple, but I can't even wrap my

head around the conversations I need to have. Will Dad forgive me for leaving? Will Mom? Can I forgive *them*? There's so much to work out. But I want to do it. I need to.

"So this is why you've been afraid of me?" Gideon says, after a moment. "You think I'll pull a move like your dad. That I'll head for the hills when you need me to be there for you?"

"First of all, I've never been afraid of *you*. I've been afraid of *being with* you. Secondly, you have it backward. I knew you wouldn't run. I was afraid *I* would. I was afraid I don't have the 'stick-around' gene, and that I'd just check out like my dad. By keeping things superficial, I was sparing us the bigger hurt when I leave."

He leans back a little, the tension releasing from his brow. He nods. "Solid read on me, Martin. But you're wrong about you."

"I am?"

"Hundred percent. You might take the long road from time to time, but you never actually leave. You're here for Bas, aren't you? And you're going home to your family when this is over, right? You're not a leaver. Especially not when it comes to me. You're in *really* deep when it comes to me. I mean, Daryn, you infiltrated a military base to take a picture of *my ass*. You're a goner. Believe me. You're not going anywhere."

I want to disagree with him, but I just laugh.

As ridiculous as he's being, I'm comforted by what he said. And relieved. Mostly though, what I feel is the profound desire to stay right where I am.

Remember Bas's birthday cake?" Jode says as he finishes reading Sebastian's note for the third time. He passes it to Marcus, who hands it back to me.

Their earlier suspicion has eroded. As I look across the fire, the hope of finding Bas is tangible. It's in the glint in their eyes.

Their easy smiles. The way no one complained about trail mix for dinner.

Bas knows we're here. He could show up at *any moment.* We're so close now. *So* close.

We all feel it.

"You mean our collective unbirthday cake in Germany?" I say. "How could I forget?" We'd been on a train somewhere near Frankfurt, running from the Kindred, when Bas showed up in our private car with a birthday cake. An amaretto-infused cake frosted with layers of white and dark chocolate. "I think about that cake regularly."

Not just because it was so good. Bas decided that, since it was none of our birthdays, we should celebrate our unbirthdays. We did it, too. We sang the song and everything.

It was so Bas. Random and fun. He elevated ordinary moments.

As the guys retell the story, I steal a few moments to write in my journal. Tonight has grown cold and my fingers feel stiff. I have to keep stopping to hold them closer to the fire.

22. *Fires, when it's cold*
23. *Riot, to start fires when it's cold*
24. *The note from Sebastian (Come find us, Bas! We're here. We're waiting for you!)*
25. *Sebastian's unbirthday cake in Frankfurt*
26. *Home, on the horizon (I will go and I will apologize and I will be apologized to.)*
27. *Gideon, I know you're reading over my shoulder . . .*

He laughs. "I thought you said it was our list."

"It is, but you're distracting me."

"Am I distracting you, Daryn?" He smiles, his eyes going heavy.

He *is* a distraction. His smile. His attention. Everything

about him. I've kissed him and touched him and I can do both now when I want to, just like I did by the lake a little while ago. It's mind-blowing. If only we weren't in a demon realm, I could really put this new development to good use.

"Would the pair of you like to turn your backs so you exclude us more effectively?" Jode asks.

"We're just adding to the list." I hold up my journal.

"Daryn." Gideon shakes his head, pretending to be disappointed. "It's *our* list."

"A list?" Jode leans back, resting his head against his bag. "What's this list about?"

Rather than explain it, I just lean over and give it to him.

Gideon puts his hand over his heart and winces. "I hate sharing, Martin."

I lean up, whispering in his ear. "Some things are only for you."

He gives me a long unblinking look that makes my face burn and my body feel light and hot.

"This is an outrage," Jode says dryly. "I'm in here once and Gideon is here . . . two, three, *four* times?"

"Three," I say. "The last one doesn't really count."

"Oh, it counts," Gideon says.

"How many times am I in it?" Marcus asks.

"Are you guys making this a *competition*?"

"Of course."

"Yeah."

"Definitely. And I'm dominating."

"For real," Marcus says. "How many times am I on there?"

"Once, like me. For your winning smile." Jode closes the notebook and tosses it to Marcus. "But don't let it go to your head. Gideon's arse has a spot on the list as well."

Gideon looks at me and winks. "Like I said, dominating."

"Dare, you got a pen?" Marcus asks.

This catches me by surprise for a moment. "Yes." I toss it

to him, smiling. This is perfect. Whatever he adds, it's already perfect.

As Marcus writes, Jode leans back and gazes up at the trees. "You're thinking it'll be five for you after this. Aren't you, Gideon?"

"You know me well, Ellis."

Marcus finishes writing. He sets the pen in the fold and hands the journal to Gideon. I lean in and read.

Marcus's handwriting is elegant cursive—almost astonishingly elegant. And what he wrote is, as expected, perfection. Even better is that Gideon reads it aloud.

"'Twenty-eight. The family you make.'" He looks at Marcus. "Damn right, bro. This is the best one here." He looks at me. "Tied with fourteen."

"Ah, yes," Jode says. "Gideon's Super Lips."

Marcus shakes his head at me. "Why?"

"It was a mistake. I wrote it before the list went public. What's your addition, Jode? It can be anything. Anything that has significance to you."

"Full English breakfast," he says, without missing a beat. "Bacon, eggs, sausages, baked beans, grilled tomato, mushrooms, toast, marmalade. With tea, of course. One of life's undeniable pleasures."

My mouth instantly waters. "Well, it's no trail mix, but all right." I add "English Breakfast" to the list. "What else?"

"Another?" Jode narrows his eyes in thought. "Well, I don't think Super Lips will like it."

"Then don't say it," Gideon says.

"Say it, Jode." Marcus smiles. "You gotta say it now."

"Dude," Gideon says. "No."

"Number thirty," I say, as I pretend to write. "When Gideon. Gets. Flustered."

"I'm not flustered."

"Actually, you are."

"Actually, I'm *not*." He looks at Jode. "Go, Drummond. Say your thing. Number thirty."

"Fine. Since you insist. But I have to explain a bit, so you understand." Jode stretches his legs out and settles against his bag again. "Your sister is taking a course in studio art. Painting, oil on canvas. Her subject is the human figure, but her style is expressionistic. Semi-abstract. She's been sending me photos of what she's been doing. They're fantastic."

The smirk hasn't left Gideon's face. "Okay? I've seen my sister's paintings. They're all over my house." He looks at me. "Add it. Number—"

"Hold on, I haven't finished yet," Jode interrupts. "In this course Anna's taking, she's been exploring the concept of wholeness in her work. Her figures are bold, vital, but each one lacks something physical. The painting with the figure lacking eyes, for example, conveys wisdom. The one with the figure lacking a torso possesses a sense of solidity. The one with no mouth looks as though it's on the verge of breaking into song. They're all quite excellent. But the painting of the figures with no hands is Anna's finest. She thinks so and I do as well, and anyone else who's seen it.

"In that painting there are two figures. Mirror images, nearly. One is missing the left hand. The other, the right. Nothing is depicted overtly, but you can see that the figures are holding on to one another. They do not *have* hands but they are quite clearly *holding* hands. The feeling it communicates is love. It's unity . . . and it's art. In the highest sense of the word, that painting is art."

Jode scratches his jaw as he sits up and looks Gideon dead square. "So, for thirty, I propose adding that specific painting. The one she made of the two of you."

Gideon doesn't move for a long moment. Then he sits up, propping his elbows on his knees and cradling his head in his hands. He laughs. "I'm flustered." When he peers at me a moment later, his eyes are shining and his smile almost breaks my heart. The love he has for his sister is so evident. It makes me ache to see Josie. "Thirty," he says.

I add it.

And we keep going, all of us calling up our own Reasons. I'm surprised by how much the guys get into it; we easily break the fifty-item mark. With every new addition, it feels like we're restoring ourselves. Reminding ourselves that the things that are meaningful to us belong to *us*.

We choose what goes on this list.

It feels, in some small way, like pushing against the power of the Rift.

CHAPTER 22

⚊ GIDEON ⚊

In the morning, Shadow is missing.

I'm not too alarmed, though. We don't tether our horses because they don't wander away. It's their nature to protect us, so they never go far.

But after half an hour of walking around camp and calling her, staring into shadows looking for Shadow, we decide it's time to take her disappearance seriously and make a search plan.

As Jode and I strike camp and pack up, Marcus and Daryn head to the lake. Daryn will wait where she and I talked last night in case she spots Shadow along the shore. Marcus will canvass around the lake in search of her, moving in a clockwise direction. They'll stay within range of each other in case something comes up.

After they've gone, Jode looks at me. "No sign of Sebastian, and now Shadow's missing?"

"Shadow could've found Bas. He could ride up with her any minute."

"True. Things do seem to always go our way here."

We get everything packed up. I'm not even sure it's the right move. If the message really was from Bas we should be staying put, but being mobile instinctively feels better.

"What do you think?" Jode asks, swinging into Lucent's saddle. "Did we lose Marcus and Daryn, too?"

"Don't joke, man."

"It worries me when you're worried, Gideon," Jode says. "To the lake?"

"Yeah." I tie Ruin to Lucent's saddle and we leave, our count down to two horsemen, three horses, no Seeker.

"They could be there having a grand time, oblivious to our concern," Jode says.

"If that's really what's happening, they won't be oblivious for long."

We reach the lake. Daryn's not here.

Her backpack sits on the shore. The backpack with the orb, which she never lets out of her sight.

I grab it, quickly checking to make sure the orb is still inside.

"Is it there?" Jode asks.

I nod.

He exhales through his teeth. "Now what?"

As I climb back into the saddle, Riot's amber eyes watch me with unusual intensity. Because he's so focused on me, I become focused on me.

"Jode, headache."

"Me too."

"Shit." We head away from the exposed lakeshore, back under the cover of the trees. I have no idea what kind of threat we're dealing with. Another nightmarescape? The Harrows? The freaky relics we've been passing? Am I going to ride past a shoe or am I falling through the ground? "Let's move clockwise like Marcus. Maybe Daryn went with him and—"

An ear-shattering sound rings out, filling the air. It reminds me of when the plane appeared, but this is more constant, a continuous crackling. And it's coming from the lake.

We wheel around, charging back to the shore we just left behind.

Before we've even come through the trees, we see the ice forming on the lake.

It originates from the center, a patch of white spreading over blue water. The sky's reflection vanishes from the lake's surface. Replaced by frosted white.

It happens *fast*.

By the time we barrel up to the lakeshore, the water lapping against the gravel has frozen solid.

That's when I realize Riot's moving too fast.

I jam my heels down and throw my shoulders back, wrenching on the reins like I never do. *"Riot!"*

But he's a hundred times stronger than I am. The reins strip the skin of my right palm. He doesn't slow down. The lake's suddenly right in front of us—and we go airborne.

We clear fifteen feet before his hooves smack down.

For an instant.

He slips, lurches. Staggers right, then jerks back.

I launch from the saddle, flying over his ears. I hit the ice—elbows, chin, chest. Teeth slamming. Then I go sprawling on my stomach, frost kicking into my face.

I've barely come to a stop when I *feel* Riot's fall—a tremor on the ice. Hear the crunching sound behind me and his deep grunt.

I shoot to my feet, boots slipping, and I touch my chin. Bleeding, and pretty well. I've left a red strip on the ice.

I turn to look for my horse.

For a second, as Riot and I try to stay standing, it's almost funny. Like we're in some epic tap-dance battle. Then we stabilize, kind of, and every detail registers.

The powerful muscles in Riot's legs and chest tremble like he's being electrocuted. Big fogging breaths push from his nostrils. Dragon breaths. His amber eyes are huge and I can see white all around them.

I hear a sizzling sound. The dusting of frost on his red coat melts in a second. It rises into the air as steam and drips off of him as water. A few flames struggle through on his knees. Then I see his hooves, deep red with heat.

They sink like he's on quicksand, melting into the ice.

If he goes through the ice, he'll drown. He'll never get back through the crust. I'll lose him. And I'll lose me too, because I'll go in after him.

Riot lifts his head and makes a low sound, his rear hooves sliding.

Gideon, help. What do I do?

"Okay, Big Red. Steady." We're twenty feet away from solid ground. But since one step seems impossible, the distance might as well be a mile.

I step toward him. White spiderwebs crackle away from my boots, and I freeze. Riot's weight is immense. His fall has created big fracture lines across the ice. White veins directly in our path to each other—and to safety. Every move I make will stress the ice.

"Don't move!" Jode yells from shore. "Don't move or you'll fall through!"

"Thank you, Jode! I got that! Any ideas?"

"Riot, here! To me!" he yells.

Nothing happens. Riot doesn't budge. He doesn't even look Jode's way.

"Other ideas, Jode?"

"Not yet." Ruin's rattled by Riot's predicament, pulling at the lead tied to Jode's saddle. Jode hops off and sets her loose. Marcus's bronze mare immediately tears up and down the gravelly shore. Everyone recognizes the suck of this situation. And every second, it's getting worse.

"Gideon." Jode's expression goes hard with fear as he looks past me. "*Look.*"

I follow his line of sight and finally understand why Riot ran out here.

Shadow stands in the middle of the lake. Tall and still. Stark against the ice. She's watching us. Waiting.

Seeing that she's won our attention, she turns and walks away on her long, careful legs.

Away.

To the *opposite* side of the lake.

When I look toward where she's going, time stops.

Someone's there. Too far away for me to see clearly. But he's tall and still. Lanky, like his horse.

"Gideon, do you see that? Is that him?" Jode waves his arms. "Sebastian! Bas!"

I can't tell if Bas reacts. If he does, it's not obvious. He doesn't shout back or wave his arms. But I'm sure it's him.

And he's not alone.

A figure stands beside him. Samrael. I'm sure of that, too.

Every cell in me, every fiber, feels like it's incinerating.

Riot blows a hard exhale, pulling me back to the immediate problem.

"Come on, Riot. Come on." I take a step toward shore. Then another.

Riot takes a tentative step after me.

We go five steps before it happens. A huge chunk of ice breaks off, right where he'd just stood. Water splashes up, spraying Riot, and he scrambles back instinctively, startled. He gets going too fast, and that starts another slip-and-slide situation. He's going the wrong way, too. Away from shore.

I'm powerless as I watch his back legs wash out. Watch him clamber back up and slide almost ten feet on rigid legs.

His coat lights up with fire as he grows more terrified. His hooves. I see it—a terrible spiral. Him descending into panic, torching brighter, melting the very ice he's standing on.

I run after him, pushing off as quickly and lightly as I can.

There's a trail of broken ice separating him and me now. I have to jump the last stretch. I land, slide, and slam into his side, unable to stop myself.

He roars and stamps, and I almost lose my toes.

"Whoa, boy! Whoa!" I grab the reins. "It's okay, Big Red. You have to move, Riot. You have to move *now*."

I love this horse as much as I've loved anything. He gave

me my life back. He healed my soul. I look for a way through the maze of broken ice. I don't see one.

"Gideon!"

Jode is jogging a wide path across smooth ice, coming toward our position. A length of paracord is slung across his shoulders, glaring green against his white armor. Far behind him, Lucent follows, his great head bowed low, like he's smelling the ice.

I don't see anyone on the far side of the lake anymore. No Bas or Samrael.

"Jode, what are you doing?" I yell.

Ice cracks nearby. Riot and I step back. Any second he could lose his balance, wipe out, and fall right through. Any second the ice beneath us could give.

Jode stops about twenty feet away. A perfect hockey stop, like he grew up on the ice. He pulls the rope over his head and starts tying a knot. "I'll pull him out!"

"It's not going to work!" It's a terrible idea. Lucent is well back and struggling to stay upright. Hardly any better than Riot. "He won't even make it out here!"

Jode turns and sees his horse. "Oh, *hell*! Lucent, get back!"

"That wasn't part of your plan? Were *you* going to pull Riot out?"

"Yes! I was! Can we argue about this later?"

A crackling sound shatters across the lake and water arcs into the air. To the left and right. Behind me. Beneath me. The ice jolts sharply as the sheet Riot and I've been standing on separates, becomes its own island, twenty feet by twenty feet of floating frozen platform.

Riot and I crash against each other, staggering as we try to keep our feet. I grab my sword and drive it into the ice. Holding on to the pommel, I wait for Riot to slam into me; then I wrap my arm around his neck.

"Riot, stay! Riot, stop moving!"

His legs lock and he trusts me to hold him still.

Thousands of pounds of him.

Every muscle in my body strains to keep him steady until the ice floe finally stops rocking. Slushy water rushes past my boots. Riot makes defeated sounds. Awful whimpering sounds unlike anything I've ever heard from him—and that I never even thought possible.

Jode stands at the edge of our ice floe. He rises slowly, now that it's more stable. Black water surrounds us, broken chunks of ice floating by.

Jode drops the rope at his feet and draws his bow. He fires three shots into the sky. *Bzzt, bzzt, bzzt.* But we both know it's a pointless call for help.

We aren't accidental victims of peril. Peril is *after* us. The Rift is.

There's no solution. Riot's shaking with fear. I'm shaking with anger, with the effort of holding him. With powerlessness.

More chunks of ice snap and splash. "I've had about enough of this," Jode says. He draws the bowstring, calling up another arrow, and looks at me. "Say the word."

I look at Riot, fighting for his life. But we're going through anyway. It might as well be on our terms. I lift my sword from the ice, sheathe it, and firm my hold around Riot's neck. "Do it."

Jode fires at the smooth stretch of ice between us.

Nothing happens for a second. Then the world tilts.

Riot and I hit the ice. We slide into cold dark water that swallows us, and we sink in its teeth.

CHAPTER 23

─ DARYN ─

G ideon, wait." I jog to catch up to him as he rushes ahead. "Where are you going?"

"I have to find Marcus," he says without slowing down.

"Marcus? He should be—"

"I'll find him. Go back," he calls over his shoulder.

Okay, that was kind of rude. Even though he's right. I *should* go back to the lake. I left my backpack down there. But I keep after him. Something isn't right.

Five minutes ago, he stalked down to where I was sitting by the lake and asked about Marcus, not once looking at me. As I replied that I saw Marcus a little while ago, Gideon walked away. Before I'd even finished speaking.

I jumped up and followed him.

I'm still following him.

And I still don't know what's going on.

"Did you guys fight?" I jog a few steps to keep up. I can't believe I'm even asking the question. I haven't seen Gideon and Marcus so much as argue since the first days they knew each other. It was ugly then, sure. It's like they packed all the animosity their relationship was meant to have right at the beginning. But that's behind them. *Isn't it?*

"Can you just slow down for a second?" Once again, he doesn't answer me. It's like he doesn't even hear me. "*Wait.*" I grab his arm. "Gideon, what's—?"

When his blue eyes finally come to me, my legs lock and fear shoots down my spine.

They're the first things I fell for, his eyes. They're honest, soulful eyes. And they're beautiful. I've kissed his eyes. So the change I see in them now jars me.

I'm not looking at Gideon. I'm looking at someone, or something, with no soul.

I snatch my hand away.

"Go back," he repeats. "I have to find Marcus. He needs to learn a lesson."

A lesson?

He turns sharply, staring off into the dense trees for an instant, then he breaks into a run.

Behind me, toward the lake, comes a crackling noise. Shockingly loud.

Jode is probably back there, but something is horribly wrong. I make a split-second decision and follow Gideon—the thing that looks like him—chasing after him through the woods.

"Marcus!" he roars, his pace blistering, his prosthetic flashing in the morning light. "Where are you?"

The voice is different. Gritty and bent on violence. I don't know why I didn't catch that before.

He's running upslope. My thighs start to burn, but terror propels me. I stay right with him as we dodge branches and weave through trees. My gaze falls on the sword sheathed at his back. If I can take it away from him, he'll have no weapon. Less chance of hurting Marcus. I make a push, pulling out all the speed I have, and reach for it.

He whirls around and grabs my wrist so fast I nearly smash into him. His grip is like a vise, and I hear myself cry out.

"You can't stop us," he says.

Us?

Oh no.

Movement to my right draws my attention. Someone else

is running through the trees. I recognize the deep red armor and sandy blond hair. The easy athleticism of his movements.

Gideon?

As he draws nearer, I see that it *is* him.

Another one of him.

"Marcus! Where are you?" His eyes pan the woods intently. Every bit as much on the hunt. He runs right past me and Gideon—no, the *impostor* holding my wrist—without a glance or a trace of recognition.

I whirl to the pounding of footsteps behind me.

Another figure. Gideon again. Also moving swiftly, hungrily.

"Look, Seeker." The Gideon in front of me smiles—a smile full of cruel intentions. "More than me."

A chill races down my spine at the words—words the Harrow spoke to me the first time I entered the Rift.

"Who are you? *What* are you?"

"A torment. A haunting." He releases my arm and turns to the sound of Marcus's voice.

Marcus is close, and he's heard the calls for him.

"I'm here!" he calls back. "Gideon! I'm here!"

"Marcus, no!" I yell, and instantly realize my mistake. Marcus will only come faster if he thinks I'm in trouble.

With single-minded focus, the impostor in front of me shoots off. I chase after him again, launching over twisting roots, the forest blurring by me.

This can't be real, can it? What are they going to do?

Moments later, with my lungs and legs burning, I arrive at a clearing.

Marcus stands at the center with the scythe planted at his side. All around him are doubles of Gideon.

I count a dozen.

If he's stunned by the sight, Marcus doesn't show it. He

casts a steady look around, seeming almost disinterested. Then his gaze stops on me and comprehension flares in his eyes. He knows that *I'm* real, at least.

"You think we're brothers, Marcus?" says one of the doubles. "Is that what you think? Well, we're not. You're not my blood. You're nothing like me. You're worthless."

Marcus doesn't move. Not a muscle. But the words inflict a blow that even I feel.

They step closer to Marcus like a pack of wolves, working together. Flames kindle on the swords, running along the blades and up over their arms.

I've never seen Gideon like this. Burning, without Riot.

"Stop!" I yell. They don't. Why did I even try?

As they draw close, ten feet away from Marcus, I bolt forward, pushing my legs to sprint hard. I don't know how to help, but I can't let this happen.

They see me coming. Two swords shoot out, crossing in front of me.

Much lower than hurdles.

I leap over them. As I land, my momentum sends me into Marcus, who catches me with his free arm.

"Marcus," I say, trying to catch my breath. "It's not Gideon."

"You gonna believe *her*?" asks one of them. "She doesn't care about you, either. No one does, Marcus. *No one.* Your parents didn't—that's for damn sure. None of your foster families did. Your coaches didn't care. I *definitely* don't care. You think I want you living at my house? You think I like seeing you freeloading off my mom? Looking at my sister? I've got plenty of friends, Marcus. I don't need you. And we sure as hell aren't family. You're a charity case. That's all you are. What's it going to take before you get it through your skull? You're worth nothing. You aren't worth the air you breathe."

It's not just hearing the words from Gideon's mouth that's soul-crushing; it's seeing the hatred in his face. The coldness.

"You're full of lies," Marcus says.

"I'm not. It's the truth," says one.

Another adds, "You know what else is true? I'm going to kill you." He slices the air with the sword, two quick slashes to underscore the words. "Are you going to fight back? You'll lose. You'll only make it worse. You'll get Daryn hurt."

"Marcus." I step in closer. My shoulder presses against his chest and I can feel the way his heart is hammering. "They won't attack us."

"No?" says one of them.

All at once, they lunge forward, a savage blur of steel and physical force.

It's so fast. Marcus doesn't have time to swing the scythe. Maybe he can't make himself do it.

We turn in to each other, responding to some primitive instinct to huddle, protect, and be close. Then I feel it. Bright, piercing pain. Pain like lighting bolts. I feel every one of the dozen swords slashing through me. Cutting through my arms, my thighs, and my heart.

Marcus jolts in my arms—or it's me—or it's both of us. The pain is complete and it lasts lifetimes. I want it to end, to finish—or for it to finish *me*. My legs shudder. My mind shudders. And still, I hear their yelling and their taunts.

"I'll destroy you, Marcus!"

"You're pathetic!"

They come from every direction, relentless and bloodthirsty.

Then, suddenly, silence rushes in. Roaring silence.

Faintly, I hear myself gasping for air. Marcus, huffing by my cheek. The pain washes out of me with every breath. With each one, I feel stronger.

"Are they gone?" My voice is a croak. Marcus's arms are like slabs of concrete around me. He loosens them and we step back—and my balance wavers.

Neither one of us has a scratch, but my stomach's churning. My legs feel unsteady. Shaky and undependable.

The clearing is empty. No one else is here anymore.

"Marcus—" I clear my throat, trying to find my voice. "Gideon would never say that. He'd never say those things."

Marcus puts his hands on his hips and drops his eyes. I can still see the pain in him. The doubt is coiled in his body. The hurt is.

"He wouldn't, Marcus. He'd never even *think* them."

He looks up. "You don't know what's in his head."

"But I know I'm right."

"You're saying that to protect him. He could be thinking everything we just heard. It could be what he's always thinking. He could be—"

I step close and look right into his eyes. "*No.* Don't let this place ruin your friendship. Don't let it poison your heart. Gideon loves you, Marcus. Maybe he's never said it outright, but—" *But what, Daryn?* "But he's never said he loves me either, and—" *And what, Daryn?* "And I know that he likes me, at least."

A smile lights in Marcus's eyes. "At least." He shakes his head. "Daryn . . ." He looks around the clearing slowly. "I don't want to doubt him."

"Then choose not to."

"You think you choose what you believe?"

"Yes," I say without thinking. Without knowing whether I mean it. I just need him and Gideon to stay good. I need it desperately. We all do, in order to find Bas.

He wraps his hand around the staff of the scythe and pulls it out of the ground, setting it on his shoulder. "We should go back."

We're quiet on the walk. I can't help worrying about where this will lead. We're being haunted. We've managed to stay together so far and unaffected by the stress, for the most part.

But I can't see that lasting. The Rift will change us if we stay here long enough. It could destroy us, I think.

Which makes me think of Bas, who's been here eight months.

How has he survived the Rift?

CHAPTER 24

- GIDEON -

As soon as Riot and I go under, my heart stops and cold clamps down on my muscles.

Chaos swirls around us. Ice slams at us like bricks. There's no way to see through bubbles and black churning water.

When Riot yanks away from me, my arms don't respond, won't do what they're supposed to, and I can't hang on to him.

He surges away. Surges down, sinking. His legs thrash, trying to gallop underwater. Gallop up, to the surface. To me.

But he drops like an anchor.

The flames on his legs go out first. Then his body. His mane and tail, last.

My horse goes dark like a sinking ship losing its lights.

He disappears.

I know I can't yell out loud so I hold it in, which makes it sound terrible. Like a sob.

I kick and dive, but my legs have no strength and my arms are even worse. White spots burst before my eyes. My lungs start to convulse. I need air.

I stop swimming and look up. I can't see the surface anymore.

I keep swimming down. I won't lose my horse this way.

But my lungs feel like they're filling with acid, and I can't hold back anymore.

I use the last of my breath to yell for Riot.

Then I brace for ice water to shoot into the back of my mouth.

Cold air rushes in instead. My oxygen-starved lungs gulp it in, restoring, as my mind races to understand.

I'm *breathing.*

Underwater.

Or . . . I'm swimming through air?

Not the time to figure it out. Riot needs me. I keep searching for him, carving my way through freezing black water that I can somehow breathe. Eyeballs chilling. Fingers numbing. Cold knifing into the back of my throat.

Bubbles rise up from below. Swarms of bubbles that grow denser, and steal my visibility.

Then they turn green.

First pale, then bright, then dark.

All shades of green.

As I'm grappling with this, their texture grows brittle against the skin on my arms and my face. A sound rises in my ears, a rustling like shaking leaves, and I feel the slap of bending branches on my legs and back.

I'm swimming through leaves.

And I'm going too fast.

My brain provides theories—gravity, falling through air, through trees.

None of them make sense, and I'm not ready when the branches vanish. I don't even brace myself as I fall through the canopy, punching into open air.

I see the maze of branches above me, the flash of a thick tree trunk, and the next instant I slam against the ground flat on my back.

My breath pushes out of my chest in one heave, like a balloon popping. I wait for the reverse, the intake, but I'm back to burning, starved lungs that can't draw any air.

Jode's face appears over me, frowning in concern. His wet hair drips water on my forehead. "Are you all right? Gideon, can you move?"

I thump my chest.

"Breath get knocked out of you?" The worry leaves his face. "Better work it out, then, because I won't be giving you mouth-to-mouth. It would be too odd, what with Anna."

I flip him the bird.

He smiles. "There you go. Right as rain again." He straightens, but I lie there another minute. Shivering. Soaked. Freezing cold. And my chin is throbbing, too.

"Horses?" I ask, finally able to look around. We're back in the woods. Back in the clearing where we camped. Where I stood less than an hour ago.

"Just there. Blazing angry, yours. He's about to set this entire forest on fire."

"Let him."

Jode's right. Riot's not himself.

Big curls of flame roll up his legs and chest. His amber eyes are huge and distant. For the first time in as long as I can remember, I can't sense what he's feeling.

I rest my hand on his wide forehead and keep it there until his eyes start to soften. Until I feel him grow stronger, his strength relaying back to me.

"You're a good horse, Riot."

He blows a blustering breath.

You're a good human, Gideon. But you could've warned me sooner about the ice. I don't like frozen lakes.

I pat his neck. Then I hang my arms over the saddle, letting him hold my weight, which makes us both feel better.

Jode's busy doing things I can't see. I hear him walking around behind me. Zipping up bags and talking quietly to Lucent and Ruin.

"Have you finished licking your wounds?" Jode asks, bringing Lucent and Ruin over by their leads.

"Haven't even started yet."

"Well, can you wrap it up? We need to find Marcus and Daryn, and Shadow and—"

"Did you actually think you could pull Riot off that lake with a rope? That *you* could. All five-foot-ten, a buck sixty of you?"

"It seemed more promising than standing beside him on shattering ice."

"I had a plan, Drummy."

"Did you? And what was it?"

"Not die. And it worked."

He lifts an eyebrow. "I can't argue that." He sighs, shaking his head. "Why?" he says, staring across the trees.

"I don't know. I think I might have had a nightmare just like that at some point."

He glances at me. "Do you think the Rift is trying to destroy us?"

"It's trying to do something." I realize I don't trust anything here. Not the trees or even the sky. Everything feels like it could change at any second. Jode's the only thing here I trust. Jode and the horses.

Jode rubs his head, making his damp hair spike. "It was him, Gideon. Across the water. It was Sebastian. Shadow wouldn't have left us for any other reason."

"He wasn't alone."

"I saw that. Do you think they were real? Or part of the trial?"

Trial, he calls it. Felt more like torture.

"I don't know," I say. Even Shadow, out there in the middle of the ice, could've been fake. "Part of me hopes so."

Jode frowns. "You hope they *weren't* real?"

"Bas was standing with Samrael, Jode. *With* him. I could be wrong, but Bas didn't look like he was being coerced or under duress."

"You think we've lost him to Samrael," Jode says.

It sounds like a statement, and that bothers me. "I didn't say that. All I'm saying is that it's possible Samrael tried. You know that's how they operate." In the fall, the Kindred wanted to recruit me. Their leader thought I had potential. If Bas has been here with Samrael for the past eight months . . . Samrael could've tried to convert him, too. "If Samrael turned him, we have to be prepared to deal with it."

"Thoughts on how we'd 'deal with it'?"

"Working on it."

Jode lets out a long sigh. "Will nothing come easily in here?"

"No. Oh yeah, I forgot to tell you. We're out of food."

"No more trail mix? That I don't mind."

Half an hour later, we find Marcus and Daryn. Before we've even dismounted, Daryn asks about Shadow.

"Did you find her? Where is she?"

"We had some trouble on the lake," Jode says. As he describes our ice-capade, I notice the look on Marcus's face. He's wearing the same expression he used to wear all the time when we hated each other. Like he wants to kick my ass. Very thoroughly.

I interrupt Jode. "Marcus, what?"

"Nothing."

I look at Daryn. "Why is he pissed at me?"

"You attacked him," she says. "In a haunting."

Haunting? I instantly know—she and Marcus went through their own trial. "I attacked him. *I* did?"

"Yes. A dozen of you. Perfect look-alikes."

"A dozen Gideons?" Jode's eyebrows shoot up. "The sarcasm must have been intolerable."

No one laughs. Marcus walks away, heading toward the lake.

"Marcus," I call to him. He doesn't stop. "*Marcus.* Come on, man."

"Best to let him cool off," Jode says, jogging after him.

Anger builds inside me with nowhere to go. Why am I taking the blame for something I didn't do? I just *drowned*. I just watched *my horse* drown. Why the hell am *I* being punished right now?

The Rift.

It's messing with us. It's taking us down without throwing a single punch.

"How bad was it?"

Daryn glances down, hesitating. "Pretty bad."

An image flashes through my mind. Me, beating the hell out of my best friend. Pummeling the best guy I know.

"He knows it wasn't real, Gideon. But it was hard to go through. It'll take him some time to shake off."

I know she's remembering seeing her mother on the roof of the yellow bungalow. I know it'll take her some time to shake that off, too. Just like it'll take me time to forget Riot disappearing into dark water. And Daryn, banging on Dad's truck window. "You called it a haunting."

"It's just something that . . . well, that you said."

"I said stuff? Daryn, what did I say to you? Did I hurt you, too? I did, didn't I?"

She steps in and wraps her arms around me, resting her head against my chest. "Let's just hug this out."

"How about not now?" It's not *hug* time.

She lifts her head. "Okay, then let's kiss it out."

That gets my attention. My entire body's listening now. "What happens if I say no again? Does this game keep elevating? What's after kissing?"

"Are you going to say no again?"

"Martin, when you say things like that, my brain powers down. It makes it impossible for me to . . ."

The drumming sound of hoofbeats stops me. I scan the woods.

Someone's riding toward us on a black horse. On Shadow.

Bas?

Sebastian?

I can't believe what I'm seeing.

"Bas?" Daryn says, whirling to face him. "Bas!"

"Wait. It might not be him. He might not be alone."

"It's *him*."

She's smiling, buying in completely. Didn't she just see a dozen fake versions of me? It can't be him. After all this searching, there's no way he just rides up.

She breaks away from me and she's gone, running to meet him.

"Daryn—wait!" But she's pure determination.

My pulse rises to a shrill pitch in my ears. I brace myself for the ground to open up. For ice to form. For wind, Harrows, Samrael. Hauntings.

Nothing changes.

Bas—if it's him—draws closer.

As he closes in, he looks from me to Daryn. Going back and forth, like my mind is.

Are you real?

Or are you just another one of the Rift's lies?

CHAPTER 25

~ DARYN ~

I run to Bas, leaving Gideon behind me.

Caution might be the wiser move. The Rift has fooled me before. But I'll never forgive myself if I doubt Bas and it's really him. If I'm wrong, I'd rather face the consequences. After all he's been through, he needs us now.

Our trust. Our support. Our belief in him.

Sebastian stops Shadow and jumps to the ground. Tears brim in his brown eyes as he walks up, and I see an edge of pain that's new, and sharp. Then he breaks into a dashing smile that's so familiar, so precisely what I need to see, that before I know it, I'm laughing and launching myself at him. "We found you! I was so worried, Bas. We all were. *So* worried."

"You're here." He lifts me off my feet and spins me around. "I've been praying for this. I can't believe you're here."

"Of course we are. Didn't you know we'd come?"

He sets me down and looks into my eyes. "Aw, Daryn. Don't cry or I will."

"I'm just so happy."

"Not as happy as I am."

We turn as Gideon walks over. Jode and Marcus are with him, just back from the lake. They're wearing expressions that are surprisingly similar, like they're expecting Bas to lay a knife across my throat.

Bas's smile fades. "What happened to them?"

"This place did." They've forgotten how to trust.

"I understand that," Bas says.

I glance at him and see another shadow of pain flash across his face. He's changed in obvious ways. There's a maturity to his features, all traces of boyishness gone, and a new confidence in how he carries his substantial height. He has become, impossibly, more handsome. But he's picked up a quality that's less tangible. I can't pinpoint it. But it saddens me.

The guys stop a few feet away. They go still. Silent and watchful. Everyone is waiting for someone else to make a move.

I can't take it. "No offense, you guys, but this is the worst reunion ever."

"Exactly," Bas says. "The top worst. This isn't what I pictured at all."

Jode is the first to break rank. He laughs his hilarious cackle and pulls Bas into a hug, pounding him on the back as he utters the same nonsense I did moments ago.

Marcus comes next. He wears the sweetest smile that's ever been smiled in the Rift, I'm positive. "Bas. Bro . . ." They embrace, and by the time Bas steps back, he's failing at holding back the tears.

With only Gideon left, somehow the wary vibe returns. Gideon stands in silence, a look of suspicion on his face.

Bas shakes his head. "G, dude. Not a funny joke."

I see Gideon's grin for an instant before he explodes forward and flattens Bas to the ground.

It immediately turns into a dog pile. A horseman pile. Loud and full of elbows and laughs and shoves. Irresistible. I burrow my way in, and I'm swallowed up. It's blissful chaos. Intensely unifying. We're a human fireworks show.

All I can think is that we're whole again.

Complete.

As we draw apart, everyone speaks at once and Bas doesn't know where to look. He tries to answer four people's questions, but no information is actually getting across. Gideon and Marcus give up and jump all over him again.

I look for Shadow, wondering if she feels this—this profound satisfaction—and find her watching me.

In her eyes, I see gratitude, solidarity, and love. I didn't have the Sight steering me to this moment. I had a black horse that knew my pain, shared it, and stayed with me.

"Right, then, you apes," Jode says, his English sense of propriety pushed to its limit. "Can we have some order?" No one wants order. "Can we at least continue this in Nevada where there's not a single one of these bloody trees, or Harrows?"

That settles things down.

"You're right. Let's get out of here," Gideon says. His eyes shine, brilliant with happiness. "Bas, let's get you home, man. What do you say?"

Bas's smile recedes. "No—not yet. I'm not ready yet."

It's like someone has pressed pause. Everything stops.

"Bas," Gideon says. "What do you mean?"

"I'm not ready." He looks around with what I think might be distress. "I can't explain it right now. I just need some time. I was here for so long. I need to get my head right before I leave."

His words dampen our festive mood. None of us has been through what he has. None of us can begin to understand what he's feeling. He's earned this request. Suffered for it. We can do this for him. So we agree.

We set up camp for the night.

It's amazing, I think, as I gather branches and twigs for kindling. There have been so many surprises here in the Rift, but this is the biggest one yet.

We found Bas.

But we're still here.

Before long, we're gathered around the fire and sharing the food Bas produced from a leather bag. Two kinds of cheese, crusty brown bread, thick slabs of bacon, apples, and huge strawberries. After days of granola bars and trail mix, the sounds and facial expressions around the campfire almost embarrass me. Including my own.

Rather than bombard Bas with questions like before, we let him share what he wants to, but talk seems secondary at the moment anyway. All we really want to do is witness the hereness of him, and appreciate the togetherness of now.

"I was the same way in the beginning with food," he says. "I wondered if I'd starve here. I got so hungry I thought about eating dirt. I had no idea it would get better, but there's a farm where I've been living. We have fruit orchards, gardens, chickens, dairy cows, and enough livestock to . . ."

Suddenly self-conscious, he picks up a stick and traces lines in the dirt, his hair falling across his eyes. Our actor, revealing too much truth too quickly. I listen to the fire, proud of the guys for being so patient and sensitive in letting this unfold.

"So, you're alive," Gideon says, wrecking it. Done with subtlety.

Bas looks up and laughs humorlessly. "Actually, I wasn't completely sure about that until I saw you guys just now. I know you're all probably wondering what happened to me. I bet you've got so many questions, but . . ." He props his long arms on his knees. "I'd really rather hear what you guys have been up to first."

We all look at each other.

"We've been looking for you," Jode says. "We've been trying to work out how to get you back."

Bas smiles. A dashing smile, like when he first saw me. I'd

forgotten how beautiful he is. Steep cheekbones and full lips. A long straight nose. Eyes the color of dark chocolate that actually deserve to be called dreamy. I see that new quality in them again, but now I'm closer to understanding it. It reminds me of Marcus and Gideon. Of having taken some hefty knocks in life. But it only makes Bas more appealing. Added to his black armor, he's every bit the roguish warrior who will make you laugh to deflect away from his dark secrets.

"Thanks, Jode. That makes me feel good," Bas says, with the easy candor I remember. "That can't be all you did, though. Someone had to have done something more interesting."

Gideon sits forward. "Well, you probably haven't noticed, but I lost my hand."

"I did notice, in fact."

"I figured. But I got this as a replacement. It's actually pretty cool when I'm not in here. Because it works."

Bas smiles. "It suits you."

Such a simple thing to say. But it's not pity and it's not false. I can tell Gideon appreciates that. I can tell it means a lot.

"I've been in Wyoming working at a ranch," I say, trying to give Bas what he actually wants. I understand how he feels. Just over a week ago, I felt out of the loop myself. "I teach little kids to ride and rope. And we do arts and crafts."

"That reminds me." Gideon hops to his feet and goes to one of the supply bags, reaching inside. He comes back with Bastian's scales. "Here you go, man."

Sebastian's smile fades away as he takes the weapon, a chain of smoke-colored steel with scales on either end—scales that are currently interlocked. He looks at it so fondly. It makes me realize how much he sacrificed all these months without a single possession from home—not a single thing to call his. "Thank you."

"Anytime."

Bas smiles. He looks around. "What else?"

"Well, I've been at Cambridge," Jode says.

"Jode's also been with Anna," Marcus adds with a mischievous smile.

Gideon shakes his head. "A little respect?"

I'm glad to see them teasing each other. I was worried about the fallout from the haunting, but with Sebastian back, everyone's happy. United.

Bas's eyes go wide, turning from Jode to Gideon. "Wait, wait, wait. Your *sister*? *That* Anna?"

"Yes, that Anna," Jode says. "And I truly don't see why it's such an issue for you, Gideon. It's not as though I've shared the details about—"

"One more word, Jode. Seriously, man. One more."

Jode laughs. "Anyhow." He gestures between Gideon and me. "I think we're looking past the obvious here."

Bas breaks into a huge grin. "You two? The two of you? That's awesome!"

"I broke down her defenses," Gideon says matter-of-factly.

"He didn't," I say. "My defenses are perfectly secure. We're conducting friendly negotiations."

"Our negotiations are a lot more than friendly."

"On occasion."

"Such passion," Jode says. "It's electrifying."

But Bas is loving this. "I kept thinking about what you were all doing while I was in here. And I pictured this—this exact moment. The five of us together again, catching up. When Rael told me he saw you, Daryn, I knew it was only a matter of time. I knew you'd come for me. We've been riding through this area since then, looking for you. I left the note—did you get my note?"

He trails off, seeing that he's lost us. Tension rises around us, as thick as smoke in the air. I feel my face burning, my heart racing. And I want to freeze time, because I know

I'm about to lose the beautiful, peaceful moments we just had.

"I was trying to find the right time to tell you," Bas says, his voice missing its usual color.

"Now works." Gideon stares at him, unblinking. "You know what else I want to know, Bas? Who the hell is Rael? If you don't mind my asking."

He pronounces the name like Bastian did. *Rell*. But we all know the answer already. Since the moment I first saw Samrael in here, part of me has been trying to accept that this was possible. Bas was in such bad shape when he entered the Rift. It would've been a miracle if he'd survived alone.

"Gideon, you have to understand—"

"Hold on a sec. We're talking about *Samrael,* right? The demon that poisoned you? The demon that cut off my hand? Is it *that* Rael, Bas? Is that who we're talking about?"

Bastian doesn't blink. "I was going to die. I would have if he hadn't saved me. I owe him my life."

"*He* was the one who tried to *kill* you."

"He's different. He's changed. I know what you're thinking. That it's impossible he's changed. But he has. What happened with the Kindred was before. Samrael was a subject. No—it was more than that. He was a slave to Ra'om. Ra'om controlled him. Ra'om controlled all of them. You *know* that. He was in command. He gave them their power and told them how to use it. If they opposed him, he hurt them. You have no idea, Gideon. You just don't know. You can't just show up here and think you understand everything. You don't."

"Samrael commanded your *death*. Are you even hearing that? And he killed the guard in Los Angeles. We lost three people in Wyoming. He's a *killer*."

"So are *you*! So is Jode. So is Marcus. You only justify it by saying it's for the right reason."

"You want me to apologize for killing demons? Never going to happen."

"That's not what I want."

Gideon throws his arms out. "Then what is? What are you saying? Why are we talking about a demon like it matters? Why are we still in this hellhole?"

Bas jumps to his feet. "You have no clue what I've been through!"

Gideon is up just as quickly. "Why are we still here, Sebastian?" he asks again demandingly, every word punching the air.

"Because," Bas says. "I'm not leaving without him!"

I'm not leaving without him.

The words knock around in my skull like marbles in a jar. There's no order, or context, or permutation in which they make sense. It's like he just spoke a different language.

"I don't know what the hell you're saying, but Samrael's not leaving here," Gideon says. "It's not happening, Bas. He's not going anywhere."

"Then neither am I," says Bas, with finality.

Gideon sits back, that cold skepticism seeping into his blue eyes, washing away all traces of his good mood.

Marcus drops his head into his hands.

Jode shuts his eyes, like he can't believe what's just happened.

Something dark has just moved into our circle. A raw ache builds in the back of my throat, and I scramble to recover the closeness we just felt. "Sebastian, if you stay, then we all stay."

He looks at me, his expression crestfallen. "I'm sorry, Daryn. I can't leave him here, just like I couldn't leave one of you. You have to believe me. He's changed. He doesn't deserve to be stuck here. He's different."

"He's not the only one," Gideon says.

"You're right. I am, too. I'm not afraid to take a stand anymore, Gideon. I know what's right and what's wrong. I'm not leaving him. So you can just give up trying to convince me."

The anger coming off Gideon is palpable. Even Riot feels it where he stands with the other horses. The flames of his coat burn higher. His eyes are like embers in the night.

CHAPTER 26

⇀ GIDEON ↼

What happened back there? You got any explanations for me, Big Red? I could use a sound voice of reason right now."

Riot listens as he walks beside me. I had to leave the campfire. I was afraid I'd start chucking burning logs into the trees. So Riot and I are on a horseman/horse break.

I'm worried, Gideon. I'm worried and I would like to leave this place.

"Me too, horse. I'm *really* worried. And I *really* would like to leave this place."

I stop and look through the woods. I can't see the fire, just the dark shapes of the four people around it. And I can't hear their voices clearly, but it surprises me when I hear them laughing.

It offends me, actually.

How are they having fun? How are they forgetting that Samrael is a demon? That he mind-tortured me and maimed me? Why is letting him out of here even up for discussion?

"You get *ten* spots if you want, Bas! Here, you write them."

Daryn's voice rises loud enough for me to hear her. It sounds like they're indoctrinating Sebastian into "Reasons."

I want one good reason to stay here that's not totally insane. I mean—*Samrael.* We're exposing ourselves to this interactive psychosis sphere because of him?

Riot makes a soft sound, bobbing his head.

You should go back there, Gideon. I know you want to. I want to go, too.

"Doesn't matter, Riot. If I hear his name—Samrael—or wait, *Rael*—one more time, I'll go supernova. I will lose my shit."

Well, that's not good. Okay. Let's stay.

The hours roll by. I sit against a tree and come up with no solutions as it grows quiet around the fire. I've just settled into a zone where I'm half asleep when I see Daryn walking toward me.

She sits right beside me. "Hey, Riot."

I have to smile. It's awesome that she thinks of him first. He thinks so, too.

"How are you doing?" she asks, bumping me with her elbow.

"Really great. You?"

"Not great at all."

She rests her head on my shoulder and loops her arm through mine. Just having her near makes me feel better. I don't want to spoil the moment by bringing Samrael up, but I can't stop myself. "I've decided to knock Bas out and carry him out of here unconscious. Good plan, don't you think?"

"Not if you want to keep your friendship with him. I don't think he'd forgive you for doing that. He's pretty set, Gideon."

"I'm pretty set, too."

"I know."

I push out a breath, trying to loosen the knot in my chest. "So what's next, Martin? Where do we go from here?"

"Bas wants to take us all back to where they've been staying. It's a fortified settlement he calls Gray Fort."

"Sounds fun."

"He thinks if we talk to Samrael and listen to what he has to say, we'll see."

"Where to aim our arrows and blades?"

"Gideon, what Bas is saying matches up to what Samrael said to me the first time I saw him. He wanted to take me to

Bas. He offered protection. Safety. I didn't believe him at the time. But if I had, maybe this could have all been avoided. Maybe Low wouldn't have died, and we wouldn't—"

"No. You did the right thing."

She raises her head. "How can you be sure? What if Bas is right and Samrael has changed?"

"It sounds like you're trying to defend the guy who cut off my hand."

"No. I'm not. But I want to go home. I want to bring Bas home. I want us all to get out of here. I want to do the right thing, even if it's really hard, and I don't see any alternative here. People make mistakes. They deserve second chances. If I didn't believe that, then I would never have the courage to go back home. I need to believe my parents and my sister will forgive me for leaving them. Haven't you ever wanted to change something you did or said? Make up for it?"

All the damn time, I think. She's got me. I excel at losing my temper and doing or saying something I have to try to patch up later. War is not who I am, it's my vice. It's what I deal with daily. "All right. People deserve second chances. But do demons?"

"Demons were angels once. Samrael was a servant of God. A direct servant. I can't imagine feeling greater regret than turning away from that."

Another good point.

Why is she making so many good points?

"Do you have any idea what he took from me, Daryn? I've never hated anything as much as him. I'll kill him before I give him a second chance."

"You think killing him would make you feel better?"

"Absolutely."

"What about your dad? He died but you still love him, don't you?"

I don't like where this is going. "Of course."

"So it's transcended death. You could say the love you feel is eternal."

"You could say that."

"Why do you think your hate would be any different? If love transcends death, why doesn't hatred?"

"Because Samrael deserves to die and my dad didn't."

Daryn stares at me. "I don't think killing Samrael would rid you of the hatred. I think all you'd be doing is adding layers of guilt. I know you. You're not cold-blooded."

Bastian's words shoot through my mind. *You only justify it by saying it's for the right reason.* "You're giving me too much credit."

"I'm not. You have a big heart and a big conscience."

"I have a bigger sword. This isn't just about me. If we let Samrael out, we're endangering everyone. We'd be right back where we started. We know he's a mind manipulator. I know what he can do—it's not good, Daryn. He uses your worst fears against you. I only experienced it for a few weeks. Bas has been here for months."

"You think he brainwashed Bas?"

"What other explanation is there?"

"Bas is telling the truth. Samrael has changed. Why else would he want to leave here? In the fall, Samrael's entire goal was getting *in* here to amass power, remember? He wanted to form an evil army with the Kindred. Maybe he doesn't want that anymore. Maybe he wants what Bas is saying. A fresh start."

"No," I say. "It's what Samrael wants us to think, but he hasn't changed. If we let him out of the Rift, all hell breaks loose. He'll form his own little band of rebel demons and it'll be the same thing all over again. Or worse. We stopped the Kindred in the fall, Daryn. They need to stay stopped. I have no problem carrying around some personal guilt if it means keeping thousands, maybe millions of innocent people safe.

"If we do what Bas wants and go to this fortified location, the odds are I'll kill Samrael, or he'll kill me. That's just the reality here. It's the reality of this situation."

Daryn blinks at me. Then she takes my wrist and pulls my arm around her, tucking her head against my chest like she's listening for my heartbeat.

I freeze. I'm clenching my teeth so hard I'm giving myself a headache. "You're throwing me off balance here, Martin. What is this tactic, anyway?"

"I just like the way you feel."

I hear myself laugh. It sounds like the laugh of someone in pain.

She firms her grip around my waist, and her body heat reaches me. Her scent. One breath at a time, she wins. I relax and pull her all the way in. "You kill me, Martin," I whisper into her hair. "I really like you."

She reaches for my prosthetic, and weaves her fingers through its metal ones like it's part of me. "Same."

It's so quiet that I can hear her every breath. I scan the area around us, checking for relics, hauntings. Harrows. I don't know what it's like to *not* expect danger anymore.

"Gideon," Daryn says, her voice gentle and soft. "We have to leave room to consider every possibility."

I thought we were done. I wanted to be done. "I can't, Daryn. I'm not trying to be bullheaded. But I can't forgive Samrael for what he did. We could talk about this for a year. I'm never going to see this the way you do."

"Then trust me. Trust how *I* see it."

"You know I trust you. Don't put me in this position."

She leans back and looks at me. "Think about it? Just *think* about it."

How can I say no? I nod.

She smiles. "Thanks." She slides into my lap and wraps her arms around my neck. Then there's nothing else but her.

As Daryn leads me back to the campfire she tells me that nothing needs to be decided now. "At least just be near us. The important thing right now is that we're together again."

I keep my trap shut. The important thing right now is that we need to get out of here. The important thing is that we have a real problem on our hands—one we need to address quickly.

We've been lucky to avoid the Harrows since we came in last time with Cordero's group. And the hauntings have sucked, but we've survived them. All of that could change in a heartbeat. We need a firm exit plan. We need to take action.

When we get back to the campsite, Jode and Sebastian are sacked out and only Marcus is awake, keeping watch.

"I've got it," I tell him, dropping against a tree. "I'll keep a lookout."

He nods. He knows I'll be up anyway. Then he rolls into his blanket.

I'm still not sure where we stand. I can't tell if he's still pissed at me for something a dozen fake me's did.

Daryn plops down beside me. "I'll stay up with you," she says, shaping her backpack into a pillow.

"It's okay. Better for only one of us to be tired."

She smiles. "Okay. Then I'll sleep."

She stretches out beside me. I twirl the wavy hair at the base of her neck around my fingers and watch her eyes drift closed.

I wonder how it'll be when we get out of here. If things will change. If I'll still get to do stuff like this, touch her like she's mine. I imagine introducing her to Anna, and how that would go. I think they'd get along really well—a painter and a writer. I picture Mom meeting Daryn and get choked up, because there's no chance Dad will ever know her.

After a while, my thoughts grow darker. I imagine breaking earth and splintering sheets of ice. I see Low's brutalized, lifeless body.

Then my mind reaches back into my past and I see the things Samrael planted in my head once.

My mother, standing over my grave.

My father, falling to his death.

My sister, losing her mind.

Daryn, with Samrael.

With him, the same way she was with me a little while ago.

Before long I'm grinding my teeth and stressed out of my mind. I exhale a long breath, pushing the tension out, and my gaze falls on Daryn's notebook. I grab it and flip it open, turning to "Reasons."

Right away I notice that there are several kinds of handwriting. I recognize Marcus's ridiculously fancy cursive. He writes like he's signing the Declaration of Independence. I know Daryn's, of course. And Jode's, which is like a lighter version of Marcus's. My scrawl's here on the few lines I added a while ago. And then there are the lines written in block letters that slant to the left like they're leaning backward.

Bastian's writing.

From what I can tell, they passed the journal around, everyone adding to it. But somewhere along the way Sebastian took over. His additions make up the last ten entries.

I sit up, angling the page so the firelight hits it, and read.

65. The end of a long wait for something. Waiting is the worst!—S. L.

66. The way good friends don't change very much even after a long time apart. (I knew we'd get right back to this!)—S. L.

67. CHOCOLATE! Chocolate chips in trail mix! Chocolate is the king of foods!—S. L.

68. The time G and I were sock surfing in the hallways of the train in maybe Sweden?—S. L.

69. Jode's laugh. Psycho! (Have to use on a character someday.)—S. L.

70. This list! I love it!—S. L.

71. Knowing that even though someone's pissed at you, it's only temporary. Good friends forgive.—S. L.

72. Loyalty, and walking the line between old friends and new ones.—S. L.

Damn.

"What do you think?" Marcus is still awake. He sits up, rubbing a hand over his face.

"About the list?" I ask.

He shakes his head. "About what Bas wants. About us going to this place to see Samrael."

"Worst idea I've ever heard. I'm not exaggerating. The top worst." I catch myself using Bas's words. It's already happening. I'm already picking his dumb sayings up. "What do you think? And what about Jode?"

"He hasn't said. He's been listening, asking questions." Marcus shrugs. "I'm same as you."

None of that surprises me. And I already know where the last member of our group stands. Daryn has pulled her legs up and curled into a ball. She's almost smiling in her sleep. "How's she going along with this idea? She's handing out trust like it's free."

Marcus rubs a hand over his scalp. "You don't think it is?"

"No. Do you?"

"Not in my life. Not how I learned it." He lies back and stares at the patchwork of night sky, branches and leaves. "But maybe it should be."

We're quiet for a while. I debate dredging up the past. Never a good idea, but I do it anyway. "Are you still pissed at me?"

He looks at me. "I didn't like how it felt."

"You know it wasn't me. If I could I'd go back and beat all of my asses."

"I know."

"Okay. You're not breaking up with me, right?"

He smiles. "I'm gonna give you another chance."

I knew we were fine. It'd take a lot more to damage our friendship. But it's still good to hear. "Marcus, if we do this thing for Bas, I can't go anywhere near Samrael."

"You think I can?"

"No. Jode, though. I think Ellis could do it."

"And Dare," he adds.

I bite down on my bottom lip. My gut keeps telling me this is wrong, and that giving Samrael an opening is the last thing we should do. But I've learned to trust Daryn's instincts. We have to do this.

"Tomorrow, Marcus. We'll go to this place. You and I will hang back. We'll keep the orb with us. Bas, Jode, and Daryn can ride on to see Samrael."

"Dang," Marcus says, shaking his head.

"I know, man. I know." But there are no good options.

We're going to have to take some risks.

CHAPTER 27

‑ DARYN ‑

We'd been searching around the lake for a few days," Bastian says. "Rael and I knew that's where we'd find you. It's the only source of freshwater anywhere near here." He looks back and smiles at me. Then his gaze lands right over my shoulder, on Gideon, and his smile disappears.

We're on our way to meet Samrael.

Gideon is a tall and silent presence at my back. I'm riding with him, tandem, and this close, there's no escaping the tension in his body.

This morning, I was shocked to learn that everyone is on board with what Bas wants.

Jode agreed. Marcus. And most surprisingly, Gideon, who's been virtually silent all morning and is clearly not happy about it.

But we're going.

In two days, we'll reach Samrael at Gray Fort, the small fortified settlement where he and Bas have been living. At which point I'm not sure what happens.

Jode and I talk to Samrael? Make some kind of determination about whether he's worthy enough to leave here?

I'm not sure how to get that done.

How do you judge character? *Literally* judge it?

How do you ascribe some quantifiable metrics to a person's morality?

Yes, you scored in the seventieth percentile for kindness, but you're in the twenties for lying. I'm very sorry. You need to stay.

How does that work? And when did Jode and I become the morality police?

I can't fool myself, though. The real weight of responsibility falls on me. I control the orb. I'm the gatekeeper, whether I want to be or not.

Bas continues. "We saw Shadow on the ice—but I'd felt her before that." He pats her as he talks. I'd forgotten how he likes to tell stories. It's been too quiet without him. "I knew you were close, right girl? But then we saw Jode and Gideon across the lake. I was so happy I couldn't even speak. I lost it, right there. Rael and I agreed that he should let me come to you alone first, so I could explain things. He turned back, taking my horse. My normal horse. Did I tell you we have those? Not many. Just a few. Anyway, I rounded the lake and found Shadow, and then you guys. I would have come straight for you across the ice, but I knew it was a haunting. I wouldn't have been able to help."

"Whoa—hold on," Jode interrupts. "A haunting?"

Marcus and I lock eyes.

"Yeah. The changes that happen in this place? It's like this is a giant stage with moving parts and trapdoors and special effects. It can do anything. Jumble up your thoughts and spit them back at you. It's crazy. Like a nightmare that's real. I hate it. But not all the hauntings are bad. Some can be pretty cool. I've actually been through a few that are really beautiful."

"Really?" Jode says. "You've had *good* hauntings?"

"Oh, yeah. Don't ask me how they happen because I don't know. They just do. Anytime, too. There are no rules here. Anything goes."

Gideon's hand tightens on my hip. I don't like the sound of that, either.

"What about the Harrows?" Jode asks. "The cloaked spectral creatures?"

"Oh, those. I *really* hate those. We call them the Lost, but I like 'Harrows.'" Bas nods to himself. "Yeah. It fits them better. There are more of them near Gray Fort. Rael thinks it's the life in us. They're drawn to it. We'll need to be extra careful as we get closer. But don't worry. I'll get us there."

We're all worried. Every one of us.

The Rift treats us to more of our personal relics as the day goes on.

"They're like mini-hauntings," Bas says when we ride past an upside-down bicycle with spinning wheels. "Not as large-scale but they'll still mess with your head."

We continue our routine of claiming the item and providing some background. A bizarre sort of show-and-tell.

The bicycle is Bastian's. A favorite bike he left behind in Nicaragua when he moved to the States as a kid.

Marcus claims a plain bookshelf with a few binders, tattered books, and trophies, and a football encased in thick acrylic given to him by a coach that he describes as "all right."

The old Jeep with peeling paint is Gideon's, which we all know. It's the Jeep he was going to fix up with his father.

"That one's mine," I say, as we come to a big velvet couch with deep cushions and a dozen pillows piled all over it. The color of the couch is "goldenrod." I know because I helped my mom pick it out. "That's my mom's favorite spot in our house. It's right in front of a big bay window in our family room. The afternoon sun pours right onto it and makes the fabric feel so warm. It's impossible to stay awake on that couch in the afternoon."

This sets off a chain reaction of yawns and wistful glances at the couch. We're all in need of a good night's sleep.

As we file past it, a pang of nostalgia hits me. Josie and I did our movie marathons plunked on that couch on the rare occasions she actually slowed down, and wasn't driven by her responsibilities at school, cross-country, or home. We'd bake chocolate-chip cookies and binge-watch The Lord of the Rings, Harry Potter, or Star Wars. Every film and television adaptation of Jane Austen's novels ever—which is a lot.

I loved those weekends.

The desire to go home pulls at me again. I want to see the look on my sister's face when I show up after a year and a half away. Mom's face. Dad's. I want to see Isabel and Maia. I want to see Ben and Sophia and Soraya. I want to see Jared Suarez. I want to run track again. Sit in classes like Statistics and Geology, learning things I'll probably never need to know again. The pull of a structured life is like a hook caught in my chest.

For the first time, I feel like having lost the Sight is a blessing. I'm not a Seeker—and I've been seeing that as a lack. A failure. But what if it's not? What if it's a gift?

If I'm not a Seeker, I can reclaim my life.

I'm ready for that.

I want it.

To everyone's surprise except Sebastian's, the terrain actually starts to vary from the uniform and endless woods we've traveled.

We ride past glades and streams, shimmering with life. Rock clusters and shrubs, nestled together. We cross another burnt field with the dead trees, this one vast.

As we rise in elevation, riding uphill, we gain views of the endlessness of the forest ahead and behind us. In the distance, we see a pale ridge against a hazy white sky, like mountains cut from tracing paper.

Bas informs us this is our destination. Gray Fort is in those mountains.

Mom's white flowers are nearly ever-present. Sometimes they're already there as we ride past. Other times they bloom from the ground and open like anemones.

Nothing is surprising anymore.

I choose to take it as a good sign. I imagine that when I see the flowers, it means Mom is thinking of me at that very second, just as I'm thinking of her.

At sunset, we camp again and the mood is subdued. Tomorrow we'll be entering an area rife with Harrows. We'll see Samrael. And the underlying tension between Gideon and Bas is something we all feel. It only makes our group more somber.

A strained relationship between them is the last thing I'd have expected.

Gideon's relationship with Jode is a battle of dry humor. A sarcasm cage match. And they're both unapologetically competitive with each other. But there's respect between them, too. I think Gideon admires Jode's intellect, while Jode admires Gideon's decisiveness.

With Marcus, Gideon has a friendship with roots down to the earth's core. You can feel the bond between them. I've seen them look at each other and laugh for no apparent reason, like they're picking up on a frequency the rest of the world misses.

But with Bas, there was always *noise*. Buoyant, good-humored noise in the shape of stories, jokes, pranks, laughter. In the fall, Bas and Gideon entertained each other constantly and that entertained the rest of us. The absence of this feels conspicuous. The lack of their noise is loud.

Adding to my sour mood is the fact that I spent the day watching Bas ride Shadow. It was amazing to see—I've wanted to see it for so long—but the loss is beginning to hit me. For the time Bas was in here, she was mine. And I love her.

As soon as I have the thought, Shadow turns from where she stands with the other horses and looks at me.

I think she knows how I feel. I think she feels it, too.

With a fire started and food consumed, sleep is the next step. I know this routine. We've done days of this.

I'm about to lay my head on my backpack when Jode says, "Daryn? You're not sleeping yet, surely?"

I push myself back up. A quarter of my brain is already shutting down. "What? Why?"

"The list! Don't deprive me. I've been waiting all day for it. Give us the List of Life."

"Yes," Bas says, breaking into his first smile of the day. "We have to keep going. We're on seventy-three, right?"

We are. I bring out the notebook and toss it to Marcus, looking forward to more of his beautiful penmanship in my journal.

Marcus sits up and flips it open.

"Your turn, Gideon," Bas says. "We all added to it last night. You're next."

Gideon frowns, and I know why. It feels like Bas just offered him an olive branch.

"Okay." Gideon shrugs. He looks at me. At first he seems annoyed. Then I see the slightest glimmer of mischief light up his eyes. "Daryn and I have an announcement to make. It's really early for this, but we're excited about it, and . . . what the heck. Let's just tell them, don't you think?"

"Oh, definitely," I say, though I have no idea what he's up to.

"Great." His big hand swallows mine in a warm grasp and he turns back to the guys. "Sometime later this year . . . well, in a few months I should say, since we're not sure about the timing. But in a few months something really special is going to happen and we want you to be the first to know about it. The three of you. So, in a few months, like I said, we're going to have a . . ." He bows his head, resting his forehead on the back of my hand. "Sorry. I'm really emotional about this."

"The acting," Jode says. "Macbeth never felt this torment."

"So bad," Marcus says, shaking his head.

"Shh, you guys. I like this," Bas says. "Keep going. What happens in a few months?"

Gideon looks up and there are actual tears glimmering in his eyes—I think they're from trying not to laugh, though. "We're going to have a reunion in Connecticut. At Daryn's family's house. And you're all invited. That's what I want to add. Our reunion."

I look at him. "That's actually a great idea."

"Ahhh," Bas says, nodding appreciatively. "A reunion, nice. I'll be there." His eyes narrow, like he's seeing potential. "You have raw talent, Gideon. I could shape you into a great actor."

"I don't need any shaping, thanks."

I jab him in the ribs. He smiles and puts his arm around me.

"You're good, though," Bas continues, undeterred. "I've seen it before this, too. Remember the chocolate samples in Copenhagen?"

Gideon laughs. "Yeah. I remember."

Something passes between them, thawing the cool distance they've kept all day.

Jode circles his hand in an *out with it* motion. "Do share, for those of us who missed it."

Bas smiles. His shoulders relax as he settles into storyteller mode. "It was on our train journey from Rome to Norway.

I think it happened the day after I got the birthday cake. Remember that?"

Four voices. "Yes."

"Okay, yeah. So, we had like a fifteen-minute stop at a station. I forget which one, but Gideon and I went looking for food—we did that a lot."

"You did, Bas. I just went with you."

"Yeah. That's probably true. Anyway, we found a bakery and ordered two croissants. The lady behind the counter went to warm them up, so we waited at the counter. Then we saw that right in front of us there was a plate of samples. Chocolates. Little pieces cut up, kind of like fudge. We tried them and they were good, so we kept going. By the time the lady came back with our croissants, we'd taken most of them down. I think Gideon felt bad because he said, 'These samples were awesome. Thank you.'

"She replied in Danish. We didn't understand what she said but the message on her face was crystal clear: They weren't samples. We'd just polished off the scraps on someone's used plate that was just sitting there. We'd been eating someone's leftovers.

"The bakery lady was mortified for us. I think I was still chewing. I didn't know what to do. But like a true master of improvisation, Gideon looked at me and said, 'I didn't get a word of what she said, did you?' And I of course agreed. No clue what she'd said."

I can't stop laughing. None of us can. Marcus is laughing so hard my notebook slips off his lap.

"Then what happened?" I ask.

"Nothing," Bas says. "We took our croissants and walked out of there."

"And almost missed the train because we couldn't pull it together," Gideon says, grinning. "Those were good chocolates."

"I can't believe you didn't tell us that," I say.

"You don't want to know *every* story."

"If they're that funny, I do."

"Same," says Marcus.

Bas and Gideon look at each other like they're both running through mental catalogues. "Tell the one about your armor and the German guy," Bas says.

Gideon lets out a big, surprised laugh. "Oh, yeah. That's a good one."

It's the first of several stories, and each is funnier than the one before it. We laugh until we ache. We add to "Reasons" if something fitting comes up along the way.

My eyes start to burn for sleep, but I don't want to miss out. Burrowing under Gideon's arm, I shut them and listen.

Their voices are so different, capturing exactly who they are as individuals, but they make a chorus that's as comforting as Gideon's solid presence and the campfire's warmth. I'm almost totally relaxed when I hear the horses—all four—let out short, sharp snorts.

Everything stops as we scan the woods for what alarmed them.

"Harrows." Bas shoots to his feet, setting off an explosion of motion. The guys reach for their weapons. I grab my backpack, thinking of the orb.

"Do you hear them?" Jode asks.

The horses have all wheeled to face in the same direction. I look where they're looking, concentrating. I listen for the wind that precedes them. For their bloodthirsty howling. I look for their quick movements and ragged cloaks. The flash of teeth and claws. I can't hear or see anything.

There. I see movement in the darkness.

But it's not the Harrows approaching.

It's Samrael.

Stepping from the darkness with a graceful stride. His hands raised to show that he's defenseless.

"I didn't mean to startle you," he says. "I'm unarmed." He looks at Bas, then at me, and then finally at Gideon. "I have urgent news."

CHAPTER 28

⟶ GIDEON ⟵

I don't make a conscious decision to attack him. I just do it. I lunge for Samrael, my sword grasped in my hand, my shoulders torqued for maximum power.

When I'm at the end of my backswing, something clamps onto the blade.

My shoulder jolts; my sword nearly rips out of my fingers.

Confusion hits me, until I see Bas. He holds the disk on one end of the scales. The other is wrapped around the blade—the blade that should be shearing through Samrael right now.

"No, Gideon!" he yells.

Every fiber in my body demands revenge. I feel insane with it, my vision blurring at the edges. Bas's voice sounds separate from reality, echoing inside my head.

Samrael has come to a stop, waiting to see what'll happen next.

Marcus stares at him with murder in his eyes. Jode has an arrow trained on him, glowing and poised to launch.

"I'm going to let go," Bas says to me. "Don't do anything . . . just don't do anything, okay?"

With a practiced flick of the wrist, like he didn't skip a beat with the scales in the eight months he's been here, he unhooks the disk from the chain and releases my sword.

I instantly want to try again. Take another swing. Or throw the sword.

I could hit Samrael.

But Bas is waiting for me to try something. He's ready to stop me again.

"Jode, Marcus," I say. "Do it. Finish him."

Before I'm done speaking, Bas shoots in front of Samrael and spreads his arms, the chains caught up in one fist.

"*No!* I'm not letting you do this." He's decisive, challenging. Aggressive. He was none of those before. "You're going to have to kill me to get to him."

I believe him. One thing Bas has always been is selfless. He'd give his life to protect someone. That's what got him here.

"Gideon, man . . ." he says. "Just *listen* to him."

I look past him, to Samrael. The look in his eyes is emotionless. Like we're objects to him. Like he's never *felt* in his entire life.

Bas wants me to listen? No. I don't want to hear a word out of his mouth. I want nothing except to skewer his black heart.

"We had a plan, Gideon," Daryn says. "Remember?"

I don't remember. Then I do.

But I never agreed to peace talks. I never will.

The wind is rising around us, carrying the Harrows' soiled fire smell. I can hear their howling now—the hyped-out sound of pack animals on the scent.

A hot, sick feeling rises in my throat. No way I can deny it. We're in trouble. I have to change gears.

"Ten seconds," I say. "That's how long you get."

"You aren't safe here," Samrael says, launching right in. "The Lost are moving toward this location."

"Harrows," Bas supplies. "They call them Harrows."

Samrael nods. "Two bands. Thirty strong each. I saw them from the foothills. There's no time to waste. You have to follow me. If we leave now, we may be able to lose them."

"You think I'm going to do that? Follow you?"

"We have a history I regret, Gideon. I hope Sebastian has begun to explain the situation I was in. I hope he's told you that I . . . that I want to make amends."

"Are you giving me my hand back?"

He has no answer for this. The Harrows are coming closer, their cries growing louder. "Ra'om controlled us," Samrael says. "We were powerless against him. We did what he commanded, or we suffered. You can't begin to imagine what he was capable of. I understand that you may never trust me. I can't change what I did. But I know you've experienced your own regrets. You know how it feels to wish you'd behaved differently. Perhaps you can understand that."

I look at Marcus. "Is this piece of shit talking about my dad?"

Marcus's reply is to swing the scythe through the air, spinning it in front of him, then behind him, and back. The huge sickle blade slicing through the night is impressive. Something you'd see in a performance. But Marcus never does anything for show. He's loosening up. He's getting ready.

Samrael glances toward the woods. "Unfortunately, we don't have time to have this conversation now." He looks at Daryn. "Come with me. All of you. We can discuss this once we've reached safety."

"Gideon," Bas says. "He helped me. He's the only reason I'm still alive. You can trust him. If we don't leave now we'll be ripped apart. Or Daryn could bring us out of here. But then Samrael comes, too."

"No," Daryn says. "I'm not taking you through until I'm sure." She looks at me. "I'll open the portal. You guys go through. Get Bas out of here. I'll stay behind. I'm the only one who needs to be here to—"

"*No.*"

"Hell no," Marcus adds.

"Something needs to be decided quickly," Jode says.

"We need to get Bas out of here, Gideon."

"We *all* need to get out of here, Daryn. That includes you." Why do I even have to say this? What's she thinking? That I'd be okay with leaving her in here? With Samrael? "And what if the orb breaks?"

"I'm not sure. I don't know."

The howling grows louder. It's coming from two directions, like the bands are working together on a flanking maneuver.

"Either we ride now," Samrael says, "or we die."

As much as it kills me to admit, it's true. We're about to be overrun. Evasion is the only real option. "Let's get moving."

Everyone mounts up.

Samrael brings forward two horses—big dapple-grays. There's a quick discussion between Bas and Daryn that I can't hear, and then she's swinging into one of the saddles.

"Daryn, what—"

"If we have to fight, it'll be easier if we're not both on Riot."

True, but I hate the idea. I want her with me or on Shadow, but we're mobilizing before I know it.

Samrael leads the way, so. I follow him.

A demon.

CHAPTER 29

⟶ DARYN ⟵

We race through the trees at a breakneck pace. A dangerous pace.

Any stumble or unseen branch could be deadly. But the Harrows are deadly without question, so we ride like our lives depend on it.

My gray gelding is slower than Shadow and the other horses. I lose my spot near the front and fall to the back. Samrael, also on an ordinary horse, drops to the rear of the group with me.

Up ahead, Gideon sees me and tries to slow Riot. The others notice too—Jode, Marcus, Bas—all of them drawing back.

"No! Go! Keep going!" I yell, but it's useless.

In moments, it's undeniable: No matter how fast we ride, we won't be fast enough. The Harrows are closing in. Almost as though they knew exactly the direction we'd take.

When their smoky reek reaches me, I know we have minutes, maybe seconds, before we see them bounding toward us, all sharp claws and depthless eyes.

"We're too many! Too visible!" Samrael calls forward.

It's true. In the darkness, Lucent and Riot are impossible to conceal, and Ruin's bronze coat is hardly better. They're homing beacons.

My earlier idea resurfaces. I make a snap decision. "Stop! *Stop!*"

They all react instantly.

Horses squeal and twist as they come to a halt, and shouts of surprise erupt around me.

Taking advantage of the commotion, I slip my knife from the side pocket of my backpack and hide it under my shirt.

"We can't run. They're all around us," I say.

"We can't fight, either," Samrael says.

"Coward," Gideon lashes at him. "We're not lying down. We fight."

"You're hearing the scouts. There are scores more behind them."

As they argue, I maneuver my horse closer to Samrael's. Then I slip my feet out of the stirrups and count to three.

With a burst of strength, I pull my feet onto the saddle's seat and push off, leaping onto Samrael's horse. I land behind him and hook my arm around his neck.

Startled, his horse springs forward. I'm jolted back but I hold on, prepared for it. Then I lay the knife blade under his chin. "Don't move."

"I'm only steadying the horse," he says.

"Daryn, what are you doing?" Gideon asks.

My hand holding the knife is shaking. I'm sure Samrael can tell. "I'm opening the portal." I reach behind me with my free hand, into my backpack. "You guys need to go. You have to get out. I'm the only one who has to stay. Bas, I'll stay to see if what you said is true."

I don't know why I don't say what I mean specifically. *I'll stay to see if Samrael is worthy enough to be let out of here.*

The words just don't come out.

"How does that help?" Jode sounds desperate. Our situation *is* desperate. "*You'll* still be in danger."

Samrael is the one who answers. "One horse will be less visible than a cavalcade. I can hide one horse. We can evade them."

"Two." Gideon withdraws his sword with a hiss of metal. "I'm staying, too. Marcus, Jode—get Bas out of here. *Go*."

This isn't what I want, but I know I won't change his mind. I don't even have time to try.

"If you try to go through the portal," I warn Samrael, pressing the blade harder against his neck, "you'll make a killer out of me."

I toss the orb into the air before I can think about what I just said.

Samrael's back straightens as he sees it hovering there. The quest for the orb was an obsession for the Kindred last fall. It felled every one of its members except Samrael.

I open the portal, the process familiar now, instinctive.

The Harrows are so close I can feel the air trembling, the trees shuddering.

I glance at Sebastian. He watches the portal with reverence, relief already sparking in his eyes. This is his exit. His return home. But then he looks sharply at me. "We can't leave you here."

"Go, Bas. Go home," Gideon says.

"You'll give Samrael a fair chance?"

Bas asks me this, not Gideon.

"Yes. I promise I will."

"Thank you," Bas says. Then he turns to Samrael, emotion plain on his face.

It suddenly feels wrong holding the blade to Samrael's throat. I withdraw it and slide it against his back.

"I'll see you outside," Bas says. He leads Shadow into the portal.

As he disappears inside, I gasp, caught up in a rush of feeling. He's going home—it's all I've wanted to see for months. But Shadow's going with him, away from me. Her absence steals my strength. It makes all the bones in my body feel pliable.

"Go, Marcus," Gideon says. Marcus looks like he's not going anywhere. "I need you to go." He looks at Jode. "Both of you. Now."

Gideon is asking the world of them. He's asking for everything. We all know what it feels like to leave a friend in here.

They turn their horses and enter. Jode and then Marcus. Both quickly swallowed by the tumult and chaos of the portal.

Gone.

I close the portal, swiftly re-forming it into the orb. Then I call it back to me, feeling the crackle of fading energy as it settles in my palm. As I slip it back into my pack, I see that the crack is more severe, almost cleaving the orb in two.

"Can we ride?"

Samrael's voice pulls me back. "Yes. *Go.*"

Gideon stays with us as the gray builds speed. He keeps Riot nearly glued to our side.

I hold on tightly to Samrael because I have to, but I shiver at the life I feel through his shirt. He's warm, muscular, normal—and a demon.

Dread screams through my mind as branches whip past us. I keep tensing, thinking I see the Harrows. I keep waiting for them to gush through the trees like a ragged black wave. I keep wondering what I've just done.

Why am I here? Has Samrael really changed?

Looking over, I catch Gideon's eyes.

I didn't want him to stay. That wasn't part of my plan.

It should only be me.

CHAPTER 30

─ GIDEON ─

We can't outrun them.

Can't hide from them, either.

Samrael and Daryn could've, possibly, but concealment isn't an option with Riot. I didn't think this through—just reacted. But no way in hell was I leaving her in here alone.

I have no other choice. I have to take a stand. Buy time for Daryn to escape.

With my archenemy.

"Go, Daryn! Keep going!" Drawing my sword, I turn Riot and prepare for the first wave of attack.

The creatures descend immediately. Two of them. Frayed and bony. Galloping over dirt on hands and feet.

The first one leaps, giving me an easy target. I plunge my sword into its gut, withdrawing it quickly. It shrieks and tumbles to the ground. The second hesitates. It's just enough time for Riot to throw a hoof. I hear a sickening crack and the Harrow goes down. In the next instant, it's trampled.

"Gideon!"

Daryn and Samrael have stopped. "Daryn, *go!*"

Why?

Why did they *stop* rather than *escape*?

The answer is almost impossible to believe. Samrael wields a blade with speed I know all too well. Like Daryn, he's fighting. To help *me*.

I see the Harrow before either of them do—a small one, streaking at them like a bullet. "Daryn—to your left!" I yell.

But it jumps and latches onto Daryn, its cloak wrapping around her.

The horse rears as the Harrow pulls on Daryn. She clings to Samrael, screaming. He twists and buries the blade into the Harrow's shoulder. It shrieks, tumbles off, and peels into the darkness, dragging something behind it.

"My backpack!" she yells. "Gideon—the orb!"

"Go! I'll get it! Get out of here!" A band of Harrows stalks toward me. They come slowly, calculatingly. Not in their usual blind charge. I count a dozen, then stop counting.

Some have short daggers that flash amber and gold, reflecting Riot's fire as they stalk forward. But it's the ones carrying coiled chains around their necks that worry me. Chains are tough for a sword to cut through—even mine. Chain mail worked for a reason. Riot moves in jerky motions, blowing sharp breaths. He's not happy about them, either.

Daryn is shouting something as she retreats with Samrael. I can barely hear her above the shaking trees and the howling.

Then she's out of sight, swallowed by the shadows of the woods.

I can't leave the orb, and running wouldn't work, anyway. These creatures are faster than Riot.

I look around me. No backpack in sight and I'm outnumbered ten times over, but the soldier in me resists panic. The best I can do is slow them down to give Daryn a better chance at escaping. I search for the most immediate threat.

It's all of them.

They come in a swarm—suddenly and together. Throwing chains through the air that arc above me like metal flares.

They hit us everywhere.

Riot roars.

My sword is hooked at the crossbar. My hands, at the wrist. My horse, around the neck. Then a chain falls over my neck, grazing my shoulders for a second before it's pulled tight.

Pain explodes in my windpipe.

Riot's front legs swipe out sharply, and we go down like a falling tree. Tipping in an instant that lasts forever.

He falls on my leg—his full weight. My bones snap like twigs. Femur, shinbone, foot. My vision whites out and pain becomes everything.

Riot blazes, lighting up like a bonfire. I'm stuck beneath him, but I can see that his hooves have been chained and that he's being pulled at unnatural angles.

"Don't touch my horse! I'll kill you!" The chain around my neck is constricting my throat. My voice sounds like an engine that won't turn over. My threats go nowhere.

As the Harrows close around us, Riot writhes and struggles, every movement grinding my leg bones to gravel.

I feel myself passing out, sounds receding. Vision tunneling.

A decaying stench floods my nostrils like an airborne poison as one of the Harrows leans over me. It has a pale white scar across one wrinkled cheek.

If it had eyes, it'd be staring at me.

And if I still had the power to speak, I'd tell it that when I get my revenge, I'll start with it first.

CHAPTER 31

～ DARYN ～

The gray mare's coat is lathered in sweat when Samrael stops her.

Samrael, too, is damp with sweat. Beneath my hands, his shirt is hot and stuck to his skin. He's breathing fast from exertion.

But I'm not sure I'm breathing at all.

I'm not even sure if my heart's still beating. I don't feel anything except a sharp stinging in my throat, like I drank acid.

We rode a long time, I think.

What just happened?

Samrael turns slightly. The dawn light traces his profile with a thin line. Long straight nose. High brow. Cheeks and jaw like a rock quarry.

"This will likely be no comfort," he says, quietly, "but we would only have gotten killed if we'd stayed any longer. There was nothing to be done. And he's a strong fighter. I know from experience. I'm certain he was able to escape."

I scramble off the horse, seized by the need to get away from him.

I take three steps before my legs give out and I sink to my knees. Sink into the terrible feeling that's curling into every particle in my body.

Regret. Regret at a subatomic level.

Never—not even when I ran away from home, or when I lost Bas to the Rift—never have I felt this internal alarm blaring at me, telling me I've done something that needs to be undone *now*.

Gideon is back there.

Gideon.

I pull myself up. "We—" My voice has left me. I swallow and try again. "We have to go back. We have to help him."

Samrael dismounts. He walks to me. His brow is furrowed with annoyance or concern. I don't know him well enough to know which. Holding his gaze feels like locking eyes with a cobra. "I don't want to crush your hopes—"

"Then don't. Actually, you can't. Even if you try."

"I was going to say, at the risk of discouraging you, now isn't the time to go back. We're not in a position to help him. The Harrows have numbers on their side. We *will* help. But we need to think logically about this. We need to strategize. If we go to Gray Fort—"

"Gideon is back there and he needs us now." How do I know? How am I so sure? I wasn't this sure when I lost Bas. I was too scared. Too terrified of trusting myself. Without the Sight, I felt unguided. I feel guided now. *Trust, even when it's hardest. Especially when it's hardest.* "We need to go back."

Samrael looks toward the mare. The set of his jaw is hard, decided, but I'm not backing down. "Sebastian said you helped him. He told us you saved his life and that you've changed your ways. If you have, you'll go back for Gideon. He was fighting to save our lives. He stayed back there so that we could get away."

"He stayed for your life, not mine."

"You're still here because of him." My gaze drops to his forearm. Through the rips in his sleeve, I see the gash the Harrow left, so like the cuts on my back when they were fresh. Blood drips off his hand, disappearing into the dirt. Every drop marks the time we're wasting. I try a new approach. "The orb was taken. The Harrow that attacked us took it."

A glint comes to his gem-hard eyes. Genuine interest. "It was in the pack?"

"Yes. Without it, neither one of us will get out of here." For a sickening moment, I wonder if Samrael wants this—exactly this. For me to be stuck here in the Rift with him forever.

"Fine. We'll go back, but not just yet," he says. "The Lost—the Harrows—prefer to sleep by day and hunt in the dark. When they're asleep, it's the sleep of the dead. If we find them at the right time, we shouldn't have any trouble taking the backpack and looking for Gideon. We can head back in a couple of hours, to be safe, and search until dusk."

He pauses for a moment, waiting, but I'm not going to thank him for doing something that's so obviously the right thing.

He returns to the mare, taking her reins. "She needs water. There's a stream a short walk from here."

I think he expects me to come with him. I don't.

I listen to the clop of the gray's hooves receding. Then silence falls around me, making my breathing seem too loud, my anxious paces even louder.

I'm missing so much.

Gideon, who's back there somewhere. On the run? In hiding?

Captured?

The orb, which has been stolen.

Marcus, Jode, Bas, and Shadow, who are no longer here.

I feel utterly alone. A prisoner of the Rift.

I spin myself into a panic, buzzing with anxiety. I'm a bell that won't stop ringing.

I can't stand it any longer. Anything is better than stewing in my own thoughts.

I run down the path Samrael took, slowing down only when I see him through the trees.

The mare stands in the creek. Water rushes past her knees. Her long neck is lowered as she drinks. Samrael watches her from the bank.

I debate making myself known, but I don't want his company. I just don't want to be alone.

I slip behind a tree and kneel.

My mind is on Gideon. It won't go anywhere else. I wonder if he thinks I've abandoned him? No. He knows I wouldn't. Tears sting my eyes, wanting to spill as I imagine what he must be feeling, but I hold them back.

Samrael brings the mare out of the creek and tends to her affectionately, brushing her down with a swatch of burlap. He either doesn't see me, or doesn't care that I'm here. Returning to the creek, he pulls his shirt over his head and drops it on the bank, then crouches to splash water on his face. He runs his fingers through his black hair a few times and rinses the cuts the Harrow gave him on his forearm.

On his back, I see two ghastly scars. Twin scars, from shoulder blades to the middle of his ribs. Where wings might attach. Where they once did.

I know he was an angel once. But seeing proof—visible proof—sends a shiver down to my toes.

"I'm deeply gratified that Sebastian went home," Samrael says, surprising me. He doesn't turn to me. He speaks with his eyes downcast. Fixed on the shirt in his hands. "It's . . . strange to be here without him. But I'm very glad he went. Thank you."

"I didn't do it for you."

"Of course not."

I can't look away from the scars on his back. "Why did you give up so much? How could you fall from grace, fall *so far,* and become *this*?"

The questions come out of me before I know it.

"Become this?" He turns to me at last, his expression equal

parts curiosity and challenge. "Do you mean deplorable? Repulsive? Or is it simpler? Do you mean to ask me how I chose to become evil?"

"Pick one. They all work."

"I made a mistake that took me astray for a very long time," he says, almost dismissively. "And I can see I have a ways to go before you'll see me."

"I'm looking right at you."

"You're looking at what I was."

"I don't care what you were *or* who you are."

"And yet you're here to judge me," he says.

"I'm here for *Bas*. I'm here to fulfill a promise."

"As I recall, the promise was to give me a fair chance. Is this your notion of fairness?"

My face heats with anger. But I can't disagree with him. I'm not being fair. I'm being judgmental.

How do you judge character without being judgmental?

What have I gotten myself into?

He sighs. Turns back to look at the shirt in his hands. "Daryn, I apologize. I apologize for my tone. I've caused this—all that's happened. The price is all mine to pay. Every day, I regret the wrongs I've committed. I imagine the condemnation of my soul. And yet, I hope . . ." He pauses, and his shoulders rise as he draws a deep breath. "I hope to one day atone for what I've done. I hope for redemption."

I have nothing to say in response. I can't tell if he's being honest, or putting on a show as he calculates how to fool me. I've burned all of the mental power I had left for the day.

Samrael rises and wades to the horse, gently leading it back to the bank. He removes a linen napkin with bread, apples, and cheese folded inside. He looks at me like he's considering offering to share.

"Don't bother."

He sits alone and eats.

My body is so spent, physically and emotionally, that I find myself sagging against the rough bark, my chin resting on a knot. I curl my legs and arms into the nook between the big roots. Beneath me, white flowers spring up, pillowing my limbs with their velvet softness.

I pray for Gideon. Then Riot.

Then Bas, Jode, and Marcus, that they're on the outside and safe.

I keep going down the list. Mom, Dad, Josie. Isabel. Maia. Ben. Low. Low's son.

The far side of the creek fills with white flowers.

Samrael's attention swings to me; he's waiting for my reaction. He doesn't know this is normal. A gift that the Rift gives me.

I close my eyes to better feel Mom's presence, and only realize I've fallen asleep when I feel a gentle jostling of my foot.

I rocket to my feet, mind racing to catch up.

Samrael stands before me—tall and straight. Watching me with marble-green eyes. The mare is saddled again, and the light slants through the trees in soft afternoon beams.

"It's time," he says.

CHAPTER 32

⤙ GIDEON ⤘

Water for you. To drink." The Harrow's voice sounds like rocks scraping together. "Drink it into your body." It brings a wood bowl to my mouth with its bony hands.

I turn my head. "Wait. Where's the girl?" I rasp, sounding worse than the Harrow. Pain flares deep into my throat. I feel like I was hit by a baseball bat on the Adam's apple. "The two people on the gray horse? Where are they?"

Tell me they got away. Tell me they're long gone.

"No talking. Water for you. To drink. Drink it into your body?"

I'm dehydrated and I need the water, so. I drink it into my body. My head throbs with every gulp but I finish every drop. Then I lean back against the tree I'm chained to.

I didn't think it was possible to hate these trees any more than I did, but I do.

I *hate* these trees.

"What about my horse?" I try to turn to see what's behind me. Explosions of pain detonate along my left leg and inside my foot.

The woods spin. The water comes back up.

Every drop I just drank.

The Harrow looks at the puddle beside me with the vacant holes where its eyes should be. How does it see? "Worry not, I bring more. Worry not?"

"Okay. I won't worry."

The thing smiles at me. Its mouth looks like the inside of a cave, teeth like stalagmites. "I return with water to drink and you worry not. You drink the water I bring."

"Good plan."

The smile goes bigger. Then it walks off, stooping, black cloak flowing behind it on invisible tides.

I make the weirdest friends.

I settle against the rock, moving centimeter by centimeter to keep my leg still. In addition to my pulverized bones and bruised windpipe, my shoulder sockets are screaming from having my hands tied behind my back for hours.

All day, I've been fading in and out.

Mostly out.

There are dozens of Harrows around me. Gathered around trunks in heaps. Pitched all over the branches, like the trees decided to wear black sweaters. They're completely still. My Harrow buddy is the only one awake. The rest are deep asleep, many of them making a sinister purring sound. Their scent is so thick I can taste it, a taste like watered-down ashtray.

Smack in the middle of the Harrow slumber party, I see Daryn's backpack. Sitting there, on the dirt, like it's nothing of value. Like it doesn't have our only hope of ever leaving here tucked inside.

I don't see Riot anywhere. I don't feel him nearby.

I can't think of him without seeing him drowning or covered in chains and pinned to the ground.

I hope he's still alive. And that I *stay* alive.

I have no idea what the Harrows have planned for me.

Why didn't they just kill me?

My situation assessment is getting too depressing, so I think of the positive things that have happened.

Bas got out. And Jode and Marcus got out.

That's pretty good. Not bad.

My buddy comes back with more water.

"You have a name?" I ask.

"Name?"

"Yeah. How do your friends get your attention?"

"Friends?"

"Shit. Never mind."

"You must sh—"

"No." I almost laugh. "I don't have to go. You're like a parrot. You ever seen *Pirates of the Caribbean*? The movie? There's a parrot in it called Cotton, I think. Talks just like you."

"Cotton?"

"Fluffy white stuff. Super soft. Perfect name for you, actually."

It says nothing. I think I've confused it.

"More water?" it says after a moment. "Drink. More for you."

As I drink, I notice its attention on my prosthetic. "You curious?" I shift a little so it can see my hand. "Go ahead."

The Harrow waits like it's expecting a trick. Good instincts, but it's too soon for that. I need to plan a little more. Let my leg heal. Finally it bends over my prosthetic and sniffs. "Touch?"

"Have at it."

Long fingernails the yellow color of wood glue tap the metal. *Tink, tink, tink.* "It moves?"

"Not here. It doesn't work here." It seems disappointed, but still interested. Still hovering around my prosthetic with fascination, like it's an alien baby. It gives me an idea. "If you take me to my horse, you can have it. All you have to do is show me where he is, Cotton. "

Pause. "Give Cotton?"

"That's right. Gideon will give to Cotton."

He straightens. He's surprisingly tall—I'm used to seeing them on all fours. He looks around at the branches draped in black. At the piles of bony rags across the clearing. None of the other Harrows stir. Their wicked purr continues, filling the woods.

Cotton frees the chains binding me to the tree, grabs me under the elbows, and pitches me over his shoulder like a sack of flour.

Pain slices up and down my broken leg, almost putting me out. Blood rushes to my head and a piercing noise floods my ears. Every step is agony. We only go about fifty paces before I'm off-loaded onto the dirt, thankfully on my right side so I can spare my busted leg most of the impact. Once again, though, the pain is all-consuming. I'm sweating cold and my body won't stop shaking.

"Horse," says the Harrow, pointing to a pond around thirty yards away. It's small. Surrounded by trees. Nothing more than a pool of rancid standing water. I can smell it from where I am.

With the patchy sunlight and scrim of branches hampering my view, I almost don't see Riot. He's submerged to the shoulders in the muck. Chains are looped around his neck and fastened to trees around the pond, keeping him immobilized. His mane is soaked. There's not a single ember or flame or glimmer of heat on him. What little I can see of his body is dark red, like wet brick. Even his eyes are lifeless. Lumps of cold coal. Without his fiery appearance, he's camouflaged, perfectly blending into the scenery.

When he sees me, he tries to move and makes only the smallest ripple across the scummy surface of the water.

Help me, Gideon. Help me.

He's too weak or too restrained—and I want to bawl, seeing him like that. My throat goes raw with desperation and anger.

I need a plan. I search for a rock or a stick. Anything. "Cotton, we need to have a real conversation. That kind of treatment isn't going to work for me."

"Hand," the Harrow says.

"What?"

"Hand." Cotton looks from me to my prosthetic, waiting for me to make good on my promise.

"Free my horse. Then untie me and I'll give it to you."

"Untie?"

"Yes. It's attached to me with a harness. I have to unstrap it before I give it to you."

Cotton creeps closer. His hands hover over the chains around my wrists for an instant. Then, quick as lighting, he's behind me, slamming his palm over my mouth.

He hauls me up a tree so fast I leave my stomach behind. Then he pushes me onto a thick branch, pinning me. "Watch," he says, still keeping his hand over my mouth. "Watch with Cotton?"

I can't see anything. Part of his weight is resting on my crushed leg. Tears are pouring out of my eyes and, once again, I'm on the verge of passing out. I blink hard and finally spot two figures moving through the woods. They're on foot, and moving stealthily.

My breath stops as I recognize Daryn. Seeing her unharmed is an intense relief. She's come for me. Another swell of emotion sweeps through me. It's amazing—and I'm not surprised.

But she brought Samrael.

Seeing them working together is like watching a nightmare. I've feared something too close to this.

Being pushed aside. Losing her to him.

They stop when they're about twenty paces away. Close enough for me to see the dark circles under her eyes and the look of determination on her face.

I try to yell, but Cotton digs his weight into my leg.

Shards of broken bone spear into my muscles and I grunt, but Cotton plugs my nose and stops any sound coming from me.

"Make noise and stop breathing. Girl stop breathing. Gideon stop breathing," Cotton says into my ear. "Make noise?"

I can't get any air. I shake my head. He releases my nose.

"They're just there," Samrael says, pointing to the main cluster of Harrows, where I was tied up less than ten minutes ago. He's so close. He's speaking in a hushed voice, but his every word is crystal clear. "Remember, if we wake one of them, we wake them all."

Not true, I think. One of them *is* awake.

"And we have to move quickly. Strange noises and scents—either will wake them. Are you ready?"

Daryn nods, never taking her eyes off the cluster of Harrows. "Yes."

Off they go.

Away.

In moments, I can't see them. The way Cotton has me pinned, the trunk is blocking the view to my right, where Daryn and Samrael are headed.

Fortunately, my new buddy gives me highlights.

"Walk, walk, walk. The bag close to girl. Close. Close. Ah, she find it. She wear it. The boy, Gideon, not close to girl. Boy with Cotton. She find boy?" Laugh. Hiss. Laugh.

Daryn and Samrael must search for fifteen minutes before they reappear. This time, almost directly below me. The day is fading. Dusk is approaching.

Daryn pulls her backpack off her shoulders, crouches on the ground, and removes the orb. It's a damaged thing now. Disintegrating, almost like she's holding dust in her hands.

I'm glad she found it. It could still get her back out. At the very least, it'll give her leverage with Samrael.

"Okay," she says. "It's here." She stuffs it back in her bag. "But I didn't see Gideon anywhere."

Her voice cracks.

My heart cracks.

"Neither did I," Samrael says. He actually looks like he feels bad for her. "Wait here. I have an idea."

He disappears again. In my ear, quiet as a moth's wings, Cotton says, "Girl pretty," and I want to make myself into a grenade and pull the pin.

Ten feet below me, Daryn is saying something over and over under her breath.

I think it's "Where are you?"

If she looked up, she'd have her answer.

If she turned the other way and walked thirty paces, she'd see the pond and Riot.

She doesn't do either.

Her *Where are you*s stop. She goes quiet, like she's thinking.

Quickly, she removes the orb from the backpack again and darts to the trunk of the tree, pushing the orb into the hollow of a knot. Then she jogs away and ties a scarf she finds inside her backpack around the branch of a nearby tree, marking it, looking between the two.

All of this without ever seeing me.

Then she zips up her pack and waits.

Samrael comes back a couple of minutes later towing a Harrow. The creature is in a similar state as me. Knife to throat. Mouth covered. Forcibly restrained.

Cotton begins to purr almost imperceptibly by my ear.

"Yell or make a sound and you will cease to exist." Samrael removes his hand from the Harrow's mouth. "Tell her about the rider with the red horse."

The Harrow turns empty eyes on Daryn. "Rider and fire horse escape."

Daryn stifles a gut-wrenching sound. "Where?" she says. "When?"

"In woods," the Harrow says. "In trees."

Daryn asks again and again, but the reply never changes.

I want to yell that I'm *in* the tree. Right now, right up here.

"I'm sorry, Daryn," Samrael says, "but we can't stay here. Go. I'll deal with this. I'll be right behind you." The Harrow in his grasp will need to be silenced; otherwise it'll wake the others. Silenced, in this case, probably means killed.

Daryn whirls and runs. Bolts, like she's trying to escape feeling.

Samrael releases the Harrow and sheathes his blade. "Back to the others," he says. "Go."

The creature shrinks away like a punished dog.

Samrael looks up, right at me. "No luck finding the rider and his burning horse. Such a shame."

Even if I could speak, there would be nothing to say.

We're past words. Now there are only two outcomes. Life and death.

One for each of us.

"Tree, look inside," says Cotton. "Look in hole of tree?"

Samrael sees the knot. He reaches inside and removes the orb.

"Clever girl, isn't she?" He slips it into the pocket of his coat. "Bring him," he says to the Harrow pinning me. "I want him there tonight."

CHAPTER 33

D aryn?" Samrael says, pulling me out of my daze. "We'll walk from here."

We've been riding for hours. They blur together. I can't remember any of them clearly. It was dusk for an instant as we left the Harrows. Then it was night and the fog rolled in—through the woods and inside my mind.

It makes me wonder if I've totally peeled away from reality. I think I might have.

Gideon is still out there. I have to find him.

The need feels like an urgent siren wailing inside me, but I have to be smart about this. Samrael said he has resources at Gray Fort. People who can help in the search and increase the odds of finding him. I have to accept the help. Anything to find Gideon.

How is it that I'm still *searching for people I love?*

"It'll be easier if you dismount first," Samrael adds, since I'm still not moving.

I jump down and land with a jarring thud, my teeth slamming together.

Every part of me feels leaden. Cold. Hard.

Samrael, on the other hand, dismounts with fluid ease. He pats the mare's rump. "Home," he says. She trots away, her gray coat disappearing into the fog.

Samrael paces away slowly, staring at the ground. He stops. He comes down on his heels and brushes dirt and leaves aside, revealing an iron handle. A wooden door is set flush to the forest floor.

Out *here*.

I'd never have found it in these woods. Not in a million years. I'd never have even *expected* to find it.

I walk over, fear seeping through my faded mind as I remember falling through the ground in the haunting with Gideon.

The iron hardware groans as Samrael lifts the trapdoor, leaves and dirt tumbling off. The earth exhales a cool breath that brushes across my cheeks. It smells musty, like wet stone, and faintly of decay.

"There are Harrows all over this area," he explains. A torch flickers below. Its light pours up uneven stone steps. "We use secret entrances, a different one every time. Otherwise they'd wait in ambush and we'd never be able to leave—or return."

He offers his hand to help me down. I don't take it.

I pull in a breath and step down.

It feels like descending into literal doom. The air wilts in my lungs. Sounds flatten. The steps are so narrow I have to turn my feet sideways.

At the bottom, a long corridor stretches before me. Stone walls. Stone floors and ceiling. Lamps at regular distances create small pools of light, breaking the overwhelming darkness. The flames wave wildly as Samrael shuts the door, then stretch tall again.

"Straight ahead."

Is he kidding? There's nowhere to go except straight ahead.

As we walk I become conscious of Samrael's nearness behind me—which is odd. I've shared a saddle with him for hours. But here there's nowhere for me to run, and a scream would go nowhere.

Who would I call for help, anyway? *Harrows*?

I think of the knife in my backpack. In my mind, I practice how I'll use it if my fears come true.

Why am I afraid? He needs me to leave the Rift. Hurting me wouldn't help him get what he wants.

The silence bears down on me, a weight pressing on my ears. It's more oppressive than the damp air or the darkness. "Why do you want to leave here? I thought this was what you wanted. To come into this place."

"It was," he replies behind me. "This is what Ra'om forced me to want. But I've changed. There is no finding peace or fulfillment here. Being here is a continuous trial. Perhaps you've noticed that yourself."

I have noticed, but I don't want to talk about me. "Why did you spare Bas when the two of you first came into the Rift?"

"We don't need to discuss this now. There's plenty of time for it later."

"I want to discuss it now."

"The easiest answer to communicate is curiosity. I've known many humans. Few are as guileless and good."

His answer is uttered with a trace of frustration.

"You spared his life because you found him *interesting*?"

"I saved his life. He was sick when he first came through. He needed care for weeks. He never blamed me during that time. He never complained about his situation. Rather, he made the best of it. I thought him a fool at first. Simple. Ignorant. This was how I used to think. Then, one day, I realized he'd become indispensable to me. At a time when I'd lost everything, he cheered me."

My mind shoots to Shadow—she was the same for me. Thinking of her, of how far away from me she is, makes my heart race. Much too fast. I feel a panic attack coming on. My lungs start to shut down like a city power grid. I can't breathe fast enough to get the air I need.

The world tilts. I walk into the wall like a drunk. Cling to it like it's the edge of a cliff.

"Daryn, are you all right?" Samrael rushes forward. "Can I help?"

I shake my head. "Just need . . . a moment."

"Take as long as you need." Samrael leans against the wall and watches me, his brow furrowed in concern. I focus on breathing. Relaxing and breathing and convincing my body that everything is okay.

When the panic finally leaves me, I straighten.

"I wondered when it would hit you," Samrael says. "I am sorry for your pain."

"He's not dead!" I snap. "Don't make it sound like he's gone!" I exhale a shaky breath, hating that he saw me in such a pathetic moment. "And why do you care? Why would you be sorry? You hate him."

He shakes his head. "I didn't mean to imply that. And I don't hate him, either. He thought me evil, which was true. If there is any feeling in me, it's envy. Gideon never yielded to Ra'om as I did. I'll always have to live with my own cowardice." As I listen, I search for false notes in his voice. Search for lies hidden in his green eyes.

He surprises me by smiling.

"What?"

"This is new for me," he says. "I've never done anything like this—bared my weaknesses. But I want to be honest with you to prove to you I've changed. I suppose I'll wind up telling you all of them before this is over."

"I won't live that long."

He laughs, taking my comment as a joke, instead of an insult like I meant it. I'm about to correct him—but I don't.

"Shall we keep on?" he asks. "This isn't the most welcoming part of Gray Fort."

We continue down the corridor. Then *up* the corridor as the ground slopes higher. We take several more turns. I try to remember them—it seems important that I should be able to retrace my steps—but our path seems too random and my composure is a tenuous thing, requiring my total concentration.

Finally, we reach wooden steps. Beside them are casks of wine, I think, judging by the pungent smell, and sacks of potatoes or grain. Samrael climbs the steps and pushes a hatch in the ceiling up with his shoulders. It slams open, detonating clouds of dust.

"Sorry," he says, frowning. "I should've warned you, it's dusty."

Yes. Because dust in my hair is a major concern for me right now.

We climb into a dim storeroom—a pantry. The door at the end is ajar, and the light spilling through illuminates the shelves against the walls stacked with ceramic bowls, wicker baskets, and thick glass jars. Smells invade my nose. Thyme, basil, and garlic. Other herbs and spices that remind me of home-cooked meals and holidays, which jars me. Nothing about this is comforting.

We enter an old-fashioned kitchen with an open cooking hearth, a long heavy wood table at the center and several more along the walls, all lit by candlelight.

"I thought there were other people?" All I want to see is a search party, gathered and ready to go.

"Asleep at the moment. You'll meet them in the morning. We'll organize then."

A cast-iron pot hangs over glowing embers of the cooking hearth. My traitorous mouth waters as its smell wafts over. Some kind of savory stew or soup. The loaf of bread on the table doesn't help. There's also a haphazard pile of fruits and vegetables scattered across the wood surface, like someone tucked the best of the day's yield into their shirt and poured it out.

"Are you hungry?" he asks.

"No."

He knows I'm lying.

"I don't want to eat."

"Tomorrow, perhaps." He hands me a candleholder, takes one for himself, and then leads me out into a foyer with sweeping dual stairs. Details glimmer from the darkness—chandeliers and crystal sconces. Ornate chairs, and fabric walls swirling with gold thread making elaborate designs. This place must have been grand once, but its glory has faded.

I wonder at its origin. The Smith Cabin is somewhere behind me, in the depths of the forest. It came from me—my life. Is this house Samrael's? From some ancient corner of his life?

"There are plenty of spare rooms on the second floor," Samrael says, stopping at the base of the stairs. "Mine is the first on the left. You can have your pick of the rest. With Sebastian gone, we'll be the only ones here."

"It's just us?" I don't like this arrangement. It's a huge house—it should be alive with other people.

"Sorry to disappoint."

"It's fine. Which room was Bastian's?"

"Turn right at the top. Then it's at the far end on the right."

I don't know what to say to him—*Good night? Thanks for letting me stay in your creepy house?* So I climb the steps without a word, conscious of his attention on me.

I slip into the room at the far end on the right. Inside, I turn the lock. Test the knob. Repeat both steps. Then I look at my new room, which was Bastian's for so many months.

The decor is like the rest of the house. Ornate but tired. Furniture spiraled and claw-footed, as though it could spontaneously animate like everything else in the Rift.

I thought that maybe by taking this room it would feel warmer or more *known* somehow, but it doesn't.

I'm not sure what I expected. It's not like Bas was able to

bring photos from home to personalize this space. There is a guitar in the corner that I'm sure he used while he lived here, but it's an odd-looking one, the body round instead of curved. When I pluck one of the strings, the tinny sound it makes sends a shiver down my spine.

I find a connected bathroom with rudimentary exposed plumbing. A claw-foot tub, of course. But I can't imagine *bathing* here. Or sleeping here. Or spending another minute here.

There's a mirror—and I scare myself with my own reflection. I look savage. Feral. Determined. And wounded.

Back in the bedroom, I push the heavy curtain aside, revealing a window full of night and indistinct shapes. A wall below, I think.

Nothing to see. Not that it's a great mystery.

I know what's out there.

Trees. Harrows. Hauntings.

Gideon.

The orb, stashed in a tree. Far away from here.

I hid it so I wouldn't be tempted to open the portal and run away from this—from here. I need to honor my promise to Bas. I *will* honor it.

And if Bas is wrong and Samrael is still evil to the bone, he won't be able to force me to open the portal. No orb, no exit. He won't leave here unless I'm positive.

The room has a chill, so I move to the fireplace and light the kindling beneath the woodpile. Invest myself in tending to the flames. Bringing them to life.

When it's crackling, I sit on the bed. I remove my jacket and drape it over the chair by the desk. I pull my boots off.

I think I've done all I can—at least for now. For today. For this moment. I slide under the heavy covers and cry as silently as I can.

CHAPTER 34

⇥ GIDEON ⇤

I've been thrown into a dungeon.

It's almost funny.

Actually, no. It's not.

A few hours ago, the Harrows pulled Riot out of the pond. They hoisted me onto another horse, tying me to the saddle. Then they led us both through the woods to a cave that turned into underground tunnels—stone-paved, stone-walled. Tunnels that wove and turned and brought me to this place—an alcove with only one open side, sealed off by corroded iron bars.

I have a mattress made of straw wrapped with worn linen. A bucket for water. Another to function as my bathroom. My hands are manacled in front of me. Even my useless prosthetic, which is kind of hilarious.

Actually, no. Not hilarious.

The only source of light is an oil lamp hanging beside a stone staircase that turns up into the darkness.

I've got a feeling I know who's up there.

My eyes move to the cell across from mine. The Harrows brought Riot here with me. He could barely fit through the corridors. Weak as he was, he kept roaring and trying to smash Harrows against the walls.

"Horse scared," Cotton had said. "Gideon scared."

"No. Horse not scared. Gideon not scared, either," I told him. "Horse and Gideon planning violent actions."

He'd smiled with his razor-sharp teeth. "Cotton like."

"Cotton like Gideon or violent actions?"

"Yes," he'd said. "Cotton like."

Now, my horse is lying on his side, breathing in short huffing breaths. He's in bad shape, but better than he was in the pond.

We'll heal—both of us. My throat's coming back to normal. I can swallow now without much pain even though my voice is still hoarse. And my leg already feels more bearable. We just need a few days. Four or five and I should be healthy again, if I'm not killed before then.

I shut my eyes and listen to Riot's breathing. Willing strength back into him. Feeling him doing the same for me.

I wonder about Daryn.

What she's doing. If she's okay. Whether she's thinking about me.

Whether she'll fall for Samrael's lies.

CHAPTER 35

⟶ DARYN ⟵

Today, I'm taking charge.

I'm going to deal with Samrael fairly. If it's right for him to leave, I'll let him out. But he's not getting out until I find Gideon.

He knows these woods. He can help me scour every inch of them. If he's truly found any form of compassion, goodness, or altruism, he'll step up.

With a plan in mind, I pull on my boots and jacket, and leave in search of him.

I find him in the kitchen with two people.

People, not Harrows. Not vacuous impostors from hauntings. A man and a woman, both about fifty years old, with friendly faces that settle on me in warm curiosity.

"Thought you might sleep all day," says the woman. "I'm Rayna, and this is Torin. We do most of the cooking round here. If there's anything you like to eat or don't like, let us know and we'll take care of it for you."

"Don't make grand promises you can't keep, Rayna," says Torin.

"Course not," she says, sending him a little annoyed glance. "We'll aim to satisfy you, within our limitations. Doubt we'll prepare food like you'll be used to, where you've come from. We're simpler, I'm guessing. But we'll do our best."

She continues, informing me of other people around the house who handle washing and cleaning, everyone playing a role in keeping the compound running, with Torin interjecting often to correct or elaborate.

As they give me the lay of the land, two gangly young men pass the kitchen carrying bundles of firewood. They're introduced. I say hello and speak when I'm spoken to, and try to listen when I should, but this situation is so unreal.

How did these people get in here? Like Bas, did they get sucked into the Rift?

And why do they seem so . . . *content* with being here?

Samrael is smiling at me. He's obviously entertained by my apparent confusion—and that only distracts me more.

"I think that's enough for now, Rayna. Torin. Thank you," he says.

They excuse themselves, and suddenly I'm alone with Samrael. Silence settles thickly over us. He drums slender fingers on the wooden table.

"Do you have any particular way you'd like to do this?"

"No." I shake my head. "Do you?"

He lifts his shoulders. "I thought perhaps I'd show you around, then we can eat outside. We can talk along the way about how we'll search for Gideon and . . . any other items we might want to cover. How does that sound?"

Even though he helped me yesterday, my initial reaction is distrust. Borderline revulsion.

You already made the decision, Daryn. Give him a chance. I need to find Gideon. And . . . I need food. My empty stomach is begging to be filled. Food needs to happen. "That sounds fine."

Samrael smiles. "Great." He lifts a linen bag off the table and slings it over his shoulder.

We leave the kitchen, exiting through a side door that passes through a neatly kept garden outside, with rows of planters overflowing with vegetables, lettuce, and herbs. I'm modestly cheered by it; it's a much brighter place than the inside of the house.

As we follow the path, I gain enough distance to get my first look at the structure where I slept the night. It's a gray stone mass, solid and squat, with deeply recessed beveled windows with diamond panes. Gray Fort is well named, more a fort than a home. The roofline is crenellated and I half expect archers to peer over.

Archery reminds me of Jode, which reminds me of Marcus, Bas, Gideon—and I realize I'm grimacing when Samrael smiles, looking from me to the house.

"Not much to look at, is it? It was the height of fashion once." He squints at the dark clouds. "We may get rained on. Do you want to stay here? We could try again later."

"No." Being stuck in a storm sounds more appealing than being stuck in that somber house. "I don't mind rain. Let's go."

Samrael leads the way, taking a trail that circles the crown of the hill where Gray Fort and its small keep perch. We pass stables. Animal pens. Gardens. Cottages and orchards.

The feeling of the place is quaint, pastoral, but also slightly sad.

It could be that my mood or the weather is affecting my perception. But I don't think it is.

Along the way, I meet several other people. A young couple with their son and daughter. Two elderly women, portly and kind-faced, mending a chicken coop with hammer and nail. A tall man driving a plow hitched to a dun-colored ox. The people are friendly, but faintly distant, too. A little mild, or muted, or faded—or all. An impression forms in my mind of simplicity, just like Rayna said. The only real objective seems to be the production of food.

I think of Maia, who instantly gave me an impression of capability, toughness, and humor. Cordero, who was so pushy right off the bat. Low, singing his twangy country songs and smiling mischievously, like he was constantly pranking people in his mind. Ben, who always tripped all over himself in his rush to be helpful.

It seems right that when you meet someone, you should feel something right away. Feel *anything* right away.

I don't for these curious Rifters. I feel nothing. Only curiosity *because* I feel nothing.

"Care to share your thoughts?" Samrael asks.

Surprisingly, I do care to. "The people we've seen—where did they come from?"

"They've been here a very long time and every one of them has a different story, but I can tell you that none came willingly."

"So do they want to leave, too?"

"Actually, no. Not a single one, in fact. They've abandoned their former selves. You could say they've given up—or accepted their new existence. If you're here long enough, you become comfortable with this. Anything else would be overwhelming. This is what they've shared with me."

"You haven't accepted this, though."

He looks at me. "No. As I told you, I have hope. I want to find the people I've hurt and make my apologies. It's not in me to give in."

"About that . . ."

"You think Gideon is still out there."

"Yes. And I need help. I need to keep searching for him. He's out there. I know he is."

"Do you see this wall?" he says as we round a bend in the trail. A high fieldstone wall comes into view, topped with wicked iron barbs, long, rusted, and twisting in all directions. "That's how we keep them out. That's how we stay safe in here. It circles the entire settlement."

"Samrael, I realize—"

"Please. Call me Rael. I prefer it. It's what Bas called me. It reminds me of a new beginning."

Yeah, right. Like I'm calling him that. "Is that how you think of what you're after? A new beginning?"

"It is."

"We'll see."

I see a flash of surprise on his face as he stops. He laughs softly. Then he catches up in a few strides. "Daryn, what you're asking is extremely dangerous—I'm sure you know that. But I'll help you find Gideon."

I'm the one who stops now. "You will?"

"Yes. I've already started evaluating the resources we can spare toward the effort. Horses, weapons. People. I'll have a search plan ready by this afternoon. I want to be helpful."

A pang of guilt hits me as I remember hiding the orb. Not trusting him. "Thank you," I say. I mean it.

The trail slopes downhill, but my mood begins to lift. My lungs feel open as I breathe the damp stormy air. With every step, stress and fear feel farther away and I feel better. I've found help. An ally. I'm on a path to finding Gideon.

Hang on, I tell him, looking across the woods that seem to go on endlessly. *I'm coming for you.*

We reach a creek that gradually broadens into a stream, crystalline water flowing over smooth stones. Following it, we arrive at a glade with a clear pool.

At the far end, there's open sky above the water, and I hear the rushing sound of a waterfall. On the opposite bank, patches of Mom's begonias cluster together under the shade of the trees. Good sign. Right track.

"Let's stop here," Samrael says. I'm surprised at how comfortable I've been in his company during our walk. "We're at the edge of our protected land." He tips his chin. "There's a sheer drop not far ahead that provides a natural defense." He drops the linen sack on the scrubby grass and sits. "We've been lucky. No rain yet."

"Right. Lucky."

He smiles. I sit a few feet away and watch as he unpacks the linen bag.

"Torin packed this, not Rayna, so who knows what we'll find."

"Eye of newt and toe of frog," I mutter.

"Wool of bat and tongue of dog." He smiles, waiting for me to pick up the next verse.

"Sorry. That's all I know."

He props his arms on his knees. "'Adder's fork and blind worm's sting,'" he continues, affecting a macabre tone, "'lizard's leg and howlet's wing, for a charm of powerful trouble, like a hell-broth, boil and bubble.'"

"Yum. Breakfast of champions. Is howlet an owl?"

"It is indeed."

"And blind worm must be a snake?"

"No. Blind worms are lizards with no legs."

"That makes sense. That's why those were added separately—the lizard legs."

"No respectable brew is complete without them."

"There should be some soft ingredients in there for flavor balance, like butterfly wings and dove's feathers."

His eyebrows rise. "You'd eat butterfly wings?"

"Never. I don't know why I said that. I *love* butterflies."

"A symbol of rebirth and resurrection, I might add."

"Subtle, Samrael. Real subtle." I catch myself smiling. But if he's good—if he's really changed—then smiling is fine. Right?

"This place likes you," he says.

That makes me laugh. "Yeah, I'm sure it loves me. That's why all these terrible things keep happening to me."

"Look," he says, tipping his chin.

Across the pool, the white flowers are shimmering. I remember this; it's familiar from the first time I saw Mom. And from when she disappeared, washed away by the flowers.

As I watch, the patches of flowers lift off the bank and take flight. It takes me a moment to see that they've formed a cloud of white butterflies. My heart climbs into my throat as they lift over the trees and circle in the dark sky, bright spots against the heavy clouds, eventually disappearing.

Long moments pass before I feel composed enough to speak. "Butterflies should be symbols of hope, too."

"I agree," Samrael says. "You said terrible things have happened to you?"

I shake my head, thinking of the hauntings. "Not just to me. And not all of it has been terrible." I think of seeing the red canoe. Mom's couch. The begonias.

"We don't have to talk about it. I know what it's like here. It's one of the reasons why I want to leave." I must smirk or make some sort of face, because he says, "Did I say something wrong?"

"No. It's just that when you said that, I realized something. As much as I don't like it here, wanting to leave isn't the strongest thing I feel. What's stronger for me is . . . wanting to be somewhere else. That probably doesn't make any sense."

"It's starting to. Tell me more."

Once again, distrust rears inside me like internal brakes. But this time, I can't help wondering: Do I feel this because he's a demon? Or is it just *me*? Is it my tendency to retreat, shut down, close up? "Well, it's more about the things I've been missing."

"Which are?"

Answer, Daryn.

Why not? What do I stand to lose?

"I miss hearing my sister laugh. I miss the hugs my mom gave me every morning, without fail. I miss having long conversations with my dad about my future, even though we never agreed. I miss Isabel, my friend. I miss Shadow. I miss school, driving a car, making milkshakes. It probably sounds stupid to you—such insignificant things. But I've denied myself them for a long time. So, that's why I want to leave. So I can do all the insignificant little things that make life awesome."

I instantly feel ridiculous. It has to be the worst meaning-of-life statement ever made. And I can't look at Samrael anymore, either. "Please stop looking at me like I'm an unsolvable riddle."

He shakes his head, saying nothing, but his gaze has turned serious. I have the strange feeling that what I've said has affected him—my silly little speech.

We eat in silence that feels oddly companionable as the dark clouds rumble over us in the sky. When we're finished, he hops to his feet. "Come. I want to show you something."

I stand, following him as he picks his way along the bank toward the waterfall on the far end of the pond. A light mist has begun to fall, making the river rocks slippery beneath the soles of my boots.

We're almost there when Samrael wobbles in front of me. His arms shoot out for balance, but his foot slides and he goes in, landing with a splash in knee-deep water. He seems so surprised by his own clumsiness that I laugh.

He looks up, smiling ruefully. "Really? Is that how it is?"

"That's how it is."

He sets his other foot into the water. "No sense trying to stay dry now."

His progress wading through the water is faster and smoother. And the mist is turning into rain, so I'll be getting soaked anyway. In about five seconds I'm convinced.

I step into the water, too.

The cool seeps into my boots and pants, chilling my skin. It feels real and exhilarating. By the time we reach the edge of the pool where the drop begins, my heart is thumping with adrenaline.

I peer over the side and my stomach does a flip. We're much higher in elevation than I expected. So high up, the woods below look like a blanket rolling out into the distance. Vast tracts are brown, marring the green like stains, and I remember the areas we passed where the trees were burnt.

There's a lot more of this kind of fire damage than I'd have guessed. Half of what I see. It spreads into the distance and encroaches on the hill where I stand. I think of Gideon. Whether he's seeing any of this up close.

"It's dying," Rael says beside me.

Rael. Did I just think of him as *Rael*?

"Some sort of blight," he adds.

"It's from fire, isn't it, Samrael? I've seen it up close. The trees are burnt."

"Yes. Scorched, but from the inside. There's no warning. It affects tracts of land at random. I'll wake to learn that acres have been destroyed. It'll reach us here eventually. This entire place will be gone. Soon, if the pace maintains. It'll ruin our crops, our gardens . . ."

"Everything," I say. "Everything will eventually be lost."

He nods.

My stomach turns again. I haven't loved it here—but to think of the Rift's total annihilation? It's chilling. "The people I just met—you said they wanted to stay. They're all right with that? They'll just accept starvation?"

"I can't make decisions for them." He turns his gaze away, staring out into the distance. "And I've lost feeling in my feet."

I smile. "So have I. I'm freezing."

"Let's go?"

Before I can reply, the clouds break and rain comes down in great, heavy waves. We run back. After a few steps, a bubble of laughter rises in my throat. Running through knee-high water feels ridiculously slow and goofy. When I look at Rael and see him grinning, I can't hold it in any longer. We look like we're running in slow motion.

We're both laughing and completely soaked by the time we reach the bank.

"Shelter here or run back?" he asks, water pouring down his face. He looks younger with his hair slicked to his head, his cheeks leaner, more sculpted. His build looks rangier.

"Run back," I answer. We take off, like a starting gun just fired, snatching up our things and sprinting back up the trail.

It's a slog. Muddy and slippery. The creek swells with water and overflows, flooding parts of the trail and forcing us to leapfrog in places. It reminds me of running track, timing my steps, launching over hurdles. My body and the terrain become my entire focus.

As we reach the big stone house and barrel into the vacuous foyer, I'm blissfully mindless. We stand inside the lamp-lit gloom, dripping and out of breath. Both of us smiling. I feel more carefree than I have in a long time.

I think he feels the same.

Then I remember that Gideon is out there in the woods.

Alone, and in danger.

CHAPTER 36

⊸ GIDEON ⊸

Finally, what I've been waiting for.

A visit with my top worst favorite enemy, Samrael.

He takes his time coming down the stairs and checks Riot's cell first.

Riot's still weak, but standing. He snorts when he sees Samrael, and the two of them have a nice little stare-down.

"Hello, Gideon," Samrael says, coming over to me. "How's your leg?"

Better. Seventy percent, I think. But like I'm telling him that.

"I'm supposed to be planning a search for you right now," he says. His eyebrows rise. "Found you."

"Where's Daryn?"

"Upstairs. She's convinced you're out there," he says, waving a hand toward the network of tunnels. "And she's worried about you, naturally. But she's fine. Unharmed." He pauses. "Is that what you want to hear?"

Of course it is. Even more, I want to believe it.

"We're off to a good start," he continues. "I think I'll have her full trust soon."

"If you hurt her—"

"I won't. I promise you. I like her, Gideon. She's a mystery to me, you know. Unlike you."

I feel myself brace. Waiting for him to get into my head.

"Besides," he continues. "Harming her would be foolish. It wouldn't get me out of here."

"You're never leaving."

"I will, Gideon. I'm ready. I've been ready. I've spent long months waiting for her to show up. The gatekeeper. My ticket out of here, as they say. I've been trapped without her—that wasn't supposed to happen. Ra'om had planned to bring her in here, knowing we needed her to come and go. But Bas's heroic actions were unexpected. Quite a few unfortunate surprises that day, don't you think? Neither one of us ended up with things the way we wanted them."

Thinking about Daryn in here for the past eight months almost makes me shudder. "Is that why you kept Bas alive? To use him as a lure? He was bait, wasn't he?"

"Yes. But I genuinely grew to like Sebastian. We became good friends."

"You think so?" I laugh. "Bas has no idea what you really are. Did he know the Harrows are yours?"

"No, and neither will Daryn. Only you know."

"Lucky me. Do you control them like Ra'om controlled you? Through torture? You were nothing but Ra'om's—"

"Careful." He finally does what I've been dreading and moves into my mind. It's a familiar feeling. Painful. Like fingers walking around my eyes, then slipping inside and prodding at my brain. He put me through this repeatedly in the fall.

"Those were good times we had, weren't they? In Rome? In California?" he asks, lining up with my thoughts. Then he withdraws from my head. Fast, like a hook releasing.

I need a few seconds to shake the edge of darkness he left behind and get full control of my own head again. "How did you keep all of this from Bas?"

"He was very ill for the first six weeks. Unconscious. Then delirious with fever. It gave me time to understand my power here. By the time he was healthy, I had arranged things the way I wanted. I had a plan. I knew having him on my side would be imperative to gaining Daryn's trust."

"You lied to him for eight months."

"I didn't enjoy it, but I had to. For a time, I thought about turning him. Bringing him to heel, so to speak. But it would've killed Sebastian. Not everyone is strong enough to hold darkness inside them." He pauses. "You could do it."

"Is this your sales pitch again? I love this."

"Think of it, Gideon. All the guilt and remorse you struggle with, going away. Violence, even if it's for good, is still violence. How do you reconcile that? How do you live with guilt? If you joined me, that would end. You'd never need to ask those questions again. We could be brothers. Can you imagine it?"

"Sure can. It looks like hell."

"Your insolence is another thing I like about you."

"You think fighting feeds me? That violence is something I *enjoy*?" I shake my head. "You're evil."

"Is that what you think evil is? The desire to do harm to another? If so, then I imagine you're feeling evil right now."

I can't argue with that.

"That reminds me . . . I've wanted to talk to you about your hand. I owe you a debt for what I've done. Someday I'll repay it."

"Your death would settle it."

"That's not an option."

"Then I don't want anything from you."

"I can't say the same."

The pressure around my eyes starts again. I feel him enter my head and plunge deep this time. Deep enough to sift through my memories.

Images blur before me—not under my power.

Samrael takes me to when I first saw Daryn in Wyoming at the Smith Cabin, after all those months away from her. I'm transported back to how I felt. Standing on the porch during that rainstorm. Watching her walk up. Telling myself not to fall for her again. I was so sure I could keep my distance.

How wrong you were.

Samrael's voice echoes in my thoughts.

My memory lurches forward, blurring again, and then crystallizing. I'm in Nevada now. Seeing the moment in the trailer when Daryn and I were all over each other. *Feeling* that moment.

I can see how she changed your mind.

That's not—it's not—

Ah, there it is. A reaction. She is such a weakness in your armor. Too easy, Gideon. Between her and your horse, much too easy. First lesson I'd teach you if I were your mentor: Never care more than you can withstand to suffer.

We blur forward again to the time Daryn and I talked about her parents after the haunting where she saw her mother on the roof of the bungalow.

I relive it fully, my surroundings dropping away. I hear myself telling Daryn that her parents abandoned her. That she was a kid who needed them. I see how it affects her all over again. Then I'm back in my skin and the pressure goes away.

"Interesting," Samrael says. "She fears abandonment. Perhaps it's why she shows such extraordinary determination not to give up on you. Thank you, Gideon. It'll be helpful."

He turns and walks away.

"*Wait.*"

He stops.

"You're mining me for information on her." I don't even ask; I know it's what he's doing. Because she's a Seeker, he can't see into her mind, so he's going through me. "You're going to use what you stole out of my head to get close to her. To win her trust, so she'll let you out of here."

"To be honest with you, I don't think I need your help. I

feel a connection with her. A kinship." He smiles at his own words; then he reaches into his pocket and removes the orb. He holds it up like he's examining it. "But I'm not going to take any chances."

CHAPTER 37

— DARYN —

Daryn?" Rael says. "I'm sorry, but it's getting late. We need to go back before the Harrows begin to stir."

I rein in the gray mare I've borrowed. A dozen riders stop around me—Rifters whose names I'm just beginning to sort out. Who have given up their day and put themselves at risk to search for Gideon.

We've spent *hours* riding, and we haven't seen anything except stupid white flowers and trees, trees, and more trees.

The disappointment is too much. To my horror, my eyes fill. I dismount and stride away before I embarrass myself.

"Go on ahead, Dunnett," Rael says behind me. "We'll catch up."

The hoofbeats recede as the posse rides back to Gray Fort. My disappointment fades away as I draw deep breaths, but I don't find calm. I find anger.

"No pep talk?" I ask without turning to face Rael. "I'm a little disappointed." My words are bitter, but I'm so tired of searching and searching and being let down.

"I was trying to give you some space, but if you'd like encouragement, I might be able to help." There's a quiet thud as he hops down from the saddle. "Would you?"

"Like encouragement?" I turn to face him, and he stops in his tracks. "Sure. Why not?"

"Okay. First, let me be sure I understand: you're discouraged because our search hasn't been successful yet, correct?"

"What kind of Seeker never finds?"

Rael stands perfectly still, regarding me with an unblinking stare. "I think 'never' may be a slight exaggeration."

I roll my eyes. I know I'm exaggerating, but being called out on it isn't exactly making me feel any better.

"All right," he says. "Bear with me as I share a small story with you." He exhales quietly and at length. "Roughly a year ago, I was in Rio de Janeiro, in one of the favelas there—the shantytowns that climb the mountains around the city. They're ramshackle settlements, the houses stacked one atop another like beehives. Poverty, crime, and hunger thrive in them. That is what had drawn me and the other Kindred.

"I had spent the previous night with them inspiring fear and inciting violence. These were the things I did then, the things that once fed me and that I must atone for.

"At dawn, with the night's chaos completed, I sat on a rock ledge overlooking the favela, the city lights and the bay spreading below me.

"As I waited for the sun to rise, I had so much anger in my heart I wondered if I might poison myself with my own hatred. I hated what I did and what I was, but I still persisted. I couldn't make myself stop. Even if I'd had the strength of will, Ra'om would've persuaded me to continue in ways so vile and painful, I sincerely hope they're beyond your imagination.

"The sun rose and it didn't assuage the horror inside me, as I'd hoped. I still felt it, destroying my soul. But then I saw a flash of sunlight in the street below me. It reflected off the golden hair of the girl who stands before me now. You, Daryn. You were there."

My breath catches with surprise. I have only been to Brazil once, but I remember it perfectly. And I can't believe that *Rael* was there. "You *saw* me?"

"Yes. You came up a dirt alley, and then dipped below a roof where I lost sight of you for a moment. Then you emerged again holding a small child at your hip. For a moment I thought you were a kidnapper. But I've seen this type of human, and though they take every shape, it didn't seem right. Perhaps that's why I followed you. Perhaps it's why I tried delving into your mind. I couldn't do it. And at that moment, of course, I knew you were a Seeker.

"In truth, I debated putting an end to your life. Daryn—I say this because I want you to know the full extent of what I was. Fueled by fear and hatred. But, for reasons that are beyond me, I did not. I followed you instead.

"You took the little girl to a cafe. There were dried tracks of tears on her grimy face. She did not speak English, and you did not speak Portuguese, but as I recall, you both spoke the language of sweets. You bought her some kind of fruit tart. Then some kind of pastry dusted with sugar. Then some kind of fried dough concoction. You wiped the girl's mouth with a napkin and smiled at her. You played a game, having her guess which of your hands held a coin. Very soon, perhaps partly because of the extreme quantities of sugar flooding her very small system, she was belly laughing. When you were finished, you took her right back to where you found her and, in that instant, on that little girl's face, I saw pure and unbridled happiness."

"She was precious. I remember her, too. I fell in love with her in that hour. Why are you telling me this?"

"You gave her more than a moment of happiness that day—you gave her hope that she could carry as long as she wished. Perhaps I'm wrong, but . . . Seeking is as much about keeping hope as it is about finding. Giving hope, sustaining it—what Seeking could be done without that? You gave that little girl hope, and you've done so for me as well. So. If you're getting that part right most of the time, which I know you are, then you're a very good Seeker indeed. And," he adds, tipping his head, "we *will* find him."

A massive wave of gratitude sweeps over me and, for an

instant, I glimpse the glory of what he once was. Feeling the impulse to hug him, I step forward before I realize what I'm doing and stop myself.

Rael's back straightens suddenly in surprise. A warm amber light glows behind him, brightening. Huge golden wings unfurl at his back, ten feet high or more. They brush past branches as they open, fanning wide.

Even in the fading daylight, they're brilliant.

Majestic.

Stunning.

The look on Rael's face as he sees them is utter disbelief.

But the wings begin to rain gold feathers as soon as they're fully extended. They flutter down one by one, then by the dozen. In seconds, there's nothing left at his back. The wings are no more than piles of feathers melting into the dirt by his feet, disappearing.

I don't dare say a word.

Silently, we mount up and ride back to Gray Fort.

I glance at him as the last of the day's light leaves the woods.

His face is pale and his eyes are distant.

He was trying to cheer me, but something far more profound just happened to *him*, and I can tell he needs time to absorb its impact.

Rael is shaken to the core.

I'm still thinking about his reaction as I submerge into the bath one last time. The water has been lukewarm for a while and my fingers are shriveled, but I feel reinvigorated. If Rael is right and Seeking is about keeping hope alive, then I can do that. I pull myself out of the tub, dress, and head downstairs.

The sound of conversation leads me to the kitchen. I find Rayna and Torin busy with food preparation. Rael is in there, too. Sitting at the farm table at the center of the room as he talks to them. I hear Sebastian's name from his lips, his voice jovial, like he's reminiscing about his friend, but he falls silent when he sees me.

He breaks into a smile. He's himself again: casually elegant, composed. No trace of the shaken Rael from earlier.

"There you are," he says, standing. "Is this all right? I thought we could eat here. It's more comfortable than the formal dining room."

He's changed into gray slacks and a loose black button-down. He's also bathed—and he looks . . . handsome. I immediately feel stupid for thinking so. First, it's irrelevant. And second, now I feel ridiculous for wearing the same clothes I've worn for a week—and coming down here with wet hair piled in a top knot.

"Of course. This is fine."

He pulls out my chair for me and sits across from me.

"Just about ready," Rayna calls over her shoulder.

"This is going to sound odd, but I feel like I haven't seen you in ages," Rael says. His fingers tap on the stem of a wineglass and I'm reminded of how ancient he is. Maybe *ages* isn't an exaggeration to him. He must think I'm so young—a child.

"I know. I feel the same way." We've spent a lot of time together over the past three days. Searching for Gideon. Touring Gray Fort. Talking. His company is beginning to feel normal. The time we spent apart just now somehow felt much longer than a couple of hours. That reminds me. "Thank you for trying to find Gideon today. I didn't get a chance to thank you earlier."

"Of course. I'm sorry we didn't find him, but we'll try again tomorrow."

I nod. "That sounds good." All I see are echoes of those golden wings spreading behind him. Had he seen a glimpse of what his future might look like if I let him leave the Rift? Had he seen his "new beginning"?

Rayna lifts a steaming pot off the stove and rushes toward the garden door. "The door, Torin. The door, the door, the door."

We both stop to watch them—two people working as a single entity. One commanding, the other obeying. It's so innocuous. Just part of how they operate. But I think of what Rael's told me about Ra'om. Another command-and-obey duo—but not at all as innocent.

"Do you miss the Kindred?" I ask.

"No."

"None of them?"

"Not at all. We weren't friends, Daryn," he says simply. "We were united by our weakness. I don't miss that. Do you miss home?"

"Yes. Terribly."

"What is that like? Terrible missing?"

"It's always with you. It never leaves you." *It's what I feel for Gideon, too.* "Haven't you ever felt that?"

"Not for a person. I feel it for my wings."

I nod, understanding. That's what I saw on his face earlier, exactly. Terrible missing.

We sit in comfortable silence for a moment.

Rayna returns with the now-empty pot. Torin, as usual, trails behind her. "Torin, the pie's going to burn. The pie, the pie, the pie," she says.

"He hears better when you say things in threes," Rael says dryly.

"I do not, Rael," Torin says. He hustles past Rayna to take the pie plate out of the wood-burning oven. It's not burnt. The crust looks golden and crispy.

Rayne slices portions of the chicken pie for us with industrious movements. Everything is a task here. Something to be done that needs to be done again the next day. I'm starting to see why Rael and Bas became so close. Bas, with all his fun and stories, would've provided sorely needed levity.

Steam breaks through the crust of the pie, and the aromas in the kitchen become even more mouthwatering.

As Rael and I eat, Rayna continues to whirl around the kitchen, prepping tomorrow's meals and ordering Torin around.

Rael smiles at me across the table. "Dinner and entertainment," he says.

"I like it, like it, like it," I say.

He grins. "You would have loved Sebastian's take on them."

"I was just thinking about that. And I *will* love it. I'll ask him about it when I see him again."

Rael nods. "You should." His gaze drops to his food, the unspoken question looming loudly between us.

Will *he* see Bas again?

I feel my face warm, and my stomach tightens. I set my fork down, the significance of my role hitting me again.

Is he forgivable?

If I'm going to do this, I need to understand better. I need to know more.

I wait until Rayna and Torin excuse themselves for the night. With them gone, the kitchen feels especially quiet. Rael slides his plate away. His expression goes from content to prepared, like he knows what's coming. I feel it, too. Like I'm rolling up my sleeves and getting down to work.

"What made you decide to change?" I ask. "Besides curiosity over Bas?"

He doesn't reply for a long moment. "Do you mind if we walk? I could use some air."

"Great idea." I could use some air, too.

We leave through the garden door and take the path toward the stables. The cool air holds the smell of freshly turned soil. There's no storm tonight or even any clouds, just stars.

The quiet woods surrounding Gray Fort.

Harrows.

And Gideon—and Riot.

We walk in silence for a while. Again, I notice how easy it is to be with him. That has to count for something. Gut feeling.

Suddenly, I see a vivid image of Gideon's left arm in my mind. The neat scars on his strong wrist that I kissed not too long ago.

Rael did that.

No. Samrael *did that.*

And he's done much worse to other people.

Do I ask him how many people he's killed?

Does it matter?

I saw several with my own eyes in the fall—isn't knowing that much enough?

"I suppose regret is a good place to begin," Rael says, interrupting my anxiety spiral. He slips his hands into his pocket, and our pace slows. We're near the stables now. The paddock, which reminds me of Shadow. "Time feels like it stands still here—maybe you haven't felt that yet. It took a few weeks before I truly felt like I was stuck. Cursed to repeat virtually the same day over and over. This . . ." He waves a hand. "It's not for me.

"I began to feel like I was mired in time, unable to take a step forward. No future ahead. So, I began to look at my past. I considered how I'd spent my days. All my thousands upon thousands of days. I thought about every one of them. Earnestly. I considered my insatiable appetite for power. My service to Ra'om. My lack of regard for life or consequence, and . . . I was sickened by myself. This place held a mirror to me and I did not like what I saw."

"So you want to change the man in the mirror."

He smiles. "Yes."

"How?"

"How?"

"Yes. How are you going to change? If you leave here what are you going to do? What do you want from a fresh start?"

"I . . . I think . . ." He looks lost. He looks like he's genuinely never been asked that question in his entire immortal life. "You ask hard questions."

"You're asking a lot of me."

"Yes. I am." He draws a deep breath, looking up at the stars. "I think I'd seek what you have." He looks at me. "I know I would."

"What do *I* have that you want?"

"The thing that binds you to friends. The thing that calls you home to your family. That's kept you here, strong, hopeful, and determined."

Easy answer. "You mean love."

"Not just love. Love that is greater."

"Greater than?"

"All else."

CHAPTER 38

‑ GIDEON ‑

Is it night yet?" I ask the man who brings me a bowl of watered-down broth. I'm starving. I'm not getting enough food that I can keep down. Rifters don't understand celiac disease.

"Soon," he answers. "An hour or so."

Cotton is gone.

Torin has taken his place.

Torin is human, which should be an upgrade, but Cotton had tons more personality than this guy, who shuffles away without another word, disappearing around a corner.

The past few nights have been brutal. No visits from Samrael. No idea how Daryn is doing.

"At least I've got you," I say, meeting Riot's amber eyes.

Always, Gideon. But I'm ready to get out of here. I'm angry that you're here.

He's showing it, too. His new thing as of a few hours ago has been striking his big hooves against the bars. He sends up sparks when he does it, and the clanging sound is so loud, it's almost blinding.

I rub the raw skin under the manacle on my right hand, pick up the bowl, and drink my dinner.

I've just finished the soup when Samrael comes around the corner.

He stands before my cell, slips his hands into his pockets, and regards me with his emotionless eyes. Behind him, Riot snorts and swipes a hoof, smacking it against the bars.

Samrael cuts a dark look his way.

"I trust you're healing? Feeling better?" he asks.

My leg is better. I can stand now, like Riot, but not for long. And it's still painful. I've got another day to go at least before I'm back in fighting shape.

"You look like you could use more food," Samrael says after a pause, carrying the conversation without me. "I'll talk to Torin about it."

More silence that I don't fill. I'm not happy with the meal plan here. But I'm not thanking him for looking into it.

Something is different about him, but I can't pinpoint what it is.

"Well. Daryn and I have been spending some time together. Searching for you, mostly, but also going on walks and sharing meals. I'm rarely not in her company lately. I think it's safe to say we're becoming close. Relax, Gideon. Not that kind of close. So possessive. But I understand. She is special.

"The knowledge I took from you last time I came to see you? Her abandonment fears, and her fears for her mother's well-being—would you believe I didn't use any of it? We seem to have no trouble relating to one another. Our talks are meaningful. I find myself going on and on when I'm with her. Telling her what I've seen. Where I've been. The truth of what I've done, and . . . she just *listens*." He drops his gaze to the stone floor like he's debating his next words. "She . . . she wants to give me forgiveness. I know for a fact that she does." He looks up, his expression faraway like he's remembering. "She almost makes me believe that my redemption is possible. *Truly* possible."

"It's not."

He smiles. "I've always appreciated your honesty. Come. It's time for a walk." He lifts the key from the hook and unlocks the door. "And before you plot escape or revenge, let me remind you that I have Daryn and Riot both in my care. Now, up. Let's see if that leg has healed."

I push myself to standing and leave my cell for the first time in days.

Revenge is on my mind, front and center, but my hands are bound and my leg is still weak. And I have a useless prosthetic. Now isn't the time. Even when I was completely healthy, I was never able to bring him down.

Samrael makes me walk ahead of him, telling me where to go. As we leave the cluster of cells behind and head into the maze of corridors, I hear Riot smashing his hooves against the bars, making a racket that echoes through the stone tunnels.

After a while, I feel the stress on the bones knitting together in my leg and start to limp. The sound of my uneven stride is too loud, and too telling. Step—*step*. Step—*step*. I fight it, trying to stay even.

"No shame in it," Samrael says. "I'd offer you my hand if I thought you'd—"

"Shut up."

"You know, I regret cutting it off."

"I don't think you do yet, but you will."

He laughs. "Never the quitter. Admirable."

Despite the pain in my leg, it's a relief to be out of the cell, moving. I try to think ahead—where's he taking me? If he wanted me dead, he could've done it in the cell.

By the time we come through a door set into a hillside, my leg is a blaring center of pain and I'm sweating.

Oh, yes. Awesome. We're back in the woods. I was really missing this.

"I think all of the confiding I've been doing has affected me," Samrael says. He gazes at the trees like they mean something to him. "It feels good to finally share the secrets I've been keeping. I feel so understood." He looks at me. "What would you like to see, Gideon? Daryn, probably. I don't even need to get into that dense skull of yours to know that, do I? Daryn it is."

My heart jolts. I look for her, but there's nothing but forest around us. We're the only ones here.

Movement draws my eye to a cluster of rocks. They're rumbling on the ground, bouncing like the earth is shaking. Then they roll and glom together. Mass into a shape that's vaguely human. Then *exactly* human.

Daryn's hair spills out in a flash of gold. Her shoulders form. Her neck and arms. All of her, solidifying. Everything is exact. Her clothing. The way she moves. Even the way she smiles at me.

It's Daryn. It's *her*.

"We've been wondering why the hauntings happen, Gideon," she says. She glances at Samrael. "It's him. He's been searching into your minds. He's found your fears and made them manifest. It's been Samrael all this time. He's been trying to scare you into leaving. He didn't want you here. He only needs me to let him out. And I will. I'm going to release him from this prison. I'm going to go with him. And I'm going to leave you here."

With no warning, she fractures into rocks again. Instantaneously, they tumble to the ground. I stare at them long after they've gone still, rage burning inside me.

Samrael. He was the one who put us through hell. He tried to turn Daryn against me. He tried to mess with Marcus . . . Riot . . .

"Shocked?" he says. "You shouldn't be. You know what I can do when I'm in your mind. My power only transmuted into something greater here—greater, and worse."

The headaches we've had make sense now. It was him, searching through our minds for our weaknesses so he could conjure them into existence.

"There's more, Gideon. Watch."

Three of the trees near us are shaking, their leaves and branches shuddering. A familiar burnt smell flows into my nose, and pressure builds in the air. A splintering sound cracks into the night, stopping my heart, as the bark splits down the center.

Inside, the wood is glowing red. Slender black figures are cocooned within the bark of each tree. They begin to unfold and bend, pulling themselves free. Turning empty eyes toward Samrael like they're awaiting their orders. Because that's exactly what they are doing.

"I'll summon you when I need you," he says, and they scurry off, melting into the darkness.

"What did you just do?" Something sickening just happened—something sinister. I feel it.

"Whenever I conjure something, they're created," Samrael replies. He sounds almost somber. "The larger the haunting, as you call it, the bigger the price. Turning that lake to ice took acreage to create. I can show you sometime. Thousands of trees, gone. Thousands of Harrows, spawned. That's the trade. It's a trade I can't stop . . . it's an addiction.

"You have no idea how it feels to be able to will something into existence, even temporarily. The draw to the power is irresistible. But it's not an endless supply. I've seen the edge of these woods. They end, and there's nothing more beyond them. When I burn through them, there will be no more left. At the end, I'll have created an army that has to destroy, is made for destruction, but has no opponent. No aim. Can you imagine what happens then?"

"Anarchy," I say. "They'll turn on each other. And you. You're destroying yourself."

"Utterly. Now you know why I can't stay here."

"Sucks for you. But you're not going anywhere."

"You wouldn't say that if you could see Daryn and me together."

"Why did you show me this? Do you expect me to be impressed? You want me to congratulate you on creating the evil army you've always wanted? Well congrats, man. You're on your way to world domination. Best of luck with this shit show.

"You know how pathetic you are, right? You do realize you'll lose control of this? Even if you do get out of here with your Harrows, you're never going to be satisfied. You're always just going to be a miserable demon, trying to find meaning in all the wrong ways. You wouldn't know happiness if it stared you in the face, Samrael."

He almost looks confused, or like what I just said actually cut deep. Then he shakes his head like he's coming out of a mental fog.

"I don't care what you think of me," he says defensively. "Now move, rider. I have to get back. I'm meeting Daryn for dinner."

As we retrace our steps through the corridors, I barely notice the aches in my leg. Something keeps nagging at me. By the time I'm back in my cell, I can't stop thinking about it.

"Daryn has seen her mother twice in hauntings," I say as he turns the key, locking me back in. "But I've never met her mother. I have no idea what she looks like, or how she speaks—none of that." I think of the couch and the canoe—other things that we came across that I've never seen before. "There's no way you got that information from me."

Samrael smiles. "Ah, good. You're paying attention. Keep going. You're almost there. If I wasn't the one, then who . . . ?"

"Daryn." The blood in my veins freezes over. "She can do what you can. Conjure things."

"Correct. She's been doing so inadvertently. She did it only yesterday. She gave me back my wings for a moment, and didn't even realize she'd done it. And you'll recall the yellow house? Where your father died? I had something special planned for you. Everyone who matters to you was going to be on that roof. Your father, your mother. Your twin sister. Daryn and your friends. Imagine how you'd have felt, seeing the end of all of them, one by one. Stepping off that roof. Powerful, isn't it? We both know your father's death has haunted you so. But before I could complete my vision, she interfered. She saw your worst fear and, I can only suppose, imagined her own. *Imposed* it. That haunting wasn't only my doing, Gideon. It was ours. Me and Daryn."

"Daryn would never have wanted to see what we saw."

"Of course not. But that's a conscious decision. The subconscious mind is a deep-running current. People are rarely fully aware of their thoughts. But she'll discover the truth eventually. Soon, she'll know about herself. Then she'll put the rest together and know about me. I can't allow that to happen. I need her trust to get out of here. And I need it because . . ." He pauses. "It's become important to me."

"You want her trust, so you're going to keep lying to her? Good approach."

"It's flawed. Believe me, I know it is. If there were an alternative, I'd take it."

"I've got an alternative. Open this gate and I'll show it to you. I can do better than just conjure your death. I can make it real."

He smiles. "Well. I imagine you'll only be more motivated when you see your horse—or I should say, *don't* see him? He was making too much noise, Gideon. I made plans earlier to

CHAPTER 39

⤙ DARYN ⤚

90. *Arriving at a very difficult conclusion, after much thought and consideration.*

I close my journal and set it on the nightstand. Then I sit back against the pillows and watch the last glowing embers in the fireplace.

I believe Rael.

At dinner tonight, we had great conversations again.

He talked openly about his regrets. How he's used people. Manipulated them. Hurt them.

Whenever he tried to stop, Ra'om was there to torture him physically or mentally to keep him in line. But still, it doesn't change the fact that he did *awful* things as a member of the Kindred—and hates himself for every one of them.

My regrets feel so minor by comparison, but I still feel like I have a lot in common with him. How long did I wait to come here for Bas? How much have I regretted that day I lost him? And how could I have left home like I did without telling my family?

We're both trying to find our way back after straying from our paths.

We're both trying to move on from big mistakes.

My mistakes deserve to be forgiven—I have to believe that.

And if I deserve forgiveness, then why shouldn't Samrael?

There isn't a sliding scale for that kind of thing, is there?

I close my eyes, realizing what this means. Maybe I will let him leave the Rift.

I'll retrieve the orb, and maybe I'll let Rael out, but I'll stay here until I find Gideon. I've been going out with the search parties daily. It's only a matter of time before we find him.

I toss and turn in bed, too anxious and worried to sleep. Doubt won't leave my body, and I've grown used to Rael's company. It'll be strange to be here without him. I think I'll miss him.

Finally, after an unsuccessful hour of trying to get myself to settle down, I climb out of bed, deciding to try Mom's trick for sleepless nights. A glass of milk might help me.

I dress, loosely tying the laces of my boots, and slip downstairs.

As I reach the foyer, voices in the kitchen stop me short. Their hushed tones send me instinctively into a corner. I listen, staring at the column of warm light pouring through the kitchen door.

"I'm telling you. He won't eat bread," Torin says.

"How'd he survive before he got here? Size he is, he looks well fed," says Rayna.

"He eats things that aren't bread. Give him more of the roasted chicken."

"Fine. So picky. Am I to slice this for him, too?"

"We ain't givin' a prisoner a knife, Rayna. Besides, even if he had a knife, how's he to cut with that metal hand?"

I slam my hand over my mouth to keep it in. The relief. The shock. The euphoria. Then the sickening, sickening betrayal that crawls through my stomach.

They keep talking, but a shrill sound has risen in my ears.

Gideon is *here*?

A prisoner *here*?

A door whines, and a cool draft sweeps out to me, carrying

the scent of herbs and spices. I instantly recognize that smell. I know where they're going.

Their conversation fades to silence. I don't move. I keep myself pressed against the wall, but a wild strength kicks to life inside me, filling my muscles and mind and heart with singular purpose.

Ten minutes later—every second interminable—Torin and Rayna return to the kitchen. They snuff out the candles, the room falling into darkness in gradations. As they exit for their home through the garden door, they take the last candle with them, leaving the kitchen moonlit and blue.

Finally. I count to twenty and dart through the kitchen, into the storeroom. I lift the door to the cellar an inch at a time to prevent its loud creaking. Then I climb into the darkness, shut the door above me, and immediately start running.

When I came through these corridors, I got an idea of how extensive they are, and I plan to cover every square foot. I have to find Gideon before the sun comes up and someone discovers me missing.

I navigate the turns through sheer faith, racing down steps and turning down corridors. The minutes tick past, but I never slow or feel panicked. Every move I make feels right. At a junction, I go left and come to a series of barred stone alcoves. They're dungeonlike and dismal, and I'm positive this is where I'll find him.

"Gideon?" I lift a lamp off its hook and run to the first one.

He's inside. Sitting on the floor. His arms are crossed over his knees, and his head is bowed.

"Gideon, it's me."

He looks up sharply. Blinks hard, his eyes narrowed at the brightness of the lamplight. He lifts himself up and stands perfectly still for a moment, giving me a long stare like he's not sure I'm real.

"The key," he rasps. "It's on a hook on that wall."

I grab it with trembling hands, open the gate, and fly at him. Joy fills me like a sun, shining inside me. Bright and powerful. "You're alive. You're okay." I kiss his lips, his cheeks, his nose. There's no way to feel enough of him; I will never satisfy my need to touch him.

The chains binding his wrists jangle as he takes my face in his hands. The tears in his eyes almost break me. "I wasn't sure I'd ever see you again."

"I knew I'd see you."

"I couldn't stop thinking about you." He drops his forehead against mine. "I was so worried about you."

"Gideon, we have to get out of here. I hid the orb. We can find it and—"

"Daryn, wait. We can't leave. Samrael has the orb. He has Riot somewhere, too."

The blood drains from my head so fast I sway. "He took the orb?"

"Right after you hid it in the hollow of the tree."

"How—how do you know this?"

"I was there, Daryn. I saw it. There's a lot you don't know. The Harrows are Samrael's. The hauntings are, too. He's doing it all."

The full weight of the betrayal hits me, and it feels like the earth is giving way beneath me. Like the haunting Gideon and I went through when we fell for what seemed like forever.

All of the fruitless search parties and his promises. All of the things he's been confiding in me. All of it is *fake*?

"The Harrows are the consequence of the hauntings," Gideon explains. "Evil creating evil. A cycle of it. He's addicted to the power—but it's finite. He'll self-destruct in time and he knows it."

"That's why he wants to leave."

He nods. "Probably to continue his work with the hordes

he's created. Take the destruction beyond the Rift." He steps back and runs his hand over his mouth. "There's something else, Daryn, and you may not like this, but . . . he said you have the same ability. He called it conjuring. He said you could do it, too. That you've been doing it."

The walls begin to collapse around me. Gideon keeps talking, but I shut my eyes and breathe. I see the flowers, and Mom, and try to think. Try to remember and understand.

Did I will them into being?

Did I make them exist without knowing it?

Suddenly, it's too much.

I rush to the water bucket in the corner and lean over it as my stomach clenches. All of my muscles are shaking. "I can't tell," I gasp. "I can't tell if I'm going to throw up or pass out."

Gideon is beside me, pulling my hair back. Placing a strong grip on my shoulder. "I'm right here. We can handle either one."

I breathe and breathe, pushing back the sobs, the terror. This is the power Samrael covets? I haven't even used it—not at will—and I loathe it. Abhor it.

I want to step out of myself.

I'm so scared—*of myself.*

How is that even possible?

When I'm no longer fighting the urge to be sick, Gideon guides me to the wall and we sit. He lifts his arms. I loop under the chains and rest against him, drawing from his strength.

We're quiet for a while. I shut my eyes and feel the pulsing in my mind—the headache I first noticed in here. I now know what it is—this ability I have in here to conjure. Seconds pass, and I'm afraid to open my eyes. What if I do, and see that I've conjured something into being?

Gideon clears his throat. "Someday I'm going to take you out. We'll do something extremely normal. Like go miniature golfing or bowling." I know he's trying to calm me. To get me to think about better things. Better days. "We'll go to the movies. See comedies and animated films only. Films with catchy songs in them and talking animals . . . Daryn, hey." He waits for me to look at him. "We'll figure this out."

"I know. I think I already know how."

"How?"

"I'll go back and search for the orb inside the house. If you're still here, and nothing changes, Rael won't suspect me. He won't know I've been here. Once I have it, I'll kill him. I'm going to kill Samrael for deceiving me and for hurting you." They're words I never thought I'd hear myself say. Ever.

My fingers start trembling.

"Daryn, don't . . ."

"Don't what? Don't be like you? Don't hate like you do? You wanted this, didn't you? For Samrael to die? Why is it okay for you to want revenge, but not me?"

"I don't want you to get hurt."

"I *am* hurt! He lied to me. And look at what he's done to *you*. He pushed me too far."

He doesn't reply.

And I've been here too long. "I have to go."

I kiss him and slip out from under his arm. He catches my wrist before I leave.

"I love you, Daryn. I want you to know that."

Beautiful words. Amazing. But I never wanted to hear them spoken with such foreboding. With fear behind them.

I bend down and kiss him again. "I'll say it back," I whisper. "I promise. But not here."

CHAPTER 40

– GIDEON –

I've managed to wade in and out of shallow sleep for a couple of hours when I hear footsteps carrying through the corridors. I run through the possibilities. Samrael. Cotton. Torin. Marcus.

Marcus?

I almost don't trust my eyes when he rounds the corner, Bas right behind him.

Marcus zeroes in on me immediately. He sets the scythe against the wall, unhooks the keys, and opens the cell door. He brings the base of the scythe down on my chains, breaking them, finally relieving the pressure on my wrists. Then he hugs me, quick and hard. The look in his eyes is fierce, contemplating the murder of the demon responsible for putting me in here, but Bas won't make eye contact with me.

"You all right to walk out of here?" Marcus asks. "Jode's waiting for us with Riot when we get outside."

"How did you get in here?"

"Later, G. We need to roll."

"Daryn's upstairs."

"I know, man. We'll regroup, then come back for her. Move."

We sprint through the stone heart of the hill. My leg has healed, so I can haul with Bas and Marcus. We're climbing into daylight in minutes.

Jode stands with the horses and Riot bobs his head when

he sees me. I swing up into the saddle and rest my hand on his withers. "You scared me, Riot."

He lights up like a bonfire. *Most of it was an act, but I'm glad to know you care. I do too, Gideon. It's very good to be with you again.*

I almost feel as whole as when we fold.

With Bas leading, we ride.

He takes us to an abandoned stone house with a sagging roof. We bring the horses right inside with us; they almost fill the single room.

Jode dismounts and climbs a wooden ladder to a loft. He sets himself up by a window with most of the glass panes missing, his bow within arm's reach as he stands watch.

Marcus moves to a boarded-up window, propping himself against the sill. Bas paces, his eyes down on the floor. Still no eye contact from him.

I stay with Riot, and lean against him as I listen to the horses settling their breathing.

I think the guys are waiting for me to speak, but I don't want to explain everything again yet—what Samrael can do, and has been doing. Or what Daryn can also do and has been doing.

"How'd you guys get back in without the orb?" I ask.

"Isabel," Marcus says. "She's at base camp. Right after we came in here together, she showed up with the missing piece of the orb—the shard that broke off when Daryn used it the first time. She told Cordero to hold on, that this wasn't over yet."

"She had that piece? And she used it to get you back in?"

Marcus nods. "She can open the portal like Daryn. It's a Seeker thing. I'm not even sure Daryn knew that. But, yeah. The broken piece was enough to get us back here. It's like Isabel knew all along she'd need it. That we'd need it."

"She probably did know."

"Probably."

"How did you know where I was?" I ask.

Bas still hasn't said a word to me. It's like I'm invisible to him.

"Riot," Jode says. "Soon after we came back in, we saw him with some Harrows, and you nowhere to be seen. We got Riot back, and let him lead the way. He came right to the entrance of the tunnels."

I pat Riot's neck. He makes a sound deep in his throat, his eyes glowing in the dim room.

"I'd seen those corridors once before," Bas says. "I'd gone exploring one day when Rael was gone. When I realized you were in there, I could only imagine one reason why." He finally meets my eyes. His expression is tragic. He looks broken up. He looks like he's rethinking his every thought over the past eight months. Like he's wondering how he could've believed a demon over his friends. "He fooled me, Gideon. And you paid the price."

"No, Bas. Don't think for one second this is your fault. No blame, no shame. We stand together and we stand strong. Agreed?"

He drops his head, pressing his fingers to his eyes.

Then he looks up and nods. "Yes. Agreed."

CHAPTER 41

The night is endless.

I pace back and forth in front of the fire in my room. Feeding it until the woodpile is gone. Alternating between soaring emotional highs and crashing lows.

Gideon is alive! He's so close!

But he's imprisoned.

Samrael lied to me!

But now I don't have to make a decision about letting him leave the Rift. Now I know what's right.

I have the power to conjure!

I have the power to conjure.

This revelation sticks with me most, terrifies me most.

I look at the fire and imagine creating Riot.

I look at the bed and imagine creating Mom, sitting against the pillows. I imagine her holding me.

I look at the stool by the desk and imagine, randomly, creating the puppy that must be at home chewing on furniture.

Can I do these things? Call these things into being here?

Have I been?

I think back to every little moment I've spent here and try to connect some sort of willful intention to create on my part, but I can't. I wasn't paying attention to my thoughts—they were just thoughts. I didn't even *think* that my *thinking* might have power.

But I should have.

We knew Rael could break into minds. Why didn't we think he could be behind the hauntings? The Harrows?

As curious as I am, and as strong as the pull is to see if I can manipulate the Rift, shape it into what I want to see, I lock it away.

I am not like Samrael. I had begun to think so. I'd begun to see how we're both fighting to reclaim things we've lost. But I am nothing like him.

As daylight finds all the cracks and parts in the drapes and infiltrates the room, that, at least, I decide. I will not misuse power—power that shouldn't be mine to begin with.

Then I leave my room and head downstairs to meet Rael for the morning walk we planned last night during dinner.

I can't leave until I find the orb.

Which means I have to act like nothing has changed.

But everything has changed.

Everything.

Rael is waiting for me in the foyer. The front door is open, and he's gazing outside at an overcast morning. I wonder if he's contemplating freedom. Or plotting the next move in his nefarious plan.

Or just thinking about the fun we'll have on our walk together because we *have* been having fun. For *days*.

He's easy to talk to. Educated. Intelligent.

Well-traveled. Well-read.

He smiles easily, laughs easily.

He's honest. Polite. Considerate.

Contrite. At least I thought so before I learned the truth. I actually believed he was through with hurting people, deceiving them, and using them for his own personal pursuit of power.

I was so wrong.

He hears me and turns, smiling as I descend the sweeping stairs. His smile vanishes as I come nearer. "Are you all right?"

Unlike Bas and Gideon, I will never be able to act my way out of anything. I've never been able to lie. Easier for me not to say anything. But in this case, I have to. "I didn't sleep well. It's nothing." I head outside before he can ask me about it.

"Sorry to hear that. Daryn, is—Daryn, wait. Please wait."

I turn, and wonder if my anger is burning through my eyes.

"Instead of a walk, I thought I might take you somewhere new. I want to talk to you about something important. I'd hoped to do it somewhere . . . special."

Fear weaves a hot thread through my sternum. I instantly regret not having my knife on me. "Sure."

"This way," he says, and motions me past the kitchen, back upstairs.

I'm painfully aware of his nearness. There's only one explanation for this.

He saw Gideon.

He knows I know everything.

He's going to kill me, or pressure me to open the portal.

Either way, something terrible is coming.

He steps past me on the second floor, and opens the door to one of the unused bedrooms. He walks to the fireplace, and opens a small door set into the wall beside it.

"It leads up to the roof." He holds the door open like a gentleman.

"You first. I don't like cobwebs or spiders."

He smiles. It's a shaky smile and he's looking in my direction but not making eye contact. "Of course. Follow me."

The inside is cramped, and smells of mold and wet stone. There's so little visibility that I bump into Rael's back twice, kick the step in front of me twice, and graze my shoulders against the walls repeatedly.

He swings open a small door and daylight sweeps in like a gust, taking me aback.

We climb out to a narrow ledge framed by a low wall with the crenels I saw days ago. The sky is gray and unsettled.

There's hardly any space up here—barely enough room for two people to stand side by side. Rael plants his hands on the ledge. He gazes at the wooded hills with a look of concentration, like he's working up the nerve to say something.

I have no idea what. And I don't know where my anger went, or why all I feel now is sadness.

He's not who I thought he was. And, I realize, I was beginning to love his triumph. It inspired me. Such a profound transformation. Such a massive positive shift. I was becoming attached to him. I wanted peace for him. Redemption. Happiness.

I step to the edge, and see a sliver of the garden beyond sloping rooflines. Another sliver of the wall, circling the hill. And much farther below, the huge sections of the woods that are blackened and gone.

"I have made a terrible mistake," Rael says. No lead-up. He comes over to me. I feel how close he is, inches away, but I don't look at him. If I do, he'll know. I won't be able to hide what I'm thinking.

You're a liar.

You're evil.

"What mistake?" I ask.

"I have not been honest with you. I—I have to admit, Daryn . . . I didn't believe that anything I could do or say to you would change your view of me. After what I've done, to Gideon, to others, I didn't think you'd be able to offer me another chance."

"I haven't."

"I know. You haven't. But I feel, Daryn . . . I feel that you might. I feel hopeful. And I want to be worthy of that hope.

You've looked at me like I am different. Like I'm better than I was. Like I'm worth something. You've given that to me freely. It means far more than any amount of respect or deference I could ever produce in others by force. So much more. And I want to feel deserving of it. I want to become what I've pretended to be."

In my peripheral vision, I see his extended hand. An offering.

The orb.

He's giving me the orb.

"I took this. The day we went into the Harrows' camp. I knew you placed it into the hollow of the tree, and I took it." He tips his chin. "Please. Take it."

I take it. I hold it in both of my hands like it's a bird that might fly away.

"I have not been honest with you," he repeats, "and this is only the beginning. I have more to tell you. If you choose to hear me, stay. Be here tonight, and I will tell you all of it. *Everything*. If you're gone, I won't fault you. I've wronged you time and again. I only hope there's still some forgiveness left in your heart for me."

He slips past me—but then stops and quickly brushes a kiss on my cheek. "Regardless of what you decide, thank you."

He leaves then, abandoning me to my thoughts. Maybe he thinks the solitude up here will help. The time to consider what he just told me. It won't help.

You're too late, Rael.

I don't believe you anymore.

I count to a hundred, and then head back inside. Down one flight of stairs, then another. Walking almost normally, despite my urge to flee this place immediately.

I don't see Rael anywhere in the house. I don't see anyone— not even Rayna, who's usually in the kitchen at this time, preparing the evening meal. It's unusual, and makes me suspicious, but I don't hesitate or slow down. I head right to the cellar door and heave it open, then plunge inside.

Triumph and relief wing into my chest as I sprint through the corridor toward Gideon's cell. My mind churns through my next steps.

Escape through tunnels. Open portal. Go home.

Turning the last corner, I race to his cell.

It's empty.

He isn't here.

Despair hits me, savagely.

Have I been *abandoned?* Did he leave me behind?

Echoes of past pain roll through me. But it can't be. Gideon would never.

So . . . did Samrael somehow learn that I found Gideon down here? Has he taken Gideon somewhere else?

Has he had Gideon *killed?*

I don't know what to think.

I *can't* think, with fear racing through my mind.

I spin and run back through the corridors. Up to the kitchen. Through the foyer and outside. Churning my legs down the path that follows the creek. Running away from reality, from the miserable unreality of the Rift. I don't stop until I've reached the pool where Rael and I came that first day when it rained.

Tears sting my eyes as I look at the begonias. At how they surround me.

It's been me. I've created them.

Suddenly I want more. Need more. An escape from the despair and loneliness.

I reach for the water, finding it in my mind.

The connection is so strong, so easy to achieve. Like hearing a musical note and adding my own, harmonizing. Then I'm leading the way and creating the melody.

The surface of the water ripples and leaps to life in hundreds of thousands of droplets. They bind together, shaping into butterflies. Butterflies made of water, wings fluttering and shimmering like glass. I make them rise and soar, schooling like fish over the water; I lose myself in their beauty.

Then I have an idea. I bring them together, combining them, and create Shadow—a crystal image of Shadow galloping over the water, her hooves kicking up splashes. I hear myself laugh. It's effortless. Pure delight. Heady, to have so much power. Electrifying.

I bring Shadow to me and reach out, feeling rippling water instead of her silky black coat.

The limit of what I can do is a distant line. I'm nowhere close to it. I could turn this pond into almost anything I can imagine.

But it's not costless. Inside, I feel a darkening, like I'm losing part of myself. Now that I know this power, how will I ever unknow it?

Suddenly, a fear hits me that I'll need it. That I won't be able to resist it.

I make Shadow rear up, sending her front hooves high in the air.

Beautiful, I think.

Terrifying.

CHAPTER 42

— GIDEON —

Dusk, then?" Bas says.

"The light will be to our best advantage," Jode says. "With our horses, the long shadows and slanting rays will provide the best camouflage we're likely to get. It might not make much difference. Then again, it might make all the difference. And if we get in and out quickly enough, we'll have a good chance of avoiding the Harrows. It's our best chance." He looks at me.

I nod. "Agreed."

Bas gives us the layout of Gray Fort, using a piece of charcoal to scratch the floor plan on one of the walls. He makes his best guesses as to where Daryn might be, and the orb. And he describes the single entry point through the wall—a gatehouse with a lone guard.

"What's inside?" I ask him. "We get through the wall, then what will we see?"

"Orchards. Houses. Animal pens. Gardens. But no security. There's nothing. I mean, the wall keeps the Harrows out. That's all we ever worried about."

"Why would you worry if you were Samrael when every threat in this place is under your command?" Jode says.

"Every threat until now," Marcus says with quiet menace.

I look from him to Jode, and then to Bas.

There's no time to absorb that we're together, the four of us. But on some soul-deep level, I feel restored. Now I just need Daryn and a ticket out of this hellhole.

We create a breaching plan and go over contingencies, reviewing everything a few times. By the time we're prepared, there are still a couple of hours before it's time to head out.

Bas offers to take over on lookout in the loft so Jode can take a break. In five minutes, both Jode and Marcus have wedged themselves into empty corners of the room to grab some sleep. I doubt they'll be very successful.

Riot and the other horses have lined up, pressed close. They're resting their heads on the horse beside them, kind of braided together that way. Also in the zone between being asleep and awake.

I sit by the front door. Scratch my jaw. Draw my knees up. For a second, I just appreciate being out of the cell. Away from the bucket and the straw mat I lived with for days.

I look at Riot. He's here. He's all right.

We haven't gotten out of the Rift yet, but we've had some victories.

"I know you don't want to hear regrets," Bas says from above. "But I can't stop thinking . . . how did I miss it? Why couldn't I see what he really is?"

I don't know how to answer him. But I do know what it's like to get fooled.

"Do you know anything about the Gold Rush?" I ask him.

Bas looks down from the loft. "The Gold Rush?" He looks back through the broken shutters. "Yeah. I auditioned for a Western once. I didn't get it. But I learned about it a little. Gold miners. Prospecting. Everyone moving out West in search of riches."

"Yep. That's about it. But, being from California, I had to learn a lot more. In third grade we spent a ton of time on it, learning all about the history. Then we went on a field trip to an old mining town to pan for gold.

"Everybody was pumped up. We wanted to *actually* find gold. Real gold. We were nine, and believed anything was possible. Anyway, I must've panned for an hour under the hot sun, but it felt like I'd been there all day. I got nothing. Rocks. Dirt. I didn't even get interesting trash like some of the other kids. I didn't like that.

"This kid in my class, Luke Miller. He was my best friend, so of course we competed at everything. Luke had pulled a rock from his pan that looked kind of shiny. *Slightly* shiny. But he was going around telling everyone he'd found the mother lode. And I had nothing, so. I got pretty mad."

Bas smiles, still looking outside.

Marcus's laugh is a quiet rumble. He already knows this story.

"But then I went to the gift shop and things turned around for me. There, I saw that, for a mere five bucks, I could get a little glass jar *full* of gold shavings. I slapped my five bucks of spending money on the counter and walked away a much richer man. I thought I'd scored big time. It seemed like such a good deal.

"I ran right over to tell Luke that I was a better prospector than him. I was bragging right back at him, right. Just shamelessly gloating. He took the jar, turned it upside down, and showed me what it said on the bottom.

"'Made in China.' He laughed and explained global commerce to me in this super condescending way. Like, how was it possible I hadn't known any better?"

Bas grins. "What did you do?"

"Nothing. I stood by my counterfeit gold. I acted like I was proud of it. I told him it was better than his stupid rock. Then I went home and cried my heart out."

Bas laughs. "That's so sad."

"Yeah."

"He still has the jar in his room," Marcus says.

I nod. "I do. Right on my dresser."

"You've kept it for ten years?" Jode asks.

"I'd spent five bucks on it. Some of us don't have jars of real gold sitting around."

Jode laughs. "Yes, that's right. I keep my bars stacked by my bedside."

"Anyway, after I was done crying, I told my dad everything. He listened to my story, then he left the room and came back with gold cuff links. He gave one to me and said, 'Here's something that's made of real gold. But one day you'll realize that's only a pretty piece of metal. Real gold is the value of truth. It's friends you respect who respect you back. It's what we have—you and me. That's real gold.'

"He was right. I had all the riches in the world when he was alive. And I still have the cuff link, too. One of them. The other one is buried with him."

It's quiet for a long time. I want to keep talking, but there's a rock lodged in my throat.

Bas breaks the silence. "Okay, I get it. You're saying I should look for real gold. Forget about Rael. Forget about the things that don't have real value."

"No. I was just trying to pass the time by telling you my gold-mining story."

Bas laughs. "I want to see your Chinese gold someday, Gideon. And the cuff link."

"Sure." I'll give him the gold jar.

If we make it out of here, it's his.

We mount up an hour before sunset and ride to the gatehouse.

Bas and I leave our horses with Jode and Marcus about a hundred yards back, and approach the rest of the way on foot.

The guy inside the stone house has a rounded back and the mild smile of a sloth, which he turns on Sebastian. "Hello, Bas," he says. "You're here. Everyone said you left."

Bas smiles back. "I tried," he says. "But I realized after about a week or two away that I missed it here too much, as messed up as this place can be." I casually walk behind the man as Bas talks.

"I could never even try to—"

I grab his wrist and get him into an armlock. He barely struggles, even as I tie him up with rope.

"Sorry," Bas says. "It's safer for you to be out of the way."

The man nods and accepts his situation.

Bas climbs down the ladder and opens the inner latch, pulling the gates open.

Marcus and Jode bring our horses over. We close the gate behind us, mount up, and charge for the main house.

We pass a few smaller homes along the way. Enclosed gardens. Stables. Everything Bas told us to expect.

People stop working in fields and look up. They stand at their front doors and watch us ride past. I get the same vacuous feeling from them, like they can't feel anything in the extreme zones of life, like love and hate. Hope and disappointment.

We reach the house and move as planned. Fast. No hesitation. Jode guards the front. Marcus sweeps through the first floor as Bas and I shoot up the stairs.

Bas rushes into Samrael's room to hunt for the orb. I bust through the other doors in search of Daryn.

As soon as I step into the last room on the right, I know it's hers.

Her journal sits on the bed.

I grab it and stuff it into my belt at my back.

I find Bas in the hallway. "I found this," he says, and tosses my sword at me. I catch it by the grip. "But no orb. It wasn't where I thought it might be."

"Neither was Daryn," I say.

"Time's up," Marcus calls from downstairs.

Bas and I rush back downstairs and head outside, joining him and Jode.

Harrows pour through the open gate in swarms. I don't know who opened it for them—maybe the guard was coerced? It doesn't matter now; there's no undoing it.

The people who gawked at us minutes ago dash for safety, shutting themselves behind doors. Their panic is bizarrely quiet—no yelling for friends or family to take shelter.

The Harrows don't miss any opportunities as they come after us. They're a rabid cluster of fangs and claws, and they don't hesitate to attack anyone in their way.

But the mass of Harrows flows with focus, and an obvious goal, thundering closer.

They're not here to wreak destruction at random.

They're coming for us.

CHAPTER 43

⁓ DARYN ⁓

I'm watching Shadow—the Shadow I've created out of water—when fear touches me like a breath, lifting the hair along my scalp.

My focus breaks. Shadow dissolves back into the pool with a splash.

I know Rael is behind me, but I can't face him. And I hate the smoky scent I smell hanging in the air.

I think of what Gideon told me about conjuring, about what Rael told him was the cost, and realize I've just created Harrows. I've created violent, mindless creatures because I needed a little bit of comfort.

I'm disappointed with myself. Disgusted.

"I wondered what you would create first," Samrael says. "Intentionally, that is. I thought it would be your mother."

I lick my dry lips. "When I see her, I want it to be real."

"I understand."

I whirl around, facing him. "How *could* you? Have you ever told the truth? Ever? Even *once*?"

"Yes," he says. "Today, I told you the truth. Yesterday, I did as well. Tomorrow, I hope to continue to. And the following day. You've changed me, Daryn."

"I don't believe you!"

He winces and looks away, staring off across the water. "I'm very sorry to hear that. I have to admit," he says, "I'm surprised you're still here."

"I wanted to leave. I would have if I'd found Gideon."

I reach into my pocket to touch the orb. "What did you do to him, Rael?"

"I held him captive. It was before, Daryn. Before you gave me hope. I had nothing to do with his disappearance last night. I wanted to explain all of this to you." He reaches for my arm. "Listen, I—"

"I don't want to *listen* to you anymore! I don't trust you!"

"Did you? Before you learned about Gideon? Before you realized I was deceiving you?"

"Yes! Yes, I did! But I don't anymore. You ruined it. You lied to me. You played me for a fool, and you—"

"You're not a fool. You're—"

"But you treated me like one. You disrespected me. Can you understand that? You *hurt* me."

Devastation breaks over his face. His eyes gloss with tears. "Then why are you still here?"

"Because I don't want to believe you're evil. And I don't want to judge you. And I don't want to turn my back on you and wonder for the rest of my life if I was wrong."

"Wrong about what?"

"*You*, Rael. I don't want to take away your future. I don't want to take away your hope. You said it yourself. Part of being a Seeker is hope. Giving it. Protecting it. If I leave you here . . ."

"I would lose it," he says, finishing for me.

As I stare into his tearful green eyes, I wish with everything in me that I could give up on him.

A sound drifts down from the hill and bleeds into the silence. My body recognizes it; my heart leaps and my muscles tense.

It's the howling of the Harrows.

I break into a run. Rael stays right beside me.

As we reach the top of the hill, I see the slashes of light

from Jode's bow first. Then the guys, mounted, fighting against a torrent of Harrows in front of the main house.

I stop, gasping for breath, my legs twitching. The guys shouldn't be here. They couldn't have gotten into the Rift without the orb and my help.

This is a haunting. It's the only possible explanation.

But as soon as Gideon looks over and locks eyes with me, I know it's real.

It's him. It's all of them.

I sprint toward them, drawing notice from several of the monstrous ragged creatures. Three gallop together, pursuing me on my right. Samrael stays behind, no longer with me.

Ahead, Gideon is driving hard in my direction, fighting Harrows as he comes, his sword a line of light. Riot's coat blazes, snaking up Gideon's legs.

Gideon won't reach me—not in time. He's too far, a hundred yards. The three Harrows are much, much closer.

In an instant, I imagine how I would fix this by reaching for the strength inside me. Raising roots from the earth and lashing them at the Harrows like whips to snare them to the ground.

I could stop the Harrows by conjuring. And I could reach Gideon and the guys.

And I have the orb.

We could leave the Rift. Leave this place behind forever.

I could do it so easily.

I could run, and never have to think about Samrael again.

Except I know I'd think about him all the time. I'd go back to living with regret.

I can't do that again.

My legs slow, some ancient part of me knowing the correct path forward before it even enters my consciousness.

I turn and see Rael where I left him. Standing at the edge of the tree line, watching me.

He sees me. He must sense that something has changed, because he begins walking toward me.

"Daryn, no!" Gideon yells behind me. "Don't do it, Daryn! This is what he wants."

Is it?

I don't know. I'm beyond considering the hatred between Gideon and Rael. The friendship between Bas and Rael. I'm beyond grudges, revenge, and lies. Nothing about this has felt right, and I know it's because I've been going about this the wrong way. I've been trying to evaluate and decide something I can't know, or see, or even begin to understand.

Who am *I* to judge Samrael?

Who am I to determine whether he's worthy of forgiveness?

This has to be simpler than that.

It *has* to be.

Isabel's words surface in my thoughts, a seashell revealed by ocean waves.

Evil is its own undoing.

I hear it over and over as Rael draws nearer until he stands before me, tall and still, his stillness amplified by the struggle behind me and the sounds of the guys fighting for their lives.

I stare into his eyes. Stare into the complexity of who he is, full of falseness or truthfulness, or both. Aren't I those things, too? Honest and dishonest? Kind and cruel? Selfless and greedy?

Trust, Isabel told me. *Especially when it's difficult.*

"Tell them to stand down," I tell Rael. "Call the Harrows off."

CHAPTER 44

I'm fighting my way to Daryn, slashing at Harrows with my sword, when the unbelievable happens.

She turns around. To *Samrael*.

And walks in his direction.

"Daryn! Daryn, *no!*"

She glances over her shoulder. There's no uncertainty in her expression. She knows what she's doing.

What's she doing?

Is she going to open the portal for him?

The roaring noise in the clearing lessens noticeably as the Harrows disengage from our battle. They retreat and cluster in groups. In less than a minute, it's nearly quiet and they're crouched together like bats. Watching us. Waiting to be unleashed again.

Without them to fight, my path to Daryn is clear.

I cue Riot and he gives me everything he has, flying toward her. "Daryn, don't!"

She whirls around at the sound of my voice. "Stop!" she yells. "Don't hurt him!" She stands in front of Samrael, her arms wide, using her body to shield him.

I check Riot. Seconds later Marcus, Jode, and Bas thunder up beside me. They look like they want to rip Samrael apart as badly as I do.

"Trust me," Daryn says. "I know what I'm doing."

She's addressing all of us, but her eyes are on me.

If I trust her, I could lose her.

If I don't trust her, I *will* lose her.

She turns to Samrael again. The way he looks at her, with adoration, sickens me.

"After I betrayed you . . . more than once. You're granting me freedom?" he asks. "You're forgiving me? Giving me a chance?"

"No," Daryn says. "You're going to do it." She slips the orb from her jacket pocket and holds it out in front of her.

"Gideon," Marcus says. I feel his desperation to make this stop.

It doesn't stop.

Daryn begins the process of opening the portal. The orb rises from her palm and dissolves, solid becoming light and color that tumbles around us. I wait for it to break into the network of threads that show everything—fields and oceans and stars—but seconds pass with no change. Then the light intensifies, growing brighter, growing heavier. Light that gains power. That passes through me, a gale whipping at the blood inside my veins.

It's a sandstorm of light.

It swallows the stone house in the distance. Then it blots out the clearing with the Harrows lurking along the edges.

Everything washes out.

Samrael and Daryn disappear, eclipsed by the brightness. Even Marcus and Ruin, who are three feet to my left, disappear.

When I can barely see Riot's ears anymore, the white glare slowly begins to recede.

"Gideon, look," Jode says.

The earth beneath us is cracked and bleached—to the dirt that should be there. As the light continues to dim, I no longer see the clearing on the hilltop in the Rift. There's no stone house, or wall in the distance. No Harrows crouched together, waiting to attack.

Night desert stretches out around us.

I know this place. It's the Nevada playa, with the ring of mountains silhouetted in the distance. Above, the sky is loaded with stars. So many stars that they give the night a glow.

It's exactly like the place we left behind, with one difference: this desert is bisected by a barrier.

The threads that have always whirled around us in our crossings are here, but they're pulled straight. They run in parallel lines that vibrate like exposed electrical currents, stretching into the sky and out across the desert as far as I can see, forming a living wall with no vertical or horizontal end.

The world—at least everything I can see—is now divided.

There's my side and the one across the barrier, and they're mirror images.

Daryn stands beside me—but she's across from me too, opposite the barrier.

And so am I.

I see myself on the other side.

I'm right there. So are Jode, and Marcus, and Bas. Our horses.

I keep waiting for this glitch to fix itself, but it doesn't. There's two of everything.

Then I see it: there's only one Samrael.

He stands at the dividing line, looking one way and then the other, his movements setting the threads of the barrier rippling out like waves. "What is this?" he asks.

"It's what you asked for," says Daryn—the one on my side. "You wanted this, Rael. You wanted a chance to prove you're worthy of leaving." She falls quiet and now the other Daryn speaks. "But I won't be the one to decide. It's up to you, Rael. *You* decide your own fate."

It dawns on me: Daryn's doing this.

She created all of this.

Samrael doesn't know where to look. He doesn't know

which Daryn to address. Then I can almost see him decide: *Pick one and stick with it*. He chooses the Daryn on my side.

"I don't understand," he says. "Am I to choose which side is real? Am I supposed to blindly guess which is which?"

"No—I'll tell you. *I'm* real," says the girl beside me. "This side is your freedom. This side is your forgiveness."

"That simple?"

"That simple. Believe me. Trust me. Or don't."

Samrael squares himself to her, to us. He laughs, but it's a bitter sound. Then his eyes move to me. I brace myself, but when he reaches into my head, there's nothing I can do.

Hello, Gideon. I've guessed right, then. She's telling me the truth.

He withdraws just as suddenly. I don't even move a muscle.

He cheated. He peeked at the cards. The Gideon on the conjured side would have no thoughts. He knows I'm real. And, of course, the real Daryn will be on the same side as me.

But she has to have foreseen this, hasn't she?

The smile on his face disappears.

"I know which side is freedom," he says to Daryn. "And I choose against it."

He takes a step backward, away from us.

CHAPTER 45

— DARYN —

Rael takes a step away, choosing not to believe me. Choosing to go back into the Rift.

Something crumbles inside me. I run for him, stopping at the barrier. "Rael!"

We stand on opposite sides, barely two feet apart. I can't hold the porthole open anymore. It's pulling at me, tearing at me. The desert behind Rael melts away. The Gideon and Riot I conjured. Everything I created begins to fade as the Rift returns.

The stone house appears again. The garden. The orchard and the paths that wander all over the hilltop. The Harrows, awaiting their next command.

"You really would have let me go," Rael says.

"Yes. I would have."

His smile holds lifetimes of sorrow.

I don't understand, and the pull to leave the Rift is breaking me. I can't hold this together anymore, the weight of worlds and souls and of the endless, endless sadness I feel for him. "Why are you staying?"

"Because it's better if I do. Better for all of the innocents I'd have harmed."

"You wouldn't have." But I know he's telling me the truth. "So this is self-sacrifice?"

"Atonement," he says. "Perhaps redemption." Rael takes another step backward. "Or perhaps, keeping hope alive. Thank you, Daryn."

"You're *thanking* me?"

He nods, his green eyes glimmering. "For showing me that deserving trust and forgiveness is worth more than having them."

Behind me, Gideon yells for me to come with him, but I can't leave Rael yet. His smile is heartbreaking. *He* is heartbreaking. "Go," he says. "Your life awaits. And, Daryn? I'll miss you. Terribly."

The portal pulls me in, my hold breaking. Brightness flashes, like the snap of a band, and I'm blind for long seconds, caught in a turbulence that reaches into my bones and rattles my ribs together.

Then stillness comes, and I find myself clinging to dusty earth. Holding on to it like I'll be swept out to sea if I let go.

The Nevada desert appears with its black mountain ranges framing the edges of the blue night. I blink at the disorientation, the rush of feeling that's sweeping over me.

A white spot of light sits on the horizon. Our camp. Where Ben will be. Maia, Cordero, and all the others.

The playa is beautiful under the light of a trillion stars.

Gideon is with the guys. They've dismounted and stand together, waiting for me.

I wonder how long I've been here. I wonder if I asked for some time to myself, some space. I think I might have.

There is no more orb. I look for where it should be, hovering in the air before me, but my eyes pull up to the stars. To all the infinite possibilities. Infinite creations.

Rael.

As I think of him, I feel awed and inspired.

If evil is its own undoing, I think, then good can be self-generating.

He did a great and selfless good tonight.

I pull myself to my feet. Gideon walks up and pulls me into a hard hug that lasts and lasts.

He steps back. "What's next?" he asks, with a soft smile.

"I think I'm actually going to stay here a little while longer."

He nods. "Okay."

I watch him rejoin the guys. Then I see Bas swing up behind Jode. Bas lifts a hand, and they ride off toward the beacon light of base camp.

Shadow ambles over to me. Long legs, all grace.

Alone, I feel the toll inside me. I know I won't ever forget Rael. And I won't ever forget the extraordinary power I had for a brief time. But I'm not powerless.

Every second, I choose who I am. I have the power to be hopeful, or trusting, or forgiving. Every second, I can create a Reason.

I pat Shadow's velvety neck, feeling her warmth and her reassuring breaths. "We did it, girl. We brought Bas home." Then I look up to find the star where a fallen angel is suffering. I think I find it.

I must, because I feel hope.

I swing into the saddle and take up the reins. "Okay, girl. Let's go home."

CHAPTER 46

— GIDEON —

W here's Gideon? Has anyone seen Gideon?"

The voice sends a bolt of panic through me. Marcus splits into a grin as I shoot behind the pool house, hopefully out of sight.

Bas laughs, shaking pool water out of his hair. "Dude. Doc Martin *loves* you."

"Yeah, but *why*?" I ask, peering from behind a hedge. "Why does he love me?"

When we planned to have a party at Daryn's place in Connecticut, I was prepared for a lot of different scenarios for dealing with her dad. But not this.

Dr. Martin has literally followed me around all day, from the minute I showed up with the guys at ten this morning. He took me on a tour of the house, then the property. I got an expert-level tour of Daryn's mom's garden. Then he took me to the dock where he keeps his boat. That led to a quick two-hour boat ride around Long Island Sound. This was all while everyone else stayed here at the house, swimming, barbecuing. Having fun.

Doc Martin has asked me seventy-two billion questions about my prosthetic, my family, my goals and dreams for life. We even spent some quality time on celiac. I think at this point he might know me better than Daryn does.

The only upside to all this is that Chief, Dr. Martin's dog, is just as into me. I look down, and the little guy jumps all over my leg, wanting me to pet him. I squat and let him attack-lick me. I'm pretty sure this dog was always meant to be in my life, just like Daryn and the guys. And Riot.

"Dr. Martin is either really smart, and knows how to keep his daughter happy, or . . . your terrific personality won him over."

Jode laughs at his own comment. *Hehehe*.

"Is he close? Should I start running?" I look across the patio. The party is a mix of people I know and people I don't.

Cordero's here. Laughing at something Ben's saying. It's good to see her having fun. For a while there, I wasn't sure I'd ever see that again.

Anna is deep in conversation with Josie, Daryn's sister, but she occasionally looks over at Jode, like she just wants to know where he is. Like Daryn and me. Like Dr. Martin and me, too.

There are family friends of the Martins' here. Some of Josie's college friends and some of Daryn's high school friends.

It's a really diverse mix of people. High-powered doctors going red at the scalp from all the sun. Kids cannonballing into the pool and throwing Frisbees on the lawn. The sun shines and there isn't a cloud in the sky.

Not many days earn the "perfect" label, but this one does. Easy.

Even though Low isn't here. And even though Mom couldn't make it out.

It'll happen someday.

For now, this is more than enough.

Maia comes over, wedging a lime into her beer bottle. "I need a Foosball partner. Suarez and Soraya are getting too cocky. Marcus." She tips her head. "Let's dominate."

"Aight." Marcus looks at me. "Better hide, G."

And just as he steps away, Dr. Martin steps up. "Gideon! There you are!" He claps me on the shoulder. "I want you to meet one of my colleagues. He was a Ranger, too. Long time ago, though. I don't think he'd know your father, but we'll see."

"Always worth a try, right?" I hear myself say, super gamely. He's really not that bad.

Behind me I hear Jode's laugh again.

Daryn's dad keeps up a steady flow of conversation as we walk. Did I try the short ribs? He checked and the seasoning is gluten-free, and it's his favorite, and I *have* to try it. Has he told me he has half a mind to give me Chief so he can stop hearing about the damage the dog's doing to his wife's flower beds?

"More than half a mind," he says. "In fact, I think it's a great idea. Don't you think?"

I look down at Chief. The puppy's trotting beside me, heeling perfectly for a few steps, then tackling my ankles. "Um, yes, sir. But don't you think Josie or Daryn might have an issue with—"

"We'll ask. I doubt it! They'll say yes, I'm sure of it." He looks down. "What do you say, Chief? Ah, look at that. He's on board! Now, where were we? Oh, yes! Rangers!"

I'm overwhelmed. I don't know how to react to this guy. He's like Sebastian times a million. "Dr. Martin? Sorry to interrupt, sir. But have you seen Daryn?"

He stops and looks at me like he's just remembered he has a daughter. "With her mother, I think. Can't separate those two since Dare's been back. Of course now that you're here, I'm sure she'll want to spend time with you. She'll have to get in line, though. We've got some great times ahead of us, right son?" He loops his arm over my shoulders, which is awkward because he's shorter.

"Absolutely, sir."

He looks at me and shakes his head. "Good kid, Gideon. Come on! Let's meet a fellow Ranger. Hooah!"

CHAPTER 47

⭢ DARYN ⭠

Oh my goodness." Mom rinses a glass and hands it to me without looking away from the window. Outside, Dad is accosting Gideon yet again, talking at him nonstop with a huge grin on his face. "I think your father is in love."

It's true. Dad's acting like he just met his new best friend. I've never seen him so open right off the bat. So engaged and enthusiastic. But I suppose that after everything, he's realized how precious time is, and how you can't waste it.

I laugh as Gideon looks up and sees me, lifting his shoulders in a helpless shrug. "That makes two of us," I say.

Mom turns to me, giving me a look that's more happy than surprised. "Daryn. That's so wonderful. I like him a lot. He's a lovely young man."

"He just got here, Mom. You've only known him one day. Most of it, he's been with Dad."

"But I can tell."

Isabel, who's drying dishes beside me, winks. "It's in his bearing."

"Yes," Mom agrees. "I think that's it. And he's hot."

"*What?* Mom, *ew.*"

She and Isabel laugh, enjoying my discomfort. I look from one to the other, wondering how I never saw it coming that these two would hit it off, too.

Isabel arrived a few days ago to spend some time with us before the party. It seemed important to bring the past year and a half home with me—and Iz was such a huge part of it.

I think it's helped Mom and Dad to see that, though I wasn't here with them, I was with great people. It's eased their minds some, even though there's so much I'm not sharing with them. Things that are better left unsaid. We're working on catching up on everything else, though. Everything we can.

Mom's been doing well lately. Her depression has been under control for the better part of a year. She's meditating and running and taking good care of herself, and the meds she's on are working well for her. She's active in the community, working on several charities that raise money for causes benefiting the families of missing children, caring for the homeless, and increasing awareness of mental disorders. She's amazing.

And she looks happy. Happier than when I left. I've heard it said that parents are only as happy as their unhappiest child, but the same is true in reverse. If she or Dad weren't happy, I wouldn't be, either. I *wasn't*. But, for now at least, they're good and I'm good—and that's *a lot* to be happy about.

Josie's stressed but it's the reasonable, normalish kind. She's taking summer courses, and it's the stress she puts on herself to make good grades. She's on track to graduate early, working really hard to achieve her goal of getting into a top medical school. I've met some of her friends from Yale and they're awesome. A small, close-knit group. I can tell they balance out her relentless drive a little bit. Just ten minutes ago, I heard them making plans to go for pizza and a movie later. After a day of lounging around the pool, that'll make an entire day of not cracking a book for Josie. It's another thing to be happy about. We all need people to look out for us.

Dad, apparently, was lost until I came home. Both Mom and Josie suffered, but somehow managed to move on with their lives. He didn't. From what I've been told, he was in agony until the second I walked back through the door.

I'd never seen Dad cry like he did that day. Big, racking sobs that shook *me*. It went on for hours, every time he'd look at me. All day, I found myself holding him, not even capable of comforting him with words. I had worried so much about their disappointment in me. Their anger. But there was none of that.

We were together again. That was everything. To all of us. The sobs and the tears and long, long hugs were just the release of all the worry and pain.

That was six weeks ago, and I still can't think of that day without getting choked up and wanting to hug him. Even though, since then, he's been overjoyed. He's been the guy outside, with his arm hanging around Gideon.

I think I gave him his life back by coming home.

I think I did that for both of us.

The Sight never came back to me after we came out of the Rift. That part of my life is finished, as far as I know. It's time for me to get on with life, not as a Seeker but as Daryn.

In the past six weeks, I've submitted applications to several colleges, trying for late admission. Gideon has, too. Some of the schools are the same. Some just close to each other geographically.

Who knows? We have no idea what's going to happen. Education is important to both of us. It's the right next step. But we're both on the same page about our relationship. We know we'll work it out so we can be together—that's our priority.

We've been lucky enough to find each other. No one makes me happier than he does. I know there are no long-term guarantees, but I also know without a doubt what I want today, and tomorrow, and the next day.

Him.

His blue eyes. His smile. His strength and sense of honor. His belief in me.

Even his temper.

I want it all. If that's not worth shaping my life around, what is?

Besides. Dad and Chief are both obsessed, and it would be cruel to break their hearts.

Mom, Iz, and I finish up this round of dishes. None of us expected the party to last hours longer than it was meant to, but we should've. These are the best people I know. I don't want this day to end, and I'm obviously not alone in feeling this way.

As Mom and Isabel take the glasses out to the bar set up at the pool house, I slip away.

"Daryn?" Mom says, stopping me at the stairs.

"I left something in my room. I'll be right out."

She smiles. "Hurry back."

I vault upstairs and into my room. My notebook is on my desk.

I grab it and bring it to my bed, flip it open, and read the last entries.

94. *Home! With Dad, Josie, Mom, Mom, Mom. Chief! My room. The big gold couch. Josie's cookies. Mom's hugs. Dad's smile. Our house. Home home home home home.*

95. *~~Making plans for the future with Gideon.~~ Making a future with Gideon via plans.*

96. *Isabel, here at home. Like she's a piece of the puzzle we always knew we'd find.*

97. *Every time I look at Sebastian. Every time.*

98. *Letting go of regret. Embracing life, the future, love.*

I write the next one.

99. *Today. This perfect day.*

I smile as I hear footsteps coming down the hall.

Gideon appears at my door and props his elbow on the frame. Chief bounces around at his feet for a second, then flops on his back, waiting for a stomach rub. "I think your dad's trying to give me your dog."

I laugh. "Not so fast," I say. "But I'll consider sharing him with you."

His eyebrows go up. "That's better than I expected." He sits beside me and takes my hand. His eyes drop to my notebook, scanning the last lines. "Nice," he says, smiling at me. "What's one hundred going to be?"

It's a really good question. I smile, closing the notebook. "I'm leaving it empty. So I never stop looking."

"I see a Reason now," he says, looking right into my eyes.

I smile. "So do I."

ACKNOWLEDGMENTS

Seeker lived up to its name. This book was most definitely a search—for the story itself *and* for what it means to me. I felt the support and guidance of Melissa Frain every step of the way. Mel, thank you for your editorial guidance and your friendship. I've been so very fortunate to work with you.

Thanks also to the entire team at Tor Teen, especially Amy Stapp, Diana Griffin, and Patty Garcia. It's been a privilege and a pleasure to work with such a warm, talented, and passionate group.

I've also been lucky to have Josh and Tracey Adams on my side. Thank you for all you've done for me. My writing friends are always there to cheer me on or pick me up. Lorin Oberweger, Katy Longshore, Lia Keyes, Kim Turrisi, and Talia Vance were particularly helpful in the writing of this book. Thank you so much.

Finally, to my family, who make plenty of sacrifices so that I can do what I love: I love nothing more than you. So, um . . . are you up for another book?